力得文化
Leader Culture

more reading power

10招

搞定閱讀

篇閱讀

主要涵蓋
自然、歷史文化、
生活、教育和商業類

U0077409

由十招所包含快速閱讀法、選項比對消去法 以及利用文意線索了解單字等…招式搞定英文閱讀

張慧文、方定國◎著

想追求高分，**閱讀理解力與答題技巧**是關鍵
想累積實力，**廣泛閱讀**不能少

● **十大招式**
由10大招式提升應試者整體閱讀能力
在五花八門的題材中釐清閱讀方向
才能依循文章指引了解文意

● **英文本文**
由40篇閱讀文章提升考生知識面
以及累積各類別主題語彙
進而建立讀者本身的閱讀詞彙庫

● **本文解析**
由學習重點進一步掌握文章中
提及的文法重點以及延伸的文法概念
從而提升應試者文法與句型使用能力

● **理解力測驗+中譯**
由40篇閱讀測驗
包羅萬象的閱讀題材增加考生應考廣度
輔以試題練習提升臨場感以及試題熟悉度

● **本文圖解**
由圖解閱讀考試的方式
搭配文法分析
方能迅速掌握文章脈絡、架構以及出題方向

由**學習小撇步**
更能避免落於文章陷阱中

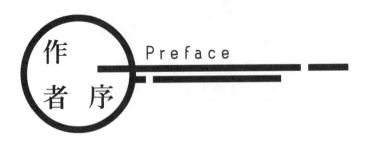

作者序　Preface

　　英文閱讀能力的培養是英文學習中重要的一環，良好的英文閱讀能力讓我們可以快速並精確掌文章中的重點，理解作者所要傳達的訊息，最後吸收成為自己的知識內涵。本書出版的目的即為有志於增進閱讀能力或是即將參加英文考試的讀者，提供英文提升閱讀能力的方法及快速有效率的答題技巧。

　　本書的內容分為「閱讀十招」及「測驗題練習」等二大部分，其中「閱讀十招」為筆者依據本身學習英文過程以及參加的各類英文考試的經驗，整理出如何可在短時間內有效並精確的掌握文章重點，以及在解答閱讀測驗題目時所應採取的策略。而在「測驗題練習」的方面，筆者依常見的十類不同的主題，精選字數約 200-300 字的短文作為閱讀練習的本文，而在每篇文章之後均有練習題及詳解供讀者小試身手。值得一提的是每篇文章的「本文圖解」，其目的是將文章閱讀時需要注意的重點，如重要文法、句型、片語、主詞及動詞位置及相關修飾語等，加以標示出來，讓讀者能真正了解英文句子的結構，日後不論是閱讀文章、參加考試、甚至自行撰寫英文都能有所助益。

　　最後，感謝倍斯特出版社給予筆者機會將畢生所學與讀者分享，並感謝各位讀者的支持，不管是工作或考試需要，都希望本書能對您有所幫助。如果有不同的意見，也請不吝指教。

方定國

幼稚園時，父親託友人自香港帶回一套學齡前學習 ABC 字母的繪本，開啟我對於英文的興趣。父母的諄諄教誨以及全力支持，讓我有機會能遠渡重洋到太平洋的彼岸，一個陌生且寒冷的國度——加拿大，延續我對英文的興趣與學習。回國之後仍投身於英文相關的工作，並且在公司擔任翻譯師多年之後，決定投入英文教學的領域，試圖把我所學可以讓莘莘學子們能簡單快樂的學習英文。目前仍擔任語文補教老師與翻譯師的工作，因此，本書 [閱讀 10 招] 是結合我多年教學的經驗，以及對於英文閱讀方面的學習技巧之大成。希望讀者能藉由本書快速、簡單與快樂地透過閱讀來學習英文。

Kevin Chang – 于 Taipei, Taiwan, 2015

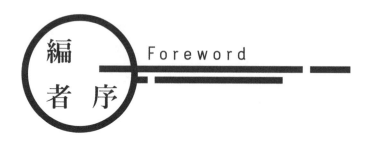

　　其實英文閱讀能力的養成並非一朝一夕，而在許多大大小小的考試中，閱讀能力影響著能否在英文考試中拿到理想的成績以及完成所有題目，相信許多學習者也在掌握基礎字彙和文法後，讀者在閱讀上其實漸漸有了一個輪廓，除了平常養成閱讀習慣之外，在既有基礎上學習者更需要良好的指引跟藉由閱讀技巧，使自己在閱讀時更快掌握文章中的重點完成作答，而此書正好提供了讀者「閱讀十招」和及「測驗題練習」，其中「閱讀十招」能使學習者更上一層樓，而「測驗題練習」則涵蓋十大主題，讀者能夠藉由十大主題中的 40 篇精選閱讀測驗擴大自己的知識面，在許多英文閱讀考試上有更好的表現。

力得文化編輯群

目次
content

人文 & 科技
Humanity & Technology

第一招 先看題目再看文章

　　考試時間有限，要在有限的時間內，將一篇文章徹底弄懂再來答題，會耗費許多時間，常因為不知道問題重點，將時間虛耗於無關緊要的段落中，且就算把文章從頭至尾努力地看完了，答題時往往看了後面又忘了前面，而考試題目出題的順序常是依照文章內容順序，此時必須再從頭去看文章，如此來回於文章及題目之間，時間就浪費掉了。所以，解決方法就是先將題目瀏覽一遍（只看題目本身，選項可先不看，因為選項中四個有三個是錯，看了不但浪費時間還可能被誤導），先在腦中浮現題目的重點，再以搜尋引導出題目正確解答的方式逐一來完成。如沒把握可以一次記住所有題目重點，可以依序看一題，答一題的方式來作答。

　　至於不同的題目類型，有不同的答題技巧，經筆者整理閱讀測驗會出現的題目主要可分為以下三類：

(一) 疑問句型

　　看到具有疑問詞的疑問句型題目時，依照疑問詞種類，歸納出文中應注意的重點資訊，如看到 when，就當注意搜尋表示日期、時間的地方；若有出現 who 時，就需注意文中有關人名或人物出現的地方；當然其它像 where（表處所、地方）, what（何事、何物），how（表方式、程度）等依此類推。

(二) 引導類型

　　針對引導類型的題目，應注意該題目句子中所包含的關鍵文字，然後注意文章中與其有相關的資訊或文句，通常答案就會浮現了。例如看到題目是：The reason that they believe in her is...，該題目中，應該注意的是 believe in her 就是關鍵字，表示文中一定有足以顯示他們會信任她的原因，這時閱讀文章時，就針對你所需注意的原因，就可以將答案選出來。

(三) 本文主旨

看到這類題目，就要了解英文寫作方式一般是直接破題，單刀直入的，不像中文講求起承轉合，所以該類型的答案大部份都是出現在第一段，甚至第一句就可以看得出來，但仍要注意少部分因為出題者故意給陷阱，而需注意一下中段文章。而就算是選項乍看之下模稜兩可，但只要注意邏輯鋪陳，並以每段為單位來整理歸納，把握每段的論述重點，不要被其他無關的字句給混淆（如舉例外情況，或牽扯到其他事情等），應該都可以順利解出。

為印證上述方式，以下舉例在國家考試中出現過的考題，來說明如何運用上述方式精準答題，讀者可以此方法靈活運用於後面的練習中。

To toot, to cut the cheese, or to pass gas. These are all funny ways to talk about something that everyone does: Farts! A normal person passes about half a liter of gas a day. That equals about 14 farts per day.

Then where do farts come from? There are several sources of fart gas. We get fart gas from the air we swallow. Gas also goes into our intestines from our blood. In addition, gas is also produced from chemical reactions and bacteria living in our intestines. Nervous people usually have more gas. This is because they swallow more air. Besides, food goes through their digestive systems faster. This means oxygen cannot be absorbed from the food in time. It turns into fart gas.

People's diet affects the stinkiness of farts. The smell has to do with the sulphur in foods such as eggs, meat, and cauliflower. Beans cause a lot of farts, but these farts aren't usually really stinky. Beans are not high in sulphur, but the sugar in them produces gas in the intestines.

Finally, people wonder, "Where do farts go when you hold them in?"

Well, these farts will not poison you. However, you may get a bad stomachache from the pressure. Farts you hold in are neither released nor absorbed. They will come out sooner or later.

1. What is this passage mainly about?

   (A) The way to reduce farts.

   (B) Facts to know about farts.

   (C) How to have a healthy diet.

   (D) The dangers of holding in farts.

2. Why do nervous people have more farts?

   (A) They eat too many beans.

   (B) They do not have enough sleep.

   (C) Their blood pressure is too high.

   (D) The food they eat is not well digested.

3. When we hold in a fart, where does it go?

   (A) It is absorbed by the intestines.

   (B) It is released from the mouth or nose.

   (C) It is just delayed and will come out later.

   (D) It goes back to the stomach and helps with digestion.

　　在第一個題目問的就是本篇主旨或大意，而事實上如果你只看第一段，其實也足以解題了，因為前面提過，英文文章一開頭通常就會破題，而第一段談的都是有關於屁的知識，所以答案應該選 (B) 認識放屁最為恰當。如果對答案有疑慮，再由全文的開始談到屁的來源，再談到味道及最後忍住不放屁的情形來判斷，都是談到對於屁的一些知識。至於其他選項中提到的飲食及忍住放屁都分別只是舉例及說明屁的常識而已，並非主旨大意。

　　在第二個題目看到問句 why 開頭（問某事的原因），這時注意文中是否有關於解釋的語句，並注意該句中的關鍵字 nervous people（緊張的人），果然文章中第二段第三句及第四句就看到：Nervous people usually have more gas. This is because they... cannot be absorbed from the food in time 這時答案 (D) 就出來了。

第三個題目中，注意題目中提到的關鍵字 hold in a fart（忍住不放屁），這時依序看下來，最後一段中你就會看到："Where do farts go when you hold them in?"找到關鍵字句後，通常答案就會出現在它後面的句子裏 (They will come out sooner or later)，甚至與題目中的字句一字不漏，如本題答案 (C)... will come out later。

1

人文 & 科技

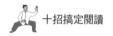
 英文本文

Article 1.1

Composites will soon be showing what they can do for the largest **aircraft** in the world will have seen, the Airbus A380. Airbus will maintain its drive to 'compositize' most of the tail section, including the empennage and fin, of the aircraft it builds. The company will have been relieved by findings from the US that the composite fin structure on the A300-600 aircraft that crashed near New York two months after 9/11, at first under suspicion, now appears to have been exonerated, so that there is no constraint on the selection of composites for this item again. Airbus Industry is clear that, although composite materials will account for some 16% by weight of the A380 airframe, saving about 15 tons over the weight of an equivalent all-metal structure (total empty aircraft weight will be around 280 tons), composite content could have been greater still had cost **not been a limiting factor.** Meanwhile, Boeing, which has today been less committed to composites than Airbus, appears about to adopt them in a big way for future airliners. Though the development of the Mach 0.95 Sonic Cruiser has been shelved, in line with the market's pre-criticizing of fuel efficiency and environment acceptability over speed, the company wants to incorporate technologies that were under development for the high-speed aircraft in a new 210-250 passenger twin jet so far designed the B7E7. These will include composite fuselage and wing structures, resulting low weight contributing to a target fuel burn 17% less than that of the similarly-sized current generation A330, and a 10% lower operating cost.

 理解力測驗

Q1. What does the term "**aircraft**" in line 2 refer to?

    (A) craftwork

    (B) vehicle

    (C) airplane

    (D) composite

Q2. According to this article, what is the total empty aircraft weight of A380?

    (A) 280 tons

    (B) 380 tons

    (C) 260 tons

    (D) 360 tons

Q3. Based on this article, which of the following statements is true?

    (A) The largest aircraft in the world will have been seen, the Airbus A330.

    (B) Boeing has been more committed to composites than Airbus.

    (C) Airbus Industry is clear that composite materials will account for some 16% by weight of the A380 airframe.

    (D) Airbus Industry wants to incorporate technologies that were under development for the high-speed aircraft in a new 210-250 twin jet passenger liner.

Q4. What does the phrase "not been a limiting factor" in line 13 refer to?

    (A) cost

    (B) weight

    (C) structure

    (D) composite contents

Q5. According to the contents, what would be the best title for this article?

    (A) Airbus Has Been Exonerated from the Accident.

    (B) A380 - the Largest Aircraft in the World.

    (C) Boeing Is the Largest Competitor to Airbus Industry.

    (D) Composites - the Next Generation Materials for Aircraft.

人文 & 科技

 本文中譯

A380 空中巴士

　　複合材料很快就會向世人顯示，可以適用於製造世界上最大的航空器，空中巴士的 A380 之中。Airbus 對於所製造之航空器，將會維持在機身尾段對於複合材料之大量需求，其中包括尾翼及安定翼。對於在 911 事件後的兩個月，鄰近紐約所發生的 A300-600 墜機事件，起先 Airbus 公司是受到懷疑的，但經由美國方面調查，發現機上複合材料安定翼的部分之後，便排除對 Airbus 公司的指控，並不再對此複合材料項目的選擇有任何限制了。Airbus 公司表明，雖然複合材料將佔 A380 機身重量的 16%，大約節省了相當於全部金屬結構之重量 15 公噸 (總空機重量約為 280 公噸)，而如果價格不是限制的因素的話，複合材料還會有相當大的使用空間。與此同時，相對於 Airbus 迄今都較為不支持複合材料的波音公司 (Boeing)，也顯露出未來將大規模採用它們來製造大型客機。儘管音速 0.95 的音速巡航者客機開發已被擱置，然對於符合市場上有關於燃油效率，以及對於速度之環境接受度的先前評估，公司方面仍希望納入到目前所開發的技術，設計新的 210-250 乘客高速雙引擎客機 B7E7。這些將包含複合材料機身與機翼的結構，其燃油目標將比同世代以及尺寸的 A330 客機還要節省約 17%，並且能降低近 10% 的營運成本。

理解力測驗中譯

1. 第 2 行的 "aircraft" 這個名稱是何意？

(A) 工藝品

(B) 車輛

(C) 飛機

(D) 複合材料

2. 根據本文，A380 的總空機重量為？

(A) **280 公噸**

(B) 380 公噸

(C) 260 公噸

(D) 360 公噸

3. 根據本文，下列哪一項陳述是正確的？

(A) 世界上最大的航空器，空中巴 A330。

(B) 迄今比 Airbus 都較為支持複合材料的波音公司。

(C) **Airbus 公司明白的表示，複合材料將佔 A380 機身重量的 16%。**

(D) 有些街道或道路僅供行人使用。

4. 第 13 行的片語 "not been a limiting factor" 是何意？

(A) **成本**

(B) 重量

(C) 結構

(D) 複合材料的內容

5. 依據本文內容，本文最佳標題為何？

(A) 空中巴士已經從意外中脫罪了

(B) A-380 - 世界上最大的客機

(C) 波音公司是空中巴士企業最大的競爭對手

(D) **複合材料 - 新一代航空器的材料**

 本文圖解

Composites will soon *be showing* **what** they can do for ③Ⓐ the largest
名詞子句當 show 的受詞，
what... the world 為該子句主詞
aircraft the world have never seen, the Airbus A380. Airbus will maintain its

drive to 'compositize' most of the tail section, including the empennage and

fin, of the aircraft it builds. The company *will have been relieved* by findings

from the US **that the composite fin structure** on the A300-600 aircraft
形容詞子句，說明 findings，composite fine structure 為該子句主詞

that crashed near New York two months after 9/11, at first under suspicion,
形容詞子句修飾先行詞 aircraft

now **appears** to have been exonerated, **so** that there *is* no constraint on the
子句動詞
表結果的連接詞，
連接第二個子句
selection of composites for this item again. ③Ⓒ Airbus Industry *is* clear **that**,
that... factor. 名詞子句，當主詞補語

although composite materials will account for some 16% by weight of the
表結果的分詞構句

A380 airframe, **saving** about 15 tones over the weight of an equivalent all-

metal structure total empty aircraft weight which will be around 280 tones,

composite content could have been greater still **had cost not been a**
與過去相反的假設句，主要子句用
could have + p.p，條件句用 had + p.p

limiting factor. Meanwhile ③B Boeing, which has today been less committed

> which 指前面的 Boeing，
> 也是本句的主詞

to composites than Airbus, *appears* about to adopt **them** in a big way for

> them 指前面所提的 composite content

future airliners. Though the development of the Mach 0.95 Sonic Cruiser has

been shelved, in line with the market's pre-criticizing of fuel efficiency and

environment acceptability over speed, ③D the company *wants* to incorporate

> the company 是
> 指波音公司

technologies that were under development for the high-speed aircraft in a

new 210-250 twin jet passenger liner **named** the B7E7. These will *include*

> p.p 當形容詞修
> 飾 liner

> 分詞片語，表示
> 達成以下的效果

composite fuselage and wing structures, **resulting** low weight contributing

to a target fuel burn 17% less than **that** of the similarly-sized current

> 指 A330 的燃油消耗率

generation A330, and a 10% lower operating cost.

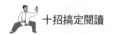

🖊 單字與片語

重要單字 Key Vocabularies

① composite（n）複合物

② composite（adj）複合的，合成的

③ aircraft（n）航空器，飛機

④ exonerate（v）免除罪責

⑤ acceptability（n）接受度

⑥ shelve（v）擱置

⑦ operating cost 營運成本

重要片語 Key Phrases

❶ under suspicion 受到懷疑的

❷ constraint on 受到…限制

❸ account for 佔…

❹ in line with 與…一致

❺ contributing to 促使

本文解析

本文先提到複合材料已用於製造世界上最大的航空器，而剛開始波音公司對複合材料的安全性有所懷疑，然事後證實複合材料的安全性無疑，且空中巴士將其大量運用於 A-380 客機上，並獲致良好成果，這使得波音公司更有信心將它運用於未來的大型客機中，故可知該文章主旨就是複合材料在飛機製造上的運用。

第一題問 "aircraft" 這是指何項交通工具，這個字在英文中是指航空器、飛行器、飛機等，在本文是指飛機。第二題問 A-380 的重量，這可由 A380 airframe, ... will be around 280 tons. 這句話得知，注意，不要被其他數據搞混了。第三題問文章中的細節，只要找出每個選項中的關鍵字，並在文章中相關處加以比對，就可得知答案，例如選項 (B) 中，關鍵字可用 Boeing has been more committed，但文章中可看到：Boeing, which has today been less committed to...，是否定之意，故選項為非。第四題問 "not been a limiting factor" 指文中何物，由 ...composite content could have been greater still had cost **not been a limiting factor**. 知道價格 (cost) 是限制複合材料使用的因素（因為複合材料價格昂貴），所以知道 a limiting factor 就是指複合材料的價格。

學習重點 ➡

關於科技類型的文章，筆者建議讀者應該注意文中的數據（數量、百分比與日期），這些通常會是測驗題目的出處。例如本文最後一句中，讀者應弄清楚其中兩個數據 17% 與 10% 所代表的含意，其中 17% 是指該波音的新型飛機會比其對手 A-330 更節省燃油的比例，而 10% 是指其操作成本可節省的比例。

學習小撇步 (Tips) ➡

閱讀測驗的題目，筆者建議讀者首先要先瞭解題目在問什麼，這是非常重要的。題目常常會有些刁鑽 (tricky)，例如本測驗的第 3 題：Based on this article, which of the following statement is true?(根據本文，下列哪一項陳述是正確的？)，有時候出題者會利用搶快的心理把題目變成：is Not true; is incorrect，所以再次提醒讀者一定要看清楚題目問什麼再作答。

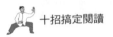

 英文本文

Article 1.2

Television was not invented by any single person. Nor did it spring into **appearing** overnight. It had evolved gradually over a long time through the ideas of many people -- each one building on the work of their predecessors. The process began in 1873, when it was accidentally discovered that the electrical resistance of the element selenium varied in proportion to the intensity of the light shining on it. Scientists quickly recognized that this provided a way of transforming light variations into electrical signals. Almost immediately a number of schemes were proposed for sending pictures by wire (it was, of course, before radio).

One of these earliest schemes was patterned on the human eye. Suggested by G. R. Carey in 1875, it envisioned a mosaic of selenium cells on which the picture to be transmitted would be focused by a lens system. At the receiving end, there would be a similarly arranged mosaic made up of electric lights. Each selenium cell would be connected by an individual wire to the similarly placed light in the receiving mosaic. Light falling on the selenium cell would reproduce the original picture, and had the necessary amplifiers and the right kind been available, this system would have worked. But it also would have required an impractical number of connecting wires. Carey recognized this and in a second proposed to "scan" the cells-transmitting the signal from each cell to its associated light, in turn, over a single wire. If this were done fast enough, the retentive power of the eye would cause the resultant image to be seen as a complete picture.

 理解力測驗

Q1. What is the best title of this article?

(A) Television in the Electronic Era

(B) The First Steps in the Invention of Television

(C) The Art of Television

(D) Harmful Effects of Television Viewing

Q2. In line 2, the word "**appearing**" could best be replaced by

(A) placing

(B) subsisting

(C) approaching

(D) existing

Q3. An important discovery in the early period was the electrical resistance of

(A) mosaics

(B) the human eye

(C) lenses

(D) the element selenium

Q4. In 1875, Carey envisioned a mosaic of selenium cells on which the picture to be transmitted would be focused by

(A) wire

(B) electric lights

(C) a lens system

(D) amplifiers

Q5. Why was Carey's first scheme for television abandoned?

(A) Because he had no the necessary and available amplifiers.

(B) Because it would have required infinite connecting wires.

(C) Because he had no mosaic of selenium calls on which the picture to be transmitted.

(D) All of the above.

 本文中譯

電視的發明

　　電視並非由任何單獨一人所發明的，它也不是一夕間出現的，它是經由一段長時間，經由許多人的創意思想而逐漸演進的，而每一項演進都是建立在前人的成就之上。這個演進歷程開始於 1873 年，當時無意間發現硒元素的電阻會隨著光照射它的強度而作等比例變化，科學家很快就認知到這是用電子訊號來傳送光影變化的一種方式。而用電纜傳送影像的計劃也在不久隨即出現（當然，那是在無線電之前）。

　　而這其中最早的一項計畫是以模仿人類的眼睛，這是由 G.R. 蓋瑞在 1875 年提出的構想。他認為將要傳送的圖片落在一個硒光電管的感光鑲嵌螢幕格點上，是可透過一透鏡系統聚焦來達成的。在接收端，將有一個類似的電子光束排列的鑲嵌螢幕，每一個硒光電格點都經由一條獨立的電線連接到相對應接收端鑲嵌螢幕的光線位置，如此則落在硒光電格點的光線點就會重現原來的圖樣，而假如有必要且正好可用的放大器，這樣的系統應該會可行。但它還是需要無數的連接線。蓋瑞認知到這一點，並且立刻提出用單一條電線，從每個格點到它對應的光線，逐次"掃描"格點來傳送訊號的想法。假如這程序做得夠快，人眼睛的暫存記憶就能將這組合的影像視為一個完整的圖像。

理解力測驗中譯

1. 下列何者為本篇最佳標題？

(A) 在電子時代的電視機

(B) 電視發明的第一步

(C) 電視的藝術

(D) 觀看電視的害處

2. 在第二行中，"appearing"這個字最適被下列何字取代？

(A) 位於

(B) 維持

(C) 靠近

(D) 存在

3. 在早期，有一項重要的發明是與什麼的電阻相關？

(A) 感光鑲嵌螢幕

(B) 人類眼睛

(C) 透鏡

(D) 硒元素

4. 在 1875 年，蓋瑞認為將要傳送的圖片落在一個硒光電管感光鑲嵌螢幕的格點上是可透過何者達成？

(A) 電線

(B) 電光源

(C) 透鏡系統

(D) 放大器

5. 蓋瑞的最初電視機的方案被放棄的原因為何？

(A) 他沒有所需且必要的放大器

(B) 這項方案需要無數的連接線

(C) 他沒有傳送的圖片所需的硒光鑲嵌螢幕

(D) 連接線的數目是不可行的

 本文圖解

Television *was not invented* by any one person, **nor** did it *spring* into

> 表否定連接詞置於句
> 首，需用倒裝句

being overnight. It *evolved* gradually, over a long period, from the ideas

of many people -- each one building on the work of their predecessors.

The process *began* in 1873, when ③ it was accidentally discovered that the

> 名詞子句當 discovered 的
> 受詞，說明發現的現象

electrical resistance of the element selenium varied in proportion to the

intensity of the light shining on it. Scientists quickly *recognized* that **this**

> this 指這種方法

provided a way of transforming light variations into electrical signals. Almost

immediately a number of schemes *were proposed* for sending pictures by

wire (it was, of course, before radio).

One of the earliest of these schemes *was patterned* on the human eye.

Suggested by G. R. ④ Carey in 1875, it *envisioned* a mosaic of selenium cells

> 分詞構句，原句為 As It was
> suggested....

on which the picture to be transmitted would be focused by a lens system.

> which 引導形容詞子句修飾 cells

At the receiving end there *would be* a similarly arranged mosaic **made up**

分詞片語修飾 mosaic，
表示由光源所組成的

of electric lights. Each selenium cell would *be connected* by an individual

wire to the similarly **placed** light in the receiving mosaic. Light **falling on** the

過去分詞當形容詞，
表示被放在…

分詞片語修飾 light，表示
落在上面的這些光線

selenium cell *would reproduce* the original picture, and **had** the necessary

amplifiers and the right kind been available, this system would have worked.

it 指蓋瑞的這個構想

But ⑤ it also *would have required* an impractical number of connecting

本句為假設語句的變形，
為與過去式時相反的假設

wires. Carey *recognized* this and in a second *proposed* to "scan" the cells-

transmitting signal from each cell to its associated light, in turn, **over** a single

over 在此意思
為透過…

wire. If this were done fast enough, the retentive power of the eye *would*

cause the resultant image to be seen as a complete picture.

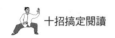

 **單字與片語**

重要單字 Key Vocabularies

① accidentally（adv）意外地

② envision（v）想像

③ propose（v）提議

④ pattern（v）仿效

⑤ recognize（v）公認

⑥ amplifier（n）放大器

⑦ impractical（a）不切實際的

⑧ retentive（a）保留的

⑨ resultant（a）組合的

重要片語 Key Phrases

❶ a number of　一些

❷ made up of　由…所組成

❸ in a second　片刻間

❹ in turn　輪流

 **本文解析**

　　本篇文章中，經由第一段一開頭即提到電視並非由任何單獨一人所發明的，也不是一夕間出現的，後面繼續針對電視發明的最初演進過程做說明，這樣更可以清楚的確定本文的主旨是有關電視機的發明過程，所以第一題有關該文章的最佳標題可為電視發明的第一步。

　　第二題問文章中"appearing"這個字，該字出現在 Nor did it spring into appearing overnight，意思是電視機不是一夕之間就出現的，所以 appearing 可以用 existing 表

示存在的意思來取代。第三題問到一項重要的發明是有關何物的電阻特性，由 it was accidentally discovered that the electrical resistance of the element selenium varied...，知是 the element selenium 的電阻。第四題問蓋瑞認為將要傳送的圖片落在一個硒光電感光鑲嵌螢幕的格點上是可透過何者達成，由文章中 Carey in 1875, it envisioned a mosaic of selenium calls on which the picture to be transmitted would be focused by a lens system，即可知道答案是經由 lens system (透鏡系統) 來達成。題目雖然看似有點專業的問題，但只要將題目 (或選項) 中的相關關鍵字找出來，一樣能輕鬆解題，以本題來說，讀者可依題目中提到的 mosaic of selenium cells... picture to be transmitted... focused 等字，快速鎖定文章中相關句子來找答案。第五題最初電視機的方案被放棄的原因，該題由文中 ...it also would have required an impractical number of connecting wires. Carey recognized this...，文中已經用不可行的 (impractical) 來形容這些所需的電線，所以該因素就造成此計畫無法執行下去，至於放大器 (amplifier) 部分，文章中並沒有明白說不可行，故不能選。

學習重點 ➡

假設語句是英文中很重要的一種句型，但假設語句不一定會出現由 if 來引導的假設句，例如本文中"... had the necessary amplifiers and the right kind been available, this system would have worked."，就是由 had 引導與過去事實相反的假設語句 (Had + S. + P.P. ..., S. + would + have + p.p)，讀者必須能一眼認出來，才不會在閱讀的過程中被困惑，或將語句意思搞混了。

學習小撇步 (Tips) ➡

基本上，不管是哪一類型牽涉到有些專業知識的閱讀測驗文章，其內容雖然有可能出現一些較專業的用語或名詞，如本文中的 selenium (硒) 及 mosaic (感光鑲嵌螢幕) 等，通常並不會成為考題的一部份，或妨礙你對本文的瞭解。但一些較為生活化或一般性的用語，如本文中的 amplifier (放大器) 及 scan (掃描) 等字，則有可能會出現比較關鍵解題的地方，所以充分的單字及字彙能力是良好閱讀能力的基礎。

 英文本文

Article 1.3

The global carbon fiber industry is once again experiencing an unhealthy cycle of tightening supply, escalating prices and uncertainties about the availability of long-term supply. This poses a serious threat to developmental momentum in several new industrial markets that are poised for commercialization and broad use.

Why is the industry repeating this all-too-familiar pattern? A major factor is unsustainable low pricing from aerospace-grade fiber suppliers. From 1999 to 2003, a period of tremendous over-capacity due to a natural down-cycle in the aerospace sector that was exacerbated by the terrorist attacks in the U.S. on Sept 11, 2001, suppliers sold aerospace-grade carbon fiber into industrial applications at cost — or even at a loss — to protect share in a **stagnant** market. In recent months, suppliers no longer able to bear the devastating effects of this strategy on their financial health instituted sweeping reforms, raised prices and warned customers about product availability limitation. Bottom line: we were again reminded that "**there is no free lunch**." Temporary prices with no basis in "cost reality" simply cannot be sustained and will eventually increase.

They need a supply community that acknowledges the extreme differences between these two markets. The aerospace sector requires fiber suppliers to configure their companies with many real and significant product and service costs in mind. It also demands significant product variety — a requirement that would create high costs in any business, and certainly do for carbon fibers.

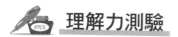 理解力測驗

Q1. According to this article, what can be inferred in this article?

(A) Why is the industry not repeating this all-too-familiar pattern?

(B) A healthy application of carbon fiber.

(C) The global carbon fiber industry is experiencing a healthy cycle again,

(D) The aerospace sector requires fiber suppliers to configure their companies with many real and significant product and service costs in mind.

Q2. What is the closest meaning of "**stagnant**" in line 12?

(A) booming

(B) still

(C) flowing

(D) floating

Q3. According to this article, when is the period of tremendous over-capacity due to a natural down-cycle in the aerospace sector?

(A) From 1999 to 2000

(B) From 1999 to 2001

(C) From 1999 to 2002

(D) From 1999 to 2003

Q4. What does the phrase "**there is no free lunch**" in line 16 refer to?

(A) Lunch is not free

(B) Nothing comes of nothing

(C) No pain, no gain

(D) No gain without pain

Q5. Who will be more interested in reading this article?

(A) Students

(B) Investors

(C) Female adults

(D) Male adults

 **本文中譯**

碳纖維

　　全球的碳纖維工業又再度面臨了因緊縮供給、逐步攀高的價格以及長期可靠供應的不確定性所造成的不良循環週期。這對於一些已經做好商品化以及準備廣泛使用之新產業市場的發展動力，造成了一項嚴重的威脅。

　　為什麼此一工業會反覆發生這種通病呢？其中一項主要的因素為航鈦級纖維供應商無法穩定維持較低的價格。由於恐怖份子於 2001 年 9 月 11 日攻擊美國，加劇了在航鈦業自 1999 至 2003 年間因為自然景氣下滑而造成的供過於求的情形，供應商只得以成本價格──甚或以虧損之價格─銷售航鈦級纖維來供產業應用，來維護其在有所停滯市場中的佔有率。在近幾個月中，供應商無法再承受這項對其財務的健全有毀滅性影響的策略，而開始的全面性改革，並提高售價及警告顧客關於產量可用的限制。最重要的一點是：我們再次被提醒"天下沒有白吃的午餐"。不是建立"價值真實性"基礎上的短期價格不僅是無法持續的，而且最終也將攀高。

　　他們要一個能夠了解兩個市場之間極大差異的供應體系。航鈦業者要求纖維供應商能夠調整生產有用且重要的產品以並注意成本，這也讓產品多樣性顯著增加──在任何行業中都會使價格提高，碳纖維也不例外。

理解力測驗中譯

1. 根據本文內容,我們可以知道甚麼?

(A) 為什麼此一工業會不會一直反覆著這種熟悉的模式?

(B) 碳纖維的健全應用。

(C) 全球的碳纖維工業又再度面臨了健全的循環週期。

(D) **航鈦業者要求纖維供應商能夠調整生產有用且重要的產品並注意成本。**

2. 下列選項何者最接近第 12 行的"stagnant"?

(A) 景氣大好

(B) **停滯**

(C) 流動的

(D) 漂浮的

3. 根據本文,哪個時期是航鈦業因為自然景氣下滑而造成嚴重的供過於求的問題?

(A) 自 1999 到 2000

(B) 自 1999 到 2001

(C) 自 1999 到 2002

(D) **自 1999 到 2003**

4. 第 16 行的片語"there is no free lunch"是何意?

(A) 午餐不是免費的

(B) 事出必有因

(C) **沒有不勞而獲的**

(D) 有所得必有所失

5. 何者最有興趣閱讀本文?

(A) 學生

(B) **投資者**

(C) 女性成人

(D) 男性成人

 **本文圖解**

The global carbon fiber industry *is* once again experiencing an

unhealthy cycle of tightening supply, **escalating** prices and uncertainties

表結果的分詞構句，表
示造成價格攀高等影響

about the availability of long-term supply. This *poses* a serious threat to

this 指前述的價格
及供應等現象

developmental momentum in several new industrial markets that are poised

for commercialization and broad use.

Why *is* the industry repeating this all-too-familiar pattern? A major factor

is unsustainable low pricing from aerospace-grade fiber suppliers. ③ From

1999 to 2003, a period of tremendous over-capacity due to a natural down-

從 , a period of... 2001, 這段話只是補充說明前面
from 1999 to 2003 發生甚麼事

cycle in the aerospace sector that was exacerbated by the terrorist attacks

in the U.S. on Sept. 11, 2001, suppliers *sold* aerospace-grade carbon fiber

into industrial applications at costs-or even at a loss-**to protect** share in

to 可視為 in order to，
表示為了甚麼目的

a stagnant market. In recent months, suppliers **no longer able to bear**

形容詞片語，修飾 suppliers，原句為：
suppliers (who are) no longer able to...

the devastating effects of this strategy on their financial health **instituted**

過去分詞當形容詞用，解釋為
"原設定的"，修飾 reforms

sweeping reforms, *raised* prices and *warned* customers about product

availability limitation. Bottom line: we *were again reminded* that "there is no

free lunch." Temporary prices **with no basis** in "cost reality" simply *cannot*

介係詞片語修飾 prices, 表示
在沒有成本現實的基礎下

be sustained and *will eventually increase.*

They *need* a supply community that acknowledges the extreme

主詞 they 指 suppliers 及
aerospace sector

differences between these two markets. The aerospace sector *requires*

these 指的是工業用及
航鈦用市場

fiber suppliers to configure their companies with many real and significant

product and service costs in mind. It also *demands* significant product variety

it 指的是 supply community

- ① a requirement that would create high costs in any business, and certainly

do for carbon fibers.
用 do 來取代前面提過的動詞 create

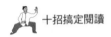

單字與片語

重要單字 Key Vocabularies

① Emerging （a）新興的

② unhealthy （a）不健全的

③ availability （n）可用性

④ commercialization （n）使商業化

⑤ all-too-familiar 似曾相識；通病

⑥ aerospace-grade （a）航鈦級

⑦ tremendous （a）巨大，極大的

⑧ stagnant （a）蕭條的；停滯的

⑨ devastating （a）破壞性的

⑩ variety （n）多樣性

重要片語 Key Phrases

❶ once again 再一次

❷ due to 因為

❸ no longer 不再

❹ there is no free lunch 天下沒有白吃的午餐

本文解析

　　本文先提到碳纖維產業的供應及價格變動會造成它後續在運用市場上的影響，而造成這種情況的原因是因為航鈦用碳纖維供應商因為 911 攻擊後，將航鈦市場上過剩的產能賣到一般工業用市場上，造成價格崩跌，而供應商受不了價格戰後開始提高售價，又造成價格大幅潑動。而解決之道是要讓供應商清楚區分這兩種市場存在許多差異，航鈦業者希望供應者能提供多樣性的有用的產品，則價格自然會提高，這也是第一題的答案。

　　第二題問單字"stagnant"，該字的意思是"停滯的"，所以選項中以 still 的意思最接近。第三題問何時在航鈦業因為自然景氣下滑而造成的供過於求,由文中 From 1999 to 2003, ... over-capacity due to a natural down-cycle in the aerospace sector 可看出答案。第四題問 "there is no free lunch" 是什麼意思,該句就是天下沒有白吃的午餐,或不勞而之意。第五題問誰可能有興趣閱讀本文,由該篇是講到產業的供應及價格等問題,故應是投資者會有興趣。

學習重點 ➡

閱讀測驗有時喜歡用複雜句 (Complex sentence) 來增加句子長度並使語意不易被讀者一次搞懂。所以遇到這種句子,一定要將句子的主要子句的主詞及動詞找出來,其餘的子句或修飾、說明語句就不會讓句意混淆不清了。例如本文中的一句:From 1999 to 2003, a period of tremendous over-capacity due to a natural down-cycle in the aerospace sector that was exacerbated by the terrorist attacks in the U.S. on Sept. 11, 2001, suppliers sold aerospace-grade carbon fiber into industrial applications at cost－even at a loss－to protect share in a stagnant market. 該句共有 54 個字,且真正的主詞及動詞出現 (suppliers sold) 在句子的非常後段,而該句前面從 From...on Sept. 11, 2001, 這一大段都只是為了說明 1999 到 2003 之間到底發生了甚麼事,中間還夾雜著一個形容詞子句 (that...)。再如這句:In recent months, suppliers no longer able to bear the devastating effects of this strategy on their financial health instituted sweeping reforms, raised prices and warned customers about product availability limitation. 主詞 (suppliers) 與動詞 (raised) 之間隔了一大段說明主詞的用語 [suppliers (who are) no longer able...]。所以還是強調讀者應對句子的結構有充分的認識,才能輕鬆面對複雜的長句子。

學習小撇步 (Tips) ➡

通常短文的最開頭幾句是該文的主要主旨及大意部份,而最後一、二句通常是該文敘述的結論,並且這二個地方常會是測驗題目的出處。所以讀者在看文章時可以把握這些英文寫作習慣,將注意力放在文章開頭及結尾部份,中間敘述方面則可以快速瀏覽過,瞭解其大意即可。

 英文本文

Article 1.4

In the later part of the 1990s the Universal Serial Bus (USB) was invented as a system of exchanging data from one storage place to another at a relatively fast speed. Today about 10 billion USB devices are in use, a figure that even **stuns** its inventor Ajay Bhatt from Intel. USB has become a common name everywhere, from schools and offices to hospitals.

Ajay Bhatt was annoyed by the different types of connections that a PC had and looked for a simpler way of linking different parts of a computer. He tried to set up a uniform connection system for all PC parts and other devices. Although it was difficult for Bhatt to convince computer makers that he had a good idea, he finally got the approval to change a computer's extension system completely.

USB has many advantages. For one, a single port can control up to 128 devices at once. They are powered by themselves and you do not have to switch off a device to make USB work. A USB object installs itself. Just plug it in and the computer automatically downloads the software you need to make it work.

When the first USB devices hit the markets in the late 1990s, they were an immediate success. In later versions the transfer speed of USB devices was drastically improved. Today's USB 3.0 standard is over 400 times faster than its original USB 1. All over the world, millions of USB devices and adapters are being sold every day.

The Intel engineer is proud of having created a standard that the computer industry has accepted and that will be here for a while to come. Today's PCs and laptops have at least 3-4 USB ports. USB connectors can be found everywhere, on printers, digital cameras, mobile phones, and tablets.

 理解力測驗

Q1. What is the best title of this article?
  (A) The Invention of USB
  (B) The Advantages of USB
  (C) The Usage of USB
  (D) The Versions of USB

Q2. What is the closest meaning of the term "**stuns**" in line 4?
  (A) amuses
  (B) overwhelms
  (C) shocks
  (D) delights

Q3. According to this article, who came up with the ideal of USB?
  (A) Intel
  (B) computer makers
  (C) Ajay Bhatt
  (D) a PC engineer

Q4. How many times is the latest USB3.0 faster than USB1.0 ?
  (A) 10 billion
  (B) 1 million
  (C) 400
  (D) 3-4

Q5. Which of the flowing statements is NOT correct?
  (A) The computer industry has accepted USB and that will be continue for a while.
  (B) The first USB devices hit the markets in the late 1990s and they had a great success.
  (C) First, computer makers were difficult to be convinced by Bhatt about the ideal of USB.
  (D) You have to turn on a device to make USB work.

 **本文中譯**

認識 USB

　　USB 是一種能相當快速地將檔案從一個儲存的地方交轉換到另一個地方的系統。今天，使用中的 USB 裝置約有 100 億個，這是連它的發明者 Ajay Bhatt 都難以想像的局面。從學校到辦公室到醫院，USB 已經成為各地方通用的語言。

　　Ajay Bhatt 曾經被個人電腦的各種不同連接方式所困擾，並想找出一種可連接一部電腦不同部分的簡單方式。他設法建立一種對所有個人電腦及其他裝置都通用的連接系統，雖然剛開始 Ajay Bhatt 要去說服電腦製造商說他有這個好主意是很困難的，但這構想終究獲得各方同意而完全改變電腦的擴充系統。

　　USB 有許多優點，其中之一是單一連接阜可以同時控制多達 128 個裝置，它們自己會驅動而無需另外關閉一個裝置同時又能使用 USB。USB 物件可以自行完成安裝，只要插進去，電腦就會主動下載所需的軟體來讓其運作。

　　當最初的 USB 裝置在 1990 年後期問市時，便一舉成功。在後來的版本中，USB 的傳輸速度更是急遽增加，今天的 USB 3.0 的速度超過它當初原本 USB 1.0 速度的 400 倍。全世界每天都還有數以百萬計的 USB 裝置及其配合裝置販售中。這位英特爾的工程師對他能創造電腦業界能接受的標準非常感到自豪，並且這套標準還會未來持續一陣子。今天的電腦或筆電都至少有 3-4 個 USB 阜，而 USB 連接器在印表機、數位相機、行動電話及桌上型電腦等每個地方都能看到。

理解力測驗中譯

1. 本文最佳標題為何？

　(A) **USB 的發明**

　(B) USB 的優點

　(C) USB 的使用

　(D) USB 的版本

2. 第四行中與"stuns"這個字意義最接近的是何者？

　(A) 使喜歡

　(B) 覆蓋

　(C) **嚇到**

　(D) 愉快

3. 依據本文，誰提出 USB 這個構想？

　(A) 英特爾

　(B) 電腦製造商

　(C) **Ajay Bhatt**

　(D) 一位 PC 工程師

4. 最新的 USB3.0 較 USB1.0 快多少倍？

　(A) 100 億

　(B) 1 百萬

　(C) **400**

　(D) 3-4

5. 下列何項敘述不正確？

　(A) 電腦製造商已經採用了 USB，並且未來將持續一陣子。

　(B) 最初的 USB 在 1990 年後期問市，並且很成功。

　(C) 剛開始，Ajay Bhatt 很難去說服電腦製造商關於她的 USB 的構想。

　(D) **你必須啟動一些裝置才能使用 USB。**

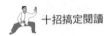

 本文圖解

① In the later part of the 1990s the Universal Serial Bus (USB) *was invented* as a system of exchanging data from one storage place to another at a relatively fast speed. Today, about 10 billion USB devices *are* in use, ③ a figure that even stuns its inventor Ajay Bhatt from Intel. USB *has become* a common name everywhere, from schools and offices to hospitals.

Ajay Bhatt *was annoyed* by the different types of connections that a PC had **and** *looked* for a simpler way of linking different parts of a computer.

and 連接 annoyed 及
looked 兩個動詞

He *tried* to set up a uniform connection system for all PC parts and other devices. Although ⑤ it was difficult for Bhatt to convince computer makers **that** he had a good idea, he finally *got* the approval to change a computer's

that 引導名詞子句當雙賓動詞 convince
的直接受詞（第二個受詞）

extension system completely.

USB *has* many advantages. For one, a single port can *control* up to 128 devices at once. They *are powered* by themselves and ⑤ you *do not have* to switch off a device to make USB work. A USB object *installs* itself. Just *plug* it in and the computer automatically downloads the software you need to make it work.

When ⑤ the first USB devices hit the markets in the late 1990s they *were* an immediate success. In later versions the transfer speed of USB devices *was drastically improved*. Today's ④ USB 3.0 standard *is* over 400 times faster than its original USB 1. All over the world millions of USB devices and adapters *are being sold* every day.

The Intel engineer *is* proud of having created a standard that ⑤ the computer industry has accepted **and that** will be here for a while to come.

and 連接二個主要子句，而 that 在句中為代名詞，
指的是前面提的創造出 USB 標準這件事

Today's PCs and laptops *have* at least 3-USB ports. USB connectors can *be found* everywhere, on printers, digital cameras, mobile phones and tablets.

人文 & 科技

①

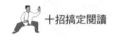

 單字與片語

重要單字 Key Vocabularies

① device (n) 裝置

② figure (n) 圖案；景像

③ stun (v) 震驚

④ annoy (v) 打擾

⑤ convince (v) 說服

⑥ approval= (n) 許可

⑦ advantages (n) 優點

⑧ plug (v) 接通

⑨ ersion (n) 版本

⑩ adapter (n) 轉接器

重要片語 Key Phrases

❶ in use 使用中

❷ switch off 關閉

❸ hit the markets 上市

❹ for a while 一會兒

❺ be proud of 以…為榮

 本文解析

　　本文第一句就提到 USB 是在 1990 年代末期發明的，然後繼續說明該發明的經過及發明者的背景，最後提到該發明對現在的影響，所以都是圍繞著 USB 發明的主題，故該文章標題應為 USB 的發明。

第二題問"stuns"這個字，在首段第三句提到現有 100 億個 USB 裝置，這是個很驚人的數字，所以發明者應該是會很震驚或驚訝，所以第二題以 shocks 最接近。同時在本句後面看到 ...its inventor Ajay Bhatt from Intel，知道 USB 的發明者是 Ajay Bhatt，而第三題題目中用 came up with(想出來這個點子) 來代表發明。接下來文章提到 USB 問市後造成極大的成功，且其傳輸的功能也有極大的進步，由 ...USB 3.0 standard is over 400 times faster than its original USB 1. 可知 USB3.0 比 USB1.0 快了 400 倍。第五題是有關於 USB 描述為非者，這些描述中，除 (D)You have to turn on a device to make USB work(你必須啟動一些裝置才能讓 USB 開始作用)，但文中提到 ...you do not have to switch off a device to make USB work，故該敘述錯誤，其餘都正確，詳圖標示處。

學習重點 ➡

被動語氣是科技技術類文章寫作常常會用到的語句，因為它能表現出人們主宰控制的意思，尤其是在論文的寫作中更是常見。如本中的 was invented...，was annoyed...，was drastically improved 等用語。主動語態的主詞是動作的執行者，其句子結構為主詞＋動詞 (及物)＋受詞 ...，而被動語態的主詞是動作的承受者，其句子結構受詞＋ be 動詞＋動詞過去分詞＋ by(或 to) 主詞 ...，而該動做承受者 (原來的主詞) 常常是被省略。並要注意被動式的變型，如本文中的 ... adapters are being sold every day 就是一個被動進行式。

學習小撇步 (Tips) ➡

閱讀測驗內容中會出現一些數字、人名等內容，這時就要注意這可能是題目的答案，而題目的選項中會有一些干擾選項，如同樣都會以文中出現的年份或數字等，來干擾粗心的答題者，有些可能需要作一些簡單的運算才能得出答案，基本上來說，這些題目都不難，只要你能看清楚再作答。

第二招
搜尋文章中的關鍵字（句）與略讀

接續前述所提，先看題目後，即可對該文章內容及所要答題重點有初步的輪廓，也知道所需留意關鍵字詞了，接下來就是回到原文中搜尋答題所需的資訊，也就是找出答題所需的關鍵字句。此時，對無關緊要的資訊可以最快的速度略讀過去即可，甚至看不懂也不用予以理會，重要的是必須經由關鍵字，確實找出與題目有相關的地方，一旦發現這些關鍵字及其相關詞語，如問某原因的 why 問句時，後面就可能出現 because 或 for the reason that…等用語時，這時閱讀速度就需稍微放慢，謹慎閱讀並確認內容，因為答案一般就在這附近，如此才能將閱讀時間用在對答題最有幫助的地方才能將閱讀的效率發揮到最大。至於何者為需要精讀的重點地方，只要回想一下這部份與題目有沒有關聯，就能研判出來。例如題目中問到一個星期中的哪一天是電視黃金時段收視最差的時間，這時必須注意的就是文章中有提到從 Sunday 到 Saturday 的字眼，而不是去注意每天的時段部分，如 0700-0830 in the morning 等部分。

要在茫茫文章中要如何將相關答題關鍵字找出來呢？這時「略讀」就是很重要的技巧（或者說觀念）。筆者認為略讀有幾個作用，首先，當然可以用它來快速掃描關鍵字詞所在處，縮小答案搜索範圍。再來，可以迅速掌握文章大義，對主旨題很有幫助，最後是去藉由略讀來掌握文章結構及內容，對相關綜合型考題（如下列敘述何者為是／非）答題有所幫助。而在略讀文章時，基本上只需要注意每一段的前兩句話，因為那往往就是整段的討論主題，其他部分則是衍生的論點，原則上不需理會（如果前兩句話還沒出現明確意義，只要繼續讀到有論點出現即可）。另外還有一個很重要的地方，那就是以群體或整段來讀，因為對於考試者而言，你只需要了解文章各段落的大意與少部份的細節即可，如果一直拘泥於部分難懂的語句或生字，只會讓寶貴的時間流逝，而對解題甚至毫無幫助。

至於如何可以加快略讀速度而不致於有讀沒有懂，甚至於誤讀，平時就要對考試出題方向的文章多加以注意，對較為不拿手的領域在平時練習時要多精讀，讓文章的類型能浮現腦海中，考試時就能以果決心態來閱讀文章並找出關鍵句加以解題。另外，快速閱讀時尤其要注意文章中的像 it, this, that, so 等指示代名詞所代表的確實含意，以免因誤判而造成誤解文章真正意思，或因邏輯不通根本無法了解文章，況且有些題目還會直接問這些指示代名詞所指的是文章中的何項名詞，所以不可不慎！以下為測驗文章中一段，可以說明如何用本段所敘述的觀念及方法來解題：

After 16 weeks of labor contract disputes, Wang Metals workers say they have had enough. At 10:30 this morning, hundreds of workers walked out of work and onto the picket line. Wang Metals has more than 800 workers, and the union says about 90 percent of them are participating in the strike. They plan to continue to picket factory office here in four-hour shifts. The union representative claims workers have taken these measures as a last resort. "We had met and decided to wait for the company to put a decent offer on the table, and when it finally did last night, it turned out to be unacceptable. So, we voted to strike." The representative said that workers intend to strike as long as necessary. Extra security has been ordered by the plant, and guards are blocking passage through the main entrance to the factory. Local business leaders are concerned because any kind of prolonged dispute could have a negative effect on other sectors of the community as well. "Wang Metals is the backbone of our local economy. Everything from food to entertainment, to houses... it all connects to the plant," says one business owner.

1. Which of the following is the best headline for this news?

(A) Wang Plant Orders Extra Security

(B) 800 Workers Stage Walkout at Wang

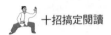
(C) Wang Metals Loses Money During Strike

(D) Wang Workers Start Strike Today

2. What triggered the strike?

(A) The company being the backbone of the local economy.

(B) An offer by the company that the union found unacceptable.

(C) 90 percent of the workers picketing the factory offices.

(D) The company ordering extra security guards.

3. How long do the workers intend to strike?

(A) For four weeks.

(B) A number of weeks.

(C) Indefinitely.

(D) Late into the night.

　　第一個題目問該報導的最佳標題，其實就是說該文章的要旨，由開頭第二句 At 10:30 this morning, hundreds of workers walked out of work and onto the picket line 應該就可以知道該篇主要報導這家公司今天上午的罷工 (walked out of work) 行動。如果你還不放心，那就以略讀的方式快速瀏覽全文，就可以知道報導一開始就指出今天上午數以百計的工人示威罷工，再來說明罷工的原因是因為待遇的談判已經破裂，最後是當地企業對該公司罷工對當地經濟影響的憂慮，故答案為 (D) 今天王式金屬員工開始罷工。另外，也許你不知道第二句後面出現的 picket line（警戒線）這個字，但它不會妨礙到你閱讀，因為由面前 walked out of work 及後面提到的 strike 都是講有關罷工，所以根本沒影響。第二個題目中看到 what，就是要找與 strike 發生相關的字眼，由 ... We had met and decided to wait for the company to put a decent offer on the table, and when it finally did last night, it turned out to be unacceptable. So, we voted to strike...，知道罷工的原因是 it turned out to be unacceptable，而這 it 是指 a decent offer（一個合理的待遇）。第三個題目中看到 workers intend to strike 可視為關鍵字，由文中"The representative said that workers intend to strike as long as necessary...." 可輕易看出答案應該是 (C)

Indefinitely(無限期)，這邊需注意的是該選項用 Indefinitely，而文章中是用 as long as necessary，這是一種改敘手法，後面會談到這方面的問題。

2

心
理
&
健
康

 英文本文

Article 2.1

Have you ever felt an unexplainable feeling when you first experience something? It seems as if you have experienced it before. That strange feel is déjà vu. You may have heard a story from one of your family members who correctly sensed a problem with another family member who was far away. Was this **extraordinary** instinct a form of telepathy? Telepathy, or mind reading, is thought of as extrasensory perception, or ESP. It is possible a form of communication from one mind to another by extrasensory means instead of through the normal five senses. Telepathy is also known as déjà vu, thought transference, the 6th sense, the third eye, or a gut feeling.

The world telepathy was invited by the French researcher Fredric W. H. Myers in 1882. In 1885 the American Society for Psychical Research was founded and began to study telepathy scientifically. A sender tries to transmit a number a test, or an image to another person in a separated room who tries to receive the information. So far, the research hasn't proved the existence of telepathy. Nonetheless, the famous psychiatrists Sigmund Freud and Carl G. Jung believed in telepathy. Freud said it was a primitive ability which could sometime occur.

If telepathy is real, it doesn't happen all the time. However, superheroes and super-villains with reliable telepathic abilities are found in many novels and movies. In the popular Harry Potter series of book by J. K. Rowling, telepathy is just one of the many possible magic abilities. Movie series, such as Star War and Star Trek, also have individuals capable of telepathy. Telepathy is definitely and exciting idea.

Does communication occur between the minds people who are separated? Can you read someone's mind? What do you think?

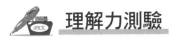 理解力測驗

Q1. Which of the following statements summarizes this article?

(A) Sometimes, people feel as if they have foreknowledge when they first do something.

(B) Telepathy is perhaps a form of communication from one mind to another by extrasensory means.

(C) Telepathy is one of the many possible magic abilities.

(D) Instinct is a form of knowledge.

Q2. This article is mainly about

(A) American Society for Psychical Research.

(B) mind-to-mind communication.

(C) the result of telepathy research.

(D) the famous psychiatrists Sigmund Freud and Carl G. Jung.

Q3. The purpose of the last paragraph is to

(A) emphasize your important role in this research of telepathy.

(B) offer an explanation of telepathy.

(C) encourage you to think about the subject.

(D) explain that you have the final say about the subject.

Q4. According to this article, what is telepathy?

(A) It's a real and ordinary instinct.

(B) It's communication between minds through the five senses.

(C) It refers to knowledge conveyed from one person to another by means of the normal sense.

(D) It refers to possible thought transference.

Q5. In the first paragraph, the word "**extraordinary**" means

(A) amazingly regular.

(B) extremely ordinary.

(C) unusually and amazing

(D) having special responsibility.

2

心
理
&
健
康

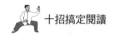

 **本文中譯**

心靈感應

　　你是否曾經對某種初次經歷到的事情有一種莫名的感覺？彷彿之前就已經經歷過的。這種奇怪的感覺就是"幻覺記憶"，這是一種似曾相似的感覺。或許你曾經聽過你的某個親人可以感覺到另一個身在遠方親人遭遇麻煩，這種奇異的本能就是一種心靈感應嗎？心靈感應又稱之為讀心術，被認為是一種超感官知覺，這可能是種非透過一般五種感官而在心靈間傳遞的超感官溝通方式。心靈感應也是一般常說的似曾相似、傳心術、第六感、第三隻眼、或直覺。

　　心靈感應這個術語最早出現於 1882 年，由法國科學家佛雷德克・邁爾斯所提出。1885 年美國心理研究學會成立，開始用科學方法研究心靈感應，由一個人用念力發送數字、味道或圖像，傳送給另一個房間內的接收者。到目前為止，這項研究還無法證明心靈感應的存在。不過，著名的心理並理學家佛洛依德和卡爾・容格都相信心靈感應的存在。佛洛依德表示，心靈感應是一種偶而會發生的原始能力。

　　就算有心靈感應的存在，也不一定時時都會發生，不過，在小說和電影裏，倒是常常可以見到擁有良好心靈感應能力的超級英雄或超級惡棍。在 J. K. 羅琳廣受歡迎的哈利波特系列中，心靈感應不過是眾多神奇能力的一種。在星際大戰和星際旅行的電影系列中，有些人物也擁有心靈感應的能力，心靈感應無非是一個會讓人興奮的點子。各處一方的人，可以用心靈感應來溝通嗎？你能讀別人的心思嗎？你如何看的？

理解力測驗中譯

1. 下列何者為本文的大意？

(A) 有時候，人們第一次做一些事情時會感覺他們好像有預知的能力。

(B) 心靈感應可能是一種用超感官的方法將人的想法傳給另一個人的傳達方式。

(C) 心靈感應是許多神奇能力的其中一種。

(D) 直覺是一種知識的形式。

2. 本文主要談到？

(A) 美國心靈研究社。

(B) 心靈對心靈的溝通。

(C) 心靈感應研究的結果。

(D) 有名的心理學家 Sigmund Freud 與 Carl G. Jung。

3. 最後第一段的主要目的在於

(A) 強調在這個心靈感應研究中你的重要地位。

(B) 提供心靈感應的解釋。

(C) 鼓勵你思考一下這主題。

(D) 解釋你有對這個主題的最終說法。

4. 依據本文，何為心電感應？

(A) 它是一種真實且尋常可見的本能。

(B) 它是經由五種感官來溝通心靈。

(C) 它意味著經由一般的感官來將知識由一個人傳至另一個人。

(D) 它意味著移情作用的可能性。

5. 在第一段中，"extraordinary" 這個字的意思是

(A) 令人驚訝地尋常。

(B) 極度地平常。

(C) 不尋常且令人驚訝。

(D) 有特殊的責任。

 **本文圖解**

Have you ever *felt* an unexplainable feeling <u>when you first experience</u>

<u>something</u>? It seems as if <u>you have experienced it before</u>. That strange feel *is*

déjà vu. You may *have heard* a story from one of your family members

<u>who correctly sensed a problem with another family member who was</u>
第一個形容詞子句修飾　　　　　　　　　　　　　形容詞子句內的形容詞
members　　　　　　　　　　　　　　　　　　　子句修飾 member
far away. *Was* ⑤Ⓐ this extraordinary instinct a form of telepathy? Telepathy,

or mind reading, *is thought of* as extrasensory perception, or ESP. ⑤Ⓒ It

is possible that a form of communication from one mind to another by

extrasensory means ⑤Ⓑ instead of through the normal five senses. ⑤Ⓓ Telepathy

is also known as déjà vu, <u>thought transference</u>, the 6th sense, the third eye,
　　　　　　　　　　這些詞都是用來說明前面的 déjà vu 代表的意義

or a gut feeling.

The world telepathy *was invited* by the French researcher Fredric W.

H. Myers in 1882. In 1885 the American Society for Psychical Research

was founded and *began* to study telepathy scientifically. A sender *tries* to transmit a number a test, or an image to another person in a separated room

who tries to receive the information. So far, the research *hasn't proved* the

existence of telepathy. Nonetheless, the famous psychiatrists Sigmund Freud

and Carl G. Jung *believed* in telepathy. Freud *said* **it** was a primitive ability

which could sometime occur.

it 指的是 telepathy，後面為
一名詞子句當成 said 的受詞，
which 再引導一型容詞子句修
飾 ability

2
心理＆健康

If telepathy is real, it *doesn't happen* all the time. However, superheroes

and super-villains with reliable telepathic abilities *are found* in many novels

with 引導的介係詞片語，表示具有…的能力

and movies. In the popular Harry Potter series of book by J. K. Rowling,

telepathy *is* just one of the many possible magic abilities. Movie series

such as Star War and Star Trek also *have* individuals Capable of telepathy.

Telepathy *is* definitely and exciting idea.

Does communication *occur* between the minds of people who are

separated? Can you *read* someone's mind? What do you *think*?

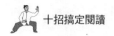

 單字與片語

重要單字 Key Vocabularies

① extraordinary (a) 非常的

② instinct (n) 本能，天性

③ telepathy (n) 心靈感應

④ definitely (adv) 明確地

⑤ transference (n) 轉移

⑥ transmit (v) 傳送

⑦ psychiatrist (n) 精神醫學者

⑧ superhero (n) 超級明星

⑨ extrasensory perception 超感官知覺

⑩ yield (v) 出產；產生

⑪ satisfactory (a) 令人滿意的

⑫ behavior (n) 行為

重要片語 Key Phrases

❶ as if 就如同…一樣

❷ instead of 替代

❸ believed in 認為存在

❹ all the time 一直，向來

 **本文解析**

本文開始未立刻點出主題，而是藉由一些現象描述，像是聽過親人間的感應等故事帶領讀者進入主題，之後就談到心靈感應是一種超感官的溝通方式，並且有心理學家進行研究，但都尚無法確定這種能力的真實存在，所以對此現象仍有懷疑，信者恆信。故第一題問本文的要點，就是心靈感應可能是一種用超感官的方法將人的想法傳給另一個人的傳達方式。

第二題問主要談到的內容就是心靈之間 (mind-to-mind) 的溝通。第三題問本文的最後一段目的為何？因最後一段是連續三個疑問句，且對照前面段落可知，這種心靈感應雖然有些專家如 Freud 等人相信，但都未被證實，所以文中並未提供明確的答案，而是要讀者自己思考一下 (think about the subject)。第四題問有關於心靈感應的敘述，除了 It refers to possible thought transference. (它意味著移情作用的可能性)，其他敘述都為錯誤，請對照本文圖解示處。而最後第五題的 "extraordinary" 這個字是非常、極度的之意，句中表示這種能力是一種不尋常的本能，所以選項中以 (unusually and amazing，不尋常且令人驚訝) 最恰當。

學習重點 ➡

介係詞片語是由介係詞開頭，後面接名詞或代名詞等兩個或兩個以上的字群所組成。可當名詞、當形容詞或當副詞使用，修飾動詞、形容詞、其他副詞或修飾整句，最常用得是當形容詞用，修飾在它前面的名詞 (注意：與一般形容詞放在名詞前面的用法不同) 例如：However, superheroes and super-villains with reliable telepathic abilities are found in many novels and movies. 句中 with reliable telepathic abilities 就是一組由 with 引導的介係詞片語，當形容詞用來修飾前面的名詞 superheroes and super-villains (主詞)。

心理&健康 ②

 英文本文

Article 2.2

In the United States, flu season occurs between October and following May, with the peak of the season occurring between late December and March. An estimated 5% to 20% of the US population gets the seasonal flu, and more than 200,000 individuals are hospitalized for complications related to the influenza virus. Although the majority of healthy individuals will recover from the influenza virus in a few days to a week, there are approximately 23,600 flu-related deaths annually. Patient populations, include individuals older than 65 years; those with **chronic** health conditions, such as diabetes, asthma, chronic obstructive pulmonary disease, cardiovascular disease, sickle cell anemia, renal or hepatic disorders, and pregnant women; and young children are at an increased risk for developing complications associated with the influenza virus and should obtain yearly vaccinations. Possible flu-related complications include bacterial pneumonia, dehydration, and ear and sinus infections, as well as the exacerbation of certain chronic medical conditions, such as congestive heart failure, asthma, and diabetes. Certain populations should not be vaccinated without consulting a physician first. In 2009, an estimated 12,000 flu-related deaths were due to the H1N1 pandemic in the United States. In contrast to seasonal flu, approximately 90% of the deaths were among those younger than 65 years. Individuals between the ages of 50 and 64 years were the most affected by the 2009 H1N1 virus, with an estimated 80% of this patient population having 1 or more medical conditions.

 理解力測驗

Q1. What does the word "**chronic**" in line 8 refer to?

   (A) Short-term.
   (B) Long-term.
   (C) Acute.
   (D) All of the above.

Q2. According to the information, when is the peak of flu season in the U.S.?

   (A) Between October and May.
   (B) Between late December and March.
   (C) Between late December and May.
   (D) Between October and March.

Q3. Based on the contents, how many flu-related deaths approximately in the U.S. every year?

   (A) 200,000.
   (B) 23,600.
   (C) 12,000.
   (D) None of the above.

Q4. Which of the following descriptions is NOT true?

   (A) The flu season occurs between October and May in the U.S.
   (B) Possible flu-related complications include bacterial pneumonia.
   (C) Certain populations could be vaccinated without consulting a physician first.
   (D) About 90% of the H1N1 pandemic deaths were younger than 65 years.

Q5. Regarding the information, in 2009, an estimated 12,000 flu-related deaths in the United States resulted from?

   (A) Seasonal Flu.
   (B) H1N1 virus.
   (C) Influenza virus.
   (D) Chronic disease.

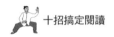

 本文中譯

流感疫苗

　　在美國，流感季節發生介於 10 月至隔年 5 月，季節高峰期則發生介於 12 月底到隔年 3 月之間。估計約有 5% 至 20% 的美國民眾會得到季節性的流感，並且超過 200,000 的人住院治療流感病毒相關的併發症。即使大多數健康的人會在幾天到一週的時間內自流感病毒中恢復健康，但每年仍有大約 23,600 人死於流感相關的疾病。患者人口包括 65 歲以上的人。患有慢性病健康狀況的人，例如糖尿病、氣喘病、慢性阻塞性肺病、心血管疾病、鐮刀型貧血症、腎臟或肝臟疾病，和懷孕的婦女和幼童都處於染上與流感病毒相關併發症增加的風險中，並且都應接受每年一次的疫苗接種。可能與流感相關的併發症包括細菌性肺炎、脫水、耳朵以及鼻竇感染，以及某些慢性醫療狀況的惡化，例如鬱（充）血性心臟衰竭、氣喘病與糖尿病。某些族群若未經醫師諮詢不應注射疫苗。2009 年，估計大約有 12,000 件與流感相關的死亡案例是由美國流行疾病 H1N1 所造成。對照季節性流感，大約有 90% 的死亡案例是小於 65 歲的人。介於 50 歲與 64 歲的人是最容易受到 2009 H1N1 病毒的侵襲，估計有 80% 的這種患者人口會一種或多種醫療狀況。

理解力測驗中譯

1. 第 7 行的 "chronic" 是何意？

(A) 短期的

(B) 長期的

(C) 急性的

(D) 以上皆是

2. 根據本文中的資訊，何為美國流感冒季節的高峰期？

(A) 介於 10 月至隔年 5 月

(B) 介於 12 月底至隔年 3 月

(C) 介於 12 月底至隔年 5 月

(D) 介於 10 月至隔年 3 月

3. 根據本文內容，美國每一年大約有多少人死於流感相關的疾病？

(A) 200,000

(B) 23,600

(C) 12,000

(D) 以上皆非

4. 下列何者不是正確的敘述？

(A) 在美國，流感季節發生介於 10 月至隔年 5 月。

(B) 可能與流感相關的併發症包括細菌性肺炎。

(C) 某些人可以未經諮詢醫師就注射疫苗。

(D) 約有 90% 的 HIN1 流感死亡的人是未滿 65 歲的。

5. 根據本文資訊，2009 年在美國估計有 12,000 的流感相關死亡案例是起因於？

(A) 季節性流感

(B) H1N1 病毒

(C) 流感病毒

(D) 慢性疾病

 本文圖解

In the United States, ④A flu season *occurs* between October and May,

② **with** the peak of the season **occurring** between late December and

with 引導介係詞片語，說明　　分詞片語，修飾 season
伴隨著…的情況

March. An estimated 5% to 20% of the US population *gets* the seasonal

flu, and more than 200,000 individuals *are hospitalized* for complications

related to the influenza virus. Although the majority of healthy individuals

過去分詞片語修飾 complications，
表示與某方面有關

will recover from the influenza virus in a few days to a week, ③ there *are*

approximately 23,600 flu-related deaths annually. Patient populations

include individuals older than 65 years, those with chronic health conditions,

第一個主要子句動詞 include 的受詞為 individuals... or hepatic disorders

such as diabetes, asthma, chronic obstructive pulmonary disease,

such as 後面的疾病名稱為舉例說明說何謂
chronic health conditions(慢性病健康狀況)

cardiovascular disease, sickle cell anemia, renal or hepatic disorders, **and**

pregnant women and young children *are* at an increased risk for developing

complications **associated with** the influenza virus **and** should *obtain*

and 連接第二個主要子句
的第二個動詞 obtain

yearly vaccinations. ④B Possible flu-related complications *include* bacterial

pneumonia, dehydration, and **ear and sinus infections**, as well as the

對等連接詞 and 連接第二個主要子句

exacerbation of certain chronic medical conditions, such as congestive

heart failure, asthma, and diabetes. ④C Certain populations should not *be*

vaccinated without consulting a physician first. In 2009, ⑤ an **estimated**

過去分詞當形容詞，表示被
估計的，修飾後面的名詞

12,000 flu-related deaths *were* due to the H1N1 pandemic in the United

過去分詞片語，表示與某方面有關聯

States. ④D In contrast to seasonal flu, approximately 90% of the deaths *were*

among **those** younger than 65 years. Individuals between the ages of 50 and

本句原為：those (who are) younger than 65 years.，
表示那些年紀超過 65 歲的人

64 years *were the most affected* by the 2009 H1N1 virus, **with** an estimated

with 表示附帶…狀況之下
(80% 的病人有其他醫療狀況)

80% of this patient population having one or more medical conditions.

該組字視為一個專有詞，也就是耳鼻竇感染，
需與前面的對等連接詞 and 做區分

② 心理 & 健康

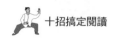
單字與片語

重要單字 Key Vocabularies

① peak (n) 高峰；山峰

② seasonal flu 季節性感冒

③ hospitalized (v) 住院治療

④ complications (n) 併發症；複雜化

⑤ influenza virus 流感病毒

⑥ chronic (a) 慢性的；長期的

⑦ yearly (a) 每年一次的

⑧ vaccinations (n) 接種

⑨ exacerbation (n) 惡化

重要片語 Key Phrases

❶ the majority of 與…形成對比

❷ such as 例如

❸ associated with 與…有關聯

本文解析

　　本篇由開頭第一句便可看到 flu season (流感季節) 這個字，且後面不斷提到有關美國流感死亡人數及應特別注意的族群等，故可知該文為一篇有關美國流感發生的醫學報告 (導)。

　　在第八行中的 "chronic" 這個字是慢性的、長期的意思，所以第一題答案很明顯為 long-term(長期)。第二題答案可由第一句中得知，流感高峰期則發生介於 12 月底到隔年 3 月之間。第三題有關於流感每年死亡人數可由第七行 there are approximately 23,600 flu-related deaths annually 中得到答案，但注意別與後面 an estimated

12,000 flu-related deaths were due to the H1N1 pandemic...，這邊的死亡人數是指 H1N1 禽流感引起的，這也是第五題的答案，所以要注意數字間的關係。第五題是有關本篇的敘述何者為非，只要將選項中的關鍵字在文章內中找出，即可看出答案。請注意，本題選項 C 要看文章中 Certain populations should not be vaccinated without consulting a physician first...，意思是這些人沒有醫生允許不可注射疫苗，也就是要有允許才可注射疫苗，其餘請參考本文圖解所示。

學習重點 ➡

　　本篇文章的結構並不複雜，沒有讓人害怕搞不清楚的關係詞結構，但其中有些句子很長，如果沒有清楚的句型概念，恐怕讀起來會很辛苦。如這句 Patient populations including... and should obtain yearly vaccinations. 一共有 54 個單字，但是經分析後就是 Patient populations include ＋（受詞 1），such as（舉例說明受詞 1 有哪些）and pregnant women(受詞 2)；and（對等連接詞連接第二個句子）young children are(動詞 1) and should obtain（用 and 連接動詞 2) yearly vaccinations。這樣就能一目了然了，所以如何將句中真正的主詞動詞找出，並弄清楚連接詞連接的對象是非常重要的，而這有賴於清楚的文法句型概念。

學習小撇步 (Tips) ➡

　　本篇文章雖然看似有很多有關疾病的專有名詞，但其實那都只是障眼法，讓人看得眼花撩亂，但真正需要知道的也只有 flu, influenza virus, pandemic 等幾個基本常用的字。所以就算對於較少見的醫學報告的文章，只要將基礎的一些醫學及疾病等相關用語記起來，如 clinic(診所)、cough(咳嗽)、contagious(傳染的)、diabetes(糖尿病、肥胖)、malaria(瘧疾) 等，就不用擔心會被考倒，因為閱讀測驗不是考你專業的知識，只是考你閱讀能力。

2 心理 & 健康

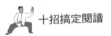

 英文本文

Article 2.3

Bone is constantly remodeled through the balanced activities of osteoblasts and osteoclasts. Whereas genetic defects of bone-forming osteoblasts typically **result in** delayed bone development and osteoporosis, mutational inactivation of bone-resorbing osteoclasts leads to osteopetrosis, a condition of high bone mass accompanied by immunologic defects due to bone marrow displacement. Through their ability to release calcium from the mineralized bone matrix, osteoclasts are also involved in calcium homeostasis, which is mediated mostly by the action of parathyroid hormone (PTH) triggering increased bone resorption. Likewise, hypocalcemia and hyperparathyroidism have been observed in individuals with infantile malignant osteopetrosis, and there are a few case reports describing rachitic widening of the growth plate, a phenotype that has been termed osteopetrorickets. Because osteoclasts resorb bone through extracellular acidification, it is not surprising that most of the known human osteopetrosis mutations affect genes involved in acid production and secretion.

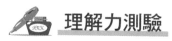 理解力測驗

Q1. According to the passage, bone will be constantly remodeled through
(A) mutational inactivation.
(B) bone-forming activity.
(C) balanced activities of osteoblasts and osteoclasts.
(D) bone marrow displacement.

Q2. What is the closest meaning of "**result in**" in line 3?
(A) outcome
(B) cause
(C) enter
(D) reason

Q3. Based on the information, osteoclasts are also involved in
(A) calcium homeostasis.
(B) bone sorption.
(C) growth plate wideness.
(D) acidification.

Q4. Who will be interested in responding to this article?
(A) Male readers
(B) Female readers
(C) Medical students
(D) Seniors

Q5. Which of the following statements is NOT true?
(A) Osteopetrosis is a condition of high bone mass accompanied by immunologic defects because of bone marrow displacement.
(B) Genetic defects of osteoblasts typically result in delayed bone development and osteoporosis.
(C) Most of the known human osteopetrosis mutations affect genes involved in acid production and secretion.
(D) Hypocalcemia and hyperparathyroidism have hardly been observed in individuals with infantile malignant osteopetrosis.

②
心理&健康

 本文中譯

骨質疏鬆症

　　經由成骨細胞與蝕骨細胞的平衡活動，骨骼會不斷的重組。有鑒於骨骼成形的成骨細胞之基因缺陷通常會導致遲緩性骨骼生長與骨質疏鬆症，而蝕骨細胞的突變則會導致骨質疏鬆症，這是一種因骨髓替換產生免疫性缺陷所伴隨而來的高骨質的症狀。經由蝕骨細胞可自富含礦物質的骨母質中釋放鈣離子的能力，蝕骨細胞也牽涉到鈣離子的恆定，這是大多由副甲狀腺素 (PTH) 觸發行為所增加骨骼的溶蝕來調節的。同樣地，在罹患嬰兒惡性骨質疏鬆症的個體中，也觀察到低血鈣症與副甲狀腺高能症，並且有少數的病例報告則是描述生長板的佝僂病性的增寬，這是一種被稱做石骨症的表現型態。因為蝕骨細胞經由細胞外的酸化作用來溶蝕骨骼，所以大多數已知的人類骨質疏鬆症的突變缺陷基因都與酸的產生以及分泌物有關這並不意外。

 **理解力測驗中譯**

1. 根據本文,骨頭會經由何者不斷地重組?

(A) 突變鈍化

(B) 成骨活動

(C) 成骨細胞與蝕骨細胞的平衡活動

(D) 骨髓替換

2. 下列何意最接近第 3 行的"result in"?

(A) 結果

(B) 造成

(C) 進入

(D) 原因

3. 根據本文資訊,蝕骨細胞也涉及?

(A) 鈣離子的恆定

(B) 骨吸收

(C) 生長板增寬

(D) 酸化

4. 下列何者會較有興趣回應此文?

(A) 男性讀者

(B) 女性讀者

(C) 醫學院學生

(D) 老年人

5. 下列何者陳述為非?

(A) 骨骼會經由成骨細胞與蝕骨細胞的平衡活動而不斷的重組。

(B) 基因缺陷則會典型的導致遲緩性骨骼生長與骨質疏鬆症。

(C) 大多數已知的人類骨質疏鬆症的突變缺陷基因都與酸的產生以及分泌物有關。

(D) 在罹患嬰兒惡性骨質疏鬆症的個體中,很少觀察到低血鈣症與副甲狀腺高能症。

 本文圖解

① Bone *is* constantly *remodeled* through the balanced activities

of osteoblasts and osteoclasts. **Whereas** genetic defects of bone-

連接詞引導的副詞子句，表示有鑑於…情形

forming ⑤Ⓑ osteoblasts typically result in delayed bone development and

osteoporosis, mutational inactivation of bone-resorbing osteoclasts *leads*

to ⑤Ⓐ osteopetrosis, a condition of high bone mass **accompanied by**

分詞片語，修飾前面的
condition

immunologic defects **due to** bone marrow displacement. Through **their**

介係詞片語，修飾 defects，
表示歸因於…

their 指的是
osteoclasts

ability to release calcium from the mineralized bone matrix, ③ osteoclasts

are also involved in calcium homeostasis, which is mediated mostly by the

action of parathyroid hormone (PTH) **triggering** increased bone resorption.

表結果的分詞片語，意思為激發出…

Likewise, ⑤Ⓓ hypocalcemia and hyperparathyroidism *have been observed* in

individuals with infantile malignant osteopetrosis, and there *are* a few case

reports describing rachitic widening of the growth plate, a phenotype that has been termed osteopetrorickets. Because osteoclasts resorb bone through

extracellular acidification, it *is* not surprising **that** ⑤ⓒ most of the known

> that 引導的名詞子句，事
> 實上就等於該句主詞 it

human osteopetrosis mutations affect genes **involved in** acid production

> 分詞片語修飾 genes，
> 表示與…有關的

and secretion.

2 心理 & 健康

單字與片語

重要單字 Key Vocabularies

① remodeled（v）重塑

② balanced activities　平衡活動

③ mutational（a）突變的

④ inactivation（n）鈍化

⑤ bone mass　骨質

⑥ accompanied（v）伴隨

⑦ bone marrow　骨髓

⑧ displacement（n）替換；位移

⑨ Likewise（adv）同樣地

⑩ Termed（v）稱作

重要片語 Key Phrases

❶ result in　導致

❷ leads to　造成

❸ release A from B　自 B 釋放出 A

❹ involved in　涉及；專注於

❺ it is not surprising　不令人意外的

本文解析

　　本文首先提到骨質疏鬆症與成骨細胞與蝕骨細胞息息相關。而在罹患嬰兒惡性骨質疏鬆症的個體中，有低血鈣症與副甲狀腺高能症的現象，且有生長板的佝僂病性的增寬，這是因為蝕骨細胞影響而造成的，最後提到人類骨質疏鬆症的突變缺陷基因與酸的產生以及分泌物有關。該文主要就是提到成骨細胞與蝕骨細胞二者對人體及相關疾病的影響。

　　第一題問到骨頭會經由何者不斷地重組，由題目關鍵字 bone will be constantly

remodeled，很快在第一行就可以得到答案，讀者可以不用知道何謂 osteoblasts 及 osteoclasts。第二題提到與"result in"意思最近的字，它的意思是"造成…結果"，所以答案是 cause(造成)。第三題是說蝕骨細胞與何有關？你可以在文中由題目關鍵字 also involved in，在第六行中找到相關的字句，讀者也許不知道 calcium homeostasis 的意思，但沒關係，那就是答案。第四題問誰會對本文有興趣，本篇都是講述相關醫學上的現象，所以應該是醫學院學生會有興趣來看。最後一題問敘述何者為非，同樣用每一選項中的關鍵字去找文中的相關地方，就可以比對出來了，但要注意可能會經過改寫。另外，要注意否定及肯定的用語，否定不見得會出現 not 字眼，例如本題答案就是用加 hardly，來將原來的肯定變成否定，相關句子請參考標示處。

學習重點 ➡

句子中常會看到 (N ＋分詞) 這種結構，最常見的是過去分詞，這是由形容詞子句簡化而來，稱為分詞修飾語或分詞片語，如本文中的一段"it is not surprising that most of the known human osteopetrosis mutations affect genes involved in acid production and secretion."，這時 involved in acid production and secretion 就是一個分詞片語，修飾前面名詞 genes。而該分詞片語也可視為形容詞子句 (which is) involved in acid production and secretion. 的省略型式。

例句：It is hard for him to understand a letter written in English.

（看懂一封英文信對他來說 是一件困難的事。）

= It is hard for him to understand a letter which was written in English.

學習小撇步 (Tips) ➡

本篇為有關於醫療相關資訊的題型，且其中有不少醫學專業用語，如 osteoblasts、osteoclasts、immunologic、parathyroid hormone 等，讀者除非有醫學背景，否則應該不會認識這些單字，但是作為一篇閱讀測驗的題目，這些專業用語應該不會成為閱讀及解題的障礙，讀者只要把它們當成一個專有名詞來看待就行了，必要時給個代號以資區別，如 A 代表 osteoblasts，B 為 osteoclasts 等。

2 心理 & 健康

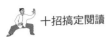

 英文本文

Article 2.4

Children with Craniofacial differences are at a higher risk of developing psychosocial issues related to anxiety, self-esteem, and depression, as well as being targets of teasing, bullying, and social isolation. The number of resources available to address the psychosocial concerns specific to Craniofacial populations are limited. Studies have shown that children with chronic conditions who receive support from those who share their experience can be beneficial, particularly within specialized camps that create opportunities for patients to connect. Craniofacial camp programs provide safe, therapeutic environments that promote self-esteem, confidence, social awareness, and normalization of any physical or facial disfigurements. The collaboration between Craniofacial teams and established children and family camps increases therapeutic experiences for our Craniofacial populations. This presentation highlights how our Craniofacial team went about establishing a relationship with the Painted Turtle camp in Lake Hughes, CA. The Painted Turtle is a non-profit organization member of the Paul Newman Serious Fun Camps, formerly the Association of Hole in the Wall Camps. As of March 2012, the Painted Turtle began serving children and families with Craniofacial conditions. The camp is providing opportunities for our patients and their families to connect and share experiences. This presentation describes the steps that were taken to help qualify our patient population for the Craniofacial camp experience, which may be applicable both nationally and internationally. Criteria for consideration of inclusion of our patient population are discussed. Strategies are offered for identifying and **keeping track of** candidate patients and families that come for Craniofacial team visits on average once per year. Collaboration with existent local children camps is essential to help expand the opportunity for Craniofacial patients and families to connect with each other and to increase therapeutic resources to this patient population.

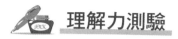 理解力測驗

Q1. According to the contents, which of the followings is NOT the possible psychosocial issue for children with Craniofacial differences?

(A) anxiety

(B) bullying others

(C) self-esteem

(D) depression

Q2. What is the main purpose of a Craniofacial camp program?

(A) It provides a safe and therapeutic environment.

(B) It promotes a medical treatment of any physical or facial disfigurements.

(C) It gives the patients a specific experiment.

(D) None of the above.

Q3. Based on the contents, what can we learn about the Painted Turtle camp?

(A) It is a non-profit organization member of the Paul Newman SeriousFun Camps.

(B) It began serving children and families with Craniofacial conditions on March 2012.

(C) It provides opportunities for Craniofacial patients and their families to connect and share experiences.

(D) All of the above.

Q4. What is the meaning of "**keeping track of**" in line 24?

(A) running

(B) walking

(C) recording

(D) making

Q5. According to the passage, how often do the candidate patients and families come for Craniofacial team visits?

(A) Once a year.

(B) Twice a year.

(C) Three times a year.

(D) No mention.

 本文中譯

顱顏夏令營

　　患有顱顏差異的孩童有呈現出焦慮、自我以及憂鬱等等心理問題的高度風險，並且常常容易成為嘲弄、霸凌以及社會孤立的目標。但用於關懷心理層面，特別是對顱顏差異患者的可用資源數量卻是有限的。研究報告顯示，具有慢性狀況的孩童，如經由來自其他患者自身經驗的分享支持，對他們是非常有益處的，尤其是在讓患者有機會可彼此接觸聯繫的特定夏令營隊中。顱顏夏令營計畫提供安全的、有療效的環境，可促進自尊、自信、社會自覺以及身體或顏面缺陷的正常化。透過顱顏小組及組織完善的親子夏令營隊共同合作，可增進對於顱顏異常病患治療的經驗。這篇介紹中強調我們的顱顏小組是如何著手進行建立與位於加州修司湖的錦龜 (Painted Turtle) 夏令營隊之間的關係。錦龜夏令營是一個非營利性組織，保羅紐曼極度趣味夏令營隊 (Paul Newman Serious Fun Camps) 的成員，原為希望之光夏令營協會 (Association of Hole in the Wall Camps)。到了 2012 年 3 月，錦龜開始服務患有顱顏狀況的孩童及其家屬。該夏令營隊提供機會，讓我們的患者及其家屬可以彼此接觸聯繫，並且分享自身的經驗。這篇介紹詳述我們協助讓患者有資格參加該顱顏夏令營體驗的步驟，這些步驟也能適用於全國性或國際性的活動。關於患者的考慮內容標準也有討論到。這些策略是用來作為追蹤及驗證這些平均每年一度來到顱顏團隊的候選病患及家屬們。與在地現有孩童夏令營隊的合作主要是來協助展開顱顏異常的患者及其家屬互相的聯繫與接觸，並且可以增加對於該病患的治療資源。

理解力測驗中譯

1. 根據本文內容，下列何者不是患有顱顏差異的孩童有可能有的心理問題？

(A) 焦慮

(B) 霸凌別人

(C) 自我

(D) 憂鬱

2. 何者為顱顏夏令營計畫的主要目的？

(A) 提供一個安全以及有療效的環境

(B) 促進一個身體或顏面缺陷的醫療

(C) 給予病患特定的實驗

(D) 以上皆非

3. 根據本文內容，我們可以瞭解關於錦龜夏令營的是

(A) 它是一個非營利性組織，保羅紐曼極度趣味夏令營隊的成員

(B) 2012 年 3 月，錦龜開始服務患有顱顏狀況的孩童及其家屬

(C) 錦龜提供機會，讓顱顏患者及其家屬可以彼此接觸聯繫，並且分享自身的經驗

(D) 以上皆是

4. 第 22 行的"keeping track of"是何意？

(A) 跑步

(B) 走路

(C) 記錄

(D) 做

5. 根據本文，顱顏小組應進行平均一年幾次的訪問候選患者及其家屬？

(A) 一年一次

(B) 一年兩次

(C) 一年三次

(D) 沒有提到

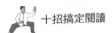

 **本文圖解**

① Children with Craniofacial differences *are* at higher risk of developing

psychosocial issues **related** to anxiety, self-esteem, and depression, as well as
　　　　　　　分詞片語修飾 issues

being targets of teasing, bullying, and social isolation.

The number of resources **available to** address the psychosocial concerns
　　　　　　　分詞片語修飾 resources，可視為省略關係
　　　　　　　詞的句型 (which are) available to...
specific to Craniofacial populations *are* limited. Studies *have shown* **that**
　　　　　　　　　　　　　　　that 引導的名詞子句
　　　　　　　　　　　　　　　當 show 受詞
children with chronic conditions who receive support from those who share

their experience can be beneficial, particularly within specialized camps that

create opportunities for patients to connect. ② Craniofacial camp programs

provide safe, therapeutic environments that promote self-esteem, confidence,

social awareness, and normalization of any physical or facial disfigurements.

The collaboration between Craniofacial teams and **established** children
　　　　　　　　　　　　　　　　過去分詞當形容詞用，表示已確定的

and family camps *increases* therapeutic experiences for our Craniofacial

populations. This presentation *highlights* **how** our Craniofacial team
　　　　　　　　　　　　　　　how 引導的名詞子句當 highlight 的受詞

went about establishing a relationship with the Painted Turtle camp in Lake

go about 表示從事於某工作

Hughes, CA. ③A The Painted Turtle *is* a non-profit organization member of the Paul Newman SeriousFun Camps, formerly the Association of Hole in the Wall Camps. ③B **As of** March 2012, the Painted Turtle *began* serving children and

as of 表示自⋯時候開始

families with Craniofacial conditions. ③C The camp *is providing* opportunities for our patients and their families to connect and share experiences. This presentation *describes* the steps that were taken to help qualify our patient population for the Craniofacial camp experience, which may be applicable both nationally and internationally. Criteria for consideration of inclusion of our patient population *are* discussed. Strategies *are offered* for identifying and keeping track of ⑤ candidate patients and families that **come for**

come for 表示為（目的）而來到

Craniofacial team visits on average once per year. Collaboration with existent local children camps *is* essential to help expand the opportunity for Craniofacial patients and families to connect with each other and to increase therapeutic resources to this patient population.

2

心
理
&
健
康

 **單字與片語**

重要單字 Key Vocabularies

① craniofacial （a) 顱顏的

② anxiety （n) 焦慮

③ self-esteem （n) 自尊

④ depression （n) 沮喪

⑤ social isolation 社會孤立 (隔離)

⑥ therapeutic environments 療癒環境

⑦ social awareness 社會自覺

⑧ normalization （n) 正常化

⑨ disfigurements （n) 毀容；缺陷

⑩ collaboration （n) 共同合作

⑪ Formerly （adv) 從前；以前

⑫ criteria （n) 標準

重要片語 Key Phrases

❶ The number of 一些

❷ keeping track of 紀錄

❸ on average 平均上

❹ once per year 每年一次

❺ connect with 連接；聯繫

 **本文解析**

　　文章開始指出患有顱顏差異的孩童可能會患有心理上的問題，但社會上能投注在他們的資源有限，因此如果能藉由與其他相同患者接觸的機會，就可以改善一些身心理狀況，而接下來介紹其中一個媒合的慈善組織，這個組織以舉辦夏令營方式，讓患者及其家屬與

其相同狀況的家庭有接觸的機會，並共同分享經驗。而本文就是詳述其協助患者參加該顱顏夏令營的報告。

第一題問何者不是患有顱顏差異的孩童有可能有的心理問題，由第一個句子即可知患有顱顏差異的孩童會有焦慮、自我以及憂鬱等問題。第二題問顱顏夏令營的主要目標，可由第七行中的 Craniofacial camp program... 看出答案。第三題問錦龜夏令營隊的敘述何者為真，由關鍵字 Painted Turtle 找到文章中間部份 The Painted Turtle is...，由後面的描述對照題目選項即可得到答案。第四題問到"keeping track of"這個詞組的意思，該詞組是表示"追蹤"的意思，所以選項中以"記錄"最為相近。第五題問到候選患者及其家屬來到顱顏小組拜訪是多久來一次，由倒數第四行中可知其頻率平均為一年一次 (... visits on average once per year)。

學習重點 ➡

本文中出現大量的關係詞引導的子句，讀者需能清楚認識關係詞在句中扮演的角色，才能分析句子，並將文章內容徹底弄清楚。關係詞分為關係代名詞及關係副詞，其引導的子句則依其用途分為名詞子句，形容詞子句及副詞子句三大類，而一般閱讀測驗中，最常出現的大概就屬名詞子句及形容詞子句二種。

使用關係代名詞時，期前面一定會出現一個名詞（或代名詞），稱之為先行詞，而關係代名詞的作用則為修飾、說明該先行詞，同時做為該關係子句之主詞或受詞。以下為關係詞引導的形容詞子句，這是最常見的一種關係詞的運用。

主格用法：

This is the soldier who fought to defend our country before.

（這個士兵以前曾挺身保衛我們國家。）

所有格用法：

The workers whose salaries were cut were very angry.

（薪水被削減的員工非常生氣。）

受格用法：

She was the woman whom everyone admired.（她就是那個人人稱讚的婦人。）

第三招 選項比對消去法

　　閱讀測驗題目中，除上述所提問句型式、引導類型及主旨（大意）等三大主要類型外，另外有一種題目會問下列何項敘述為是（或非），或考文章推論，例如：What can be inferred about the article? 通常這類問題比較麻煩，一般無法一眼直接看出來某項就是正確解答，尤其是如果題目敘述字數多，且經文意經過改敘，非常容易造成混淆，碰到這種題目真的沒辦法了，光看完主題句可能沒有用，這種題目往往需要你整個文章看完才能解。不過還好這種題目不會有太多（一篇閱讀測驗中可能只會有一題），所以這種題目雖難，可以先放著，等該篇其它題目做完再回來做。而要解該類題目只能以「消去法」，一個一個與原文句比對後，排除不要的選項，而重點是要善用題目選項中的關鍵語句與原文中的關鍵語句做比對，才能迅速得到正確答案。此外，該類型題目的選項次序與文章內容中的先後順序，一般說來也是相同的，這點可以好好運用，可節省一些搜尋的時間。

　　另外，要順利解決此類問題，還需具備相當程度的同義字及反義字的能力，而這也是這類題目考試的重點。一般較常見的改寫類型有以下幾型：

1. 單字（或詞彙）：如 weekly 改寫成 once a week 或將 domestic visitors 改成 visitors from local area。

2. 比較類型：比較的寫法是英文中常見的論述方式，主要是將焦點放在兩個或多個之間比較出其差異性，例如：

   原文：A is much preferable to B

   選項：A is better than B

3. 大小關係或變化：將變化情況由數據變成文字描述等，例如：

原文：... which accounts for 40%...

選項：... it is less than one half...

4. 全句改述：就是將文章中的答案部分在選項中作部份或全部改述，讓人一時摸不著頭緒，例如：

原文：She applied for the position of custodian at the local mall

選項：she put in an application for the janitor's job at the neighborhood shopping center.

以下為一實際考題，讓我們看看如何用消去法的技巧來解題吧！

The term Black English is a relatively "new" word in American English. During the Civil Rights Movement in the 1960s, the adjective "black" became popular. It replaced "Negro," which recalled the memories of slavery. Black was considered a more dignified word. Americans began speaking about Black English, Black studies, Black Power, Black History, and so forth.

The origins of Black English really go back to West Africa. The English slave traders were often unfamiliar with the various African languages. They needed a common language to deal with the slaves. The slaves, who came from many different tribes, needed a common language to communicate. This mixture of English and the various African languages was the foundation of Black English.

During the long trip to the New World, the slaves spoke this "new" language. They built new friendships through this common bond. More important still, they kept some of their African traditions and customs alive in this "new" language. Some of the slaves went to the West Indies. Today Caribbean English has its own grammar, vocabulary, and pronunciation. Despite the common origins, there are differences between the English of a Caribbean Black and an American Black.

3 經濟 & 政治

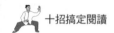

1. According to this passage, which of the following is NOT true about the origins of Black English?

(A) The slaves, who came from different tribes, couldn't communicate with each other without a common language.

(B) The slave traders were not familiar with the various African languages, so they invented a whole new language.

(C) The birth of Black English has much to do with the slave trade in West Africa.

(D) Black English came from the mixture of English and African languages.

2. According to the passage, which of the following statements is true?

(A) The origins of Black English can be traced back to West Africa.

(B) With a "new" language, the slaves couldn't keep their old traditions and customs alive.

(C) Black people in different parts of the world speak the same language.

(D) Black English is derived from the one used in the West Indies.

　　第一題問敘述何者為非，選項 (A) 的關鍵字 common language，由第二段第三行 The slaves, ... needed a common language to communicate. 可推斷一開始他們沒有溝通的共通的語言，敘述為真。選項 (B) 的關鍵字可視為 invented a whole new language，重點是要看新語言是否為這些販子所創的，由二段最後一句 This mixture... was the foundation of Black English 可知新語言不是由奴隸販子創造的，故敘述為非。選項 (C) 的關鍵字可視為 slave trade in West Africa，由由第二段第一行 The origins... go back to West Africa. 及後面一句 They(指奴隸販子) needed a common language to deal with the slaves. 可推知該種語言與西非的奴隸交易有很大關聯，敘述為真。選項 (D) 的關鍵字可視為 mixture of English and African languages，由第二段第一行 This mixture of English... the foundation of Black English 可知黑人語言來自於英語及非洲語言的混合體，敘述為真。故敘述為非者為 (B)。

　　在第二題問敘述何者為真，選項 (A) 的關鍵字可視為 origins of Black English，由第二段第一行 The origins of Black English really go back to West Africa，敘述為真。注意：此時原文中的 go back to 被改敘為 be traced back to。選項 (B) 的關鍵字可視為 traditions and customs alive，由第三段第二行 they kept... traditions and customs alive...，可知奴隸們保留存他們老傳統及慣用語並活用在新的語言中，敘述為非。選項 (C) 表示世界各地黑人都說同一種語言，但由本文第二段中得知：黑人在世界不同的地區原本並非是講相同的語言，所以才要有一種共通語言來溝通，所以敘述為非。選項 (D) 的關鍵字可視為 derived(衍生) from... West Indies，由本文第三段第三行到最後 Some of the slaves went to the West Indies...，可知文中提到有些奴隸去了西印度，而加勒比黑人英文與美式黑人英文起源相同，並沒說黑人英文是源起於西印度，敘述為非。故敘述正確者為 (A)。

3
經濟 & 政治

 英文本文

Article 3.1

For the first time in history, more cars have been sold in China than in the United States. One of the reasons is that the economic crisis has not hit China as badly as the United States. Although sales are also down compared to the figures of last year, there are still many customers in Chinese car showrooms.

China has a lot to **catch up on**. Car analysts point out that in the United States there are 800 cars per 1000 people; however, in China, the same figure is only 20 cars. For many Chinese, buying a car is a big event because most of them have never had one before. It's not just a transportation tool like in the US or Europe. In China, it's still a status symbol. With the growth of over 20% per year, China has the fastest-growing automobile market in the world. Even though sales have been down due to the recession, they are still better than anywhere else in the world.

In order to encourage growth, the government has offered to help motorists and the smaller carmakers of the country. Tax on smaller vehicles has also been reduced and there are subsidies for those who want to exchange an old car for a new one. Even though most Chinese buy smaller local models, those who can afford it will still buy American and European cars.

 理解力測驗

Q1. According to the article, why more cars have been sold in China than in the United States?

(A) The economic crisis has not hit China as badly as the United States.
(B) Chinese people is becoming richer.
(C) There are more customers in Chinese car showrooms.
(D) There is a growth of over 20% car sale rate per year China.

Q2. How many cars do the Chinese have for every 1000 people?

(A) 20
(B) 200
(C) 400
(D) 800

Q3. Which is the closest meaning of the term "**catch up on**" in line 6?

(A) keep up with
(B) make up
(C) keep on
(D) come over

Q4. According to this article, why do many Chinese think buying a car as a big event?

(A) Because it's just a transportation tool.
(B) Because cares are very expensive.
(C) Because many of them have never had one before.
(D) Because cars aren't a status symbol.

Q5. Which of the followings is NOT the offerings the government has done to encourage the growth of cars?

(A) offering help to motorists and the smaller carmaker
(B) reducing tax on compact vehicles
(C) giving found for those who want to exchange an old car for a new one
(D) helping those who can afford buying American and European cars

3

經
濟
&
政
治

 本文中譯

中國汽車銷售

　　有史以來第一次，中國境內的汽車銷售比美國多，原因之一是經濟危機對中國的影響並沒有比對美國的影響來的嚴重。雖然與去年相比的銷售數字仍呈現下滑，仍有許多顧客光顧汽車展示中心。

　　中國仍有很大的成長空間。汽車分析家指出，在美國，每千人有 800 輛汽車，但在中國，同樣每千人只有 20 輛。對許多中國人而言，買車是件大事，因為他們大多以前從未擁有過車子。在美國或者歐洲，汽車不過是一種運輸工具，在中國，汽車仍是一種身分象徵。中國每年以 20% 的成長率而成為世界上成長最快速的汽車市場，雖然是銷售額受到經濟衰退的影響，它還是比世界上其他地區表現來的要好。

　　為了要促進銷售額的成長，政府已試圖來幫助國內的用車人及小型汽車製造業者，小型車的關稅也已經降低，並且對那些要將舊車換新車的人提供補助。儘管大部份中國人會買較小的本土車，那些對買得起的人還是會買美國車或歐洲車。

理解力測驗中譯

---

1. 依據本文，為何中國汽車銷售較美國汽車銷售為多？

(A) **中國經濟危機的衝擊沒有美國來的嚴重。**

(B) 中國人變的更有錢。

(C) 有更多的消費者出現在展示中心。

(D) 每年中國汽車成長率有 20% 根據。

---

2. 中國每千人有多少部汽車？

(A) **20**

(B) 200

(C) 400

(D) 800

---

3. 何者與第六行中的"catch up on"這個字意義最相近？

(A) 趕上

(B) **補足**

(C) 持續

(D) 帶來

---

4. 依據本文，為何中國人認為買車事一件重要的事？

(A) 因為那是一種運輸工具。

(B) 因為車子很貴。

(C) **因為他們很多以前從沒有擁有過車子。**

(D) 因為汽車不是身分的象徵。

---

5. 下列何者不是政府為了提高汽車成長率而做的措施？

(A) 提供協助來幫助國內的用車人及小型汽車製造業者

(B) 降低小型車的關稅

(C) 對那些要將舊車換新車的人提供資金

(D) **幫忙買得起美國車或歐洲車的人**

③
經濟＆政治

 本文圖解

For the first time in history, more cars *have been sold* in China than in the

United States. One of ① the reasons *is* that the economic crisis has not hit

China as badly as the United States. Although sales are also down

compared to the figures of last year, there *are* still many customers in
分詞構句，原句為 (when it is)compared
to…，表示與原來數據做比較
Chinese car showrooms.

China *has* a lot to catch up on. Car analysts *point* out that in the United

States there are 800 cars for 1000 people; however, ② in China the same

figure is only 20 cars. For many Chinese ④buying a car *is* a big event because

most of them have never had one before. It's not just a transportation tool

like in the US or Europe. In China it's still a status symbol. **With** a growth of
like 在這裏當介係詞用，意思是   with 引導介係詞片語，
就如同…，修飾前面的 tool   表示在甚麼情形下
over 20% per year, China *has* the fastest-growing automobile market in the

world. Even though sales have been down due to the recession, they *are* still
                                                            they 指的是前
                                                            面的 sales
better than anywhere else in the world.

In order to encourage growth, ⑤Ⓐ the government *has offered* to help motorists and the smaller carmakers of the country. ⑤Ⓑ Tax on smaller vehicles *has also been reduced* and ⑤Ⓒ there *are* subsidies for those who want to exchange an old car for a new one. Even though most Chinese buy smaller local models, those who can afford it would still *buy* American and European cars.

3

經濟 & 政治

 單字與片語

重要單字 Key Vocabularies

① economic crisis　經濟危機
② showroom　(n) 展示間
③ analyst　(n) 分析師
④ figure　(n) 圖表，數據
⑤ transportation　(n) 運輸
⑥ status　(n) 身分
⑦ symbol　(n) 象徵，符號
⑧ motorist　(n) 汽車駕駛人
⑨ exchange　(v) 交換，替換
⑩ subsidy　(n) 補助，補貼

重要片語 Key Phrases

❶ catch up on　補足
❷ point out　提出，指出
❸ due to　由於，因為 (介係詞片語)

本文解析

　　文章先談到中國汽車銷售比美國來的多，其原因就是因為經濟危機對中國影響較歐美來的小，第二段中主要談到相較於歐美市場，中國汽車市場成長仍有很大的空間，最後第三段提到中國政府對汽車銷售有些鼓勵措施，但是許多人對歐美車比對本土車情有獨鍾。所以文章的主題就是中國汽車銷售發展的情形。

　　第一題問到中國汽車銷為何會比美國多，由第二句 One of the reasons is... 即點出原因在於經濟危機的影響因素。第二題問中國每千人的汽車擁有數，這直接從文章中就可看出答案，但需注意 figure 這個表示"數據"的字要看的懂。第三題中，"catch up on" 這個字有二個意義，一個是"得到…"，另一個義是"彌補，補足"之意，在文章中因為主要提到的是汽車銷售數據，所以在此當成第二個解釋，表示仍有可增加的空間，另選項中的 keep up with 為"趕上"之意，雖然意思相近，但考量前面有 a lot，是指許多成長空間，故用 make up 較適合。第四題問為何中國人認為買車是一件重要的事，由 because most of them... 可以看出答案。最後一題問何者不是政府為了提高汽車成長率而做的措施，文章中清楚點出有幾個措施，但最後一句中 Even though..., those who can... 並非上面所指的協助措施，而是描述有些人有錢也不願去買國產車，與政府提高汽車成長率的努力沒關係。

學習重點 ➡

　　科技或商業類的文章中，使用到比較用法的比例很高，所以應瞭解比較用語的句型，如本文中有用到的 ... more cars have been sold... ，... hit China as badly as the United States. ，... they are still better than... ，及 ... also down compared to the figures…等句子中，都有使用到比較的概念，以下是一些常用的比較級句型。

(一)原形

1.not as ＋形容詞或副詞原形＋ as...(不像…那麼)

　例句：August is not as hot as July.(八月不像七月那麼熱。)

2.表示倍數：倍數＋ as ＋形容詞或副詞原形＋ as... (…的幾倍)

　　例句：The laptop is twice as expensive as the desktop.

　　　　　(筆記型電腦的價格是桌上型電腦的二倍。)

3.as ＋形容詞原形＋ a/an ＋名詞＋ as... (與…一樣是…)

　　例句：Tom is as experienced a carpenter as his father used to be.

　　　　　(湯姆也和他父親一樣是個老經驗的木匠。)

(二)比較級

1.比較級＋ than any other ＋名詞 ... (比其它所有的…還…)

　　本句型雖用比較級用法，但意義卻是最高級 (超過其他所有，那就是無人能敵了)。

　　例句：She is smarter than any other worker in her office.

　　　　　(她比辦公室其他人更聰明。)

3.部分比較及後面介係詞不用 than，而是用 to，包括：superior, inferior, senior, junior 等。

　　例句：Mr. Walker is senior to me in the company.

　　　　　(華克先生在公司裡比我資深。)

③ 經濟＆政治

學習小撇步 (Tips) ➡

　　文章中的代名詞有時也可能是考題之一，或是看懂文章的關鍵因素，如果搞錯對象，那可能文章意思就完全不同了，或是無法合乎邏輯。以本文為例，如 Even though sales have been down due to the recession, they are still better than anywhere else in the world. 句中 they 指的就是前面的 sales，這除了用文義判斷外，還可用其他輔助方式來判斷，如名詞的單複數用法等。

 英文本文

Article 3.2

The use of money is an indispensable part to our daily life; however, money is not only a currency tool apparently, but also the in-depth aspect about inherent mind and attitude of individuals that money involved. According to different individual backgrounds and experiences, it may not only give different meanings to money, but also hold different attitudes. Formerly, some scholars have proposed various viewpoints on the money attitude, such as an expert had once proposed that the money connotation included the following three facets: safety, preservation and power-fame. The development of money attitude issue so far is mainly to construct the effective money attitude assessment scale, and the current money attitude scales that comprehensively used by scholars are the MAS (Money Attitude Scale). Some scholars employed the using status for credit card to understand the relationship between money attitude and **excessive** consuming behavior, and through the MAS to test, they verify that people who have the tendency toward more money representing power-fame may have the excessive consuming behavior more easily. People distrusting tendency toward money may not have the excessive consuming behavior comparatively. However, people regarding money as the tool of relieving anxiety may have the status of excessive consuming behavior. As a result, it showed that the individual attitude toward money will influence his/her excessive consuming behavior. Thus, to sum up the theoretical bases of previous studies and researches, we will understand the money attitude of consuming lenders through investigating the influence on their loan behavior.

理解力測驗

Q1. According to the contents, which of the following is NOT the fact of money connotation an expert once proposed?

   (A) safety

   (B) preservation

   (C) power-fame

   (D) attitude

Q2. What is the closet meaning of the term "**excessive**" in line 13?

   (A) expressive

   (B) exaggerative

   (C) exercisable

   (D) exercise

Q3. Based on this article, which of the following descriptions is true?

   (A) Use of money is an indispensable part to our daily life.

   (B) Money is one of currency tools.

   (C) Money involves in individual's inherent mind and attitude.

   (D) All of the above.

Q4. According to the author, which of the following may have the excessive consuming behavior more easily?

   (A) People has the tendency toward the more money representing safety.

   (B) People has the tendency toward the more money representing power-fame.

   (C) People has the tendency toward the more money representing preservation.

   (D) People has the tendency toward the more money representing consumption behavior.

Q5. Based on the contents, which of the following has mainly constructed by the development of money attitude issue so far?

   (A) Effective money attitude

   (B) Effective money attitude assessment scale

   (C) Effective consuming behavior scale

   (D) Effective consuming behavior

③ 經濟 & 政治

本文中譯

金錢態度

　　金錢的使用是生活中不可或缺的部分，然而其並非只是表面上的貨幣工具而已，金錢所涉及的是與個人內在想法和態度有關之內心層面。由於個人背景與經驗的不同，會賦予金錢不同的意義，且所抱持的態度也會有所差異。過去學者也會針對金錢態度提出不同的看法，如某位專家曾提出，金錢的涵意包含安全、儲備以及權力 - 名望等三個層面。金錢態度議題發展至今，主要是建立有效之金錢態度評估量表。而有些學者則以信用卡使用情形來瞭解金錢態度與過度消費行為間之關係，並透過 MAS 金錢態度量表驗證出，具有較高之金錢代表權利 - 名望傾向的人愈容易有過度消費行為產生。對金錢存有較不信任感傾向者，較不會有過度消費情形產生，然而，視金錢為降低焦慮工具者容易有過度消費狀況，這顯示出個人對於金錢的態度會影響其過度消費之行為。因此，綜合過去研究之理論基礎，可藉由瞭解消費性貸款者之金錢態度來審視其對貸款行為之影響。

理解力測驗中譯

1. 根據本文內容，下列何者不是某位學者提出關於金錢涵意的層面？

    (A) 安全

    (B) 儲備

    (C) 權力 - 名望

    (D) 態度

2. 第 13 行的單字"excessive"最接近下列何意？

    (A) 可表達的

    (B) 誇張的

    (C) 可用的

    (D) 運動

3. 根據本文資訊，下列何者敘述為真？

    (A) 金錢的使用是生活中不可或缺的部分

    (B) 金錢是一項貨幣工具

    (C) 金錢涉及個人內在的想法和態度

    (D) 以上皆是

4. 根據本文作者，下列何者可能會容易有過度消費行為產生？

    (A) 具有較高金錢代表安全傾向的人

    (B) 具有較高金錢代表權利 - 名望傾向的人

    (C) 具有較高金錢代表儲備傾向的人

    (D) 具有較高金錢代表消費行為傾向的人

5. 根據本文內容，金錢態度議題發展至今，主要是建立下列何者？

    (A) 有效的金錢態度

    (B) 有效的金錢態度評估量表

    (C) 有效的消費行為評估量表

    (D) 有效的消費行為

3 經濟 & 政治

 本文圖解

③Ⓐ The use of money *is* an indispensable part to our daily life; however,

③Ⓑ money *is* not only a currency tool apparently, **but also** ③Ⓒ the in-depth

but also 用於連接二個
主詞補語

aspect about inherent **mind and attitude** of individuals that money involved.

According to different individual background and experience,

it may not only *give* different meanings to money, but also *hold* different

it 指的是 the use of money

but also 用於連接二個動詞：
give 及 hold

attitudes. Formerly, some scholars *have proposed* various viewpoints on

the money attitude, such as an expert had once proposed that ① the

名詞子句當 proposed
受詞

money connotation included the following three facets: safety, preservation

andpower-fame. ⑤ The development of money attitude issue so far *is* mainly

to construct the effective money attitude assessment scale, **and** the current

and 連接二個句子

money attitude scales that comprehensively used by scholars *are* the MAS

(Money Attitude Scale). Some scholars *employed* the using status for credit card to understand the relationship between money attitude and excessive

consuming behavior, **and** through the MAS to test, they *verify* that ④ the
they 指的是 scholars

people who has the tendency toward the more money representing power-

fame may have the excessive consuming behavior more easily. People

distrusting tendency toward money *may not have* the excessive consuming
分詞片語，修飾 people，表示
對金錢存有較不信任的人
behavior comparatively. However, people regarding money as the tool of

relieving anxiety may *have* the status of excessive consuming behavior. As

a result, it *showed* that the individual attitude toward money will influence
　　　　it 指前面所說的這件
　　　　有關金錢使用的事
his/her excessive consuming behavior. Thus, to sum up the theoretical bases

of previous studies and researches, we will *understand* the money attitude

of consuming lenders **through** investigating the influence on their loan
　　　　through 經由⋯，介係詞片語修飾全句

behavior.

3
經
濟
&
政
治

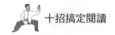

 單字與片語

重要單字 Key Vocabularies

① indispensable（a）不可或缺的

② apparently（adv）表面上

③ facets（n）構面

④ power-fame 權力 - 名望

⑤ employed（v）使用

⑥ distrusted（v）不信任

重要片語 Key Phrases

❶ money attitude　金錢態度

❷ excessive consuming behavior　過度消費行為

本文解析

　　本文先提到每個人對金錢的想法及態度都不同，有學者提出金錢有安全、儲備以及權力 - 名望等三個層面，學者利用金錢態度評估量表來評量人們對金錢的使用態度，結果顯示而對金錢較不信任感者較不會有過度消費，而視金錢為降低焦慮工具者容易有過度消費狀況。故本文主要是講述有關於不同金錢使用態度對消費行為之影響的研究。

　　第一題問何者非學者提出關於金錢涵意的層面，由關鍵字 money connotation，可直接在文章中找到答案。第二題中，"excessive"的意思是"非常的"，所以答案的選項最近為"誇張的"。第三題問敘述何者為非，依各選項的關鍵字在文章中尋找出處，即可找出答案。第四題問誰可能會容易有過度消費行為，該題目關鍵字為 excessive consuming behavior more easily，由 … who has the tendency toward the more money representing power-fame may have… 可得到答案。最後一題問金錢態度議題發展至今是建立何者？該題目關鍵字為 development of money attitude issue so far，在文章中第七行：The development of money... effective money attitude assessment scale...，很容易可以看出答案。

學習重點 ➡

有些文章中，常常用對等連接詞來表達研究之間的連貫關係，但同時也加長了文句的長度，增加閱讀者的負荷。本篇來説，在文章中連用了二次 not only..., but also...（不僅……而且）的句型，所以要了解文意，需要清楚知道連接的對象是何者，是連接兩邊動詞還是受詞（名詞）？

例如："it may **not only** give different meanings to money, **but also** hold different attitudes."便是連接兩個動詞 give 及 hold，而第二句"money is **not only** a currency tool apparently,**but also** the in-depth aspect about inherent mind"，便是連接兩邊名詞 a currency tool 及 the in-depth aspect，而且二者都是當動詞 is 的補語。

學習小撇步 (Tips) ➡

解題目時，如果能充分運用心理戰，有時會有意想不到的結果，例如問題是在文中有清楚表明的 ABC 三者，而題目要問何者為非，則在四個選項中，通常正確者會是前三者，出題者一般會將答案選項放在第四個。而相同的，如果題目為下列何項敘述為非（為真），如果看到選項有以上皆是（或皆非）者，通常就是這答案了！

3
經濟 & 政治

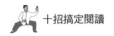

 英文本文

Article 3.3

In the US, partisan politics has also become a factor in the policy-intelligence relationship. Although there were differences in emphasis from administration to administration (such as a great emphasis on political covert action during Eisenhower's administration), there was common consistency in intelligence policy. Moreover, until 1976 intelligence was not seen as part of "spoils" of an election victory. In general, each Director of the Central Intelligence Agency (CIA) was automatically replaced during every new administration. Richard Nixon (administration 1969-1974) tried to use CIA for some political purposes when he attempted to curtail the investigation on Watergate scandal. However, another policy administration (administration 1977-1981) ended the political "separateness" of the intelligence community. Jimmy Carter, in his 1976 presidential campaign, lumped Vietnam War, Watergate scandal, and recent investigations of US intelligence together. When Cater won, George Bush (administration 1976-1977), the current director of CIA offered to stay on and eschew all partisan politics, saying the CIA needed some consistencies after the investigations and four directors in as many years. President-elect Carter said that he wanted to select the director of CIA by himself. This was the first time a current director of CIA had been asked to **step down** by a new ruler.

理解力測驗

Q1. According to the article, which of the following is the emphasis during Eisenhower's administration?

(A) Political purpose
(B) Political covert action
(C) Political investigation
(D) None of the above

Q2. Regarding the contents, when was the time the intelligence still was not seen as part of "spoils" of an election victory?

(A) 1969
(B) 1977
(C) 1981
(D) 1988

Q3. According to the writer, which of the following political purpose that Richard Nixon tried to use CIA to get?

(A) End the political "separateness" of the intelligence community.
(B) Lump Vietnam War, Watergate scandal, and recent investigations of US intelligence together.
(C) Curtail the investigation on Watergate scandal.
(D) None of the above.

Q4. Based on this article, who lumped Vietnam War, Watergate scandal, and recent investigations of US intelligence together in 1976 presidential campaign?

(A) Eisenhower
(B) Richard Nixon
(C) Jimmy Carter
(D) George Bush

Q5. What does the phrase "**step down**" in line 19 refer to?

(A) resign
(B) abdication
(C) quit
(D) all of the above

 **本文中譯**

美國政黨政治

　　在美國，政黨政治已成為政策 - 情報關係中的一項因素。儘管在不同執政期間所重視的事項存有差異 (例如在艾森豪任期中對於政治秘密行動的重視)，在情報政策上仍有其一貫的連續性。此外，在 1976 年以前，情報並未被視為選舉勝利的"戰利品"。通常在每個新的政權期間，中央情報局長都會被自動的更換。理查‧尼克森 (任期為 1969- 1974) 試圖阻撓對於水門案的調查時，就想利用中央情報局來達成一些政治目的。然而，另一個政權 (在 1977-1981 執政) 終結了政治上對於情報單位的"隔離"。吉米‧卡特在他的 1976 年總統競選活動中，將越戰、水門案以及最近美國的情報調查混為一談。當卡特勝選後，時任中央情報局長的喬治‧布希 (任期為 1976-1977) 意圖想留任，以脫離政黨政治，其理由是歷經許多的調查以及四年中換四位中央情報局長後，中央情報局有其必要維持其一貫性。但是總統當選人卡特說他想自己來遴選中央情報局長。這是首次現任中央情報局長被新上任的執政者要求下台。

 理解力測驗中譯

1. 根據本文，下列何者是在艾森豪 (Eisenhower) 任期中所重視的事項？

　(A) 政治目的

　(B) 政治秘密行動

　(C) 政治調查

　(D) 以上皆非

2. 根據本文內容，在何時情報並未被視為選舉勝利的"戰利品"？

　(A) **1969**

　(B) 1977

　(C) 1981

　(D) 1988

3. 根據本文作者，理查‧尼克森 (Richard Nixon) 試圖利用中央情報局 (CIA) 來達成下列何項政治目的？

(A) 結束了政治上對於情報單位的"隔離"

(B) 將越戰、水門案以及最新的美國情報調查混而為一

(C) 企圖阻撓對於水門案的調查

(D) 以上皆非

4. 根據本文資訊，誰在 1976 年的總統競選活動中，將越戰、水門案以及最新的美國情報調查混而為一？

(A) 艾森豪

(B) 理查‧尼克森

(C) 吉米‧卡特

(D) 喬治‧布希

5. 第 19 行的片語 "step down" 是下列何意？

(A) 辭職

(B) 退位

(C) 離職

(D) 以上皆是

本文圖解

In the US, partisan politics *has also become* a factor in the policy-

intelligence relationship. Although there were differences in emphasis from

administration to administration (such as ① a great emphasis on political

covert action during Eisenhower's administration), there *was* common

consistency in intelligence policy. Moreover, ② intelligence *had not been*

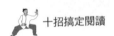

seen as part of "spoils" of an election victory until 1976. In general, each

director of the Central Intelligence Agency (CIA) *was automatically replaced*

during every new administration. ③ Richard Nixon (administration 1969-

1974) tried to use CIA for some political purposes **when** he attempted to

when 引導副詞子，
意思為當時…

curtail the investigation on Watergate scandal. However, another policy

administration (administration 1977-1981) *ended* the political "separateness"

of the intelligence community. ④ Jimmy Carter *lumped Vietnam* War,

Watergate scandal, and the recent investigations of US intelligence together in

his 1976 presidential campaign. When Cater won, George Bush (administration

1976-1977), the current director of CIA, *offered* to stay on and *eschew*

all partisan politics, **saying** the CIA needed some consistencies after the

分詞構句，表示附加狀況認為…
saying 後面子句的關係詞 that 被省略

investigations and four directors in **as many** years. President-elect Carter *said*

as many 指的是與前面提到的
數一樣多

that he wanted to select the director of CIA by himself. This *was* the first time

a current director of CIA had been asked to step down by a new ruler.

名詞子句修飾 time，關係詞 that 被省略

單字與片語

重要單字 Key Vocabularies

① curtail （v) 縮減；縮短

② scandal （n) 醜聞

③ eschew （v) 避開；避免

重要片語 Key Phrases

❶ presidential campaign　總統競選活動

❷ lumped... together　將…混為一談

❸ step down　辭職；退休

本文解析

　　本文一開始就點出美國的政黨政治是與國家情報體系是有關係的，而在 1976 年以前，情報系統 CIA 還未成為選舉的戰利品，尼克森當年也無法用 CIA 來干擾水門案的調查，但直到卡特在 1976 年當選總統後，當時 CIA 局長布希原希望留任，但卡特仍要自己提名新人選，而讓布希成為首位被要求下台的 CIA 局長。本文主要是敘述美國政黨政治中，總統對情治系統掌握上的演變。

　　第一題問有關艾森豪任期中強調的事，在第三行括弧中即可看出。第二題是要讀者判別哪一年情治系統還沒成為政黨的戰利品 (spoils)，由文中可知在 1976 年後，情治系統即成為政黨的戰利品，所以選項在 1976 年以前的年份即是答案。第三題問到尼克森希望 CIA 去幫他做的事，由文中第七行看到有關 Richard Nixon 的描述即可知他要 CIA 阻撓調查水門案。第四題問誰將越戰、水門案以及最新的美國情報調查混為一談，答案在文中就可以看出是布希。第五題中"step down"就是"下台"之意，而選項中前三者均有辭職下台的意思，所以均可以用。

學習重點 ➡

　　英文用語中如要表達緊鄰的二個數字是相同的，常先説一個數字，然後用 as many 來説數目上和這數字相同的事物，例如本文的 ... after the investigations and four directors in as many years. 這句話中，在 as many 就是指前面出現的數字 four，後面再接年 (years)，如此可避免重複，並讓文句看來簡潔有力。

3 經濟 & 政治

 英文本文

Article 3.4

Almost all futurists thought that 21st Century will be the era of bringing rapid and substantial change in people's life, and **it** will be eliminated through such competition if not well-prepared. In addition, continuous development of technologies, as well as the diversification of social groups, cultures and religions will also have great impact on societies, economies, and firms, among which nothing is better than "Digital Economy System" or "Internet Economy" to urge and make such a tremendous change. In fact, the Digital Economic Era really not came out from nowhere but adopted the development of Information Technology (IT) that has been a force for change since the 1980s when it changed not only the nature of competition, but also the original value system of each activity inside a company and the correlation between activities. Through the digital technology, "Digital Economy" made the communication methods, such as telephone, computer and broadcasting, provided the comprehensive information via the common interface, and then produced the unprecedented brand-new media and application systems. Moreover, unceasing growth of Internet has already brought a whole new learning, operation and lifestyle of mankind.

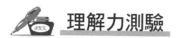 **理解力測驗**

Q1. Based on the content, which urge and make tremendous change on societies, economies and firms?

(A) Digital Economic Era
(B) Digital Economy System
(C) Information Technology
(D) Digital Economy

Q2. What does the term "**it**" refer to in line 2?

(A) 21st Century
(B) the era
(C) people's life
(D) change

Q3. According to the article, which of the followings is true?

(A) Almost all fortunetellers thought that 21st Century will be the era of bringing rapid and substantial change in people's life.
(B) Digital Economy Era is developed based on the development of Information Technology since the 1980s.
(C) The Digital Economic Era really came out from nowhere.
(D) "Digital Economy" provided the comprehensive information via the common media.

Q4. According to the author, what brand-new method for human has been brought by the unceasing growth of Internet?

(A) learning method
(B) operating method
(C) living method
(D) all of the above

Q5. Regarding this article, which of the followings doesn't cause great impact on societies, economies and firms?

(A) individualized religion
(B) unceasing growth of technologies
(C) diversification of social groups
(D) diversification of cultures

3 經濟 & 政治

107

 **本文中譯**

數位經濟

　　幾乎所有未來學家都認為，二十一世紀人類生活將會有急遽、實質的變化，而假如沒有做好適應這些生活方式的準備將會被淘汰。不但社會族群、文化及宗教的多元化等因素，而且科技的不斷進步更會對政治、經濟及團體帶來很大的衝擊，而驅使此劇烈變動的莫過於是「數位經濟體系」或「網際網路經濟」。事實上，數位經濟時代並非憑空而來，而是承襲了自1980年代以來資訊科技的發展。這時資訊科技的運用不僅改變了競爭的本質，也改變公司內部每項活動原有的價值體系及各種活動間的關係。經由數位科技，「數位經濟」得以促成各種通訊方式發展，像是電話、電腦和廣播等，透過共通介面提供全面的資訊，並從而創造出前所未有的嶄新媒體和應用系統。另外，網際網路的不斷成長，已為人類帶來全新的學習、經營及生活方式。

理解力測驗中譯

1. 根據本文內容，何者驅使並對政治、經濟及團體帶來劇烈變動？

   (A) 數位經濟時代

   (B) 數位經濟系統

   (C) 資訊科技

   (D) 數位經濟

2. 第 2 行的"it"是指何事物？

   (A) 21 世紀

   (B) 年代

   (C) 人們的生活

   (D) 改變

3. 根據本文資訊，下列何者敘述為真？

   (A) 幾乎所有預言家都認為，二十一世紀將為人類生活帶來急遽、實質的變化

   (B) 數位經濟時代是以 1980 年代以來資訊科技的發展為基礎

   (C) 數位經濟時代只是憑空而來

   (D) 數位經濟以透過共通媒體來提供全面的資訊

4. 根據本文作者，因為網際網路的不斷成長而為人類帶來何種全新的方式？

   (A) 學習方式

   (B) 經營方式

   (C) 生活方式

   (D) 以上皆是

5. 根據本文，下列何者不會對於社會、經濟與公司帶來很大的衝擊？

   (A) 宗教的單一化

   (B) 科技的不斷進步

   (C) 多樣化的社會群體

   (D) 多樣化的文化

③ 經濟 & 政治

 本文圖解

③A Almost all futurists *thought* that 21st Century will be the era of bringing

rapid and substantial change in people's life, **and** it will *be eliminated*

連接前後二個句子

through such competition **if** not well-prepared. In addition, ⑤ continuous

分詞構句，表示如果
沒有作好準備

development of technologies, **as well as** the diversification of social groups,

cultures and religions, *will also have* great impact on societies, economies

and firms, **among which** ① nothing is better than "Digital Economy System"

表示在這些衝擊的因素之中，
關係詞的先行詞是 impact

or "Internet Economy" to urge and make such tremendous change. In fact,

③C the Digital Economic Era really not *came* out from nowhere **but** *adopted*

but 連接二個主要子句的
動詞 came 及 adopted

③B the development of Information Technology (IT) that has been a force for

change since the 1980s when **it** change **not only** the nature of competition,

it 是指上一行　　不但…而且，
所提的 IT　　主要強調前者

but also the original value system of each activity **inside** a company and

but also 連接 when 子句的動詞　　介係詞片語修飾
change 的二個受詞　　activity

the correlation between activities. Through the digital technology, "Digital

Economy" *made* the communication methods, such as telephone, computer and broadcasting, ㉚ *provided* the comprehensive information via the common interface, and then *produced* the unprecedented brand-new media and application systems. Moreover, ④ unceasing growth of Internet *has already brought* a whole new learning, operation and lifestyle to mankind.

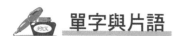 ## 單字與片語

重要單字 Key Vocabularies

① futurists （n) 未來主義學家；未來主義者

② eliminated （v) 排除

③ diversification （n) 多樣化　　　④ urge （v) 促成

⑤ tremendous （a) 極度的；劇烈的　⑥ Information Technology （n) 資訊科技

⑦ interface （n) 界面　　　　　　⑧ unprecedented （a) 空前的

⑨ brand-new （a) 全新的

重要片語 Key Phrases

❶ from nowhere 從不知名處　　　❷ digital technology 數位科技

本文解析

　　本文一開始提到 21 世紀人類生活方式將會有巨大變革，科技的不斷進步更會對社會經濟等造成巨大衝擊，而驅使此劇烈變動的就是「數位經濟體系」或「網際網路經濟」。在數位經濟的時代，將改變原有企業內各項活動的價值體系及關係，而且它也造成了各項通訊技術的進步，而最後造就了網際網路的成長，帶給人類全新的生活方式。所以本文的主題就是 21 世紀的數位經濟時代將帶給人類社會巨大的變化。

　　第一題問到何者驅使並對政治、經濟及團體帶來劇烈變動？由關鍵字 urge and make such tremendous change 找到 nothing is better than "Digital Economy System" or... 這句話，注意句中用 nothing is better than(沒有甚麼比⋯)，那就是肯定的意思。第二題問 it 是指何事物，由該句要表達的意思是：如果做好適應這些生活方式的準備將會被淘汰⋯，所以 it 是指人們的生活，而這也可以由該句後面 ... if not well-prepared. 中得到驗證，因為該假設句省略主詞及動詞，這種情形只會發生在假設句與主要子句的主詞相同，所以該假設句的主詞也必定為 it，而 it 表示人們的生活 (people's life) 才合理。第三題考細節，只要留意各選項中的關鍵字，並在文章中找出各選項的段落即可用排除法得到答案，但要注意選項與原句的改變，如選項 (A) 中是用 Almost fortunetellers，但文章中應該是 Almost futurists，所以該選項不能選。第四題問網際網路的發展為人類帶來哪方面的生活方式，這在本文最後一行可看出答案。最後一題問甚麼不會對於社會、經濟與公司帶來很大的衝擊，題目問句中用 doesn't cause great impact on...，這是將原句改寫的問法，但仍可由文中找到 continuous development of technologies... also have great impact on societies... 這一句話而看出答案，但要注意選項 (A) 中 Individualized(單一的) 這個字，文章中應該是 diversification of religions(多元的宗教)。

學習重點 ➡

　　本文中的 ... it will be eliminated through such competition if not well-prepare. 其中 if not well-prepared 稱為分詞構句，係由副詞子句所引導表附帶狀況的子句轉換而來，用以表示時間、原因、條件、讓步、附帶狀況。

例如：

1. 一般分詞構句：

   兩邊主詞相同時，將副詞子句的從屬連接詞及子句的主詞去掉，再將子句內的動詞依主動改為 Ving，被動改為 Vp.p.。

   例句：

   While I walked along the street, I met my ex-girlfriend.

   （當我沿著街上走時，我遇見我前任女友。）

   → Walking along the street, I met my ex-girlfriend.

2. 如果需要連接詞的意思時，可以將連接詞保留。

   例句：

   Having finished my work, I went to play basketball.

   （當完成我的工作後，我就去打籃球。）

   After finishing my work, I went to play basketball.

   （在完成我的工作之後，我就去打籃球。）

   故該句中，兩邊的主詞都是 it，且有必要表達連接詞 if 的意思，所以就形成 if (it is) not well-prepared 這種結構。

3 經濟 & 政治

第四招 劃線、圈字、給代號

在閱讀時（尤其是測驗時的略讀），筆可充當指路的工具及提升閱讀專注力；再來是，遇到明確或重點的概念便加以劃線註記，有助於作答時的回頭檢查。這種方式對於詢問細節描述的題目非常有用，前面提過：先看題目再看文章，看到題目才知道問題的重點或關鍵字，在略讀時遇到便可以馬上圈起來，回頭做題目時便可輕易的找到重點來答題。

很多時候甚至考題直接會以文章上的某字的意思與選項何字意義相近，這時除了考驗文章理解程度，還要考驗單字的功力。此外，遇到不懂的單字或片語時先不要慌張，因為你如果能把握文章的內容大意，除非本身單字能力太差，否則單獨一處的生字應該不會妨礙對整段文章的閱讀理解。但如果該單字或片語剛好是個關鍵詞（或甚至就是前面所述要考你的單字或詞），沒辦法避的掉，便需要以前後文來理解，這時最少也需知道該單字的詞性為何，並先用筆給該關鍵字一個代號，例如 A，在翻譯時便是以「A 在哪裡如何，在什麼時間怎麼樣」，再設法從後面的字句中推敲出這字（詞）代表的意涵。接下來同樣是一段考試出過的文章，以下將示範如何用上述方式來解決閱讀測驗題目的步驟。

When thousands or even millions of people get together, what will be the biggest health concern? Traditionally, doctors and public health officials were most concerned about the spread of infectious diseases. Robert Steffen, a professor of travel medicine at the University of Zurich, says that infectious diseases are still a concern, but injuries are a bigger threat at so-called mass gatherings.

According to Professor Steffen, children and older people have the highest risk of injury or other health problems at mass gathering events.

Children are at more risk of getting crushed in stampedes, while older people are at higher risk of heat stroke and dying from extreme heat.

Stampedes at mass gatherings have caused an estimated seven thousand deaths over the past thirty years. The design of an area for mass gathering can play a part. There may be narrow passages or other choke points that too many people try to use at once. The mood of a crowd can also play a part. Organizers of large gatherings need to avoid creating conditions that might lead to stampedes and heat stroke.

1. Which of the following would be the most appropriate title for this passage?
   (A) How to avoid mass gatherings
   (B) Mass gathering: New escape skills
   (C) Infectious diseases: New cures found
   (D) Health risks in a crowd: Not what you may think

2. Which of the following is closest in meaning to stampede in the passage?
   (A) A plane crash
   (B) A steamy factory
   (C) A sudden rush of a crowd
   (D) Heat stroke due to mass gathering events

4 地球科學

　　我們將文章略讀並畫線，用筆畫線如文內所示。而回到第一題中，要找出最佳標題，由一開始提到眾多人群聚集場合的健康風險，一般認為最大的風險應該是傳染病，然而一位學者認為事實上意外傷害才是最大的風險，後面分別提到孩童及老人可能遭受的傷害及如何避免造成傷害，都與一般人想像的不一樣，所以最適合的標題為選項中 (D) 在人群中的健康風險：跟你想的不一樣。第二題就是考單字 stampede，這個單字也許你不懂它的意思，但由句子結構知它是個名詞 (當主詞用)，我們先給它個代號 A，然後往下看：可知該句已經提到這件事會造成人員傷亡，而這是因為場地的設計使太多群眾同時在一個空間中所造成的…，所以我們可以合理推斷該名詞應該是指 " 群眾推擠 " 的意思！所以選項中意思最接近的應該是選 (C) 群眾突然狂奔。

 英文本文

Article 4.1

Milk. Not only do we drink it or take it in our coffee, but we also make many different things from it: ice cream, butter, and cheese, to name but a few. It seems that people are drinking more milk than ever these days. Around the world, studies show that people are drinking 20 percent more milk than a few years ago. As you might imagine, this depends a lot on milk cows. Farmers are constantly trying to find ways to improve the **yield** of milk from their cows, and they have found that happy cows produce more milk.

If you are like most people, listening to your favorite music and sitting in a comfortable chair relaxes you. Actually, what is true for most people is also true for cows! Milk cows need to lie down twelve to fourteen hours a day. Cows that do this are healthier and produce more milk. Unfortunately, most cows have to lie on the cold, hard dirt or concrete floor of their stalls. However, thanks to scientists in Europe, some cows now have another option—the cow water bed! These water-filled mattresses can.

be put on the ground of cow stalls, providing a soft place for cows to lie on. Cows seem to love this added comfort. One farmer found that within two weeks of putting in the water beds, his milk production went up by 20 percent!

Giving cows a comfortable place to lie down is not the only way to make them more comfortable. Psychologists in England have been studying the effect of music on milk production. By playing slow and fast music to cows while they were being milked, psychologists found that the yield of milk has increased with the cows listening slow music.

"It relaxes the cows in much the same way as it relaxes humans," said Dr. Adrian North, who carried out the study. What was at the top of the cows' playlist? Beethoven's pastoral symphony.

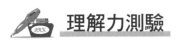 理解力測驗

Q1. What is the main idea of this reading?

(A) Cows are very much like people.

(B) Happy cows make more milk.

(C) One cow has a very comfortable life.

(D) Scientists are studying how cows relax.

Q2. Which of the following is TRUE according to the reading?

(A) Beds for cows should be made of dirt.

(B) Cows can sleep in water.

(C) Cows sleep while standing.

(D) Many cow stalls have concrete floors.

Q3. What does the word "**yield**" in line 6 of the reading refer to?

(A) allow

(B) amount

(C) be careful

(D) surrendering

Q4. Who is Adrian North?

(A) a farmer

(B) a psychologist

(C) a musician

(D) a player

Q5. What kind of music do cows seem to enjoy?

(A) classical music

(B) fast country music

(C) piano music

(D) rock music

4 地球科學

 本文中譯

牛的心情影響牛乳產量

　　牛奶，我們不僅可以飲用或是加進咖啡內，也讓我們可以做出很多不一樣的東西：例如是冰淇淋、奶油及起司等等這些食物。現代人們似乎比以前喝更多的牛奶，在全世界中，研究顯示人們每天比幾年前多喝了 20% 的牛奶。你能想像，這需要依賴相當多的乳牛。農人們持續不斷嚐試去發掘如何讓他們的乳牛可以增加牛乳生產的方法，而他們已經發現快樂的乳牛可生產較多的牛奶。

　　如果你與多數人一樣，那麼聽著你喜愛的音樂並坐在舒適的椅子會讓你放鬆。的確，對大多數人們有用的東西對乳牛們也是一樣有用。乳牛一天中需要躺下來 12 到 14 個小時，如此一來，乳牛會比較健康並產出更多牛乳。而很不幸的，大多數乳牛必須躺在牛棚中冰冷且堅硬的髒混凝土地板上。然而，這要多虧歐洲的科學家，現在一些乳牛有其他的選擇——乳牛水床。這些充滿水的氣墊可以放到牛棚的地板上，作為牛隻躺在上面的柔軟地方。牛隻似乎也喜歡這外加的舒適設備，有個酪農發現乳牛放上水床的兩個星期內，牛奶產量增幅多達 20%。

　　給牛隻一個讓牠們可以躺下的舒適空間並非讓牠們感到舒適的唯一方式，英格蘭的心理學家一直在研究音樂在牛奶產出上的效應。在乳牛們擠奶的同時，以播放快或慢節奏的音樂的方式，心理學家發現乳牛聽慢節奏的音樂時有較高的產量。"音樂讓乳牛感到舒緩，就像音樂可以舒緩人類一樣的道理"，執行這項研究的亞恩裏恩‧諾斯博士說。那什麼是乳牛最喜歡聽的音樂呢？答案是貝多芬的田園交響曲。

理解力測驗中譯

1. 本篇主要大意為何？

(A) 乳牛跟人很像

(B) 快樂的乳牛產出更多牛乳

(C) 乳牛有一個快樂的生活

(D) 科學家正在研究如何讓乳牛放鬆

2. 依據本文，下列何者為真？

(A) 給牛睡的床必須用泥土做成。

(B) 牛隻可以睡在水中。

(C) 牛可以邊站邊睡。

(D) 許多牛棚都有混凝土地板。

3. 在本篇文章第 6 行"yield"這個字指的是什麼？

(A) 允許

(B) 總額

(C) 小心的

(D) 投降

4. Adrian North 是什麼人

(A) 農人

(B) 心理學家

(C) 音樂家

(D) 歌手

5. 什麼樣的音樂是牛隻喜歡的？

(A) 古典樂

(B) 快板鄉村音樂

(C) 鋼琴樂曲

(D) 搖滾音樂

4
地球科學

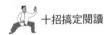

 **本文圖解**

Milk. Not only do we *drink* it or *take* it in our coffee, but we also *make*

many different things from it: ice cream, butter, and cheese, to name but

a few. It *seems* that people are drinking more milk than ever these days.
　　　　it 就是指 that 引導的名詞子句

Around the world, studies *show* that people are drinking 20 percent more

milk than a few years ago. As you might imagine, this *is* quite demanding on
　　　　　　　　　　　　　　　　　this 就是指前面的這項
　　　　　　　　　　　　　　　　　研究顯示的事
milk cows. Farmers *are* constantly trying to find ways to improve the yield of

milk from their cows, and they *have found* that happy cows produce more milk.

If you are like most people, listening to your favorite music and sitting in

a comfortable chair *relaxes* you. Actually, what is true for most people *is* also
　　　　　　　　　　　　　　　　　　What 引導的名詞子句當句子主詞

true for cows! ⑳ Milk cows *need* to lie down twelve to fourteen hours a day.

Cows that do this *are* healthier and produce more milk. Unfortunately,

⑳ most cows *have* to lie on the cold, hard dirt or concrete floor of their stalls.

However, thanks to scientists in Europe, ②B some cows now *have* another

option—the cow water bed! These water-filled mattresses can *be put* on the

ground of cow stalls, **providing** a soft place for cows to lie on. Cows *seem* to
分詞構句，表示提供水床的目的

love this added comfort. One farmer *found* that within two weeks of putting

in the water beds, his milk production went up by 20 percent!

Giving cows a comfortable place to lie down *is* not the only way to make

them more comfortable. Psychologists in England *have been studying* the

effect of music on milk production. **By playing** slow and fast music to cows
By 引導介係詞片語，
表示採用何種方法

while they were **being milked**, psychologists *found* that the yield of cows
milk 在此當動詞
擠奶的意思

listening to slow music was higher.

"It *relaxes* the cows in much the same way as it relaxes humans," ④ *said*

Dr. Adrian North, who carried out the study. ⑤ What *was* at the top of the

cows' playlist? Beethoven's pastoral symphony.

④
地
球
科
學

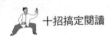
單字與片語

重要單字 Key Vocabularies

① imagine（v）想像

② yield（n）產量

③ comfortable（adj）舒適的

④ relax（v）放鬆

⑤ unfortunately（adv）不幸的

⑥ stall（n）牛棚

⑦ mattresses（n）墊子

⑧ option（n）選擇

⑨ improve（v）增進

⑩ psychologist（n）心理學家

⑪ pastoral symphony 田園交響曲

重要片語 Key Phrases

❶ to name but a few 僅以這些為例

❷ carried out 執行

 **本文解析**

　　本文開始談到牛奶除了可以喝以外還可做成許多食品，需求量很大，所以人們不斷想如何可以讓乳牛增加牛乳的產出，而增加乳牛產量的一種方法是讓乳牛可以躺在較舒適的墊子上，而心理學家提出另外一種方式，就是讓牛聽古典音樂。所以總結來說，本文主要大意就是讓乳牛愉快舒適就能增加牛乳產量，這是第一題的答案。

　　第二題是問文章中的細節題，只要將選項中的關鍵字找出文章中出現的地方就可以得出答案。第三題問"yield"（產量）這個單字指的是何者，選項中以"總額"最適宜（同樣類屬數量的統計）。第四題問誰是 Adrian North，由文中 ... said Dr. Adrian North, who carried out the study，且前面有提到這是一項心理學家的研究，所以推斷它就是心理學家。最後一題問牛可能喜歡何種音樂，文中是提到 Beethoven's pastoral symphony，但選項中沒有這項，那就是屬於一般常識性的推斷問題，比較選項中所提各類型音樂，田園交響曲應該是屬於古典音樂。

學習重點 ➡

　　本文中有一些句子，其主詞非為單獨一個名詞或片語，而是一長串的分詞片語及其修飾語所組成，或是由關係詞引導的名詞子句，如果對句子結構不瞭解，很容易誤判主詞與動詞之關係，應特別注意。例如：... listening to your favorite music and sitting in a comfortable chair relaxes you. 這句中，主詞是由分詞片語及其後的連接詞及介係詞修飾語所組成。而另一句：Actually, what is true for most people is also true for cows!，該句乍看之下似乎有二個動詞 is，但經仔細看可看出第一個 is 是名詞子句中的動詞，而該 what 引導的名詞子句即是本句主詞。另外，在最後一句：What was at the top of the cows' playlist? 該句主詞是介係詞片語 at the top of the cows' playlist，動詞是 was，而 what 只是疑問副詞，所以要看懂文章第一步就是搞懂主詞及動詞。

④ 地球科學

 英文本文

Article 4.2

Icebergs are among nature's most spectacular creations, and yet most people have never seen one. A vague air of mystery envelops them. They come into being-somewhere-in faraway, line frigid waters, amid thunderous noise and splashing turbulence, which in most cases no one hears or sees. They exist only a short time and then slowly go away just as unnoticed.

Objects of sheerest beauty, they have been called. Appearing variety of shapes, they may be **dazzlingly** white, or they may be glassy blue, green, or purple, tinted faintly or in darker hues. They are graceful, stately, inspiring in calm, sunlit seas.

But they are also called frightening and dangerous, and that they are in the night, in the fog, and in storms. Even in clear weather one is wise to stay at a safe distance away from them. Most of their bilk is hidden below the visible top. Also, they may roll over unexpectedly, churning the waters around them.

Icebergs are parts of glaciers that break off, drift into the water, float about a while, and finally melt. Icebergs afloat today are made of snowflakes that have fallen over long ages of time. They embody snows that drifted down hundreds, or many thousands, or in some cases maybe a million year ago. The snows fell in polar regions and on cold mountains, where they melted only a little or not at all, and so collected to great depths over the years and centuries.

As each year's snow accumulation lay on the surface, evaporation and melting caused the snowflakes to fall slowly on the top of the old, and it too turned to icy grains. So blankets of snow and ice grains mounted layer upon layer and were of such great thickness that the weight of the upper layers compressed the lower ones. With time and pressure **from above,** the many small ice grains joined and changed to larger crystals, and eventually the deeper crystals merged into a solid mass of ice.

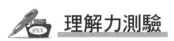 理解力測驗

Q1. Which of the following is the title of the passage?

    (A) The Name and Origin of Icebergs

    (B) The Size and Shape of Icebergs

    (C) The Dangers of icebergs

    (D) The melting of Icebergs

Q2. The author states that iceberg are rarely seen because they are

    (A) broken by waves soon after they are found.

    (B) hidden beneath the mountains.

    (C) located in remote regions of the word.

    (D) surrounded by fog.

Q3. The expression "**from above**" in line 5, paragraph 5, refers to

    (A) sunlit seas

    (B) polar regions

    (C) weight of mountains

    (D) layers of ice and snow

Q4. According to the passage, icebergs are dangerous because they

    (A) usually melt quickly.

    (B) can turn over suddenly.

    (C) may create immense snowdrifts.

    (D) can cause unexpected avalanches.

Q5. "**Dazzlingly**" in line 2, paragraph 2 probably means

    (A) brilliant

    (B) faint

    (C) beautify

    (D) sick

4

地球科學

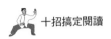

 本文中譯

冰河的名稱及起源

　　冰山可以説是自然界中最壯觀的產物，而大多數人都未曾目睹。一股神祕模糊的氣氛包圍著它。它們從不知名的遠方悄然出現，漂浮在冰冷水域中，在轟隆巨響之間激起亂流，這在大多數情況下，是沒人看得到或聽到。它們僅存的時間短暫，然後就慢慢不知不覺的消失。

　　它們曾經被稱為最純淨美麗的物體，它會以各種不同形狀出現，可能是耀眼的白色，或是如玻璃的藍、綠或紫色，帶有微微的色彩或更深的顏色，它們是優雅的、莊嚴、安詳，給人海面是平靜且陽光照耀的想法。

　　但它們也被認為是既恐怖又危險的，而且在它們會在夜晚、盲霧中及暴風雨中出現。就算在晴朗的天氣中，人們還是要和它保持一段安全的距離。它大部分可見的冰是藏在頂端冰層下方的海裡，更有甚者，它們會不預期的翻轉，使得它周遭的海水猛烈翻攪。

　　冰山就是冰河所裂開的部分，被推入海中並漂流一陣子，最後融化。今天在漂流的冰山是由長時間落下的雪花所形成的，它們將數百年、數千年、甚至有些是幾百萬年前的雪固化起來。這些落在極地與嚴寒山中的雪，在那裡只有些許會融化，有的甚至完全不會融化，所以這些雪收集了過去幾世紀以來的許多秘密。

　　當每年的雪累積在表面上，蒸發及融化作用使得這些雪花慢慢落在舊的雪的頂部，而雪最後也成為冰晶粒。如此雪層及冰晶粒一層一層堆疊上去，且它是如此的厚重以致於上層的重量壓縮了下層。上述冰雪層經時間與壓力累積之下，許多小的冰晶粒融合並變成較大的結晶體，最後較深層的結晶體沒入一整塊實體的冰層中。

理解力測驗中譯

1. 何者為本篇文章的標題？

(A) **冰山的名稱及起源**

(B) 冰山的體積及形狀

(C) 冰山的危險性

(D) 冰山的融化

2. 作者說冰山很少見是因為它們

(A) 在它們被發現後很快就被海浪打破了

(B) 藏在山底下

(C) **位在世界的偏遠地區**

(D) 被霧所包圍著

3. "from above" 這個字指的是

(A) 陽光照射的海域

(B) 極地區域

(C) 山的重量

(D) **冰與雪的累積層**

4. 依據本文，冰山危險是因為

(A) 通常融化很快

(B) **會突然間翻轉**

(C) 可能產生巨大的雪堆

(D) 會造成無法預期的雪崩

5. "Dazzlingly" 這個字可能意味著？

(A) **明亮的**

(B) 黯淡的

(C) 漂亮的

(D) 生病的

4 地球科學

 本文圖解

Icebergs *are* among nature's most spectacular creations, and yet most

people *have never seen* one. A vague air of mystery *envelops* them. ② They

come into being-somewhere-in faraway, *line* frigid waters, **amid** thunderous

<small>line 在此當動詞，　amid 為介係詞"在…
意思是"沿…排列"　之中"</small>

noise and splashing turbulence, which in most cases no one hears or sees.

<small>which 指的是前面提到的 noise 及
turbulence</small>

They *exist* only a short time and then slowly away just as unnoticed.

Objects of sheerest beauty, they *have been called*. **Appearing** variety of

<small>倒裝句，受詞放於最前面　　　　　　　　分詞片語修飾全句，表
示"以…形狀出現"</small>

shapes, they *may be* dazzlingly white, or they *may be* glassy blue, green, or

purple, tinted faintly or in darker hues. They *are* graceful, stately, **inspiring** in

<small>表示"給人…想法"</small>

calm, sunlit seas.

But they *are also called* frightening and dangerous, and that they are in

<small>that 名詞子句，
當主詞 they 補語</small>

the night, in the fog, and in storms. Even in clear weather one *is* wise to stay at

<small>one 的意思是指人們</small>

a safe distance away from them. Most of their bilk *is hidden* below the visible

top. Also, ④ they may *roll* over unexpectedly, churning the waters around them.

Icebergs *are* parts of glaciers that break off, drift into the water, float

about a while, and finally melt. Icebergs **afloat** today *are made* of snowflakes

afloat 為浮在…之上，置於被修飾名詞之後

that have fallen over long ages of time. They *embody* snows that drifted

down hundreds, or many thousands, or in some cases maybe a million year

ago. The snows *fell* in polar regions and on cold mountains, where they

where 引導副詞子
句修飾全句

melted only a little or not at all, and so *collected* to great depths over the

years and centuries.

As each year's snow accumulation lay on the surface, evaporation and

as 引導副詞子句，表示當…的時候

melting *caused* the snowflakes to fall slowly on the top of the old, and it too

④

地球科學

turned to icy grains. ③ So blankets of snow and ice grains *mounted* layer

turn to 表示"轉變成"

upon layer and *were* of **such** great thickness **that** the weight of the upper

such... that 意思為如此…以致於，與 so that 類似

layers compressed the lower ones. **With** time and pressure from above, the

介係詞片語當副詞用，表示在這種情況下

many small ice grains *joined* and *changed* to larger crystals, **and** eventually

連接詞連接第二個
主要子句

the deeper crystals *merged* into a solid mass of ice.

 單字與片語

重要單字 Key Vocabularies

① iceberg (n) 冰山

② spectacular (adj) 壯觀的

③ frigid (adj) 寒冷的

④ thunderous (adj) 雷鳴似的

⑤ splash (v) 潑；濺

⑥ turbulence (n) 渦流

⑦ dazzlingly (adv) 耀眼地

⑧ merge (v) 合併；吞沒

⑨ tinted (adj) 著色的

⑩ hue (n) 色調

⑪ churn (v) 翻攪

⑫ snowflake (n) 雪花

⑬ embody (v) 包含；體現

⑭ accumulation (n) 累積

⑭ evaporation (n) 蒸發

⑯ grain (n) 晶粒

⑰ blanket (n) 層；墊

⑱ mount (v) 登上

⑲ compress (v) 壓縮

⑳ glassy (adj) 玻璃狀的

重要片語 Key Phrases

❶ come into 開始於

❷ being-somewhere-in 在某處

❸ in most cases 大多數情況下

❹ are made of 由…組成

❺ roll over 翻過來

❻ drifted down 飄落

本文解析

　　本文一開始提到冰山有一股神祕的色彩，它們發源於未知的地方，漂浮於冰冷的海域，然後消失無形。而冰山看似純淨漂亮，但是卻暗藏危險，人們是要遠離它的。再來談到冰山形成的過程，它是由冰河裂開後被推落海中的，而冰山的形成最初是由落在嚴寒的山地的雪長年不會融化，所以年復一年的堆積的結果，因壓力的作用最後結成一大塊冰山。故本文主要是介紹冰山及其的形成過程，故文章標題以冰山的名稱及起源最恰當。

　　第二題問到冰山很少被看見的原因，在文中 They come into being-somewhere-in faraway... in most cases no one hears or sees. 這段話可看出是因位它生成的地

方很遙遠，所以很少見。第三題問"from above"這個字指的是何物，在這邊 above 是當名詞用，意思是"以上的東西"，在文中一句中提到雪層及冰晶粒一層一層堆疊上去，而上層的重量壓縮了下層，故"from above"應是指冰與雪的累積層。第三題問冰山危險的原因，由文中 they may roll over unexpectedly, churning the waters around them 可知冰山會突然翻轉，使周圍海水猛烈翻攪，要注意 turn over=roll over 都是翻轉之意。第五題問"Dazzlingly"這個單字，它是"耀眼地"，所以選項中以"brilliant"(明亮的) 最接近其意。

學習重點 ➡

　　本文中中的這段句子：... and were of **such** great thickness **that** the weight of the upper layers compressed the lower ones. 其中"so... that"和"such... that"都有"如此…所以"的意思。但在用法上有些差別。簡單說明如下：

例如：

(1)so... that：so 的後面使用簡單的形容詞，而 such...that 中，such 以 such(a/an)
　　＋形容詞＋名詞。如：

She is so beautiful that everyone likes her.
(她是如此美麗，所以每個人都喜歡她。)

She is such a beautiful girl that everyone likes her.
(她是如此一個美麗的女孩，所以每個人都喜歡她。)

(2)so... that 後面可加 a/an ＋單數可數名詞，用來加強語氣例如：

She is so beautiful a girl that everyone likes her.
(她是如此美麗的一個女孩，所以每個人都喜歡她。)

但如果是複數名詞，則不能用 so that 句型，例如：

They are such good boys that all teachers love them.
(他們是如此乖的孩子，所以所有的老師們都愛他們。)

不能寫成 They are so good boys that all teachers love them.(×)

4 地球科學

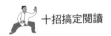
 英文本文

Article 4.3

Antarctica is a mostly unpopulated continent. It is the coldest, driest, and the most remote place in the world. And it is the world's only continent that does not have a native population. No single country owns the Antarctic. In 1997, however, a number of countries, including Argentina, Australia, Chile, New Zealand, France, and the United Kingdom, have already laid claim to the Antarctic and others will probably follow. In some areas of the continent, two countries claim the same land.

The Antarctic Treaty was signed in 1959 and creates the rules for the exploration of the Antarctic. The treaty forbids military activity in the Antarctic, as well as mining. Many countries, however, think that there are valuable materials and minerals locked up under the frozen Antarctic ice. In addition, the treaty bans nuclear testing as well as dumping nuclear waste. The Antarctic Treaty was made to protect the continent and avoid further disputes. By 2048, the treaty must be renewed. New rules and regulations could be **imposed** by then.

Currently, almost all of the 70 bases in the Antarctic are used for research and scientific activity. The snow-covered continent is perfect for tracking satellites and space research because it offers clear blue, cloudless skies. Climatologists are studying the development of the ozone layer with growing concern. It was here that a hole in the layer was discovered for the first time. More than 4000 scientists operate the research stations in the Antarctic summer, while only about a thousand populate the continent during the harsh and severe winters.

Environmentalists fear that exploiting Antarctica for military and economic reasons will damage the environment. At present, there is no economic activity in Antarctica, except for cruise ships that travel around the continent. This could change, if a new treaty allows mining in the Antarctic. As mineral resources are dwindling in other areas, nations could turn to Antarctica to find and exploit valuable raw materials.

Some geologists say that there are over 200 billion barrels of oil under the Antarctic ice. At the moment getting at these reserves would be very expensive. In addition, economic experts claim that there are large amounts of coal, nickel, and copper under the Antarctic ice.

理解力測驗

Q1. According to this article, which of the following countries hasn't laid claim to the Antarctic ?

(A) Australia

(B) Chile

(C) France

(D) America

Q2. When was The Antarctic Treaty signed?

(A) 2013

(B) 2000

(C) 1997

(D) 1959

Q3. What is the closest meaning of "**imposed**" in line 8, paragraph 2?

(A) implied

(B) improved

(C) executed

(D) extended

Q4. According to this article, which is NOT true about the Antarctic Treaty?

(A) It is the rules for the exploration of the Antarctic.

(B) The treaty forbids only military activity in the Antarctic.

(C) The treaty bans nuclear testing and dumping nuclear waste

(D) By 2048, the treaty must be renewed.

Q5. According to this article, which of following statements is true?

(A) Economic experts fear that exploiting Antarctica for military and economic reasons will damage the environment.

(B) The continent is perfect for tracking satellites and space research because it is snow-covered sky.

(C) More than 4000 researchers station in the Antarctic summer, while only less a half of that number stays up during winters.

(D) No economic activity is allowed in Antarctica, including cruise ships.

4

地球科學

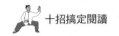

 **本文中譯**

南極洲

　　南極洲是一個幾乎杳無人煙的大陸，它是世界上最冷、最乾與最偏遠的地方，也是世界上唯一沒有原住民人口的大陸。沒有一個國家擁有南極，然而，一些國家，包括阿根廷、澳洲、智利、紐西蘭、法國及英國都已經插旗南極了，其他國家將來也可能跟進。在這塊大陸的有些地區，同一塊地有二個國家同時都宣稱擁有權。

　　南極洲條約簽訂於 1959 年，並成為探勘南極的規則，條約中不僅禁止在南極採礦，而且也禁止從事軍事活動。然而，許多國家認為在南極冰封底下藏有許多珍貴的物質及礦產。除此之外，條約中還禁止從事核子測試以及沉放核廢料。南極洲條約是用來保護這塊大陸並且避免進一步的紛爭，到 2048 年，該條約將會被更新，而新條約及規則到時會開始適用。

　　目前幾乎所有 70 個在南極洲的基地都用於科學研究活動。這塊冰雪覆蓋的大陸對於追蹤衛星及太空研究是很理想的，因為它提供了一個晴朗清澈的天空。氣象學者正在研究日益受關注的臭氧層發展，而最初發現臭氧層有個破洞就在這裡發現的。有超過 4000 位科學家及研究人員在南極洲的夏天於研究站作業，然而僅有約一千人會在嚴寒的冬天還待在這塊大陸。

　　環境學家擔心用軍事及經濟的理由來開發南極洲會危害到環境。目前，在南極洲並沒有商業活動，除了環繞這座大陸旅遊的遊輪外。假如新條約允許在南極洲採礦，這一切就可能改變，當礦業資源在其他地方逐漸沒落後，各國就可能轉向南極洲來尋找並開發珍貴的稀有原物料。

　　有些地質學家認為在南極冰層下面藏有超過二千億桶石油，而目前開採這些蘊藏非常昂貴。而且，經濟專家宣稱南極洲冰層底下也有大量的煤、鎳、銅等物產。

理解力測驗中譯

1. 依據本文，下列哪一個國家尚未在南極洲宣稱擁有主權？

(A) 澳洲

(B) 智利

(C) 法國

(D) **美國**

2. 南極洲條約是何年簽訂的？

(A) 2013

(B) 2000

(C) 1997

(D) **1959**

3. 在第二段第五行中的"imposed"與哪一個意思最為接近？

(A) 暗示

(B) 改進

(C) **執行**

(D) 延長

4. 依據本文，有關南極洲條約的敘述何者為不正確？

(A) 它是探勘南極的規則

(B) **此條約只有禁止在南極進行軍事活動**

(C) 此條約禁止核子試驗及丟棄核廢料

(D) 到 2048 年時，這條約將被更新

5. 依據本文，下列敘述何者為正確？

(A) 經濟專家擔心用軍事及經濟的理由來開發南極洲會危害到環境

(B) 這塊大陸對於追蹤衛星及太空研究是很理想的因為它的天空是冰雪覆蓋著

(C) **在南極洲的夏天有超過 4000 位研究人員駐點，然而僅有不到那數目一半人到冬天還待著**

(D) 在南極洲並不允許商業活動，包括旅遊的遊輪

4 地球科學

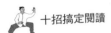
 本文圖解

Antarctica *is* a mostly unpopulated continent. It *is* the coldest, driest and most remote place in the world. And it *is* the world's only continent that does not have a native population. No single country *owns* the Antarctic. In 1997, However, ① a number of countries, including Argentina, Australia, Chile, New Zealand, France and the United Kingdom, *have already laid* claim to the Antarctic and others *will probably follow*. In some areas of the continent, two countries *claim* the same land.

② The Antarctic Treaty *was signed* in 1959 and ④A *creates* the rules for the exploration of the Antarctic. ④B The treaty *forbids* military activity in the Antarctic, as well as mining. Many countries, however, *think* that there are valuable materials and minerals **locked up** under the frozen Antarctic ice. In

分詞片語，修飾前面 minerals，表示蘊藏的礦物

addition, ④C the treaty *bans* nuclear testing as well as dumping nuclear waste. The Antarctic Treaty *was made* to protect the continent and avoid further disputes. ④D By 2048, the treaty must *be renewed*. New rules and regulations could *be imposed* by then.

Currently, almost all of the 70 bases in the Antarctic *are used* for research and scientific activity. ⑤B The snow-covered continent *is* perfect for tracking

satellites and space research because **it** offers clear blue, cloudless skies.

it 指的是 snow-covered continent

Climatologists *are studying* the development of the ozone layer with growing

concern. It *was* here **that** a hole in the layer was discovered for the first time.

it 就是 that 所引導的名詞子句

⑤C More than 4000 scientists *operate* the research stations in the Antarctic

summer, **while** only about a thousand *populate* the continent during the

表示轉折語氣"可是"的連接詞 while 連接第二個句子

harsh and severe winters.

⑤A Environmentalists *fear* that exploiting Antarctica for military and

economic reasons will damage the environment. At present, ⑤D there *is* no

economic activity in Antarctica, **except for** cruise ships that travel around the

表示除…之外

continent. This could *change*, if a new treaty allows mining in the Antarctic.

As mineral resources are dwindling in other areas, nations could *turn* to

as 在此為"當…時候"，引導一副詞子句

Antarctica to find and exploit valuable raw materials.

Some geologists *say* that there are over 200 billion barrels of oil under

the Antarctic ice. At the moment getting at these reserves *would be* very

expensive. In addition, economic experts *claim* that there are large amounts

of coal, nickel and copper under the Antarctic ice.

4

地
球
科
學

 **單字與片語**

重要單字 Key Vocabularies

① unpopulated （adj）無人居住的　　② continent （n）大陸

③ native （adj）本地的　　④ remote （adj）遙遠的

⑤ exploration （n）探險　　⑥ forbid （v）禁止

⑦ mineral （n）礦物　　⑧ mining （n）採礦

⑨ renew （v）更新　　⑩ impose （v）把…強加於

⑪ climatologist （n）氣象學家　　⑫ ozone layer 臭氧層

⑬ geologist （n）地質學家　　⑭ cruise ship （n）郵輪

⑮ environmentalist （n）環境學家

重要片語 Key Phrases

❶ as well as　不但…而且

❷ by then　到那時

❸ at the moment　目前

本文解析

　　本文先提到南極洲是一個無人居住的冰封大陸，但有許多國家宣稱擁其有主權，而南極洲條約是規範各國在這邊的探勘規則，條約中禁止採礦及軍事活動等。而南極的地理條件是作為觀測研究的絕佳地點，且在此發現臭氧層的破洞。最後談到因為南極洲有豐富的資源蘊藏，專家擔心未來如果開發南極將危害到其生態環境。

　　第一題問哪個國家尚未在南極洲宣稱擁有主權，答案從文章中第四行可以看出美國並沒有宣稱擁有。第二題問南極洲條約何年簽訂，本題也是直接可從文章中看出，但要注意不要被其他提到的年份給弄錯了。第三題問"imposed"單字的意思，它的解釋是"把…強加於"，在文中的意思就是要將新的條約加以執行，所以與"executed"最接近。第四題及第五題都是問文中的細節題，只要從選項中的關鍵字，找到文章中對應的句子比較後，用消去法即可判別出答案，但要注意選項的意思可能經過改寫，例如第五題選項 (C)...while only less a half of that number stays up during winters.，此時 that number 就是前面提到的那 4000 人，所以該句的意思就是不到 2000 人留下來，符合文章的說法（雖然文中說約有 1000 人，但少於 2000 人就包含 1000 多人的意思）。

學習重點 ➡

在本文中的一句：It was here that a hole in the layer was discovered for the first time.（最初發現臭氧層有個破洞就在這裡發現的）。這是一種英文中常見的強調句型，其句型結構為：It is(was) + adj + ... + to + V（或 Ving 或 that 子句）... 句子強調的是後面 to + V（或 Ving 或 that 子句）的事，但動詞不可強調

例句：

It was nice to see him again.

（能再次看到他真好。）→強調再次看到他

It is my great pleasure meeting such a nice speaker.

（能會見這麼好的演講者是我的榮幸。）→強調會見這麼好的演講者

It is evident that he's telling a lie.

（他很明顯的正在說謊。）→強調他正在說謊

就上述本文中句子而言，可復原成：

A hole in the layer was discovered for the first time here.

依強調不同的部分分別改寫如下：

= It was here that a hole in the layer was discovered for the first time.

（第一次發現破洞就在這邊。）

= It was a hole in the layer that was discovered for the first time here.

（第一次在這邊發現的東西就是破洞。）

= It was for the first time that a hole in the layer was discovered here.

（一個破洞在這邊被發現是頭一回。）

④ 地球科學

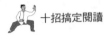

 英文本文

Article 4.4

Acid rain is one of the biggest environmental problems today. It has many long-term effects, like its damage to trees and buildings. It can lead to skin and breathing problems. It can also cause animals to become extinct.

Acid rain is caused by air pollution from cars and factories. These machines burn fuel for energy. When fuel burns, it produces smoke and invisible gases that mix with clouds. These dark clouds rain harmful chemicals onto the earth. Although the rain is not acidic enough to **corrode** skin, it coats tree leaves, buildings, and the ground with toxic water.

Acid rain has actually been around since the mid-1800s. It was discovered by Robert Angus Smith. Smith found a relationship between acid rain and air pollution. However, scientists did not start studying acid rain seriously until the 1950s. Acid rain can be prevented by burning less dangerous fuels. Factories have also experimented with special filters that remove harmful chemicals from the smoke. These are good solutions, but governments have to act fast; otherwise, the damage may be unstoppable.

理解力測驗

Q1. What is the main idea of the passage?

(A) The cause and environmental disaster of acid rain.

(B) The dangerous forms of air pollution.

(C) The environment in the mid-1800s.

(D) The discovery of acid rain by Robert Angus Smith.

Q2. According to the passage, which of the following is NOT correct?

(A) Acid rain is a serious problem these days.

(B) Acid rain may cause the climatic change.

(C) Cars and factories are main reasons for acid rain.

(D) Acid rain has been known for more than 150 years.

Q3. Which of the following is correct about acid rain?

(A) It can cause humans to become extinct.

(B) Toxic water from cars and factories causes acid rain.

(C) Serious research on acid rain only started around 60 years ago.

(D) It can make people get lung cancer.

Q4. Who should act fast to prevent the acid rain?

(A) scientists

(B) Robert Angus Smith

(C) governments

(D) factories

Q5. Which of the following words is closest in meaning to "**corrode**" in paragraph 2?

(A) comfort

(B) convict

(C) convert

(D) corrupt

4

地
球
科
學

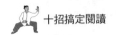

 **本文中譯**

酸雨

　　酸雨是現在最大的環境問題之一，它有許多長期的影響，像是為害樹木及建築物，它也會導致皮膚及呼吸問題，也可能導致動物滅絕。

　　酸雨起因於汽車及工廠的空氣汙染，這些機器燃燒燃料以取得能源，當燃燒時，燃料產生煙霧以及看不見的氣體而與雲混在一起。從這些黑雲下了含有有害化學物質的雨進入土壤裡。雖然雨沒有酸到會侵蝕皮膚，但它會和有毒的水附著在樹葉、建築物及地上。

　　酸雨自從 1800 年代中期起就一直存在，它是被羅伯安格斯史密斯所發現的，史密斯發現酸與空氣汙染之間的關係。然而，科學家直到 1950 年代才開始認真地研究酸雨，燃燒少一點的危險燃料可以避免產生酸雨，工廠已經完成可以從排煙中過濾有害化學物質的特殊過濾器實驗了，這些都是好方法，但政府必須快點行動，否則，危害可能會無法停息。

理解力測驗中譯

1. 本篇文章的大意為何？

(A) **酸雨的起因及對環境的危害**

(B) 空氣汙染的危險形式

(C) 在 1800 年代中期的環境

(D) 羅伯安格斯史密斯發現酸雨

2. 依據本文，下列敘述何者為非？

(A) 酸雨近來是一個嚴重的問題

(B) **酸雨可能導致氣候變遷**

(C) 汽車及工廠是酸雨的主要原因

(D) 酸雨已經被發現超過 150 年了

3. 下列關於酸雨敘述何者為真？

(A) 它可能使人類滅亡

(B) 從汽車及工廠中的有毒的水造成酸雨

(C) **大約從 60 年前才開始對酸雨作認真的研究**

(D) 它可能讓人們得到肺癌

4. 誰需快速行動來預防酸雨？

(A) 科學家

(B) 羅伯安格斯史密斯

(C) **政府**

(D) 工廠

5. 下列哪一個字意思與第二段中的 "corrode" 最接近？

(A) 舒適

(B) 犯罪

(C) 轉換

(D) **使腐敗**

4
地球科學

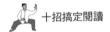

 **本文圖解**

②A Acid rain *is* one of the biggest environmental problems today. It *has* many long-term effects, like damage to trees and buildings. ③D It can *lead to* skin and breathing problems. ③A It can also *cause* animals to become extinct.

②C ③B Acid rain *is caused* by air pollution from cars and factories. These machines *burn* fuel for energy. When fuel burns, it *produces* smoke and invisible gases that mix with clouds. These dark clouds *rain* harmful chemicals onto the earth. Although the rain is not acidic enough to corrode skin, it

表讓步的連接詞引導的副詞子句，修飾全句

coats tree leaves, buildings, and the ground with toxic water.

②D Acid rain *has actually been* around since the mid-1800s. It *was discovered* by Robert Angus Smith. Smith *found* a relationship between acid rain and air pollution. ③C However, scientists *did not start* studying acid rain seriously until the 1950s. Acid rain can *be prevented* by burning less dangerous fuels. Factories *have also experimented* with special filters that remove harmful chemicals from the smoke. These *are* good solutions, ④ but governments have to act fast. If they wait, the damage may *be* unstoppable.

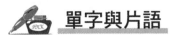 **單字與片語**

重要單字 Key Vocabularies

① environmental（adj）環境的　　② damage（n）損害

③ extinct（adj）已消失的　　　　④ pollution（n）汙染

⑤ invisible（adj）看不見的　　　⑥ chemical（n）化學品；（adj）化學的

⑦ acidic（adj）酸的　　　　　　⑧ filter（n）過濾，濾紙

⑨ unstoppable（adj）無法停止的

本文解析

　　本文一開始談到酸雨的危害，再來談到酸雨形成的原因及過程，及酸雨發現的經過，最後結論是防治酸雨，政府必須快點行動，否則危害可能會無法停息。故第一題的答案，本文大意應為酸雨的起因及對環境的危害。

　　第二題問到敘述為非，第三題問到有關酸與敘述為真者，這兩題都是有關內容的細節題，方法都一樣，就是找出選項中的關鍵字，對照文中的敘述，用排除法得到正確解答。第四題問到誰需快速行動來預防酸雨，由文由 … but governments have to act fast…，知政府必須快速行動來解決問題。第五題問到單字"corrode"，意思為腐蝕（動詞），故選項中以 corrupt(使腐敗) 最接近。

學習重點 ➡

　　本篇有關自然科學的文章，文法結構較簡單，其中用的比較多的部分還是有關被動式的使用，所以對被動式及其變化應有清楚認識，看文章就會容易且自然的多了，例如本文中的這一段：Acid rain has actually been around since the mid-1800s，這是一句現在完成式的被動語態 (has / have ＋ been ＋及物動詞的過去分詞)，要注意的是後面看到介係詞 since ＋時間，這種敘述從某一段過去時間以來的事物，動詞時態用完成式，再加上表示被動存在 (been around) 的意思，所以用完成式的被動語態。如以下例句：

　　A lot of soldiers in Iraq have been wounded(since 2001).

　　（ 自從 2001 以來，）許多在伊拉克的士兵已經受傷了。

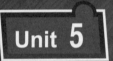

自然＆環保

Natural & Environmental Protection

第五招 答題技巧

當您具有豐富的字彙及良好的閱讀能力後，要在閱讀測驗中拿高分，還需熟悉解題過程中的一些小技巧，這些技巧可以讓你在解答閱讀測驗中，更快速的找出題目的重點，鎖定答案，達成快速正確的解題，說明如下：

1. 先找出題目（或選項）的關鍵字句，再搜尋文章內的相關文句，並注意關鍵字是否有改寫。

2. 讀每段話時，要抓住該段話的開頭一、二句主題句和關鍵字。答案常常是主題句的關鍵字（或其改寫）。

3. 段落中未展開說明的細節內容是幾乎都是干擾選項，不需要浪費時間去判斷。

4. 看到 Although/While/Despite/Despite the fact/Besides…等表示語意的轉折、讓步等地方，要特別注意其後面的語句，測驗的題目常常會出現在這些地方。

5. 主題句中如有 show 和 suggest 等詞，其後的受詞名詞子句往往是要說明的觀點，也是該段的主旨，故常是考題的答案。

6. 如果主句是 not only... but also 句型，重點是在強調後面的部分，所以要注意 but also 後面部分的說明。

7. 舉例子的句子不會是主題句，幾乎可以忽略不看。

8. 舉凡看到如反覆出現的詞、括號裡的詞、引號裡的詞、黑／斜體字等，應視為閱讀重點，題目常會出現於這些地方。

以下為一篇閱讀測驗題題目，讓我們看看如何用上述技巧有效率的解題：

Many US bird populations are in decline, some of which are even on the brink of extinction. Of the 800 species of birds in the United States, 67 are listed as endangered or threatened; another 184 are listed as "species of conservation concern" because they have small distribution, are facing high threats or have a declining population. Hawaiian birds and ocean birds appear most at risk. More than one-third of all US bird species are in Hawaii. However, 71 Hawaiian species have gone extinct since A.D. 300 and about 10 species have not been seen in the past 40 years. The declines of US bird populations can be traced to a variety of factors, including agriculture, climate change, unplanned urban development, and overfishing. In the grasslands, for example, intensified agricultural practices have hurt bird populations. Grassland cannot support many birds if it is overused or burned too frequently. Besides, public lands and parks are mowed too frequently and the grass is too short to provide a habitat for birds.

While many bird species are in decline, some other species are thriving. Research shows that wetland bird species began to increase in the late 1970s, which reflects the importance of the artificial habitats to the survival of many bird populations. The results prove that investment in wetlands has paid off and that it is now necessary to invest similarly in other neglected habitats where birds are undergoing steepest declines.

1. What is this passage mainly about?
   (A) Variety of bird species in Hawaii.
   (B) The decline of bird species in the US.
   (C) The habitat of bird species in the US.
   (D) The need for stricter bird protection laws.
2. Which of the following is NOT mentioned as a reason for the decline of the bird population?
   (A) Agriculture.
   (B) Climate change.

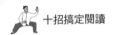
(C) Harmful chemicals.

(D) Overfishing.

3. How many bird species inhabit Hawaii?

(A) About 70.

(B) About 120.

(C) About 180.

(D) About 270.

4. According to the passage, which measure can effectively protect bird species?

(A) To monitor bird migration.

(B) To increase and preserve wetlands.

(C) To promote education in bird conservation.

(D) To develop medicine that can help birds live longer.

5. Which of the following statements is true?

(A) All of the US bird species are declining.

(B) Long grass provides ideal habitats for birds.

(C) Mowing can help birds to build their nests.

(D) In Hawaii 71 bird species have disappeared for three decades.

　　在第一題中問本文主旨是甚麼？依答題技巧 (2) 的觀念來看，開頭第一句便說許多美國鳥類正在減少，第二句也表示有鳥類然後說明鳥類族尋減少的說法 (have a declining population)，再看第二段第一句談到的是很多鳥類正在減少，但有鳥類增加…，這些句子都圍繞在有關美國境內鳥類減少的事，故答案為 (B)。

　　在第二題中問何者不是鳥類族群減少的原因？該句的關鍵字是 decline of the bird population，依答題技巧 (1) 我們很快在第一段第七行中間看到這個關鍵字，然後就可以很快發現 (C) 有害的化學物質沒有在說明的項目中。

　　在第三題中問夏威夷有幾種鳥類棲息？該句的關鍵字是 species inhabit Hawaii，依答題技巧 (1)，我們很快在第一段第五行中間看 More than one-third of all US bird species are in Hawaii.，但只有説有三分之一的鳥是在夏威夷，所以要回到前面第二行找到美國有約 800 種鳥類，所以答案為 (D) 約 270 種。解該題的技巧仍是要注意開頭一、二句 (答題技巧 2)。

在第四題中問哪一項方法可以有效地保護鳥類？由第二段第一行看到 Research shows that wetland bird species began to increase in the late 1970s, which reflects the importance of the artificial habitats to the survival of many bird. 依答題技巧 (5) 知 show 後面的名詞子句中應該就會有該題答案，該處提到人造棲息地 (artificial habitats)，而其它選項並沒提到，不用去理會或聯想 (答題技巧 3) ，故答案為 (B)。

第五題問下列何項敘述為真？依序來看：(A) 全部美國的鳥類都在減少──由各段前二句便可知道該選項為非 (答題技巧 2)(B) 長草地提供鳥類理想的棲息地──該選項的關鍵字為 grass，可以在第一段倒數第二句看到：Grassland cannot... Besides, public lands... 依邏輯判斷：草也太短無法供給鳥類棲息，故長草地提供鳥類理想的棲息地，敘述正確。這亦可印證答題技巧 (5)：看到語意的轉折、讓步等地方，要特別注意其後面的語句。(C) 割草可以幫助鳥類築牠們的巢──關鍵字為 Mowing 同樣由第二段最後一行 Besides, public lands and parks are mowed too frequently and the grass is too short to provide a habitat for birds. 所以割草無法幫助鳥類築巢，該選項是干擾選項 (答題技巧 4)，且一樣要注意 Besides 後面的句子 (答題技巧 5) (D) 在夏威夷有 71 種鳥類已經消失了三世紀之久──關鍵字為 Hawaii 71 bird species ，由第一段第六行：However, 71 Hawaiian species... 得知 71 種夏威夷鳥類自西元 300 年起就已經消失了，非消失了三世紀，敘述錯誤。要注意本題關鍵字經過改寫 (答題技巧 1)，且選項的答案出現在轉折語氣 besides 後面 (答題技巧 4)。

5
自然 & 環保

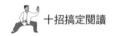

 英文本文

Article 5.1

In August 2009, Typhoon Morakot had heavily damaged these mountain areas, as well as the seafront in central and south regions of Taiwan. This typhoon had carried with extremely heavy rainfall which caused enormous and mass land **collapse**. The landslides and mudflows submerged villages and farmlands, and devastated roads and bridges. In the seafront, flooding and sea water encroachment had submerged the urban area, farmland and fishponds. After the typhoon disaster, government had immediately implemented urgent repairment and reconstruction for the public facilities, such as roads and bridges. NGOs and enterprises were also actively devoting themselves to helping reconstructing campus and residence. However, with the continuous recovery in these disaster areas, the living issues of the local residents had gradually emerged; as a result, the industry reconstruction, which is the key of whether the regular life of these victims can be recovered or not, has become the greatest concern for the result in the entire disaster recovery. Industry Reconstruction is one of the three major reconstruction plans for the disaster caused by Typhoon Morakot. It is also the last piece of jigsaw puzzle of completing the post-disaster reconstruction of industry. In addition, the goal of industry reconstruction is to recover or improve the production functions and then achieve the purpose of living and working in peace and joy for these communities. The feature of industry reconstruction is to satisfy individual living requirement for the residents. However, those requirements above are irrelevant to the public interest; therefore, the expenses of these requirements are difficult to be paid by government, so it might need more time-consuming reviewing and auditing by non-government organization (NGO). Thus if enterprises can provide assistance in time, then, with their excellent efficiency, they can promptly resolve the living issues for the residents by more economic and effective methods.

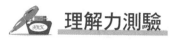 理解力測驗

Q1. Based on the content, which of the following areas was not heavily damaged by Typhoon Morakot in August 2009?

(A) Central mountain areas

(B) Seafront area

(C) Southern mountain areas

(D) Northern mountain areas

Q2. What is the closet meaning of the term "**collapse**" in line 3?

(A) fail

(B) crash

(C) break down

(D) all of the above

Q3. Regarding the author, which of the following description about the recovery in these disaster areas after Typhoon Morakot is NOT true?

(A) It is one of three major reconstruction plans after the disaster.

(B) It is the first piece of jigsaw puzzle of completing the post-disaster reconstruction.

(C) Its goal is to recover or improve the production functions for these communities.

(D) Its purpose is to achieve living and working in peace and joy for these communities.

Q4. According to the information, why the budgets of industry reconstruction are difficult to be paid by government?

(A) Because they might need more time-consuming reviewing and auditing.

(B) Because enterprises can promptly resolve the issues by more economic and effective methods.

(C) Because those requirements are irrelevant to the public interest.

(D) All of the above.

Q5. According to the article, which of the following descriptions about enterprises providing assistance in time after disaster is correct?

(A) Enterprises have better efficiency.

(B) Enterprises are more careful.

(C) Enterprises can use longer reviewing method to resolve the living issues for the residents.

(D) None of the above.

 本文中譯

企業與救災

　　發生在 2009 年 8 月的莫拉克颱風，重創中、南部山區及濱海地區。這個颱風挾帶超大的降雨，在山區造成大量的土石崩塌，土石流淹沒村落、農田，摧毀道路、橋樑。在濱海地區則因洪水氾濫及海水侵蝕而淹沒市區、農地、及漁塭。風災後，政府部門立即進行道路、橋樑等公共設施的搶修和重建，而 NGOs 和企業也積極投入校園、住宅等家園重建的工作。但是在災區逐漸復原之後，居民的生計問題也逐一浮現，因此，關係著災民是否真正可以恢復正常生活的產業重建，攸關著整個災害復原的成敗。產業重建是莫拉克風災災後三大重建計畫之一，也是完成災後重建的最後一塊拼圖。其目標在恢復或提升社區的生產機能，進而達到社區居民安居樂業的目的。產業重建的特色在於滿足居民個別的生計需求，而這些各式各樣的需求，由於和公共利益無關，所以很難由政府部門支付其費用，透過 NGO 也可能需要較長的審核時間。所以企業若能及時伸出援手，那麼以他們的執行效率來看，便可以較快的速度、和經濟有效的方法，來解決居民的生計問題。

理解力測驗中譯

1. 根據本文內容,下列哪一項不是發生在 2009 年 8 月的莫拉克颱風所重創的地區?

   (A) 中部山區

   (B) 濱海地區

   (C) 南部山區

   (D) 北部山區

2. 第 3 行的單字"collapse"是下列何意?

   (A) 失效

   (B) 瓦解

   (C) 崩潰

   (D) 以上皆是

3. 根據本文作者,下列關於莫拉克風災災後產業重建的敘述何者為非?

   (A) 災後三大重建計畫之一

   (B) 完成災後重建的第一塊拼圖

   (C) 目標在恢復或提升社區居民的生產機能

   (D) 目的是達到社區居民安居樂業

4. 根據本文資訊,為何產業重建的經費很難由政府支付?

   (A) 因為他們需要長時間的審核

   (B) 因為企業可以用較快的速度、和經濟有效的方法解決問題

   (C) 因為這些需求和公共利益無關

   (D) 以上皆是

5. 依據本文,下列哪一項關於企業在災難發生時及時伸出援手的敘述為真?

   (A) 企業有較好的效率

   (B) 企業的較為謹慎

   (C) 企業可利用較長的審核時間方法,來解決居民的生計問題

   (D) 以上皆非

5
自然 & 環保

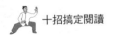
 本文圖解

In August 2009, ① Typhoon Morakot *had heavily damaged* these mountain areas, as well as the seafront in central and south regions of Taiwan. This typhoon *had carried* with extremely heavy rainfall which caused enormous and mass land collapse. The landslides and mudflows *submerged* villages and farmlands, and *devastated* roads and bridges. In the seafront, flooding and sea water encroachment *had submerged* the urban area, farmland and fishponds. After the typhoon disaster, government *had immediately implemented* urgent repairment and reconstruction for the public facilities, such as roads and bridges. NGOs and enterprises *were* also actively devoting themselves to help reconstructing campus and residence.

However, **with** the continuous recovery in these disaster areas, the living
介係詞 with 指在…情況下
issues of the local residents *had gradually emerged*; as a result, the industry

reconstruction, <u>which is the key of whether the regular life of these victims</u> <u>can be recovered or not</u>, *has become* the greatest concern for the result in the entire disaster recovery. ③Ⓐ Industry Reconstruction *is* one of the three major reconstruction plans for the disaster **caused** by Typhoon Morakot.

分詞片語，修飾 disaster，表示
由颱風引起的災害

③Ⓑ It *is* also the last piece of jigsaw puzzle of completing the post-disaster reconstruction of industry. In addition, ③Ⓒ the goal of industry reconstruction *is* to recover or improve the production functions and then ③Ⓓ *achieve* the purpose of living and working in peace and joy for these communities. The feature of industry reconstruction *is* to satisfy individual living requirement for the residents. However, ④ those requirements above *are* irrelevant to the public interest; therefore, the expenses of these requirements *are* difficult to be paid by government, so it might *need* more **time-consuming** reviewing

耗費時間的，修飾後面的二個名詞

and auditing by non-government organization (NGO). Thus <u>if enterprises</u>

5

自
然
&
環
保

can provide assists in time, then, ⑤ **with** their excellent efficiency, they can

介係詞 with 在此
解釋為以…方式

promptly resolve the living issues for the residents by more economic and

effective methods.

 單字與片語

重要單字 Key Vocabularies

① extremely （adv）極端地

② enormous （a）巨大的

③ landslides and mudflows （n）土石流

④ submerged （v）淹沒

⑤ devastated （v）毀壞

⑥ reconstruction （n）重建；復原

重要片語 Key Phrases

❶ land collapse　土石崩塌

❷ sea water encroachment　海水倒灌

❸ jigsaw puzzle　拼圖

❹ irrelevant to　不相關

❺ non-government organization(NGO)　非政府組織

本文解析

本文主要講述莫拉克颱風在台灣中南部造成淹水及土石流的災害，而政府雖然在災後立即進行重建工作，但都主要是在公共建設方面，而與居民生計息息相關的一些產業重建，卻因與公共利益較無關而不便由政府來推動及支付費用，結論是企業如能即時伸出援手，並運用其靈活迅速的效率及執行力，便可解決災後產業重建的問題。

第一題問哪些區域非為莫拉克颱風所重創的地區，答案在 ... seafront in central and south regions of Taiwan 即可看出。第二題問單字"collapse"，它是的意思是"奔潰，倒塌"等，選項中前三者均有相近意思。第三題問於莫拉克風災的災後產業重建敘述，本題是細節題，需依各項敘述中的關鍵詞，在文中找到相對應的詞句，用排除法即可得到答案。第四題問為何產業重建的經費很難由政府支付，由 ... those requirements above irrelevant to the public interest; therefore, ... are difficult to be paid by government，可知原因是因產業重建與公眾利益無關，要注意題目中將費用以"budget"來替代文章中使用的"expense"。最後問企業在災難發生時及時伸出援手的敘述，答案在最後一段話可看出來：if enterprises can provide assists in time, then, with their excellent efficiency, they can promptly... effective methods.

學習重點 ➡

本文與句結構較簡單，沒有太多相關修飾的子句或分詞結構，其中比較要注意介係詞片語的用法，如文中有二處用到介係詞片語的地方，但其解釋並不相同，在 ... with the continuous recovery in these disaster areas...，介係詞 with 解釋為"在這種情況之下"，而在 ... with their excellent efficiency...，介係詞 with 解釋為"具有…的狀況"。

5
自然 & 環保

157

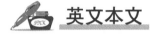 英文本文

Article 5.2

Increasing reliance on renewable energies is the way to achieve greater CO_2 emission sustainability and energy independence. As such energies are yet only available intermittently and energy cannot be stored easily, most countries aim to combine several energy sources. In a new study in EPJ Plus, French scientists have come up with an open source simulation method to calculate the actual cost of relying on a combination of electricity sources. Bernard Bonin, from the Atomic Energy Research Centre CEA Saclay, France, and his colleagues demonstrate that the cost is not directly proportional to the demand level. Although recognized as crude by its creator, this method can only be tailored to account for the public's interest, and not solely for economic performance, when optimizing the energy mix. The authors consider wind, solar, hydraulic, nuclear, coal, and gas as potential energy sources. In their model, the energy demand and availability are cast as random variables. The authors simulated the behavior of the mix for a large number of tests of such variables, using so-called Monte-Carlo simulations.

For a given mix, they found the energy cost of the mix presents a minimum as a function of the installed power. This means that if **it** is too large, the fixed costs dominate the total and become overwhelming. In contrast, if it is too small, expensive energy sources will need to be frequently solicited.

The authors are also able to optimize the energy mix, according to three selected criteria, namely economy, environment, and supply security.

The simulation tested on the case of France, based on 2011 data, shows that an optimal mix is 2.4 times the average demand in this territory. This mix contains a large amount of nuclear power, and a small amount of fluctuating energies: wind and solar. It is also strongly export-oriented.

理解力測驗

Q1. What does the article refer to?

(A) The renewable energies

(B) The cost of the mix energy

(C) The Monte-Carlo simulations

(D) The potential energy sources

Q2. Who may be Bernard Bonin?

(A) a researcher in France

(B) an economist

(C) an author of Monte-Carlo simulations

(D) a tailor

Q3. The authors are able to optimize the energy mix by several measures, except

(A) supply security

(B) environment

(C) sustainability

(D) economy

Q4. The term "it" in line 2, paragraph 2, refers to?

(A) the energy cost

(B) the installed power

(C) a given mix

(D) a function

Q5. According to this article, which of the followings is true?

(A) Renewable energies can be stored easily.

(B) French scientists have developed a simulation method to calculate the cost of a combination of electricity sources.

(C) Bernard Bonin and his colleagues demonstrate that cost is proportional to the demand level.

(D) The energy cost of the mix presents a maximum as a function of the installed power.

 **本文中譯**

再生能源

　　逐漸仰賴使用再生能源是一項可以獲致更大的二氧化碳排放永續性及能源獨立性的方法，但因為這些能源只能間歇性的使用且無法輕易存取，大部分國家都想要合併使用多種能源。在 EPJ Plus 的一項研究中，法國科學家們已經想出一項可用來計算於依各種組合電力來源時，其真實費用的資源共享模擬方法。法國 CEA Saclay 原子能研究中心的 Bernard Bonin 以及他的同僚證實了費用並不是直接與需求程度成正比的。雖然設計者也認為這個方法尚嫌粗糙，但這個方法可為公眾利益而量身定做，且當在最佳化能源的組合時，不會完全僅考量經濟效能。作者將風能、太陽能、水力、核能、煤以及汽油當成潛在的能源來源，在他們的模型中，能源需求及可獲得性被當成是隨機變數，作者用一種叫做蒙地卡羅模擬法模擬出一大堆這些變數的試驗在這組合的表現。

　　對一個特定的混合，他們發現這個組合的能源價格最小值可表示成一個安裝功率的函數。這意味著假如它太大，固定成本主導著全部結果且是壓倒性的。相反的，如果它太小，就時常需要靠各種昂貴的能源來源。

　　作者也能最佳化能源混合，依據所選定的這些三個則準，分別是經濟、環境及供應安全性。

　　就對法國所作的模擬測試來說，這是以 2011 年資料作為基礎，顯示出最佳的組合是在這個區域中平均需求的 2.4 倍，這個混合包含大量的核能以及少量的變動能源，如風與太陽能，它同時也是強烈的出口導向型。

理解力測驗中譯

1. 本文主要談到甚麼？

   (A) 各種再生能源

   (B) 混合能源的價格

   (C) 蒙地卡羅模擬法

   (D) 各種潛在的能源

2. Bernard Bonin 可能是甚麼人？

   (A) 一位法國研究人員

   (B) 經濟學家

   (C) 蒙地卡羅模擬法的作者

   (D) 裁縫師

3. 作者可以用一些標準讓混合能源的價格得到最佳化，除了何者以外？

   (A) 供應的安全性

   (B) 環境

   (C) 持續性

   (D) 經濟性

4. 第三段第六行的 it 指的是

   (A) 能源價格

   (B) 安裝功率

   (C) 一個已知電網

   (D) 一個方程式

5. 依據本文，下列敘述何者正確？

   (A) 再生能源可以很容易被儲存。

   (B) 法國科學家已發展出一種模擬方法來模擬各種電力來源組合的價格。

   (C) Bernard Bonin 及他的同事證明了價格與需求水準是成比例的。

   (D) 組合的能源價格呈現最大值，會是一個已安裝電力的函數。

⑤
自
然
＆
環
保

 本文圖解

Increasing reliance on renewable energies is the way to achieve greater

不定詞片語修飾
the way

CO_2 emission sustainability and energy independence. As ⑤Ⓐ such energies

As 引導副詞子句，
表示因…原因

are yet only available intermittently and energy cannot be stored easily, most

countries aim to combine several energy sources. In a new study in EPJ Plus,

⑤Ⓑ French scientists have come up with an open source simulation method

to calculate the actual cost of relying on a combination of electricity sources.

② Bernard Bonin from the Atomic Energy Research Centre CEA Saclay, France,

and colleagues ⑤Ⓒ demonstrate that cost is not directly proportional to the

demand level. Although recognized as crude by its creator, this method can

分詞構句，表示雖然被…認為

be tailored to account for the public's interest, and not solely economic

performance, when optimizing the energy mix. The authors consider wind,

solar, hydraulic, nuclear, coal and gas as potential energy sources. In their

model, the energy demand and availability are cast as random variables. The authors simulated the behavior of the mix for a large number of tests of such

variables, using so-called Monte-Carlo simulations.

For a given mix, they found ⑤ⅅ the energy cost of the mix presents a

found 後面接一名詞子句，　　　　　　present... as 意思
that 被省略　　　　　　　　　　　為將…表示成為

minimum as a function of the installed power. This means that if it is too

large, the fixed costs dominate the total and become overwhelming. In

contrast, if it is too small, expensive energy sources need to be frequently

solicited.

③ The authors are also able to optimize the energy mix, according to

three selected criteria, namely economy, environment and supply security.

The simulation tested on the case of France, based on 2011 data, shows
分詞片語當形容詞，修飾 simulation，表示在以…來測試

that an optimal mix is 2.4 times the average demand in this territory. This mix

contains a large amount of nuclear power, and a small amount of fluctuating

energies: wind and solar. It is also strongly export-oriented.

5
自
然
&
環
保

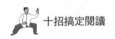

 單字與片語

重要單字 Key Vocabularies

① renewable energies 再生能源

② achieve（v）實現

③ emission（n）排放

④ sustainability（n）可持續性

⑤ intermittently（adv）間歇地

⑥ simulation（n）模擬

⑦ calculate（v）計算

⑧ colleague（n）同事，同僚

⑨ demonstrate（v）展示，證明

⑩ proportional（adj）與…成比例的

⑪ recognize（v）承認

⑫ performance（n）表現，行為

⑬ optimize（v）最佳化

⑭ solar（adj）太陽的

⑮ hydraulic（adj）水力的

⑯ potential（adj）潛在的

⑰ availability（n）可用性

⑱ random variables 變數

⑲ behavior（n）表現，行為

⑳ minimum（n）最小

㉑ dominate（v）支配，主導

㉒ solicit（v）乞求；懇求

㉓ criteria（n）準則（criterion 的複數型）

㉔ territory（n）領域，範圍

㉕ fluctuate（n）起伏，變動

㉖ overwhelming（adj）壓倒性的

重要片語 Key Phrases

❶ be tailored to 依需要調整

❷ account for 對…負責

❸ in contrast 相反地

❹ export-oriented 出口導向

 本文解析

　　本文開始提到再生能源只能間歇性的使用且無法保存，所以需要以混合方式來使用，法國研究人員提出一套方式，可以估算出使用這些組合能源的真實費用，後面介紹這個估算組合能源費用估算的方法及其發現的結論，所以本篇文章主要是談到混合能源的價格問題，這也是第一題所要問的。

　　第二題問 Bernard Bonin 可能是什麼身份，由文中可知他是在法國的研究機構，且提出一套計算費用方式，故研判應為研究人員。第三題問到有些準則讓混合能源的價格得到最佳化，文中既有提到三項，分別是經濟、環境及供應安全性。第四題問句中的 it 是指何者。it 一定是指前面有提過的名詞，所以這種題目一定要從前句來看：For a given mix, they found the energy cost of the mix presents a minimum as a function of the installed power. This means that if it is too large...。前面提到組合的能源價格最小值可表示成一個安裝功率的函數，而這個函數的結果與 fixed cost（固定成本）息息相關，也就是與現有電廠的安裝功率有直接關係，故 it 指的就是 installed power。第五題考細節題，將選項關鍵字找出，並在文中找到對應的部分即可得到答案。

學習重點 ➡

　　假設語氣是指在一種特定的情況下，推斷（或必定）會發生的事情的句子結構，其結構包含條件子句（或稱 if 子句）及主要子句（或稱結果子句）。if 子句是副詞子句的一種，其可分三大類，一是跟現在或未來事實相符（純粹假設性質），二是與現在或未來事實相反，三是與過去事實相反。以本文中出現的句子為例，如 ... if it is too large, the fixed costs dominate the total and become overwhelming. In contrast, if it is too small, expensive energy sources need to be frequently solicited.。這兩句均屬與現在或未來事實相符的假設句（或稱純粹假設性質），假設子句 if 引導的子句為現在式，它的結果子句可能為現在式（通常表習慣）、未來式（多用 will 加原形）、表達語態（使用語態助動詞 might, should 等）或祈使句。

例如：

If it rains, my dog barks.
（假如現在下雨，我的狗就會吠。）

If it rains tonight, I might not go to the party.
（如果今天晚上下雨，我可能就不會參加聚會。）

If it rains tonight, take a taxi to the party.
（如果今晚下雨，坐計程車參加聚會。）

5 自然 & 環保

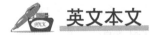 英文本文

Article 5.3

Zebra's stripes make it a very handsome animal, but what are the stripes really for? Zoologists have long been interested in the same question, and they have come up with several possibilities.

Firstly, they think stripes act as "camouflage", which means they help the zebra to hide. On the African plains, lions are the zebra's main predator, so hiding from them is very important. The shape of the stripes helps the zebra to hide in the long grass that is common on these plains. Black and white zebras are able to hide in brown and green grass because lions are color-blinded! This means that lions see everything as black, white, or gray. Even though the Zebra's stripes are black and white, they are good camouflage.

More recently, it has been proven that stripes are an effective means of confusing the blood-sucking tsetse fly as well. The tsetse fly is another resident of the African plains. They fly around and use their big eyes to find a tasty meal. Because horses, cows, and other animals with warm blood have a shape that is easy to see, the tsetse fly has no problem spotting them. However, in the case of the zebra, the stripes disguise the zebra's shape. This means that they are much less likely to be seen by the tsetse fly.

Finally, stripes are also believed to play a role in attracting female zebras. Wounds caused by fighting change the pattern of the stripes, so potential partners can see which male zebras are the best fighters. Apparently, female zebras are attracted to male zebras with lots of scars!

Useful for both camouflage and finding mate, a zebra's stripes are more than just a handsome accessory. They are an important aid to life on the African plains.

理解力測驗

Q1. Who is the zebra's main predator?

  (A) the lion

  (B) the tsetse fly

  (C) other grazers like horses and cows

  (D) animals with warm blood

Q2. Why are the zebra's stripes an important aid to life on the African plains?

  (A) Because they look nice.

  (B) Because they are useful when zebras fight each other.

  (C) Because they are good camouflage.

  (D) Because they can confuse female zebras.

Q3. Lions are color-blind. What does this mean?

  (A) Lions are short-sighted.

  (B) Lions see everything as black, white or gray.

  (C) Lions can see all colors except black and white.

  (D) Lions are blind to color at night

Q4. Which sentence about the zebra's stripes is true?

  (A) The most important role of the stripes is to make the zebra look handsome.

  (B) The pattern of the stripes can cause a fight between zebras.

  (C) The tsetse fly can recognize the zebra's shape easily because of the stripes.

  (D) Female zebras are attracted to male zebras with many scars

Q5. Which sentence about the zebra's stripes is NOT true?

  (A) They help the zebra to hide in the long grass.

  (B) Lions can see the zebra's stripes because they are color-blind.

  (C) Zoologists have been studying Zebra stripes for a long time.

  (D) They are believed to play a role in mating with female zebras.

5

自然&環保

本文中譯

斑馬條紋

斑馬的條紋讓牠成為一種很漂亮的動物，但是這些條紋是做什麼用的呢？動物學家一直以來對這問題都感到興趣，他們也想到幾個可能性。

首先，他們認為條紋是一種"偽裝"，這意味著條紋能讓斑馬隱藏起來。在非洲平原，獅子是斑馬的主要獵食者，所以躲避獅子是很重要的。條紋的形狀讓斑馬可以躲藏在草原中隨處可見的長草中，黑白相間的斑馬可以躲藏在棕綠色的草叢中，因為獅子是大色盲！這意味著獅子看每件東西都是黑、白或灰色的。縱使斑馬的條紋是黑白色的，那也足夠牠們偽裝了。

近來已證實這些條紋是一種迷惑吸血舌蠅的有效的方式。舌蠅是另外一種非洲草原的原住者，這些蒼蠅四處飛行，並用牠們的大眼睛來找尋美味的大餐，因為馬、牛及其它溫血動物的體型容易辨識，舌蠅可以輕易找到牠們。然而，對斑馬而言，這些條紋就混淆了斑馬的外型，這表示斑馬就不容易為舌蠅所見。

最後，條紋在吸引雌性斑馬中也被認為扮演一個重要角色。因為打鬥而受傷會改變條紋的型態，所以這些潛在的配偶們能由此看出哪些雄性斑馬是最好的戰士，顯而易見的是，母斑馬會為有許多傷疤的公斑馬所吸引。

由於同時具有偽裝及求偶的作用，所以斑馬的條紋不只是一種好看的裝飾品而已，對牠們生活在非洲草原也是一大助益。

理解力測驗中譯

---

1. 誰是斑馬的主要獵食者？

(A) **獅子**

(B) 舌蠅

(C) 其它草食性動物如馬和牛

(D) 溫血動物

---

2. 為何斑馬條紋對她們生活在非洲草原上是一大助益？

(A) 因為條紋好看

(B) 因為條紋在斑馬打鬥時是有用的

(C) **因為條紋是一種很好的偽裝**

(D) 因為條紋能混淆母斑馬

---

3. 獅子是色盲，這意味著甚麼？

(A) 獅子都是近視

(B) **獅子看任何東西都是黑、白或灰色**

(C) 獅子能看到除了黑色與白色外的所有顏色

(D) 獅子在晚上看不到東西顏色

---

4. 哪個有關於斑馬條紋的句子為真？

(A) 條紋最重要的作用就是讓斑馬看起來好看

(B) 條紋的型態可能導致斑馬之間的打鬥

(C) 由於有這些斑紋，舌蠅可以輕易認出斑馬的外型

(D) **母斑馬會被有許多傷疤的公斑馬所吸引**

---

5. 下列有關般碼條文的敘述何者不正確？

(A) 條紋讓斑馬可以隱藏在長草中

(B) **獅子可以看到斑馬的條紋因為牠們是色盲**

(C) 動物學家已經研究斑馬條紋很長一段時間了

(D) 條紋被認為在與公斑馬交配時扮演重要角色

5
自然 & 環保

169

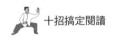

 本文圖解

The *zebra's stripes* make **it** a very handsome animal, but what are

it 就是指斑馬，
後面為其同位語

the stripes really for? ⑤Ⓑ*Zoologists* have long been interested in the same

question, and *they* have come up with several possibilities.

Firstly, *they* think stripes act as "camouflage," **which** means they help the

think 後面省略了 that　　　　　　which 指的是前面這件事

zebra to hide. On the African plains, ① *lions* are the zebra's main predator, so

hiding from them *is* very important. ⑤Ⓐ The *shape* of the stripes *helps* the zebra

to hide in the long grass that is common on these plains. **Black and white**

是指黑白相間的，
修飾 zebras

zebras *are* able to hide in **brown and green** grass because lions are color-

是指棕綠相間的，修飾 grass

blind! *This means* that ③ lions see everything as black, white, or gray. Even

though the Zebra's stripes are black and white *they are* good camouflage.

More recently, *it has been proven* that stripes are an effective means

of confusing the blood-sucking tsetse fly as well. The *tsetse fly is* another resident of the African plains. *They fly* around and *use* their big eyes to find

a tasty meal. <u>Because horses, cows, and other animals with warm blood have</u>

<u>a shape that is easy to see</u>, the *tsetse fly has* no problem spotting them.

However, in the case of the zebra the *stripes disguise* the zebra's shape. *This*

means <u>that they are much less likely to be seen by the tsetse fly.</u>

Finally, ⑤D *stripes are also believed* to play a role in attracting female

zebras. *Wounds* **caused** by fighting *change* the pattern of the stripes,
分詞片語修飾 wounds，表示由…所造成的

so *potential partners* can *see* <u>which male zebras are the best fighters.</u>
which 引導名詞子句，當 see 受詞

Apparently, ④D *female zebras are attracted* to male zebras with lots of scars!

② **Useful** for both camouflage and finding a mate, a *zebra's stripes are*

more than just a handsome accessory. They *are* an important aid to life on

the African plains.

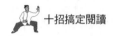

單字與片語

重要單字 Key Vocabularies

① stripe （n）條紋

② handsome （adj）漂亮的

③ zoologist （n）動物學家

④ possibility （n）可能性

⑤ camouflage （n）偽裝

⑥ predator （n）掠食者

⑦ color-blind 色盲

⑧ effective （adj）有效的

⑨ confuse （v）使混亂

⑩ resident （n）住民，居民

⑪ tasty （adj）美味的

⑫ spot （v）發現，標定

⑬ disguise （v）掩飾

⑭ female （adj）雌性的；male 雄性的

⑮ scar （n）傷疤

⑯ accessory （n）配件，零件

重要片語 Key Phrases

❶ come up with 想出來

❷ as well 也，同樣地

❸ be attracted to 被…所吸引

本文解析

　　本文提到斑馬為什麼會有黑白相間的條紋，連動物學家也只能用幾種可能性來推斷，其一是認為條紋能讓斑馬在非洲草原中，面對他們主要掠食者－色盲的獅子時，能有隱蔽的效果。其二是對非洲的舌蠅而言，斑紋讓斑馬的外型模糊化，不容易被找到。最後則認為公斑馬條紋與母斑馬擇偶有密切關係。所以本文主要是探討斑馬條紋的可能功用。

　　第一題問到何者為斑馬的主要獵食者，文中有清楚說明就是獅子。第二題問為何斑馬條紋對生活在非洲草原上是一大助益，由文章最後一句 Useful for both camouflage... They are an important aid to life... 可以看出是原因是因為偽裝的功用。第三題是問獅子色盲是何意思，文中提到 ... lions see everything as black, white, or gray，也就是說獅子看到的只有黑、白及灰的影像。第四及第五題都是考細節題，同樣地由每個選項中的關鍵字來找文中相對應的文句，即可得出答案。

學習重點 ➡

分詞構句

　　本文中最後一段：Useful for both camouflage and finding a mate, a zebra's stripes are more than just a handsome accessory. 該句就是一個分詞構句形式。分詞構句由副詞子句所引導表附帶狀況的子句轉換而來，用以表示時間、原因、條件、讓步、附帶狀況。

一般分詞構句：

　　兩邊主詞相同時，將副詞子句的從屬連接詞及子句的主詞去掉，再將子句內的動詞依主動改為 Ving，被動改為 Vp.p。

例句：

　　While I walked along the street, I met my ex-girlfriend.

　　（當我沿著街上走時，我遇見我前任女友。）

→ Walking along the street, I met my ex-girlfriend.

　　Animals can do lots of amazing things when they are properly trained.

　　（當施以適當的訓練，動物可以做很多令人驚異的事。）

→ Animals can do lots of amazing things when properly trained.

　　Not knowing what to do, she began to cry.

　　（由於不知道怎麼辦，他開始哭了起來。）

　　而本文中的句子中前面省略了（Because zebra's stripes are）等字，故便成為：Useful for both camouflage and finding a mate, a zebra's stripes are...（由於同時具有偽裝及求偶的作用，所以斑馬的條紋不只…），讀者需能看出來，才能真正理解句意。

5
自
然
&
環
保

173

 英文本文

Article 5.4

Snakes have a bad reputation. Most people do not like to look at them, much less touch them! However, many of the stereotypes that people have about snakes are incorrect. Snakes are not really the slimy, scary creatures that most people imagine. The truth about snakes would probably surprise most people.

Although many people imagine that a snake's skin is slimy and soft, it is really dry and hard like fingernails. In fact, a snake's skin is made of the same stuff that fingernails, hairs, and feathers are made of. None of these things are slimy. Most people also imagine that a snake's skin is cold, but snakes really can be cold or warm. If a snake is found in water, it will probably feel cold. On the other hand, if a snake is found on a warm rock in the sun, it will feel warm. The body temperature of a snake depends on where and when it is found.

Another incorrect idea that many people have about snakes is that all snakes act fast. It is true that snakes are fast when they strike. However, when snakes are moving normally, such as when they are trying to get away undetected, very few of them can go faster than 10 kilometers per hour (km/hr). That is about twice the normal walking speed of a person. Of course, that might seem fast to a person **frozen in fear** at seeing a snake. Keep in mind, though, that snakes do not normally attack humans. They are usually moving away to hide when people see them.

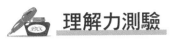 理解力測驗

Q1. What is the main idea of this reading?

(A) Not all snakes are the same.

(B) People have some wrong ideas about snakes.

(C) Snakes are dangerous animals.

(D) Some people like to keep snakes as pets.

Q2. Which of the following is NOT similar to a snake's skin?

(A) A feather

(B) A fingernail

(C) Fish scales

(D) Frog skin

Q3. According to the reading, what can be said about the body temperature of snakes?

(A) It is always cold.

(B) It is never actually cold.

(C) It is cold when snakes swim.

(D) It is warm when snakes are moving.

Q4. What does the phrase "frozen in fear" in the reading refer to?

(A) Afraid to spend time in places that are cold.

(B) Not able to move because one is scared.

(C) Feeling suddenly very cold from fear.

(D) Not being able to think about one's fears.

Q5. According to the reading, how fast is the normal walking speed of a person?

(A) 5 km/hr

(B) 10 km/hr

(C) 20 km/hr

(D) No mention

 本文中譯

認識蛇

　　蛇的聲名狼藉，大部分的人不想觀察牠們，更不用說摸牠們。然而，人們許多有關於蛇的觀念是不正確的，蛇並不真的像人們所想的是黏呼呼而令人害怕的動物，有關於蛇的真實性可能會讓大多數人感到驚訝。

　　雖然許多人對蛇的印象是濕滑且柔軟的，但蛇其實是乾燥且像指甲一樣堅硬。事實上，蛇的皮膚的組成要素與組成指甲、毛髮及與毛的要素是相同的，而這些沒有一項是黏黏的。許多人印象中蛇是冰冷的，但真實的蛇其實可以是冰冷或溫熱的。假如蛇是在水中被發現，那牠可能會是冰冷的，反過來說，假如蛇是在太陽下的岩石中被發現，則會感覺牠是熱的。蛇的溫度取決於牠是在何時何地被發現的。

　　另一個許多人對蛇的不正確觀念就是認為蛇的動作很快。當牠們在作攻擊時，蛇的動作確實是很快，然而，當蛇在一般正常活動時，像是當牠們正要毫無聲息地離開時，很少會有蛇類的行動會超過時速 10 公里，而那是人們一般正常行走速度的二倍快。當然，對一個看到蛇就因害怕而呆住的人來說那似乎是算快的了。可是記住，蛇一般不會攻擊人類，當人們看到牠時，蛇通常會離開而躲藏起來。

理解力測驗中譯

1. 本篇主旨大意為何?

　(A) 不是所有的蛇都是一樣的

　(B) 人們對蛇有些錯誤的觀念

　(C) 蛇類都是危險的動物

　(D) 有些人喜歡把蛇當寵物

2. 下列何者與蛇皮膚不相類似?

　(A) 羽毛

　(B) 指甲

　(C) 魚鱗

　(D) 青蛙皮膚

3. 根據本文,有關蛇類的體溫說法為何?

　(A) 蛇的體溫總是冷的

　(B) 蛇的體溫總是不會冷的

　(C) 當蛇在游泳時,牠的體溫是冷的

　(D) 當蛇在活動時,牠的體溫是熱的

4. "frozen in fear"這個片語在文章中指的是?

　(A) 害怕耗在冰涼的地方

　(B) 人因為驚嚇而無法行動

　(C) 因為恐懼而突然感到寒冷

　(D) 無法想像一個人的恐懼

5. 依據本文,正常人步行的速度為多快?

　(A) 5 km/hr

　(B) 10km/hr

　(C) 20 km/hr

　(D) 沒有提到

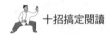

 本文圖解

Snakes have a bad reputation. *Most people* do not like to look at them, much less touch them! However, *many of the ideas* that people have about snakes are incorrect. *Snakes* are not really the slimy, scary creatures that most people imagine. *The truth* about snakes would probably surprise most people.

Although many people imagine that a snake's skin is slimy and soft, *it* is

that 引導名詞子句當 imagine 受詞

really dry and hard like fingernails. In fact, a *snake's skin* is made of the same stuff that fingernails, hair, and feathers are made of. *None of these things* are slimy. *Most people* also imagine that a snake's skin is cold, but *snakes* really can be cold or warm. If a snake is found in water, *it* will probably feel cold. On the other hand, if a snake is found on a warm rock in the sun, *it* will feel warm. The *body temperature* of a snake depends on where and when it is

where 及 when 二個名詞子
句當 depend on 的受詞

found.

Another incorrect idea that many people have about snakes is that all

snakes are fast. *It* is true that snakes are fast when they strike. However,

when snakes are moving normally, such as when they are trying to get away

undetected, *very few of them* can go faster than 10 kilometers per hour (km/

hr). *That* is about twice the normal walking speed of a person. Of course, *that*

  that 在此為代名詞，指的
  是前面提過的 10km/hr

might seem fast to a person **frozen in fear** at seeing a snake. Keep in mind,

     frozen in fear 為過去分詞   祈使句，省略
     片語，修飾前面 person   主詞 (you)

though, **that** snakes do not normally attack humans. *They* are usually moving

  that 引導名詞子句當 keep 受詞

away to hide when people see them.

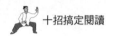

 單字與片語

重要單字 Key Vocabularies

① reputation （n）名聲

② slimy （adj）黏黏的

③ scary （adj）驚嚇的

④ creature （n）生物

⑤ fingernail （n）指甲

⑥ stuff （n）原料，要素

⑦ normally （adv）正常地

⑧ attack （v）攻擊

重要片語 Key Phrases

❶ look at 觀察

❷ much less 更不用說

❸ Keep in mind 勞記在心

❹ be made of 由…組成

❺ depends on 依賴於

本文解析

　　本文先提到人們許多有關於蛇的觀念是不正確的，接下來舉例說明人們對蛇的錯誤印象，像是蛇是黏呼呼的、蛇都是冰冷的、以及蛇跑得很快等等，而這都是不正確的觀念，最後提到蛇一般不會攻擊人類，牠們看到人會安靜地離開。所以本文大意是講人們對蛇有些錯誤的觀念。

　　第二題問何者與蛇類皮膚不相似，由文中得知蛇的皮膚的組成要素與組成指甲、毛髮及與羽毛的要素是相同的，選項中不屬於這三類的就只有青蛙的皮膚。第三題問到有關蛇體溫的敘述，由文中提到假如蛇是在水中被發現，那牠可能會是冰冷的，所以推斷蛇在游泳時體溫是冰冷的。第四題問 "frozen in fear" 這個片語的意思，該片語是指 "因驚嚇過度而動不了"。最後一題問正常情況下人行走速度，在文中有提到 That is about twice the normal walking speed of a person，（那是人們一般正常行走速度的二倍快），這句的 that 指的是前面提到的 10km/hr，所以正常情況下人行走速度應該是 10km/hr 的一半，也就是 5km/hr。

學習重點 ➡

　　本文中出現大量的關係詞代名詞及連接詞引導的子句，作為修飾名詞，或當名詞子句做為動詞受詞，或引導副詞子句修飾全句等情況，如對句子結構有清楚概念，應該不難理解本篇文章，其相關用法在此不再贅述。但提醒讀者一種介係詞＋關係代名詞用法，如本文中 In fact, a snake's skin is made of the same stuff that fingernails, hair, and feathers are made of。這句中 that 引導形容詞子句修飾 stuff，但該句可改寫成：In fact, a snake's skin is made of the same stuff of which fingernails, hair, and feathers are made。也就是將子句中的介係詞提置於子句前面，而原來的關係詞 that 則要改成 which（可當受格使用），而變成 of which，這種用法在正式文章很常見，且在文法考試中亦常考，讀者應熟悉其用法。

5
自然 & 環保

第六招 解題策略

為了免於時間不夠用，以下提供了三項解題策略。

1.從簡單的題目作答

疑問句型題目掌握問句關鍵字，例如數字和費用。再來是含較短選項的問題，這類問題通常題目內容長一點，但基本上也可以從文章中直接找出，只是注意問題中的關鍵字，但通常題目中的關鍵字是語文章中的用語相同的，例如：What is his company working on? (planning a series of promotions nationwide)，該問句關鍵字為 company working on，這時在文章的某處應該會有這些字，而答案就在這些地方。

2. 含NOT的題目留待最後作答

含 NOT 的題目一般來說，需要不斷比對題目與文章來作消去法，才能確認答案。因此，建議將此類題目留待該篇其他有把握的題目做完後再做 (就算沒時間，用猜的也沒損失)。另外，有些題目如：According to the passage, which of the following statements is true? 也是一樣，常常需要用消去法來解，也建議留待其它題目完成後再處理。以命題老師的立場，他們不會輕易把正確答案放在第一個選項中，讓受考者一試就中，所以第一個選項非為正確答案的機率頗高。

3. 善用關鍵字來解題

關鍵字一般指的是影響句意的動詞或名詞，但這邊的關鍵字就是指連接題目與文章的一組字詞。簡單的說，就是題目中及文章中所共有的部分。甚至是一模一樣的一組字詞，碰到這種情形，答案就很明顯了，不論詞組相同與否，掌握關鍵詞原意就能快速解題。

以下用一篇實際考題，來實際演練一下吧！

The Saisiyat people—one of Taiwan's officially recognized aboriginal groups—have a unique ritual ceremony called Pas-ta'al. That ceremony is said to have been carried out for as many as 400 years. Today, it takes place every two years.

And every ten years, it is larger and takes on added significance. The most recent ten-year ceremony was held in 2006 at two complementary and overlapping sites in northern Taiwan during the full moon of the 10th lunar month.

6

Thousands gathered for the first day of the ceremony in Wufeng, Hsinchu County. Tourists from all over the island joined the local villagers in the elaborate ceremony in an open field. Men and women were dancing and singing, arms crossed, hand-in-hand, and moving in and out of a huge circle. Native Saisiyat people all wore bright red and white traditional costumes with intricate weaving and beading. Some had ornate decorations at the back, from which hung mirrors, beads, and bells that rang and clanged as the dancers moved. Tourists were welcome but were asked to stay away from particular areas where secret rituals were performed by village elders. They were also advised to tie Japanese silver grass around their arms, cameras, and recorders.

1. What is Pas-ta'al?
   (A) It is an annual ritual ceremony of the Saisiyat people.
   (B) It is a Saisiyat wedding ceremony in which people sing and dance.
   (C) It is a Saisiyat ceremony in which Japanese silver grass is used as sacrifice.
   (D) It is a Saisiyat ceremony that has a history as long as four hundred years.
2. When or where is Pas-ta'al normally held?
   (A) It is held in October every two years.
   (B) It takes place in two major sites in northern Taiwan.
   (C) It is held only when the Japanese silver grass is fully grown.
   (D) It takes place only at Wufeng, Hsinchu County.
3. Which of the following statements is NOT true about the ceremony?
   (A) Tourists and villagers dance in a big circle in an open field.
   (B) Local villagers wear traditional red and white costumes.
   (C) Tourists are welcome, and they can join the elders in secret rituals.
   (D) Tourists are advised to tie Japanese silver grass around their arms and cameras.

　　第一題很簡單，就是 Wh 開頭的題目，用關鍵字 Pas-ta'al 搜尋，由首段一、二句可知 Pas-ta'al 是一個宗教慶典名稱，且該儀式有四百年了，答案為 (D)。第二題也是 Wh 開頭的題目，問 when 及 where 的問題，由第二段第二句可知所以答案為 (B)，注意：不能選 (A)，因為文中只說舉行時間為農曆十月的滿月的日子，不一定是十月份。第三題為 NOT 的題目，需用消去法一個一個找出來，各選項的關鍵字分別為 (A)... an open field (B)... red and white costumes (C)... secret rituals (D)Japanese silver grass。讀者可以自行練習依選項的關鍵字搜索筆對文中內容來消去選項，並注意該題為 NOT 題，是找出不對的選項，本題答案為 (C)。

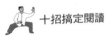

 英文本文

Article 6.1

It would be hard to imagine Britain without its daily **routine** of afternoon tea. Afternoon tea has been a British tradition for almost two centuries.

This tradition originated with Anna Maria Russell, the seventh Duchess of Bedford. A long time ago, the English had only two main meals a day. By the middle of 18th century, dinner had shifted from noontime to eight or nine at night. It was in 1840 that Anna introduced the practice of afternoon tea. It is said that Anna used to feel a little hungry and grumpy around 4 p.m. She found it difficult to wait for the late dinner. The Duchess then started having a pot of tea, some bread and butter, and cakes brought to her room every afternoon. Later, She began to invite her high society lady friend to join her for some tea and a light afternoon meal. Soon her habit of having afternoon tea gained widespread influence. It spread among the British upper classes and then to the common people. Thus, the tradition of afternoon tea came into being Afternoon tea, also called low tea, and is served on low coffee tables in a drawing room.

Low tea is the same as high tea. The custom of high tea began with the British common people in the 19th century. In the early evening, workers came back home hungry and exhausted after a day of hard work. The evening meal was served on a high dining table with tea, meat, cheese, and bread and butter. Because dining tables were higher than drawing room table, the term "high tea" was used.

This pleasant old tradition of afternoon tea remains an important part of British life to this day. Whenever you visit British, remember to put "afternoon tea" on your list of things to do.

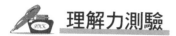 理解力測驗

Q1. The topic of this article is about

(A) Anna Maria Russell
(B) A brand of well-known British tea
(C) The origin of the British tradition of afternoon tea
(D) The difference between high tea and low tea

Q2. Which of the following statements is true from this article?

(A) In the 19th century, low tea was known as the working man's suppers.
(B) Low tea and afternoon tea stemmed from different origins.
(C) The tradition of high tea dates back to the middle of 18th century.
(D) The names of high tea and low tea probably stemmed from the height of the tables where they were served.

Q3. The author gives the reader a good understanding of afternoon tea by

(A) Recalling personal experiences
(B) Offering personal opinions
(C) Telling about its origin
(D) Using comparisons

Q4. According to this article, what is true about afternoon tea?

(A) It is the evening meal, including tea, meat, and bread.
(B) It was first enjoyed by British ladies form the upper social classes.
(C) It is usually served on a dining table.
(D) It was first enjoyed by the British working class

Q5. The word "**routine**" in the first paragraph means

(A) practice
(B) frequency
(C) route
(D) dullness

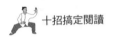

 **本文中譯**

下午茶的傳統

　　很難想像英國如果少了每日必喝的下午茶會是怎樣的情形。英國人喝下午茶的傳統已經延續了二個世紀之久。這項傳統是由貝福德的第七位公爵夫人安娜·瑪麗亞·羅賽爾所創立。古時候英國人每天只吃兩餐，到十八世紀中葉，主餐從中午時段移至晚上八、九點鐘。1840 年，安娜夫人開啟了喝下午茶的習慣。據說安娜夫人到了下午四點多就會感到有點飢餓和煩躁，她實在沒辦法等到那麼晚才吃晚餐。於是，這位公爵夫人每天下午都請人送上一壺茶、一些奶油麵包及蛋糕到她房間裏，後來她開始邀請一些上流社會的女性朋友與她共用下午茶與小點心。她的這項習慣隨即影響全英國，先是流行於上層社會，爾後也普及到一般民眾身上。喝下午茶的這項傳統就此形成。下午茶又叫做"low tea"，茶和點心通常放在起居室的小茶几上。

　　low tea 就如同 high tea，起源於十九世紀英國的普羅大眾。工人們在傍晚時分回到家中，辛勤工作一天後又餓又累，晚餐就在高度較高的餐桌上享用，餐桌上擺著茶、肉、起司、奶油麵包等。因為餐桌比起居室的茶几來的高，因此產生了 high tea 這樣的名稱。

　　直到今天，下午茶這個令人感到愉快的古老傳統仍是英國人生活重要的一部分。日後造訪英國時，記得把下午茶列為一項非做不可的行程。

理解力測驗中譯

1. 本文的主旨為何？

    (A) 安娜‧瑪麗亞‧羅賽爾

    (B) 一種知名的英國茶

    (C) 英國下午茶傳統的起源

    (D) 高茶和低茶的區別

2. 由本文中何項的敘述是正確的？

    (A) 在 19 世紀，低茶被認為是工人們的晚餐

    (B) 低茶與下午茶的源起不同

    (C) 高茶的傳統可追溯到 18 世紀中期

    (D) 高茶與低茶的名稱可能源自於桌子的高度

3. 作者用甚麼來讓讀者對下午茶有更深刻的認識？

    (A) 回想起個人的經驗

    (B) 提供個人的意見

    (C) 告訴有關它的起源

    (D) 使用比較法

4. 依據本文，有關下午茶何者為真？

    (A) 就是晚餐，包括茶、肉類及麵包

    (B) 最初是由英國上層社會名流貴婦享用的

    (C) 通常在餐桌上享用

    (D) 最初是由英國工人階級享用的

5. 在第一段的 "routine" 這個字表示何種意思？

    (A) 習慣

    (B) 頻率

    (C) 路程

    (D) 遲鈍

 **本文圖解**

It *would be* hard to imagine Britain without its daily routine of afternoon

It 指的就是後面的不定詞片語
to imagine...

tea. Afternoon tea *has been* a British tradition for almost two centuries.

This tradition *originated* with Anna Maria Russell, the seventh Duchess of

Bedford. A long time ago, the English *had* only two main meals a day. **By** the

到…時間
的時候

middle of 18th century, dinner *had shifted* from noontime to eight or nine

at night. It *was* in 1840 that Anna introduced the practice of afternoon tea. It

is said that Anna used to feel a little hungry and grumpy around 4 p.m. She

found it difficult to wait for the late dinner. The Duchess then *started* having

a pot of tea and some **bread and butter** and cakes **brought** to her room

意思是指麵包夾奶油，
視為一體

過去分詞，表示被帶到…

every afternoon. Later, She *began* to invite her high society lady friend to

join her for some tea and a light afternoon meal. Soon her habit of having

afternoon tea *gained* widespread influence.

It *spread* among the British upper classes and then to the common
It 指喝下午茶這件事

people. Thus the tradition of afternoon tea *came* into being Afternoon tea,
本句有三個動詞：came, called 及 is served
also *called* low tea, **and** *is served* on low coffee tables in a drawing room.

㉘ Low tea *is* the same as high tea. ㉒ⓒ The custom of high tea *began* with

the British common people in the 19th century. In the early evening, workers

came back home hungry and exhausted after a day of hard work. ㉒Ⓐ The

evening meal *was served* on a high dining table with tea, meat, cheese, and

bread and butter. ② Because dining tables were higher than drawing room

table, the term "high tea" *was used*.

This pleasant old tradition of afternoon tea *remains* an important

part of British life to this day. Whenever you visit British, *remember* to put

"afternoon tea" on your list of things to do.

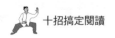

 **單字與片語**

重要單字 Key Vocabularies

① imagine （v）想像

② routine （adj）例行的；日常的

③ Duchess （n）公爵夫人

④ shift （v）改變；移動

⑤ introduce （v）引導；介紹

⑥ practice （n）習慣

⑦ grumpy （adj）脾氣粗暴的

⑧ gain （v）得到

⑨ widespread （adj）普遍的

⑩ influence （n）影響

⑪ drawing room 起居室，客廳

⑫ exhausted （adj）疲憊的

⑬ pleasant （adj）愉悅的

重要片語 Key Phrases

❶ originate with 源自於…

❷ used to 過去經常

❸ came into 誕生

❹ to this day 直到今日

 **本文解析**

　　本文開始就指出英國人喝下午茶的傳統是由一位英國公爵夫人安娜所開創的，原因是因為十八世紀時英國人的晚餐時間需到晚上八、九點，這位公爵夫人在下午時間就感到飢餓難耐，於是叫人送上茶及小點心到她房間內享用，從此這項習慣從上流社會一直流行到

一般民眾。而下午茶又稱為 low tea，而 high tea 同樣源起於十九世紀的，是指一般工人階級下班回家吃晚餐是在比較高的餐桌上吃而得名。所以本篇主要是講述英國人喝下午茶的源起。

第二題問文章中相關敘述何者正確，由各選項所提部分於文章中均可找出相對應的內容，讀者自行比較即可得出答案。第三題問作者用什麼方式讓讀者對下午茶有更深刻的認識，由本篇文章均著重在介紹下午茶的起源，故是用下午茶的起源讓讀者有深刻認識。第四題問有關下午茶敘述何者為真，由文中知下午茶並非晚餐，它是在起居室的小茶几上享用的，且最初是由英國上層社會的人先流行起來的。第五題問"routine"的意思，這個字有例行公事、習慣等含意，讚文中是指習慣之意，即與 practice 相同。

學習重點 ➡

使役動詞（have, make let)，後面接受詞＋原形動詞，其意思為讓…去做某事。

例如：

Let them train the new guide dogs.(讓他們訓練這隻導盲犬。)

但如受詞為物且後面接動詞過去分詞，則表示讓…去被做某事

例如：

Mary had her car repaired yesterday.(瑪莉昨天將車子送去修理。)

句中 had 為使役動詞，受詞 her car 為受詞，補語應用過去分詞表示被修理，不可用原形動詞。

在本文中：

The Duchess then started having a pot of tea and some bread and butter and cakes brought to her room every afternoon. 本句中動詞為 started，having 為其受詞，在此雖然是用動名詞型式，但仍保有動詞的特性，故其後面遇到需要表示"送到"的動詞則需用過去分詞 (bought)，表示是被動的意思。

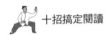
 英文本文

Article 6.2

The word "aerobic" means "with oxygen." Aerobics is a form of physical exercise that conditions your heart and lung by increasing the efficiency of oxygen absorption by the body. Aerobics activities are performed at a **moderate** level of intensity over a relatively long period of time. For instance, a long-distance run at a moderate pace is a form of aerobics exercise, but a sprint or a similar short burst of activity is not.

Typical aerobics activities, include swimming, jogging, long distance running, cycling, and fast walking. Tai Chi and Yoga are also aerobics activities. Distance aerobics combines the rhythmic steps of aerobics with beautiful distance movements. Step aerobics is a popular kind of aerobics that can be practiced in a class or at home. During the hot summers, doing aerobic activities in an indoor swimming pool is an excellent way to exercise. Depending on your age and level of fitness, you may choose regular low-impact forms of aerobics, such as Tai Chi or high impact ones, such as jumping rope. You may enjoy individual activities, such as swimming or prefer group activities such as aerobics class. Exercise regularly and make safety your highest priority. Aerobic activities can cause injuries and sprains. Before you start doing aerobics, get a checkup to make sure you don't have any health problems.

There are many benefits of doing aerobics, as following:

*Help your heart become stronger and more efficiency.

*Burn up fat and help you maintain suitable weight.

*Improves your digestion, sleep patterns, immunes, and high blood pressure.

*Decrease your risk of developing diabetes, heart disease, and high blood pressure.

*Reduces "bad" cholesterol and increase "good" cholesterol.

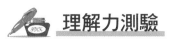 理解力測驗

Q1. What is the main point of this article?

(A) While exercise, you need to make safety your highest priority, because aerobic activities can cause injuries and sprains.

(B) There are many types of aerobics, and doing aerobics regularly can bring you many health benefits.

(C) Aerobics helps you condition your lungs by consuming oxygen more efficiency.

(D) Visit your doctor for a checkup before you choose an aerobic exercise.

Q2. What is referred from this article?

(A) All types of aerobics are safe for everyone.

(B) A high-impact form of aerobics is a perfect choice for people who have problems with their knees, back, or hands.

(C) A race at full speed for a short distance is a typical type of aerobics.

(D) Most of the older should choose low-impact aerobic activities.

Q3. In the first paragraph, the meaning of aerobics is explained through its definition and

(A) contrasting examples.

(B) a question and answer.

(C) a list of author's opinions.

(D) a list of metaphors.

Q4. Which of the following statements is NOT true?

(A) Aerobic exercise can help your heart become stronger and more efficiency.

(B) Aerobics includes both low-impact and high-impact activities.

(C) Aerobics is a type of moderate intensity physical exercise that lasts over a certain period of time and uses oxygen in the process.

(D) Aerobic exercises are high intensity activities which last for less than one minute

Q5. The word "**moderate**" in the first paragraph means

(A) tolerant

(B) extreme

(C) modern

(D) modest

 **本文中譯**

有氧運動

　　"aerobic"這個字的意思為有氧的，有氧運動是一種經由增加氧氣被人體吸收，使心肺處於良好狀態的運動。有氧運動的時間持續較久，且運動強度中等。例如用中等速度的步調所進行的長跑是有氧運動的一種，但是衝刺等類的瞬間爆發性活動則不屬於有氧運動。

　　典型的有氧運動有游泳、慢跑、長跑、騎腳踏車和快走等。太極拳和瑜珈同樣也屬於有氧運動，有氧舞蹈結合了有氧運動有節奏的步伐及美妙的舞蹈動作。階梯有氧是一種熱門的有氧運動，參加訓練或在家做都可以。炎炎夏日中，在室內游泳池中做有氧運動式一種絕佳的運動方式。可視你的年紀或健康程度而定，你可以選擇一般的低衝擊有氧運動，例如太極，或者你也可以選擇高衝擊的有氧運動，例如跳繩。或許你喜歡像游泳這類單獨活動，偏好團體活動的人，則可以參加有氧課程，要定期活動，並將安全放在第一位，有些有氧運動可能造成傷害或扭傷。在要做有氧運動前，先去做身體檢查確認你沒有任何身體問題。做有氧運動有許多好處，例如以下：

* 強建心臟，增進功能

* 消耗脂肪，維持適當體重

* 促進消化，改善睡眠，增強免疫系統、增加關節及肌肉的柔韌性。

* 降低患糖尿病、心臟病和高血壓的風險。

* 減少不好的膽固醇，增加好的膽固醇。

理解力測驗中譯

1. 本文重點為何？

    (A) 運動時，你必須把安全性放在第一位，因位有氧運動可能造成傷害及扭傷。

    (B) 有氧運動有許多種，而做有氧運動可有助於你的健康。

    (C) 有氧運動使養氣消耗更有效率而讓你心肺處於良好狀態。

    (D) 在你選擇一項有氧運動前，先諮詢一下你的醫生。

2. 從本文中有提到甚麼？

    (A) 所有形式的有氧運動對每個人都是安全的。

    (B) 高衝擊性的有氧運動對有膝蓋、背部及手部問題的人來說是一項很好的選擇

    (C) 一種於短距離內全速的跑步運動是一種有氧運動。

    (D) 大部分年長者應該選擇低衝擊性的有氧運動

3. 在第一段文章中，用以解釋有氧運動是以其定義以及

    (A) 對照舉例

    (B) 問答方式

    (C) 作者的一系列看法

    (D) 一系列的比喻

4. 下列敘述何者為非？

    (A) 有氧運動可幫助你的心肺更加強健並有效率。

    (B) 有氧運動包含高衝擊和低衝及活動。

    (C) 有氧運動是一種中等強度的身體運動，而它需持續一段時間並在過程中消耗氧氣。

    (D) 有氧運動是一種持續時間小於一分鐘的高強度的活動。

5. 在第一段"moderate"這個字意思是？

    (A) 忍受的

    (B) 極度的

    (C) 現代的

    (D) 適當的

 **本文圖解**

The word "aerobic" *means* "with oxygen." Aerobics *is* a form of physical

exercise that conditions your heart and lung by increasing the efficiency of

oxygen absorption **by** the body. ④ⓒ Aerobics activities *are performed* at a

by 在此表示經由⋯之意

moderate level of intensity over a relatively long period of time. For instance,

a long-distance run at a moderate pace *is* a form of aerobics exercise, but a

sprint or a similar short burst of activity *is*n't.

Typical aerobics activities *include* swimming, jogging, long distance

running, cycling, and fast walking. Tai Chi and Yoga *are* also aerobics

activities. Distance aerobics *combines* the rhythmic steps of aerobics with

beautiful distance movements. Step aerobics *is* a popular kind of aerobics

that can be practiced in a class or at home. During the hot summers, doing

aerobic activities in an indoor swimming pool *is* an excellent way to exercise.

Depending on your age and level of fitness, ④ⓑ you *may choose* regular

分詞構句，省略主詞 you 及連接詞 as

low-impact forms of aerobics such as Tai Chi or high impact ones such as jumping rope. You *may enjoy* individual activities such as swimming or *prefer* group activities such as aerobics class. *Exercise* regularly and *make* safety your highest priority. Aerobic activities *can cause* injuries and sprains. <u>Before you start doing aerobics</u>, *get* a **checkup** to make sure you don't have any

checkup 在此為身體檢查的意思

health problems.

There *are* many benefits of doing aerobics, as following:

* ④A *Help* your heart become stronger and more efficiency.

Burn up fat and helps you maintain suitable weight.

Improve your digestion, sleep patterns, immunes, and high blood pressure.

Decrease your risk of developing diabetes, heart disease, and high blood pressure.

Reduce "bad" cholesterol and increase "good" cholesterol

 單字與片語

重要單字 Key Vocabularies

① aerobic （adj）有氧的

② condition （v）使處於良好狀態

③ absorption （n）吸收

④ moderate （adj）和緩的

⑤ intensity （n）強度

⑥ sprint （n）全速快跑

⑦ burst （n）爆發

⑧ rhythmic （adj）有節奏的

⑨ fitness （n）健康

⑩ priority （n）優先（權）

⑪ immune （n）免疫

⑫ cholesterol （n）膽固醇

重要片語 Key Phrases

❶ make sure　確認

本文解析

　　本文先解釋有氧及有氧運動的意思，也就是長時間用中等強度的運動方式，接下來列舉一些有氧運動的項目，及做這些有氧運動的方法。而有氧運動也分為低衝擊性及高衝擊性，參加運動的人應該視自己的年紀及健康狀況來選擇適合的運動，且有氧運動也有受傷的可能，需要先做健康檢查確認後才能去做，而結尾作者列了一些做有氧運動的好處。本篇文章主要在述說有氧運動內容及種類，以及而做有氧運動對健康的好處，所以第一題答案為 (B)。

第二題問到有關有氧運動相關內容，本題不易直接由文中找到出處，但可以用文中有關有氧運動的相關敘述綜合出來：有氧運動還是可能會受傷 (Aerobic activities can cause injuries and...)，而高衝擊性的有氧運動對身體衝擊大，應不適合有膝蓋及背部有問題的人，且有氧運動需要長時間運動，所以短距離的全速跑步不是有氧運動，而年長者應該選擇低衝擊性的有氧運動應該是合理的敘述。第三題問本篇的寫作方式，作者主要用有氧運動的定義以及相關運動舉例說明來讓讀者了解何謂有氧運動。第四題問敘述何者為非，本題選項中的敘述均能於文中找到相關出處，請參考本文圖解部分。第五題問 "moderate" 的意思，該字有穩建的、溫和的之意，在文中意思應為普通中等的 (a moderate level) 之意，所以與選項中 modest(適度的) 最接近。

學習重點 ➡

在本文中：

Depending on your age and level of fitness, you may choose regular low-impact forms of aerobics such as Tai Chi or high impact ones such as jumping rope.

這是分詞構句的使用，分詞構句由副詞子句引導表附帶狀況的子句轉換而來，用以表示時間、原因、條件、讓步、附帶狀況。兩邊主詞相同時，將副詞子句的從屬連接詞及子句的主詞去掉，再將子句內的動詞依主動改為 Ving，被動改為 Vp.p.。

例句：

While I walked along the street, I met my ex-girlfriend.

（當我沿著街上走時，我遇見我前任女友。）

→ Walking along the street, I met my ex-girlfriend.

Not knowing what to do, she began to cry.

（由於不知道怎麼辦，她開始哭了起來。）

本文中的句子可還原為：

As you can depend on your age and level of fitness, you may choose...

英文本文

Article 6.3

Running a marathon is the ultimate goal for a hobby athlete. But there can be dangers involved in running a 26.2 mile or 41.2 km race. Most health problems that happen during a marathon race are not very severe - mainly strains and sprains.

In some cases, however, heart problems have led to deaths during or immediately after a marathon. In the United States researchers found out that of 11 million runners who have taken part in marathons or half marathons in the last decade 42 died. Most of them had heart problems or heart-related diseases.

Many health experts advise beginners to see doctors before they **take up** training for a race. People with heart problems or diabetes should also consult doctors before running long distances at all.

Many hobby athletes do not prepare themselves in the right way for a race. Getting yourself in good physical shape over a period of months is not always easy and requires a lot of self-discipline. Training must start slowly, with short distances, so that your body can get used to the physical stress. Runners often make the mistake of running too fast at the beginning. Rest periods should follow days of training. Running advisors say that about a month before a marathon you should be able to run 15 miles, or almost three quarters of the marathon distance, at a comfortable speed. Having enough reserves at the end is also a sign that you are in a good shape.

Training too much; however, can lead to stiffness in your muscles or other injuries. In such a case, you should lower your training rate and take a few days off.

Shortly before a marathon starts warming up and stretching can be important for your overall performance. One of the biggest problems that marathon runners face during a race is dehydration, not getting enough to drink. If it's very hot your body can lose up to four liters of fluid through sweating and breathing out air. One of the most important tasks for a runner is to drink enough throughout a race.

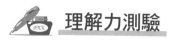 理解力測驗

6
體
育
&
休
閒

Q1. What is the best title of this article?

(A) Running the Marathon - Health Risks
(B) Running a Marathon - Ultimate Goal for Athlete
(C) Heart Problems- a Hobby Athlete May Happening
(D) Heart-related Diseases- Killer of Marathon Runner

Q2. Which of the following is the closest meaning of the term "**take up**" in line 1, paragraph 3?

(A) undergo
(B) execute
(C) exercise
(D) start

Q3. If you have heart problems and want to attend a Marathon race, what should you do first?

(A) to see health experts
(B) to consult doctors
(C) to find running advisors
(D) to have a physical checkup

Q4. According to the article, why should the Marathon training start slowly?

(A) Because you'll be in good physical shape over a period of months.
(B) Because you can begin from short distance.
(C) Because your body can be accustomed to the physical stress gradually.
(D) Because you will have enough reserves at the end of a running.

Q5. Which of the followings is correct about Marathon race?

(A) A marathon race may cause very severe health problems.
(B) Three quarters of the marathon distance is about 15 kilometers
(C) Dehydration is one problem that marathon runners may face during running training.
(D) When the weather is very hot, your body can lose as many as four liters of fluid during a Marathon race.

 本文中譯

馬拉松運動

　　跑馬拉松對一個業餘運動員來可說是一個終極目標，但是一場 26.2 英哩或是 41.2 公里的跑步也是潛藏危險。大部分在跑馬拉松比賽中會發生的問題都沒有非常嚴重一主要是拉傷以及扭傷。

　　然而，在一些案例中，於跑馬拉松過程中或緊接著跑步後曾經有因心臟問題而導致死亡。在美國，研究人員發現過去的十年中，參加全馬或半馬的一千一百萬跑者中有 42 人死亡，他們大部分有心臟問題或與心臟有關的疾病。

　　有許多專家勸初學者在他們開始進行比賽訓練前應該先去看醫生，有心臟問題或是糖尿病的人要進行長距離跑步本來就一定要去諮詢醫生的意見。

　　許多業餘運動員本身並沒有依正確的準備方式來參加比賽，在幾個月中讓你自己處於良好的身體狀況不是一件容易的事且需要許多自我約束。訓練必須慢慢來，先用短距離讓你的身體可以適應肉體上的壓力。跑者常犯的錯誤是在一開始跑的太快，在幾天的訓練後應伴隨有休息的時段。跑步教練認為在參加馬拉松比賽前一個月，你應該要能以舒適的速度跑上 15 英哩，或者大約是四分之三的馬拉松距離，而在終點時還能有足夠的儲備體力就象徵你體能狀況是良好的。

　　然而，過多的訓練可能造成你的肌肉僵硬或其他傷害，在這樣的狀況下，你應該要減低你的訓練頻率並休息幾天。

　　在馬拉松開始前的不久時間，熱身及伸展對你整體表現將是很重要的。馬拉松跑者在賽程中碰到的其中一個最大問題就是脫水，也就是沒有喝足夠的水。如果在天氣很熱時，你的身體可能會經由流汗及呼吸吐氣而損失多達四公升的水份，對一個跑者而言，在比賽全程喝足夠的水是其中一項最重要的事。

理解力測驗中譯

1. 本文最佳標題為何？

(A) **跑馬拉松—健康的風險**

(B) 跑馬拉松—業餘運動員的終極目標

(C) 心臟問題—業餘運動員可能發生的

(D) 心臟相關的疾病—馬拉松跑者的殺手

2. 第二段第一行中"take up"的意思與下列何者最接近？

(A) 進行

(B) 執行

(C) 練習

(D) **開始**

3. 假如你有心臟問題而想要參加馬拉松比賽，你首先應該做甚麼？

(A) 去拜訪健康專家

(B) **去諮詢醫生意見**

(C) 去找跑步顧問

(D) 去做個健康檢查

4. 依據本文，馬拉松訓練為何開始要慢慢來？

(A) 因為你在幾個月的一段期間你的體能會變好

(B) 因為你可以從短距離開始

(C) **因為你的身體會逐漸地適應肉體上的壓力**

(D) 因為你在跑步終點將會有足夠的儲備體力

5. 下列何者關於馬拉松比賽的敘述是正確的？

(A) 馬拉松比賽可能造成非常嚴重的健康問題

(B) 四分之三的馬拉松距離約是 15 公里

(C) 脫水是馬拉松跑者在訓練中會發生的一個問題

(D) **當天氣很熱時，在一場馬拉松比賽中你的身體可能會損失多達四公升的水份**

 **本文圖解**

Running a marathon *is* the ultimate goal for a hobby athlete. But there

can be dangers **involved** in running a 26.2 mile or 41.2 km race. ⑤A Most
　　　　　分詞片語修飾前面的 dangers，表示與…有關的

health problems that happen during a marathon race *are* not very severe -

mainly strains and sprains.

In some cases, however, heart problems *have led* to deaths during

or immediately after a marathon. In the United States researchers *found*

out that **of** 11 million runners who have taken part in marathons or half
　　　　介係詞 of 在此意思為
　　　　在…之中的
marathons in the last decade 42 died. Most of them *had* heart problems or

heart-related diseases.

Many health experts *advise* beginners to see doctors before they take

up training for a race. ③ People with heart problems or diabetes *should also*

consult doctors before running long distances at all.

6

Many hobby athletes *do not prepare* themselves in the right way for a race. Getting yourself in good physical shape over a period of months *is* not always easy and requires a lot of self-discipline. Training must start slowly, with short distances, ④ **so that** your body can get used to the physical stress.

so that 引導一表目地的副詞子句

Runners often *make* the mistake of running too fast at the beginning. Rest periods *should follow* days of training. Running advisors *say* that about a month before a marathon you should be able to run ⑤ⓑ 15 miles, or almost three quarters of the marathon distance, **at** a comfortable speed. Having

at 在此表示以⋯(的速度)

enough reserves at the end *is* also a sign that you are in good shape.

Training too much, however, *can lead* to stiffness in your muscles or other injuries. **In such a case** you *should lower* your training rate and *take* a

表示在這種情況下

few days off.

Shortly before a marathon starts warming up and stretching *can be*

important for your overall performance. ⑤Ⓒ One of the biggest problems that marathon runners face during a race *is* dehydration, not getting enough to drink. ⑤Ⓓ If it's very hot your body *can lose* up to four liters of fluid through sweating and breathing out air. One of the most important tasks for a runner *is* to drink enough throughout a race.

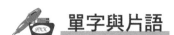 單字與片語

重要單字 Key Vocabularies

① marathon（n）馬拉松　　② ultimate（adj）終極的
③ strain（n）拉傷　　　　　④ sprain（n）扭傷
⑤ diabetes（n）糖尿病　　　⑥ consult（v）諮詢
⑦ physical shape　體能狀況　⑧ self-discipline　自我約束
⑨ stiffness（n）僵硬　　　　⑩ dehydration（n）脫水
⑪ fluid（n）液體　　　　　　⑫ task（n）任務，工作

重要片語 Key Phrases

❶ led to　導致於　　　　　❷ take up　建立
❸ at all　根本，完全　　　　❹ get used to　習慣於

 **本文解析**

　　本文開始提到跑馬拉松會有一些拉傷及扭傷等的運動傷害，也有致死的案例，但這大都與跑者本身患心臟疾病引起的。而要避免運動傷害，必須聽從專家或運動指導的指示來進行準備，一開始應慢慢讓身體適應壓力，需要有足夠的休息，過多的練習份量可能造成肌肉僵硬等傷害，而賽前的熱身也很重要，最後提到比賽中需補充水分以防發生脫水。所以本篇的主要內容就是提到跑馬拉松所需注意到的一些身體健康應注意的事項，故最佳標題以選項中"跑馬拉松一健康的風險"最為恰當。

　　第二題問"take up"的意思，take up 有開始、建立或接受等許多意思，而在文中指的是說開始進行馬拉松訓練的事，所以是當"開始"的意思，故選項中以 start 意思最接近。第三題問有心臟問題而想要參加馬拉松應該先要做甚麼，由文章中 People with heart problems or diabetes should also consult doctors before running...，知道有這方面的疾病的人要長跑前一定要徵詢醫生的意見。第四題問馬拉松訓練為何開始要慢慢來，由 Training must start slowly... so that your body can get used to...，該句後面的 so that 就是表示原因（理由）的副詞子句，所以原因是要讓身體適應壓力。第五題問何者敘述為真，選項均在文中的句子可以找到，但許多都經過改敘（改寫），讀者可自行從中比較並找出答案。

學習重點 ➡

　　能否精確掌握介係詞在文章的運用是影響閱讀文章理解的一大挑戰，以本文中的一句為例：In the United States researchers found out that of 11 million runners who have taken part in marathons or half marathons in the last decade 42 died. 該句的 that 之後一直到結束是一個名詞子句當動詞片語 found out 的受詞，而子句中另有一個關係帶名引導的形容詞子句 who... in the last decade 來修飾 runners，而該名詞子句的真正主詞是 42(42 個人)，動詞為 died，所以前面 of 所引導的介係詞片語是當子句的副詞片語修飾全句，介係詞 of 表示在…中。需注意不能將本句中的 that of 當成是一組片語（事情就像…），例如：The utilization of the outdoor space, compared with that of the indoor space, is quite low（戶外空間的運用相較於室內空間而言是相當低的）。

 英文本文

Article 6.4

Street Art is a very popular form of art that is spreading quickly all over the world. You can find it on buildings, sidewalks, street signs, and trash cans from Tokyo to Paris, from Moscow to Cape Town. Street art has become a global culture and even art museums and galleries are collecting the work of street artists.

Art experts claim that the movement began in New York in the 1960s. Young adults sprayed words and other images on walls and trains. This colorful, energetic style of writing became known as graffiti. Graffiti art showed that young people wanted to rebel against society. They didn't want to accept rules and travelled around cities to create paintings that everyone could see. In many cases, they had trouble with the police and the local government.

One well-known New York Street artist is Swoon. She cuts out paper images of people and puts them on walls and or sets them up on sidewalks. Swoon didn't start her career as a street artist. She studied art but, as time went on, got bored with the works she saw in museums and galleries. People in New York enjoy Swoon's strong and imaginative style. Some museums have already bought some of her work.

Street artists do their work for a reason. Some of them do not like artists who make so much money in galleries and museums. They choose street art because it is closer to the people. Some artists try to express their political opinion in their work. They often want to protest against big firms and corporations. Others like to do things that are forbidden and hope they don't get caught.

Advertising companies also use street art in their ads because it gives you the impression of youth and energy. The New York department store Saks Fifth Avenue recently used a street artist's design for their shop windows and shopping bags.

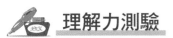 **理解力測驗**

Q1. What is "graffiti"?

(A) a collecting of museum

(B) a kind of writing

(C) a kind of art creation

(D) people who rebel against society

Q2. Where did the street art originate from?

(A) Tokyo

(B) New York

(C) Paris

(D) Moscow

Q3. Which of the following statements about Swoon is correct?

(A) She is a well-known New York street art collector.

(B) She started her career as a street artist.

(C) She studied art but latter worked in museums and galleries.

(D) Some of her works have already been collected by museums.

Q4. Why do advertising companies intend to use street arts in their ads?

(A) Because it is very cheap.

(B) Because it makes customers a dream of youth and energy.

(C) Because it is closer to the people.

(D) Because it protests against big firms and corporations.

Q5. According to this article, which of the following statements about street artist is NOT correct?

(A) They do not like artists who make so much money in galleries and museums.

(B) They try to express their political believe in their work.

(C) They like to do things that are not allowed and hope they get caught.

(D) A street artist's design has been used by a department store.

本文中譯

街頭藝術

街頭藝術是一種很普遍而正在全世界中快速傳播的藝術。從紐約到巴黎、從莫斯科到開普敦，你都可以在建築物、人行道、街頭號誌、垃圾桶等地方發現它。街頭藝術已經成為一種全球性的文化，且甚至博物館及藝廊也開始蒐集這些街頭藝術家的作品。

藝術專家認為這種活動開始於 1960 年代的紐約。青少年們在牆上及火車上噴圖文字及其他影像，而這些色彩繽紛的、充滿活力風格的作品就是為人所知的"塗鴉"。塗鴉藝術展現出年輕人想要從社會中解放出來，他們不要受規矩的束縛，而到處在城市中遊蕩去創作這些人們所看到的圖畫，他們時常受警察及地方政府的干預。

其中一個廣為人知的紐約街頭藝術家就是席翁，她把人像剪影剪下在牆上展示或者是擺放到人行道上。席翁並不是靠街頭藝術起家，她唸藝術，但隨著時間一久，她對她在美術館或藝廊看到的作品感到厭煩。紐約的居民感受到席翁強烈的風格，有些博物館已經開始購買她的一些作品。

這些街頭藝術家都有他們的理由，有些人是因為他們不喜歡那些在博物館或藝廊中賺大錢的藝術家，他們選擇街頭藝術是因為它更貼近一般民眾，而有些藝術家想要在他們的作品中表達他們的政治觀點，他們通常抗議的是大公司及財團，有些人則是想做一些被禁止的事但不想被抓到。

廣告公司也在他們的廣告中使用街頭藝術作品，因為它給人們年輕而有活力的印象，紐約的百貨公司最近在他們店的櫥窗及購物袋上用了一位街頭藝術家的設計作品。

理解力測驗中譯

1. 甚麼是"塗鴉"？

(A) 一種博物館珍藏品

(B) 一種著作

(C) **一種藝術創作**

(D) 反抗社會的人

2. 街頭藝術源起於何處？

(A) 東京

(B) **紐約**

(C) 巴黎

(D) 莫斯科

3. 下列有關於席翁的敘述何者為真？

(A) 她是一位著名的紐約街頭藝術收藏家。

(B) 她是以街頭藝術起家。

(C) 她是研讀藝術但後來在博物館及藝廊工作。

(D) **她的一些作品已經由博物館收藏。**

4. 為何廣告公司會想在他們的廣告中用到街頭藝術？

(A) 因為那很便宜。

(B) **因為那使人想像成年輕有活力。**

(C) 因為那接近民眾。

(D) 因為那表示對抗大公司及財團。

5. 依據本文，下列有關街頭藝術家的敘述何者為非？

(A) 他們不喜歡那些在藝廊及美術館中賺大錢的藝術家。

(B) 他們想要在作品中表達政治的看法。

(C) 他們想做一些不被允許的事並希望被抓。

(D) **一位街頭藝術家的設計已經被一家百貨公司所採用。**

 **本文圖解**

Street Art *is* a very popular form of art that is spreading quickly all over the world. You *can find* it on buildings, sidewalks, street signs and trash cans from Tokyo to Paris, from Moscow to Cape Town. Street art *has become* a global culture and even art museums and galleries *are collecting* the work of street artists.

Art experts *claim* that ② the movement began in New York in the 1960s. Young adults *sprayed* words and other images on walls and trains. ① This colorful, energetic style of writing *became* **known** as graffiti. Graffiti art

become 在此當成 be 的意思，也就是被…所認知的

showed that young people wanted to rebel against society. They *didn't want* to accept rules and *travelled* around cities to create paintings that everyone could see. In many cases they *had* trouble with the police and the local government.

③A One well-known New York Street artist is Swoon. She *cuts* out paper

省略 that 的形容詞子句

images of people and *puts* them on walls and or *sets* them up on sidewalks.

③B Swoon *didn't start* her career as a street artist. ③C She *studied* art but, as time went on, *got* bored with the works **she** saw in museums and galleries. People in New York *enjoy* Swoon's strong and imaginative style. ③D Some museums *have already bought* some of her work.

Street artists *do* their work for a reason. ⑤A Some of them *do not like* artists who make so much money in galleries and museums. They *choose* street art because it is closer to the people. ⑤B Some artists *try* to express their political opinion in their work. They often *want* to protest against big firms and corporations. ⑤C Others *like* to do things that are forbidden and hope they don't get caught.

Advertising companies also *use* street art in their ads because it gives you 在此當 people 的意思，指一般民眾

you the impression of youth and energy. ⑤D The New York department store Saks Fifth Avenue recently *used* a street artist's design for their shop windows and shopping bags.

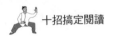

單字與片語

重要單字 Key Vocabularies

① gallery（n）藝廊

② movement（n）活動；運動

③ spray（v）噴塗

④ energetic（adj）精力旺盛的

⑤ graffiti（n）(在火車或牆壁上的)塗鴉

⑥ rebel (against)(v) 反抗

⑦ paper images　紙上剪影

⑧ career（n）職業

⑨ imaginative（adj）富想像力的

⑩ opinion（n）看法，意見

⑪ firm（n）公司行號

⑫ impression（n）印象

重要片語 Key Phrases

❶ cuts out　剪下來

❷ as time goes on　隨著時間的演進

❸ get bored with　對…感到厭煩

本文解析

　　文章先提到街頭藝術已經成為一種流傳全世界的藝術活動，而街頭藝術的發源被認為應該是在六〇年代的美國紐約，青少年們藉著在火車及牆上的塗鴉來表達他們充滿活力不受規矩的限制。作者提到其中一位街頭藝術家席翁，她的作品深受人們喜愛，連博物館也開始收藏她的作品。這些街頭藝術家都有他們創作的理由，像是要讓藝術接近大眾或是表達政治訴求，而廣告商也看到看見這個商機，利用街頭藝術讓人充滿青春活力的印象來設計廣告及商品。所以本文主要是談到街頭藝術的起源及存在的意義，以及後續的發展。

　　第一題問甚麼是"graffiti"，這個字讀者可能以前沒看過，但文章中會有說明：This colorful, energetic style of writing became known as graffiti.，可知它是一種藝術創作。第二題問街頭藝術源起於何處，文章中先是提到很多地名，但不要被混淆了，由 the movement began in New York...，知其發源於紐約。第三題問關於席翁的敘述何者為真，選項中的敘述均可在文章中出現，讀者請自行參閱，但需注意語意的差別，例如選項中 (C) 說她研讀藝術但後來在博物館及藝廊工作。她確實是研讀藝術，但沒有說她曾經有到博物館或藝廊工作，而是説她對裡面的作品 (works) 感到厭煩 (She studied art but, as time went on, got bored with the works she saw in museums and galleries)。第四題廣告公司為何想用到街頭藝術作品，由文中 Advertising...because it gives you the impression of youth...，知其原因是這些作品充滿年輕有活利的印象。第五題問有關街頭藝術家敘述為非者，選項均可由本文中找到，請讀者自行參閱。

學習重點 ➡

我們時常在文章中看到像「動詞＋介係詞」組合的動詞片語，其實文法上是可分為片語動詞 (phrasal verbs) 及介係詞動詞 (prepositional verbs) 等二種不同形式及意義。

一、片語動詞

及物形的片語動詞與介係詞是可分隔的 (因為事實上該介係詞是當副詞用，稱為介副詞)，這種片語動詞特點是介副詞可能會造成原動詞意義的改變。而當動詞的受詞是名詞時，可放在動詞與介副詞之間，也可以在介副詞之後。但當受詞是代名詞時，一定要放在動詞及介副詞中間 (也就是不可分隔性)。

例如當片語動詞用時：turn off = 關上 (瓦斯…)

John turned off the gas.

John turned the gas off.

John turned it off. (注意：不可寫成 tured off it)

二、介係詞動詞

這是不及物動詞為接受詞而加上介係詞所形成的，其特點是介係詞不會造成原動詞意義的改變。而介係詞動詞的受詞，不論是否為名詞或代名詞，均只能放在介係詞之後 (因為該受詞是其實是介係詞的受詞，所以一定要放在介係詞後面)。

例如當介係詞動詞用時：turn off = 開離 (高速公路…)

John turned off the freeway.

John turned off it. (注意：不可寫成 John turned it off from the freeway.)

歷史 & 人物

History & Characters

第七招 快速閱讀法

要在閱讀測驗中拿到好成績，除了解題技巧要學會外，快速的閱讀技巧也是關鍵因素之一。

1. 熟練英文五大句型：

英文五大句型是學習英文的人一開始就教的，事實上英文句再長，如果把其它形容詞（子句）、說明、修飾等等作用的詞句刪掉（或省略不看），最後就是只剩下主詞及動詞之間的變化，那不就是五大句型，舉例如下：

Customers who choose hotels often enjoy the advantages of brand recognition, familiar reservation processes, and on-site service, while booking a vacation rental may mean stepping out of that comfort zone in order to get privacy, peace and quietness they offer -- things that are hard to obtain in a hotel room.

這句共有 51 個字，對具有良好句型概念的讀者來說，一點都不難，因為該句說穿了就是用連接詞 while 連結起兩個 S + Vt 的句型而已。第一句的主詞 Customers，動詞 enjoy 而容詞子句 (who choose hotels) 修飾主詞 Customers，advantages 為 enjoy 受詞，後面 of... service 一長串是為了說明 advantages 有哪些。再來表示轉折語氣的連接詞 while 連接第二句，其主詞是 booking a vacation rental，動詞 mean，後面 stepping... zone 為 enjoy 受詞，後面 in order to 副詞片語修飾全句，而破折號後面示為了要說明前面的 offer 等等。

2. 看到句子先找主詞及看動詞

主詞及動詞就是一個句子的靈魂及心臟，其它字詞只是用來形容、修飾、補充、說明等作用，其中尤其動詞更是關鍵，因為動詞掌管該句中主詞相關的活動描述。一個句子只能有一個動詞（除非有對等連接詞連接）。所以快速有效的看出主詞及動詞，就是掌握快速閱讀的關鍵之一，而其方法就是將其它修飾、說明用的字語找出來，那就可以很清楚看出主詞及動詞了，例如下列句子：

The courses operated by local government at smaller Thai cooking schools in Bangkok offer an ideal home-style learning environment that is different from most of the hotels and restaurants in Thailand.

該句子單一句就有 31 個單字，乍看之下好像很複雜，其實只要將主詞及動詞找出來，要看懂其實很容易。主詞應該很容易就能看出是 The courses，該句動詞就是 offer，且由主詞 courses 為第三人稱複數，所以現在式動詞用原形這點來更加確認。確認了主詞及動詞後，該句就簡化成了：The courses(主詞)... in Bangkok offer(動詞) an ideal... environment(受詞) that is different... in Thailand.(形容詞子句，修飾 environment)，這時主要的意思就很明確了。

3.有效處理關係子句及分號

出題者運用關係子句及用分號的說明等方式，便可以加長語句，達到混淆閱讀的效果。既然如此，破解之道就是先想辦法把這些加諸原來簡單句型結構上的語句先暫時拿掉（忽略），然後依據前面所提的分析句子結構並找出真正主詞及動詞。如此必能有效加快閱讀速度，如以下例子：

The research, based on a survey of more than 3,000 teens, found that the students who had taken music lessons outside school scored significantly higher in terms of cognitive skills, had better grades and were more conscientious and ambitious than their peers.

該單一句子就有 41 個單字，看似有些複雜，但如果將關係子句、分號內的補充說明及其它修飾詞拿掉，就會變成：

The research found that the students scored significantly higher, had better grades and were more conscientious and ambitious.

這時就只有 18 個單字要看，減少一大半以上。

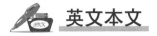 英文本文

Article 7.1

Emile Jaques-Dalcroze was born in Vienna on July 6, 1865. He started to learn playing piano at the age of 6 from a madam who lived next door. He didn't like the uninteresting practice of fingering, but played improvisatorially; however, he still strongly loved music and made huge progress in it. When he was 10 years old, Emile moved with his entire family to Geneva from Vienna, and completed the most part of music learning over there. In Geneva, he had successively completed high school and pre-college educations, and later entered the University of Geneva in 1883, as well as studied the music curriculum in Conservatoire de musique de Genève (Geneva Music Conservatory). One year later, he transferred to Paris for learning drama, but still continuously learned music during after-school time. Afterward, he was able to make some money by playing piano in cafeterias, or playing an accompaniment of vocal artists or instrument performers. Then, he gradually shifted his learning from drama to music. Emile returned to Geneva in 1886, and took the **position** of the associate conductor in Théâtre des Nouveauté, Algiers at that summer, and he did many short-term jobs all over the world then, which really influenced him a lot. As in the same period of time, he added "Dalcroze" to his family name in order to differentiate from a composer who named Emile Jaques. However, even Algiers offered him a long-term work at that time, Emile still decided to go back to Europe for continuous learning. Thus, he entered the Vienna Conservatory (now is University of Music and Performing Arts Vienna) being a student of Anton Bruckner. Emile had been stayed in Vienna till 1889, and then he returned to Paris being a student of Fauré and Leo Delibes till 1891.

 理解力測驗

Q1. What does the word "position" in line 15 refer to?

(A) place

(B) height

(C) job

(D) direction

Q2. According to the passage, when was Emile Jaques-Dalcroze born?

(A) 18th century

(B) 19th century

(C) 20th century

(D) 21st century

Q3. Based on the contents, which of the following statements is NOT true?

(A) Emile had successively completed high school and pre-college educations in Geneva.

(B) Emile moved with his entire family to Geneva from Vienna at the age of 10.

(C) Emile transferred to Paris for learning drama in 1883.

(D) Emile returned to Geneva in 1886, and he took the position of associate conductor in Théàtre des Nouveauté, Algiers.

Q4. Who is Emile Jaques?

(A) a teacher

(B) a student

(C) a musician

(D) a composer

Q5. According to the author, when did Emile start to learn playing piano?

(A) 1865

(B) 1871

(C) 1883

(D) 1886

 本文中譯

律動音樂教學

　　Emile Jaques-Dalcroze 於 1865 年 7 月 6 日生於維也納。六歲開始向一位鄰居婦人學鋼琴，雖然他不喜歡枯燥的手指練習，而是喜歡即興亂彈，他還是強烈地喜愛音樂而且進步神速。Emile 十歲時全家從維也納搬到日內瓦，並在日內瓦完成了大部分的音樂學習。在此他先後完成中學及大學預備科並在 1883 進入日內瓦大學，同時一直在 Conservatoire de musique de Genève 中學習音樂課程。一年之後他轉學到巴黎去學習戲劇，課餘仍繼續學習音樂，並逐漸能靠著在咖啡館中彈琴及幫聲樂家或演奏家伴奏賺得一些錢。他慢慢的將重心從戲劇轉移到音樂上。Emile 於 1886 年回到日內瓦。當年夏天他接下在阿爾及爾的 Théàtre des Nouveautés 樂團副指揮及合唱指揮的工作，從此他一連串地在各地有許多短期的工作，而這對他有很大的影響，也是在這一時期將「Dalcroze」加在姓氏上，以便與另一位叫 Emile Jaques 的作曲家有所區別。隨然阿爾及爾提供他長期的職位，他還是決定要回到歐洲繼續學習，並進入維也納音樂學院（現在的維也納音樂及戲劇表演大學）成為 Anton Bruckner 的學生。他一直在維也納待到 1889 年，之後又回到巴黎成為 Fauré 與 Leo Delibes 的學生直到 1891 年。

理解力測驗中譯

1. 第 15 行的單字"position"是何意？

(A) 地方

(B) 高度

(C) 工作

(D) 方向

2. 根據本文，Emile Jaques-Dalcroze 是何時出生的？

(A) 18 世紀

(B) **19 世紀**

(C) 20 世紀

(D) 21 世紀

3. 根據內容，下列何者敘述為非？

(A) Emile 於持續完成中學與大學預備科教育

(B) Emile 十歲時全家從 Vienna 搬到 Geneva

(C) **Emile 於 1883 年轉學到巴黎去學習戲劇**

(D) Emile 於 1886 年回到日內瓦並接下在 Algiers 的 Théàtre des Nouveautés 樂團副指揮及合唱指揮的工作

4. Emile Jaques 是甚麼人？

(A) 一位老師

(B) 一位學生

(C) 一位音樂家

(D) **一位作曲家**

5. 根據本文作者，Emile 何時開始學鋼琴？

(A) 1865

(B) **1871**

(C) 1883

(D) 1886

 本文圖解

② Emile Jaques-Dalcroze *was born* in Vienna on July 6, 1865. ⑤ He *started* to learn playing piano at the age of 6 from a madam who lived next door. He *didn't like* the uninteresting practice of fingering but *played* improvisatorially; however, he still strongly *loved* music and made huge progress in it. ③B When he was 10 years old, Emile *moved* with his entire family to Geneva from Vienna, and *completed* the most part of music learning over there. ③A In Geneva, he *had successively completed* high school and pre-college educations, and later *entered* the University of Geneva in 1883, as well as *studied* the music curriculum in Conservatoire de musique de Genève (Geneva Music Conservatory). ③C One year later, he *transferred* to Paris for learning drama, but still continuously *learned* music during after-school time. Afterward, he *was* able to make some money by playing piano in cafeterias, or playing an accompaniment of vocal artists or instrument performers. Then,

he gradually *shifted* his learning from drama to music. ㉚ Emile *returned* to

Geneva in 1886, and *took* the position of associate conductor in Théàtre

des Nouveauté, Algiers at that summer, and he *did* many short-term jobs all

over the world then, **which** really influenced him a lot. As in the same period

which 是指前面所提的到處從
事短期工作這件事

of time, he *added* "Dalcroze" to his family name in order to differentiate

from ④ a composer who named Emile Jaques. However, even Algiers *offered*

him a long-term work at that time, Emile still *decided* to go back to Europe

for continuous learning. Thus, he *entered* the Vienna Conservatory (now is

University of Music and Performing Arts Vienna) **being** a student of Anton

分詞片語 being 當受詞補語，說明
Vienna Conservatory 的目的

Bruckner. Emile *had been stayed* in Vienna till 1889, and then he returned to

Paris being a student of Fauré and Leo Delibes till 1891.

7

歷史＆人物

 單字與片語

重要單字 Key Vocabularies

① fingering（n）指法

② improvisatorially（adv）即興地

③ successively（adv）連續地

④ Conservatory（n）音樂學院

⑤ accompaniment（n）伴奏

⑥ conductor（n）指揮

⑦ composer（n）作曲家

重要片語 Key Phrases

❶ took the position of 接下…的工作／職務

❷ differentiate from 與…區別

本文解析

　　本文是一篇敘述一位維也納音樂家 Emile Jaques-Dalcroze 在他成長及學習過程的文章，文章從他出生背景、學習音樂過程中經歷的各階段一直寫到他在 1891 到巴黎成為 Fauré 與 Leo Delibes 的學生為止。本文有許多不常見的專有名詞，如地名、人名及機構名稱，但都只需將他視為名詞處理即可。

　　測驗中第一題問"position"是何意，該字可當位置、方位或工作職位等解釋，在文中意思應解釋為工作。第二題問 Emile Jaques-Dalcroze 生於何時，文章第一句就可看出答案，但需注意題目問的是世紀，1800-1899 都屬於 19 世紀。第二題問敘述為非者，從這些選項中提到的關鍵部分，如年代、地名、人名等，可在文中找到這些提到的部分，經比較後即可得出答案，請參考本文圖解。第四題問 Emile Jaques 的身分，由 ... a composer who named Emile Jaques. 可知這位 Emile Jaques 是一位作曲家，注意不要與本文主角音樂家 Emile Jaques-Dalcroze 搞混了。第五題問 Emile 何時開始學鋼琴，由文中 He started to learn playing piano at the age of 6... 可知他六歲學琴，再加上他的出生年份即可得知他在哪年開始學琴。

學習重點 ➡

在本文中的句子：However, even Algiers offered him a long-term work at that time, Emile still decided to go back to Europe for continuous learning. 該句中動詞後面可以看到有二個名詞 him 及 long-term work，這二個都當動詞 offer 的受詞，但分別為間接受詞 him(指人) 及直接受詞 long-term work(指事物)，這類型的動詞必須牽涉到兩個人事物，因此這類型的動詞叫做「雙賓動詞」。

例句：

I gave you a book.(我給你一本書。)

He bought Mary flowers.(他買花給瑪莉。)

She cooks her husband dinner everyday.(她每天幫她先生煮晚餐。)

注意：

以第一個例句而言，「給」的動作通常牽涉兩件事：給誰？給何物？故該動詞就需要兩個受詞，否則句子的意思就不完整了。

如果將雙賓動詞中的直接受詞即間接受詞對調，則要加上適當的介係詞在間接受詞前。

例如：

I gave a book to you.(我給你一本書。)

He bought flowers for Mary.(他買花給瑪莉。)

歷史 & 人物 7

 英文本文

Article 7.2

Calligraphic art has the long and well-developed history as the using of Han characters. Since the invention of inscriptions on bones or tortoise shells (oracle), Calligraphic art characters had developed in sequence of Seal Character, Li Character, Cursive Script, Regular Script and Running Script. There were many outstanding calligraphers and calligraphic artworks in each stage, which composed of profound tradition for Calligraphic art. From ancient times, Calligraphic art had already become a mature art that contained abundant, integral, and theoretic systems that derived from the same origin. Many theories and literatures are the summarization of implementing such art of calligraphers, which had greatly influenced calligraphy learning and creating for later generations. Calligraphic art is a kind of writing art of Han characters. According to the viewpoint of Han characters, Calligraphic art is a unique visual art, but such uniqueness will not deter those who are unfamiliar to Han characters from appreciating Calligraphic art. Han character is an important factor for Calligraphic art because Calligraphic art was derived and developed from Chinese culture, and it is also one of the basic factors in Chinese culture. Based on Han characters, it is the main symbol of Calligraphic art that is distinct from other calligraphic types.

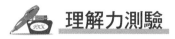 理解力測驗

Q1. According to the passage, what is the closest meaning of "**calligraphy**"?
   (A) Scripts
   (B) Character
   (C) Handwriting
   (D) All of the above

Q2. Based on the contents, which of the following descriptions is NOT true?
   (A) In ancient times, Calligraphic art had already become a mature art.
   (B) Calligraphic art is a writing art of Han characters.
   (C) Before the invention of inscriptions on bones or tortoise shells (oracle), calligraphic art had composed of the profound tradition.
   (D) Han character is an important factor for calligraphic art.

Q3. According to the author, what is calligraphic art in accordance with the viewpoint of Han characters?
   (A) a character
   (B) a unique visual art
   (C) an inscription
   (D) a script

Q4. Based on the information, which of the following scripts is NOT a calligraphic art?
   (A) Li Character
   (B) Running Script
   (C) Block Script
   (D) Cursive Script

Q5. In this article, which is the main symbol of calligraphic art that is distinct from other calligraphic types?
   (A) Oracle
   (B) Regular script
   (C) Seal character
   (D) Han character

7
歷
史
&
人
物

 本文中譯

書法的發展

　　書法藝術的歷史源遠流長，和許多文字使用的歷史一樣悠久。自從甲骨文發明以來，書法藝術的字體經歷了由篆書到隸書、草書、楷書、行書的發展階段。每個階段都產生了數量眾多的書法家和書法作品，這些書法家和書法作品構成了書法藝術的深厚傳統。書法藝術在古代已經是一門成熟的藝術，有豐富、完整、一脈相承的理論體系，很多理論著作是書法家藝術實踐的總結，深深地影響了後人的書法學習和創作。書法藝術是漢字的書寫藝術。從以漢字為的角度看，書法藝術是一種很獨特的視覺藝術，但是這種獨特性並不妨礙不認識漢字的人欣賞書法藝術。漢字是書法藝術中的重要因素，因為書法藝術是在華人文化裡產生、發展起來的，而漢字是華人文化的基本要素之一。以漢字為基礎，是書法藝術區別於其他種類書法的主要象徵。

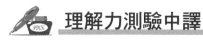 理解力測驗中譯

1. 根據本文，下列何意最接近"calligraphy"？

(A) 字跡

(B) 字體

(C) 書寫體

(D) 以上皆是

2. 根據內容，下列何者敘述為非？

(A) 書法藝術在古代已經是一門成熟的藝術

(B) 書法藝術是漢字的書寫藝術

(C) 在甲骨文發明之前，書法藝術就已經構成了深厚的傳統

(D) 漢字是華人文化的基本要素之一

3. 根據本文作者，以漢字的角度來看，書法藝術是一種？

(A) 字體

(B) 獨特的視覺藝術

(C) 銘文

(D) 筆跡

4. 根據本文 資訊，下列哪一種字體不是書法藝術？

(A) 隸書

(B) 行書

(C) 印刷體

(D) 草書

5. 本文中何者是書法藝術區別於其他種類書法的主要象徵？

(A) 甲骨文

(B) 楷書

(C) 篆書

(D) 漢字

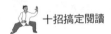
 本文圖解

Calligraphic art *has* the long and well-developed history as the using of

Han characters. ②ⓒ Since the invention of inscriptions on bones or tortoise

shells (oracle), Calligraphic art characters *had developed* **in sequence of**

in sequence of
指一系列的意思

Seal Character, Li Character, Cursive Script, Regular Script and Running

Script. There *were* many outstanding calligraphers and calligraphic artworks

in each stage, which composed of profound tradition for Calligraphic

art. ②Ⓐ From ancient times, Calligraphic art *had already become* a mature

art **that** contained abundant, integral and theoretic systems that derived

that 引導形容詞子句，修飾 art

from the same origin. Many theories and literatures *are* the summarization

of implementing such art of calligraphers, **which** had greatly influenced

which 是指 summarization，
而非指 calligraphers

calligraphy learning and creating for later generations. ②Ⓑ Calligraphic art

is a kind of writing art of Han characters. ③ According to the viewpoint of

Han characters, Calligraphic art *is* a unique visual art, but such uniqueness

will not deter those who are unfamiliar to Han characters from appreciating

Calligraphic art. ⑳ Han character *is* an important factor for Calligraphic art

because Calligraphic art was derived and developed from Chinese culture,

and it *is* also one of the basic factors in Chinese culture. ⑤ Based on Han
　　it 是指前面所提的 Calligraphic art

characters, it *is* the main symbol of Calligraphic art that is distinct from other
　　　　本句為 it is …that 的強調用法，強調 main symbol of Calligraphic art

calligraphic types.

 ## 單字與片語

重要單字 Key Vocabularies

① calligraphic （adj）書法的　　② well-developed （a）健全的；發展良好的

③ characters （n）字體；特色　　④ inscriptions （n）銘文；刻印文字

⑤ scripts （n）筆跡；字體　　　⑥ profound （a）深刻的；深度的

⑦ summarization （n）總結　　　⑧ appreciate （v）欣賞

重要片語 Key Phrases

❶ in sequence of　按照順序

❷ unfamiliar to　不熟悉的

❸ distinct from　與…不同／有區別的

本文解析

本文是一篇有關敘述書法藝術的短文，作者先敘述書法的起源及書法類型，並指出書法藝術是漢字的書寫藝術，是一種很獨特的視覺藝術，且是有具有豐富、完整、一脈相承的理論，這種獨特性不會影響不懂漢字的人欣賞書法藝術，而以漢字為基礎是書法藝術區別於其他種類書法的主要象徵。所以本文主要重點在於敘述源自於漢字的書法這種獨特的藝術的內涵。

第一題問到"calligraphy"這個字的意思，calligraphy。原來是指寫字的筆跡，藉以表示中國的書法，選項中的三者都有類似含意。第二題問敘述何者為非，從這些選項中提到的關鍵字部分，找到文中的提到的部分並比較後，即可得出答案。第三題問以漢字的觀點 (viewpoint of Han characters) 來看，書法藝術是何物，由 ... the viewpoint of Han characters, Calligraphic art is a unique visual art...，故知他是一種視覺藝術。第四題問哪一種字體不是書法藝術，由 Calligraphic art characters had developed in sequence of Seal Character, Li Character, ...，其中沒提到 Block Script。第五題問書法區別於其他種類書法的主要象徵 (main symbol of Calligraphic art) 為何，由 Based on Han characters, it is the main symbol of...，知道區別於其他種類書法的主要象徵就是指 Han characters。

學習重點 ➡

分詞構句由副詞子句及所引導表附帶狀況的子句轉換而來，用以表示時間、原因、條件、讓步、附帶狀況。

1. 一般分詞構句：

兩邊主詞相同時，將副詞子句的從屬連接詞及子句的主詞去掉，再將子句內的動詞依主動改為 Ving，被動改為 Vp.p.。

例句：

Animals can do lots of amazing things when they are properly trained.

（當施以適當的訓練，動物可以做很多令人驚異的事。）

→ Animals can do lots of amazing things when properly trained.

Not knowing what to do, she began to cry.

(由於不知道怎麼辦，他開始哭了起來。)

注意：

(1) 完成式的主動中，直接將 has/have/had ＋ Vpp 改為 having ＋ Vpp

(2) 如果需要連接詞的意思時，可以將連接詞保留。

例句：

Having finished my work, I went to play basketball.

(當完成我的工作後，我就去玩籃球。)

After finishing my work, I went to play basketball.

(在完成我的工作之後，我就去玩籃球。)

7

歷史&人物

 英文本文

Article 7.3

The greatest recent social changes have been in the lives of women. During the twentieth century, there has been a remarkable shortening of the proportion of a woman's life spent in caring for children. At the end of the nineteenth century, they would probably have been in her middle twenties, and would be likely to have seven or eight children, of whom four or five lived till they were five years old. By the time the youngest was fifteen, the mother would have been in her early fifties and would expect to live a further twenty years, during which custom, opportunity, and health made it unusual for her to get paid work. Today women marry younger and have fewer children. Usually a woman's youngest child will be fifteen when she is forty-five years and is likely to take paid work until retirement at sixty. Even while she has the care of children, her work is lightened by household appliances and convenience foods.

This important change in women's life-pattern has only recently begun to have its full effect on women's economic position. Even a few years ago most girls left school at the first opportunity, and most of them took a full-time job. However when they married, they usually left work at once and never returned to it. Today the school-leaving age is sixteen, many girls stay at school after that age, and though women tend to marry younger, more married women stay at work at least until shortly before their first child is born. Very many more afterwards return to full- or part-time work. Such changes have led to a new relationship in marriage, with the husband accepting a greater share of the duties and satisfactions of family life and with both husband and wife sharing more equally in providing the money, and running the home, according to the abilities and interests of each of them.

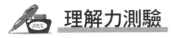 理解力測驗

Q1. According to the article, women nowadays probably

(A) marry men younger than themselves.

(B) do not do housework.

(C) do not want to give birth to children.

(D) provide the money to the family like her husband.

Q2. For women at the twentieth, the amount caring for children

(A) was shorter than in previous centuries.

(B) was longer than in previous centuries.

(C) was considered to be surprisingly long.

(D) accounted for a great part of their lives.

Q3. According to the article, an average family in 1900

(A) many children died before they were five.

(B) seven or eight children lived to be more than five.

(C) the youngest child would be fifteen.

(D) four of five children died when they were five.

Q4. When she was over fifty, the late nineteenth century mother

(A) was unlikely to find a job even if she wanted one.

(B) would not expect to work.

(C) was very healthy and beautiful.

(D) was considered to have a rest at home.

Q5. Why the woman of today may return to take a job?

(A) Because she is younger when her children are still young.

(B) Because she does not like caring for children.

(C) Because she need not worry about food for her children.

(D) Because she is younger when her children are old enough to look after himself.

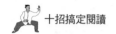

 **本文中譯**

婦女的地位

　　近來社會上最大的改變就在婦女的生活上面。在二十世紀期間，婦女一輩子花在照顧小孩時間的比例已經有顯著的縮短了。在十九世紀結束時，她們也許是在二十幾歲的時候，就可能有七到八個小孩，這些小孩中有四到五個可以活到五歲。而在這些小孩最小的到十五歲時，這時媽媽可能已經五十歲出頭，並約可以再活個十二年左右。而在這段期間內，風俗、工作機會已及健康問題讓她們不大可能會有支薪的工作。今天的婦女結婚更早且有較少的小孩。通常，在婦女四十五歲左右時，她最小的孩子已經十五歲了，且一直到她六十五歲退休都還可以有支薪的工作。甚至於當她必須照顧小孩時，她的工作可藉由家電及方便的食物來減輕負荷。

　　這項婦女生活型態的重大改變，直到最近才開始顯現出它在婦女經濟地位的全面影響。就算在一些年以前，大部分女孩都儘早離開學校，且她們大部份都從事全職工作。然而，當他們結婚後，她們通常馬上離開職場並且從此不復返。今天，完成學業的年紀是在十六歲，但許多女孩們在超過這年紀時仍在學，且雖然婦女們傾向早些結婚，有更多的已婚婦女仍至少持續工作到它們第一個小孩出生為止，而很多人後來重新回到全職或兼職的工作。隨著丈夫可以擔負較多家庭生活的責任及滿意度，且不管丈夫與妻子，都可依據他們個人的能力及興趣，更為平等共享賺錢養家及經營家庭，這樣的改變已經造成婚姻中的一種新的關係。

理解力測驗中譯

1. 依據本文，在今日婦女們可能

   (A) 嫁給比她們更年輕的男性。

   (B) 不做家事。

   (C) 不想生小孩。

   (D) **像她們丈夫一樣賺錢養家。**

2. 對二十世紀的婦女而言，照顧小孩的份量

   (A) **比之前幾個世紀要來的短。**

   (B) 比之前幾個世紀要來的長。

   (C) 被認為是非常的長。

   (D) 佔了她們生命中的一大部分。

3. 由本文可以看出在 1900 年時，一般家庭

   (A) **許多孩子在五歲之前死亡。**

   (B) 有七到八個小孩可以活超過五歲。

   (C) 最年輕的小孩都是十五歲。

   (D) 五分之四的小孩在她們五歲時死亡。

4. 當一個在十九世紀末的媽媽超過五十歲時，

   (A) **就算她想要，也不太可能找到一個工作。**

   (B) 不會想要去工作。

   (C) 仍然非常健康美麗。

   (D) 被認為應該在家中休息。

5. 為何現代婦女可能會重新回來找工作？

   (A) 因為當他孩子還小時，她還很年輕。

   (B) 因為她不喜歡照顧小孩。

   (C) 因為她不需要為他小孩的食物煩惱。

   (D) **因為當她小孩夠大可照顧自己時，她還年輕。**

7 歷史 & 人物

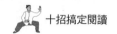

 **本文圖解**

The greatest recent social changes *have been* in the lives of women.

② During the twentieth century there *has been* a remarkable shortening of

the proportion of a woman's life **spent** in caring for children. At the end

分詞片語修飾 life，表示花費在照料小孩的時間

of the nineteenth century, they *would probably have been* in her middle

twenties, and ③ *would be* likely to have seven or eight children, of whom

four or five lived **till** they were five years old. By the time the youngest was

till 於形容詞子句內，表示直到…時間的副詞子句

fifteen, the mother *would have been* in her early fifties and *would expect* to

live a further twenty years, ④ during which custom, opportunity and health

made **it** unusual for her to get paid work. Today women *marry* younger and

it 指後面的 to get paid work

have fewer children. Usually a woman's youngest child *will be* fifteen when

she is forty-five years and is likely to take paid work until retirement at sixty.

Even while she has the care of children, her work *is lightened* by household

appliances and convenience foods.

This important change in women's life-pattern *has only recently begun*

to have **its** full effect on women's economic position. Even a few years ago
　　　　its 指前面的 change in... life

most girls *left* school at the first opportunity, and most of them *took* a full-

time job. However <u>when they married</u>, they usually *left* work at once and

never *returned* to it. Today the school-leaving age *is* sixteen, many girls

stay at school after that age, **and** though women tend to <u>marry younger</u>,
　　　　　　　　　and 是連接第三個句子的對等連接詞

more married women *stay* at work at least until shortly <u>before their first</u>

<u>child is born.</u> Very many **more** afterwards *return* to full- or part-time work.
　　　　　　　more 在此當代名詞用，為更多的人之意

Such changes *have led* to a new relationship in marriage, **with** the husband
　　　　　　　　　　　　　　　　with 在此解釋為隨著…，
　　　　　　　　　　　　　　　　表示在這種情況下
accepting a greater share of the duties and satisfactions of family life and

with both husband and ① wife sharing more equally in providing the money,

and running the home, according to the abilities and interests of each of

them.

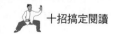

 **單字與片語**

重要單字 Key Vocabularies

① remarkable（adj）顯著的　　　② shortening（n）縮短

③ proportion（n）比例　　　　　④ retirement（n）退休

⑤ lighten（v）減輕　　　　　　⑥ household appliances 家電用品

⑦ convenience（adj）方便的　　⑧ full-time job 全時工作

⑨ afterwards（adv）後來　　　　⑩ satisfaction（n）滿足

重要片語 Key Phrases

❶ paid work　有薪工作　　　　❷ life-pattern　生活型態

❸ at the first opportunity　一有機會，儘早

❹ according to　依據

本文解析

　　本文開始就指出近代婦女在撫育子女佔其一生全部的時間的比例已較以前減少，在十九世紀時因為子女數多，而到小孩可以成年時，婦女的餘命有限且社會也不允許婦女再度去工作，而近代婦女小孩較少，到小孩可以成年時婦女都還能有重新回到工作的機會，而婦女生活型態的重大使其在社會及經濟地位有全面性的改變，也造成婚姻中的一種新的關係。所以本文主題為近代婦女育兒工作對其經濟及社會地位的影響。

　　第一題問今日婦女可能如何，選項前三者在文中並沒提到，另由文中：wife sharing more equally in providing the money...，可知他們也可以跟丈夫一樣賺錢養家。第二題提到二十世紀的婦女而言其照顧小孩的份量如何，由 ... twentieth century... shortening of the proportion of a woman's life... 知比之前幾個世紀要來的短。第三題問 1900 年時，一般家庭如何，需注意題目問 1900 年，但文中是用 nineteenth century，由 ... would be likely to have seven or eight children, of whom four or five lived till they were five years old. 這邊需注意連接詞 till 是直到…為止，該句意思是這些小孩到五歲時還活著的約只有四或五個，所以表示許多小孩在五歲之前就已經死亡了。第四題問一個在十九世紀末的媽媽超過五十歲時如何，由 ... custom, opportunity and health made it unusual for her to get paid work. 知他們不太可能找到一個工作。第五題問為何現代婦女可能會重新回來找工作，這題綜覽本文可知，現代婦女生育數少，照料小孩到可以獨立的時間較以往短，所以後面有較長的時間可以回到職場工作。

學習重點 ➡

　　本文有二處用到介係詞＋關係代名詞的用法：... would be likely to have seven or eight children, of whom four or five lived till they were five years old. 以及 ... live a further twenty years, during which custom, opportunity and health made it unusual for her to get paid work.

　　這是一種閱讀測驗或克漏字填空很喜歡用的句型。其基本上就是關係代名詞及動詞片語運用的概念而來的。使用關係代名詞一定會有先行詞，就是指這個共同的名詞，也就是如果把句子拆成兩句，一定會共同用到一個名詞。例如：

"Pet Plus" is also the place which both you and your pet will love.

拆成→"Pet Plus" is also the place.

　　　　Both you and your pet will love the place.

(the place 是 love 的受詞。合併時，the place 用 which 取代，把 which 提到第一句 place 後面，就成了 "Pet Plus" also the place which both you and your pet will love.)

但如果是以下二句要用關係代名詞來合併成一句：

This is the house. I live in the house.

　　共同的部分是 the house，一樣用 which 取代，但他前面有一個介係詞 in 不能忽略不管，所以就成為 in which，並將他一起放到一般關係代名詞的位置，也就是先行詞之後，關係子句之前。成為：This is the house in which I live。也就是說如果用 in which，拆開第二句一定會有介係詞 in。

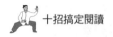
 英文本文

Article 7.4

On April 4, 2010, Apple Inc. launched its eagerly anticipated iPad **amid** great hype. The multimedia computer tablet was the third major innovation that Apple had released over the last decade. CEO Steve Jobs had argued that the iPad was another revolutionary product that could emulate the smashing success of the iPod and the iPhone. Expectations ran high. Even The Economist displayed the release of the iPad on its magazine cover with Jobs illustrated as a biblical figure, noting that,

The enthusiasm of the Apple faithful may be overdone, but Mr. Jobs's record suggests that when he blesses a market, it takes off." The company started off as "Apple Computer," best known for its Macintosh personal computers (PCs) in the 1980s and 1990s. Despite a strong brand, rapid growth, and high profits in the late 1980s, Apple almost went bankrupt in 1996. Then Jobs went to work, transforming "Apple Computer" into "Apple Inc." with innovative non-PC products starting in the early 2000s. In fact, by 2010, the company viewed itself as a "mobile device company." In the 2009 fiscal year, sales related to the iPhone and the iPod represented nearly 60% of Apple's total sales of $43 billion. Even in the midst of a severe economic recession, revenues, and net income both soared. Meanwhile, Apple's stock was making history of its own. The share price had risen more than 15-fold since 2003.

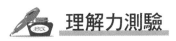 理解力測驗

Q1. According to the passage, what is the closest meaning of "**amid**" in line 1?

(A) adjacent

(B) around

(C) among

(D) all of the above

Q2. Based on the contents, what had Steve Jobs argued about iPad?

(A) The second major innovation that Apple had released over the last decade.

(B) iPad is a desktop device.

(C) Another revolutionary product that could emulate the smashing success of the iPod and the iPhone.

(D) None of the above.

Q3. According to the information, in the 1980s and 1990s "Apple Computer" was best known as its

(A) iPod and iPhone

(B) Apple Computer

(C) Macintosh PC

(D) iPad

Q4. According to the writer, what do we learn about "Apple Inc."?

(A) The company started off as "Apple Computer"

(B) Apple almost went bankrupt in 1996

(C) "Apple Computer" transformed into "Apple Inc." in the early 2000s

(D) All of the above

Q5. According to this article, why did the Economist illustrate Jobs as a biblical figure?

(A) Because Jobs' enthusiasm of the Apple faithful may be overdone.

(B) Because when Jobs favor a market, it ascends.

(C) Because Jobs' expectations ran high.

(D) Because Jobs makes Apple's share price rise more than 15 times.

7

歷史&人物

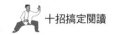
 本文中譯

蘋果的發展

　　2010 年 4 月 4 日，蘋果公司 (Apple Inc.) 在大規模宣傳活動之中推出他們被熱切期待的產品 iPad。此項多媒體平板電腦是蘋果在過去十年中第三項主要的創新產品。執行長史帝夫賈伯斯 (Steve Jobs) 一直認為 iPad 是另一項可以超越非常成功的 iPod 以及 iPhone 的革命性產品。期待是不斷的升高的。甚至經濟學人雜誌 (Economist) 將 iPad 的發表會刊登在該雜誌的封面，將賈伯斯比喻為聖經上的人物，並註明 "對於蘋果忠誠的熱情也許過頭了，但是賈伯斯先生的紀錄卻暗示，當他讚美某個市場時，該市場就會興旺起來。" 該公司以"蘋果電腦"為名開始營運，最著名的是在 1980 年代晚期以及 1990 年代的麥金塔 (Macintosh) 個人電腦產品 (以下簡稱為 PC)。儘管在 1980 年代晚期它是個強勁、快速的成長以及擁有高獲利的品牌，蘋果公司在 1996 年卻幾乎要破產。於是賈伯斯又回到工作崗位，在 2000 年的初期以創新非 PC 的產品的方式將"蘋果電腦"改名為"蘋果公司"。事實上，於 2010 年時，該公司將自己視為一間"行動裝置設備公司。"在 2009 年的會計年度，與 iPhone 及 iPod 相關的銷售額佔了將近蘋果總收入美金 430 億元的 60%。即使在嚴重的經濟衰退中，它的收益與淨收入仍是居高不下。其間，蘋果的股票達到該公司股價的歷史新高。其股價比 2003 年時漲了 15 倍。

理解力測驗中譯

1. 根據本文，下列何意最接近第 1 行的 "amid" ？

   (A) 緊鄰的

   (B) 環繞

   (C) 在…之中

   (D) 以上皆是

2. 根據內容，何者是賈伯斯先生對於 iPad 的評論 ？

   (A) 是蘋果在過去十年中第二項主要的創新產品

   (B) iPad 是一項桌上型電腦裝置

   (C) 另一項可以超越非常成功的 iPod 以及 iPhone 的革命性產品

   (D) 以上皆非

3. 根據本文資訊 "蘋果電腦" 在 1980 以及 1990 年代是以什麼產品著稱 ？

   (A) iPod 與 iPhone

   (B) 蘋果電腦

   (C) 麥金塔 PC

   (D) iPad

4. 根據本文 作者，我們得知關於 "蘋果公司 (Apple Inc.)" ？

   (A) 該公司以 "蘋果電腦" 為名開始營運

   (B) 蘋果公司在 1996 年幾乎要破產

   (C) "蘋果電腦" 在 2000 年的初期改名為 "蘋果公司"

   (D) 以上皆是

5. 依據本文，為何經濟學人雜誌將賈伯斯比喻為聖經上的人物 ？

   (A) 因為賈伯斯對於蘋果忠誠的熱情過頭了

   (B) 因為當他看好某個市場時，該市場就會興旺起來

   (C) 因為賈伯斯的期待是不斷的升高

   (D) 因為賈伯斯使蘋果股價高漲 15 倍

 本文圖解

On April 4, 2010, Apple Inc. *launched* its eagerly **anticipated** iPad amid

過去分詞當形容詞用，
表示被期待的

great hype. The multimedia computer tablet *was* the third major innovation

that Apple had released over the last decade. ② CEO Steve Jobs *had argued*

that the iPad was another revolutionary product that could emulate the

smashing success of the iPod and the iPhone. Expectations ran high. Even

The Economist *displayed* the release of the iPad on its magazine cover

with Jobs **illustrated as** a biblical figure, noting that, "The enthusiasm of

分詞片語，說明 Jobs 是被以⋯的形象來表示

the Apple faithful *may be* overdone, but Mr. ⑤ Jobs's record *suggests* that

when he blesses a market, it takes off." ④Ⓐ The company *started* off as "Apple

Computer," ③ **best known** for its Macintosh personal computers (PCs) in

分詞構句，可視為省略 (which is) best known...

the 1980s and 1990s. Despite a strong brand, rapid growth, and high profits

in the late 1980s, ④Ⓑ Apple almost *went* bankrupt in 1996. Then Jobs *went* to work, ㊵ transforming "Apple Computer" into "Apple Inc." **with** innovative

with 在此意思為
以…的方式

non-PC products starting in the early 2000s. In fact, by 2010, the company

viewed itself as a "mobile device company." In the 2009 fiscal year, sales

related to the iPhone and the iPod *represented* nearly 60% of Apple's

分詞片語修飾 sales，表示與…有關的

total sales of $43 billion. Even in the midst of a severe economic recession,

revenues and net income both *soared*. Meanwhile, Apple's stock *was making*

history of its own. The share price *had risen* more than 15-fold since 2003.

⑦

歷
史
&
人
物

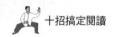

✒ 單字與片語

重要單字 Key Vocabularies

① launched（v）發行；開始　　　② anticipated（v）預期

③ amid（prep.）在…之中　　　④ hype（n）大肆宣傳

⑤ decade（n）十年　　　⑥ revolutionary（a）革命性的

⑦ emulate（v）盡力趕上　　　⑧ overdone（v）做得過分了

⑨ bankrupt（a）破產的　　　⑩ innovative（a）創新的

⑪ fiscal year　會計年度　　　⑫ soared（v）高飛

重要片語 Key Phrases

❶ a biblical figure 聖經人物　　　❷ take off 起飛

❸ start off 出發；開始　　　❹ In fact 事實上

❺ in the midst of 在…之中　　　❻ economic recession 經濟衰退

✒ 本文解析

　　本文開始先提到蘋果公司發表一款新的產品 iPad，賈伯斯認為該項產品將也是一項革命的產品，經濟學人雜誌也認為只要賈伯斯認為好的東西市場就會高度接受。而蘋果電腦公司原來是一家以生產個人電腦起家的公司，但後來幾乎倒閉，賈伯斯重新掌權後，將公司重新定位並改名為蘋果公司，並獲得巨大的成功，在經濟不景氣中，仍表現出亮眼的成績。本文主要就是談到賈伯斯對蘋果公司的貢獻及發展的影響。

　　第一題問到"amid"的意思，這是個介係詞"在…之中"的意思，所以與 among 最接近。第二題問賈伯斯對於 iPad 的評論如何，由 … Steve Jobs had argued that the iPad was another revolutionary product…，知他認為這是一項革命性產品。第三題問蘋果電腦以前是以什麼產品著稱，由 … best known for its Macintosh personal computers (PCs)…，知該公司原來是以個人電腦著稱。第四題問對蘋果公司的敘述，由選項中提到的關鍵字，找到文中的提到的部分比較後，即可得出答案。第五題問為何經濟學人雜誌將賈伯斯比喻為聖經上的人物，比喻為聖經上的人物意思其實就是高度肯定賈伯斯的眼光，也就是說他看好的市場一定不會有錯。

學習重點 ➡

　　形容詞子句（即關係子句）的關係詞在文章中常被省略，讓文章看來簡潔，但非所有狀況都可以省略，不當的省略將造成句意不清。例如本文中：The company started off as "Apple Computer," best known for its Macintosh personal computers (PCs) in the 1980s and 1990s，可視為省略 (which is) best known... 的分詞構句。

　　可以省略關係詞和／或 BE 動詞的情況有下列幾種：

(1) 關係詞在關係子句中當受詞，如 He is the man whom/ that I saw yesterday. （他是我昨天看到的男子）（句中的 whom/that 可以省略）。

(2) 關係詞在關係子句中當主詞，其後接 BE 動詞＋現在分詞或過去分詞，這時可以省略關係詞及 BE 動詞，而留下分詞：

The train now arriving (= which is now arriving) at platform 1 is the 6:36 from Taipei. （現在開抵第一月台的火車是 6 點 36 分從台北開出的）
Food sold (= which is) sold in this supermarket is of the highest quality. （這家超市所販賣的食物都是品質最好的）

(3) 若關係子句中的主動詞為普通動詞，則將這個動詞改為現在分詞，然後省略關係詞，如 Anyone touching (= who touches) these priceless exhibits will be escorted out of the museum. （任何觸摸這些貴重展示品的人都將被請出博物館），但這並不表示所有這類關係子句都可將普通動詞改為現在分詞，然後省略關係詞，如 The girl who fell down the cliff broke her leg. （那位墜落懸崖的女孩摔斷了腿）就不能省略為 The girl falling down cliff....，以免語意不通。

7

歷史&人物

第八招 培養改述能力

　　前面有提過，文章中出現的句子，如果直接出現在答案選項中的時候，往往就算沒有完全理解文章，一樣有辦法答對題目。所以，為了提高鑑別度，出題者會透過使用改述的方式，來達到混淆視聽，增加題目解題難度。所以對有心要追求高分的讀者而言，就必須注意改述句子及觀念的使用，才能真正通過閱讀測驗的考驗。

1. 歸納的改述：利用其他單字或句子，將原本多個句子濃縮歸納成一個句子的方式，這種方式會削弱考題語文章間的連結，需要多轉一道彎才能解題，舉例如下：

　　原文：The city had winter storm conditions all day, with heavy snow and winds and poor visibility. All the city streets were icy and there were many small accidents. Snowplows cleaned some of the snow away, but the piles of snow made driving more hazardous...

　　可能答案選項：There were very poor winter driving conditions.

2. 引導（推論）的改述：對句子或文章一部分進行邏輯或理論性的引申

　　原文：after three years in the position, John was promoted from assistant manager to manger of this department...

　　可能答案選項：the department manager's had been vacant.

3. 運用相似改述：使用意義相近的單字或片語，並保留相似句子的成分來傳達意思，這種方式頗為常見，難度也不算高，平時只需注意同義字詞的使用即可解決，舉例如下：

　　原文：Last week, more than five hundred thousand dollars was raised by the society that provides meals to the homeless population of the city.

可能答案選項：Over five hundred thousand dollars was raised by the organization that provides meals to the people with no homes in the city last week.

認識了題目中的改述問題後，接下來是要怎麼去解決這些題目？其實方法不外是平時多注意同義、反義字及相關片語，另外就是多作改述的練習，例如以下四句中，寫法各異，但只有一句是與其他句子不同的，你能分辨出來嗎：

(A) The factory has been accident free for the least two years.

(B) The last accident in this factory was two years ago.

(C) There have been two accidents in the factory since the least twenty four months.

(D) The plant had an accident on site twenty four months ago.

各位看出來了嗎，(A) (B) (D) 的意思都是該工廠在最近的二年內沒有發生事故，但是 (C) 是指該工廠這最近二年發生二次事故。這種用不同寫法來表達同樣意思的做法，最常出現在閱讀測驗中的下列何者為真 (或為非) 的題目，讓受考者無法一眼即分辨出答案。接下來再看一段練習，這是一句前言後，後面選項中只有依據與該前言描述意思相同，你能分辨出來嗎？

For many people, there seemed to be no escape from poverty.

(A) It seemed that many people could not change their impoverished condition.

(B) Many people found little difficulty in getting rid of poverty.

(C) Many people were poor, and they found no way to get away from the rich.

(D) It seemed that many people found no way to help those poor people.

中譯：對很多人來説，貧窮似乎是無可避免。

(A) 許多人似乎都無法改變他們困頓的情況。

(B) 許多人發現脫離貧窮沒甚麼困難。

(C) 許多人貧窮，而且他們發現無法逃離富人。

(D) 許多人似乎發現無法去幫助那些貧窮的人。

解析：注意以下用語：there seem(ed) to be（某事）... 似乎是；It seem(ed) that ＋ 子句似乎（某事發生）；get rid of 擺脫；get away from 脫逃。答案為 (A)

　　事實上，上述題目是正式的公務員考試英文考題之一，而如果將它放在全篇的閱讀測驗中的一句，就可以考你對這段（句）的理解能力。所以如果能具備良好的改敘能力，對閱讀及理解能力是具有絕對的加分效果的。

　　以下為實際考題，讓我們看看如何因應不同表述法。

As little as thirty years ago, few people questioned the gender roles that had prevailed for centuries. The conventional wisdom was that a woman's place was in the home and that a man's main responsibility to his family was to put food on the table. In the 1970s and 1980s, however, greater numbers of working women meant that men were no longer the sole breadwinners. A father's emotional involvement with his family also became more important. Forty years ago, almost no husbands were present in the delivery room when their wives gave birth. Today, it is generally expected for male partners to attend childbirth classes, to be there for the delivery, and to take more responsibility for child rearing than their fathers or grandfathers did.

In addition to society's changing views of the role men play in relation to childcare, social scientists also found that the presence of the father in the home can contribute to lower juvenile crime rates, a decrease in child poverty, and lower rates of teenage pregnancy. Differences in parenting styles between men and women are also believed to contribute to children's ability to understand and communicate emotions in different ways. The research supports the claim that the absence of a father in the family is the single biggest problem in modern society.

1. Children under the care of both parents develop good ability to communicate emotions because

   (A) there are more conflicts in the family

   (B) there are two breadwinners in the family

   (C) there are two parenting styles in the family

   (D) there are fathers and grandfathers in the family

2. The author would agree that

   (A) the increased number of working women brings about serious problems in childcare

   (B) contemporary men take more responsibility for childcare than their fathers

   (C) a father's emotional involvement with his family is not as important as a mother's

   (D) a mother's emotional involvement with her family is not as important as a father's

這二題都是在考驗改述的理解能力。在第一題的關鍵字為 communicate emotions，由第六行：Differences in parenting styles between men and women are also believed to contribute to children's ability to understand and communicate emotions in different ways. 就是答案所在，但題目中用 two parenting styles in the family 來解釋 Differences in parenting styles between men and women。第二題答案就在 Today, it is generally expected for male partner...to take more responsibility for child rearing than their fathers or grandfathers did. 句中，只是題目中用"現代男人較他們父執輩需擔負較多育兒的責任"，而文中用"今天的男性配偶需較他們父親或祖父輩負擔更多對小孩撫養的責任"。

8

藝術&文化

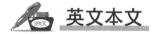 英文本文

Article 8.1

Heritage is something valuable that is passed down from our ancestors and will be passed on to our future generations. Places like the Pyramids of Egypt, the Great Wall of China, the Nazcal Lines of Peru, and the Tower of London are valuable to the world. Such universally significant places make up our world's heritage. The world's heritage refers to sites or places of outstanding universal cultural or natural value. Regardless of the territory on which the world heritage sites are located, they belong to all the people on earth. Therefore, it is in the interest of our international civilization to **safeguard** each site.

These sites are included on the World Heritage List. As of 2010, this list contains 704 cultural, 180 natural, and 27 **mixed properties** in 151 countries, called States Parties. So far, Italy has the greatest number of world heritage sites, with 45 sites on the list.

The Convention Concerning the Protection of the World Culture and Natural Heritage was adapted by UNESCO in 1972.The convention is administered by the UNESCO world heritage committee. A country must first place its important culture and natural properties on the tentative list. Then it selects a property from this list to put into a nomination file. The two bodies, The International Council on Monument and Sites and The world Conservation Union, evaluate this file and make recommendations to the world heritage committee. It is the committee that decides on whether a nominated property should be included on the world heritage list. The committee meets annually to add new sites to or delete sites from the list. It also helps states parties to protect world heritage sites by providing technical or financial assistance upon request.

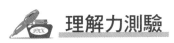 理解力測驗

Q1. Which of the following statements summarizes this article?

    (A) World Heritage Sites are listed by UNESCO and protected because the sites are special, outstanding value to human.

    (B) World Heritage Sites are included on the World Heritage List.

    (C) In 1972 UNESCO adopted the Convention Concerning the Protection of the World Culture and Natural Heritage.

    (D) As of 2010, Italy has the greatest number of World Heritage Sites, with 45 sites on the list.

Q2. This article is mainly about

    (A) a country's heritage

    (B) World Heritage Sites as places of universal cultural or natural value

    (C) how to choose a World Heritage Sites

    (D) the UNESCO World Heritage Sites

Q3. In the second paragraph, the phase "**mixed properties**" refers to

    (A) properties of both positive and negative features.

    (B) real properties

    (C) both natural and cultural properties

    (D) properties that have outstanding value

Q4. As of 2010, how many properties have been recognized by the UNESCO as "outstanding universal value"?

    (A) 180

    (B) 704

    (C) 151

    (D) 911

Q5. In the first paragraph, the word "**safeguard**" means to?

    (A) insure

    (B) lead

    (C) protect

    (D) escort

⑧

藝術＆文化

 **本文中譯**

世界文化遺產

　　遺產是指祖先遺留給我們，而我們日後也會流傳給下一代的珍貴物品。埃及的金字塔、中國的萬里長城、祕魯的那斯卡線及倫敦塔等，都是世界上的寶地。這些舉世聞名的寶地成就了世界遺產。世界遺產指的是擁有全人類公認具特殊意義和普遍價值的文物古蹟和自然景觀。這些世界遺產不論位於哪國領土，都屬於全世界每一個人。因此，保護每個地點也將有利於國際文明世界。

　　這些遺址都被納入「世界遺產名錄」中。就 2010 年來説，名錄中就包含了 704 個文化遺產、180 個自然遺產、27 個文化與自然綜合遺產，這些遺產分佈於 151 個國家，這些國家就稱為締約國。截至目前為止，義大利擁有最多的世界遺產，總共有 45 個地點列在名錄中。

　　1972 年，由聯合國教科文組織通過「保護世界文化和自然遺產公約」。公約的內容由聯合國教科文組織管理，各國家必須先將自己重要的文化和自然遺跡列出，然後從中選定一項放到提名的名單中，再由國際遺址理事會及世界自然保護聯盟來評估個案，並推薦給世界遺產委員會，最後再由該委員會決議提名的遺產是否納入「世界遺產名錄」。委員會每年開一次會，從名錄中增列或減列遺產，並協助締約國保護世界遺產，若有締約國提出要求，便會提供技術或經濟上的協助來保護這些世界遺產。

理解力測驗中譯

1. 下列何項敘述可以總括本文？

(A) **世界遺產為聯合國教科文組織所冊列及保護的，因為這些遺產對人類來說都是特殊且傑出的**

(B) 世界遺產都包含在世界遺產清冊裏

(C) 1972 年，由聯合國教科文組織通過「保護世界文化和自然遺產公約」

(D) 到 2010 年來説，義大利擁有最多的世界遺產，總共有 45 個地點列在名錄中

2. 本文主要關於

(A) 一個國家的遺產。

(B) **世界遺址是普世的文化或自然價值的一些地方。**

(C) 如何選取世界遺址。

(D) 聯合國教科文組織世界遺產

3. 在第二段中的"mixed properties"這個詞指的是

(A) 正面與負面特性的資產。

(B) 真實的資產

(C) **自然與文化資產**

(D) 傑出價值的資產

4. 就 2010 為止，有多少資產被聯合國教科文組織認為是具有"傑出的普世價值"？

(A) 180

(B) 704

(C) 151

(D) **911**

5. 在第一段中，"safeguard"這個字意思是

(A) 保險

(B) 導致

(C) **保護**

(D) 護送

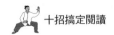
 本文圖解

Heritage *is* something **valuable** that is passed down from our ancestors

修飾 something 的形容詞需置於其後

and will be passed on to our future generations. Places like the Pyramids of

Egypt, the Great Wall of China, the Nazcal Lines of Peru, and the Tower of

London *are* valuable to the world. Such universally significant places *make*

up our world's heritage. The world's heritage *refers* to ② sites or places of

outstanding universal cultural or natural value. Regardless of the territory

on **which** the world heritage sites are located, they *belong* to all the people

which 引導形容詞子句修飾 territory

on earth. Therefore, it *is* in the interest of our international civilization **to**

it 就是指不定詞 to safeguard

safeguard each site.

These sites *are included* on the World Heritage List. ④ As of 2010, this list

contains 704 cultural, 180 natural, and 27 mixed properties in 151 countries,

called States Parties. So far, Italy *has* the greatest number of world heritage

分詞片語，修飾前面的一串名詞，表示都被稱為…

sites, with 45 sites on the list.

The Convention Concerning the Protection of the World Culture and

Natural Heritage *was adapted* by UNESCO in 1972. The convention *is*

administered by the UNESCO world heritage committee. A country must

first *place* its important culture and natural properties on the tentative list.

Then it *selects* a property from this list to put into a nomination file. The two

it 指的是前面的 The convention

bodies, The International Council on Monument and Sites and The world

Conservation Union, *evaluate* this file and *make* recommendations to the

⑧

藝
術
&
文
化

world heritage committee. It *is* the committee **that** decides on whether

it is that... 的句型，強調的是 the committee

a nominated property should be included on the world heritage list. The

committee *meets* annually to add new sites to or delete sites from the list. It

also *helps* states parties to protect world heritage sites by providing technical

or financial assistance upon request.

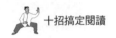

 **單字與片語**

重要單字 Key Vocabularies

① heritage （n）遺產

② ancestor （n）祖先

③ territory （n）區域，領土

④ safeguard （v）保衛

⑤ property （n）財產

⑥ administer （v）管理

⑦ tentative （adj）暫時性的

⑧ nomination （n）推薦，提名

⑨ committee （n）委員會

⑩ council （n）理事會

⑪ monument （n）遺物，紀念

⑫ recommendation （n）推薦

重要片語 Key Phrases

❶ pass down 傳下來

❷ pass on 傳遞下去

❸ make up 組成

❹ regardless of 不管，不顧

❺ as of 截至…

 **本文解析**

　　本文開頭先解釋所謂世界遺產指的是擁有全人類公認具特殊意義和普遍價值的文物古蹟和自然景觀，再來説明目前全世界已經登錄的世界遺址的狀況，最後一段説明如果一個家要申請登錄世界遺址，聯合國教科文組織對相關提出要列入保護的遺產的申請及審查流

程。所以本篇主要講的就是聯合國教科文組織如何保護這些對人類特殊且傑出的遺產,這也是第一題所問的答案。

第二題問到本文主要關於何方面,由本文前面花了許多篇幅解釋世界遺產,並說這些遺產是普世的文化或自然價值的一些地方 (places of outstanding universal cultural or natural value),所以答案以 (B) 最適宜。第三題問 "mixed properties" 這個詞指何者,因為世界遺產有分自然及文化二類,推斷有些應該是屬於混合類的,所以用 mixed properties 來表示。第四題問到 2010 為止有多少被教科文組織認定的遺產,由文中 ... contains 704 cultural, 180 natural, and 27 mixed properties...,而這些文化或自然或混合類都是已經被認定的,所以全部數量相加起來就是答案。第五題問 "safeguard" 這個字意思,它是指守護、護衛之意,所以選項中最接近的為 protect。

學習重點 ➡

一般形容詞都是緊接出現在他們所修飾的名詞或名詞片語之前。但當修飾的是不定代名詞,如 something, someone, anybody 等,則形容詞需置於代名詞的後面。

例如:

Anyone capable of doing something horrible to someone nice should be punished.

Something wicked this way comes.

而有某些形容詞與某些字結合時永遠是後置。

例如:

The president elect, heir apparent to the Glitzy fortune, lives in New York proper.

而在本文中:Heritage is something valuable that is passed down from our ancestors and will be passed on to our future generations. 句中 valuable 修飾 something 故置於其後,而該代名詞又有一形容詞子句修飾,所以該子句置於 valuable 之後,但需注意該子句為修飾 something,非修飾 valuable。

8

藝術 & 文化

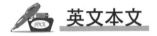 英文本文

Article 8.2

On Easter Sunday, Christians around the world celebrate the Resurrection of Jesus Christ. The Jewish, religious teacher was the son of God. He was executed by the Romans about 2000 years ago. Three days after he had died, he returned to life again and rose to heaven.

Many Christians think that they will also rise to heaven after death. That's why Easter is celebrated with joyful music and symbols of new life, like flowers and new clothes.

The name Easter may come from "Eostre", an Anglo-Saxon goddess. Every year a spring festival was celebrated in her honor. In most Christian churches, Easter is celebrated sometime between March 22 and April 25. It falls on the first Sunday after the first full moon in spring.

Easter marks the end of a time of prayer and fasting that we call Lent. It is believed that during this time Jesus Christ went through the desert for forty days without food.

The last week before Easter is called Holy Week. It begins on Palm Sunday, the day on which Jesus entered Jerusalem. His followers threw palm leaves on the streets. On Holy Thursday, Jesus had his Last Supper with his disciples or followers. The next day, Good Friday, Jesus was nailed to the cross. At 3 o'clock in the afternoon, church services around the world recall the last hours of his suffering.

On Easter morning, resurrection is celebrated. On the evening before, many people take part in processions with candles in the hands. On Easter Day the fasting period is over and people get together with their families and friends and have big meals.

理解力測驗

Q1. What is the topic of the passage?

(A) The Resurrection of Jesus Christ.

(B) The name of "Eostre"

(C) The origin of Easter

(D) The beginning of Holy Week

Q2. Why Easter is celebrated with joyful music and symbols?

(A) Because Jesus Christ was executed about 2000 years ago.

(B) Because they like flowers and new clothes.

(C) Because many Christians think they will rise to heaven after death.

(D) Because Easter marks the end of a time of prayer and fasting.

Q3. According to the passage, when is Easter?

(A) March 22

(B) April 25

(C) The first Sunday after the first full moon in spring

(D) Palm Sunday

Q4. The Christians think Easter to be the end of a time of prayer and fasting because

(A) Jesus crossed the desert for forty days without eating.

(B) Jesus called it Lent.

(C) Jesus returned to life again and rose to heaven.

(D) Jesus was nailed to the cross to die

Q5. According to the article, which of the following statements is correct?

(A) Jesus entered Jerusalem on Holy Thursday.

(B) On Good Friday, Jesus had his Last Supper with his disciples or followers.

(C) Jesus was nailed to the cross at 3 o'clock in the afternoon.

(D) On Easter evening, many people take part in parade with candles in the hands

8 藝術 & 文化

 **本文中譯**

復活節

　　在復活節的星期天，全世界的基督教徒都在慶祝主耶穌基督的重生復活。基督是宗教上的導師也是神之子，他在約 2000 年前被羅馬人處死，死後三天他再度活了過來並升天。

　　許多基督教徒相信他們在死後也將能升天，這也就是為什麼復活節會被以歡樂的音樂、以及象徵新生命的符號的鮮花及新衣來慶祝。

　　復活節的名稱來自於"Eostre"這個字，是一個盎格魯 - 薩克遜的女神。每一年，一場春季的慶典以她為名而慶祝。在大多數基督教堂中，復活節的慶祝大約介於三月 22 到四月 25 日之間來舉辦，它會落在春天第一個滿月的第一個星期天。

　　復活節象徵著一段祈禱時間以及稱為四旬齋的禁食的結束，據信這段期間內，耶穌基督穿越過沙漠而有四十天未曾進食。

　　復活節的前一個週末稱為聖週，它起源於聖枝主日，這天就是耶穌進入耶路撒冷的日子。他的信徒們將棕櫚葉灑在街道上。在聖週的星期四，耶穌與他的信徒及門生享用最後的晚餐，隔一天，也就是耶穌受難日，耶穌被釘在十字架上，在下午三點鐘，全世界的教會服務者都能感受到他受苦的最後一刻。

　　復活儀式是在復活節的早上舉辦，在傍晚時後，許多人會手執蠟燭參加遊行。復活節當天禁食結束，人們與他們的家人朋友團聚在一起並享用大餐。

理解力測驗中譯

1. 本文主旨為何？

　(A) 主耶穌的重生

　(B) "Eostre"名稱的由來

　(C) 復活節的源起

　(D) 聖週的由來

2. 為什麼復活節會被以歡樂的音樂及符號來慶祝？

　(A) 因為耶穌在約 2000 年前被處死。

　(B) 因為人們喜歡鮮花及新衣。

　(C) 因為許多基督徒相信他們死後也能升天。

　(D) 因為復活節象徵一段祈禱及禁食的結束。

3. 依據本文，復活節是何時？

　(A) 三月二十二日

　(B) 四月二十五日

　(C) 春天第一個月圓後的第一個星期日

　(D) 聖枝主日

4. 基督徒認為復活節象徵一段祈禱及禁食的結束是因為

　(A) 耶穌在四十天內未進食而穿過沙漠。

　(B) 耶穌稱它四旬齋。

　(C) 耶穌重新復活並升天。

　(D) 耶穌被釘上十字架而死

5. 依據本文，下列敘述何者為真？

　(A) 耶穌於聖週的星期四進入耶路撒冷。

　(B) 在耶穌受難日，耶穌與他的信徒及門生享用最後的晚餐。

　(C) 耶穌是在下午三點被釘上十字架。

　(D) 在復活節傍晚時分，許多人會手執蠟燭參加遊行

8 藝術 & 文化

 本文圖解

On Easter Sunday Christians around the world *celebrate* the Resurrection of Jesus Christ. The Jewish, religious teacher *was* the son of God. He *was executed* by the Romans about 2000 years ago. Three days <u>after he had died</u> he *returned* to life again and *rose* to heaven.

② <u>Many Christians *think* that they will also rise to heaven after death.</u>

That'*s* why Easter is celebrated with joyful music and symbols of new life, like flowers and new clothes.

The name Easter may *come* from "Eostre", an Anglo-Saxon goddess. Every year a spring festival *was celebrated* in her honor. In most Christian churches Easter *is celebrated* **sometime between** March 22 and April 25.
　　　表示介於…(某段)時間

③ It *falls* on the first Sunday after the first full moon in spring.
　　it 就是指復活節

Easter *marks* the end of a time of prayer and fasting <u>that we call Lent.</u>

④ It *is believed* that during this time Jesus Christ went through the desert for

it is believed…表示據信…

forty days without food.

The last week before Easter *is called* Holy Week. It *begins* on ⑤Ⓐ Palm

Sunday, the day on which Jesus entered Jerusalem. His followers *threw* palm

leaves on the streets. ⑤Ⓑ On Holy Thursday, Jesus *had* his Last Supper with

his disciples or followers. The next day, Good Friday, Jesus *was nailed* to the

cross. ⑤Ⓒ At 3 o'clock in the afternoon church services around the world *recall*

the **last hours of his suffering**.

表示這是耶穌生命前的最後一刻

On Easter morning resurrection *is celebrated*. ⑤Ⓓ On the evening before,

many people *take* part in processions with candles in the hands. On Easter

Day the fasting period *is* over and people *get* together with their families and

friends and *have* big meals.

8

藝
術
&
文
化

單字與片語

重要單字 Key Vocabularies

① celebrate（v）慶祝

② religious（a）宗教的

③ execute（v）執行，處決

④ festival（n）節慶

⑤ fasting（n）禁食

⑥ palm（n）棕梠樹

⑦ disciple（n）門徒

⑧ resurrection（n）復活

⑨ procession（n）遊行

重要片語 Key Phrases

❶ take part in 參加

❷ went through 穿越

❸ in one's honor 為慶祝⋯

 **本文解析**

　　本文開始就指出復活節就是基督教徒慶祝耶穌死後復活的節日。而復活節名稱是來藉由一場在春天舉行的以盎格魯 - 薩克遜的女神 "Eostre" 為名的慶典演變而來，而復活節紀念耶穌進到聖城耶路薩冷到受難這一段時間的經過，所以人們以慶祝復活節來紀念耶穌的重生，且復活節也代表著家人團聚的日子。所以本文主旨就是復活節的源起。

　　第一題問復活節為何會以歡樂的音樂及符號來慶祝，由 Many Christians think…. That's why Easter is celebrated… 可推知復活節會用歡樂的音樂及符號來慶祝是與信仰有關。第三題問復活節是何時？由 It falls on the first Sunday after the first full moon in spring，這個 it 指的就是復活節的日子，而非前面提的 sometime between March 22 and April 25。第四題問為何基督徒認為復活節象徵一段祈禱及禁食的結束，本題需由這兩句話來看：Easter marks the end of a time…. It is believed that…without food，其意思就是用耶穌穿越沙漠未進食而最後來到聖城，所以基督徒用復活節前一段時間的禱告及禁食來紀念耶穌這段時間的經歷。最後一題問敘述何者為非，同樣用每一選項中的關鍵字去找文中的相關地方，就可以比對出來了，但要注意所敘述的時間點是否與文中所述相符，這些錯誤的選項均將時間點以移花接木的方式讓讀者混淆，請參考各題在文章中相關句子標示處。

學習重點 ➡

　　本文是一段有關復活節的源起敘述的文章，而這種文章其中之一的重點就是要注意其發生的時間點。西方國家的節慶多半與宗教有關，且有些日期不是固定西曆的日期，而是以像某季的第一個月圓之後的星期等 (如本文所提復活節)，類似中國的節慶大都以用農曆來訂的意思。所以如果能瞭解一些西洋節慶的發源背景，對閱讀及瞭解相關文章會有很大幫助。例如真正的西洋萬聖節是每年十一月一日，而前一夜也就是十月三十一日夜晚稱為萬聖夜，這又被叫做 "All Hallow E'en"、"The Eve of All Hallows"，最終約定俗成演變成了 "Halloween"。而感恩節 (Thanksgiving Day) 源於 1620 年，五月花號船滿載清教徒到達美洲。當年冬天不少人飢寒交迫染病身亡，而在印第安人幫助下，新移民學會了狩獵、種植玉米、南瓜，並在來年迎來了豐收，所以在隔年秋末他們邀請印第安人一起慶祝並感謝其幫助。美國自 1941 年起訂感恩節為每年 11 月的第四個星期四。

8
藝術 & 文化

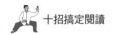

 英文本文

Article 8.3

Emilio Baracco was born in Padua (Italy) in 1946. He attended the Art Institute in Padua, a **pupil** of the goldsmith Mario Pinton and of the sculptor Amleto Sartori. From a young age he attended the latter's atelier and learned the technique of sculpting and creating theatre masks of the commedia dell'arte. From 1963 to 1967 he attended the Accademia di Belle Arti in Venice under the supervision of the sculptor Alberto Viani. He began his artistic activity in 1965 with a collective exhibition at the "Bevilacqua la Masa" art gallery in Venice where he won the prize for sculpture.

His interest in graphics led him to attend, in 1974, the International Course in Technique of Chalcographic Etching in Urbino with Renato Bruscaglia and, in 1976, the Lithography course run by Carlo Ceci. Since 1975, he has collaborated with the Centro Internazionale della Grafica [International Center for Graphics] in Venice. He was invited to the first course for artists at the Scuola Internazionale del Vetro [International Glass School] in Murano, where he worked with Maestro glassmaker Lino Tagliapietra and realized some glass sculptures. He was included in the 1979-9 and 1981-11 issues of the Grafica Italiana Bolaffi. In 1979, he joined the Associazione Incisori Veneti [Association of Venetian Etchers]. He has been included in all the editions of the "Repertorio degli Incisori Italiani [Repertory of Italian Etchers]" of the Gabinetto di Stampe di Bagnacavallo. In 1995, he realized a memorial in Piazzetta Santa Chiara, Padua, dedicated to the fallen police officers of the city. He has collaborated with a number of foundries for the casting of his bronze sculptures and since 2005 has begun a research on microfusion and created small sculptures in silver, medals, and jewels. His works can be found in important public and private collections in Italy, Europe, and the United States.

 理解力測驗

Q1. What does the word "**pupil**" in line 2 refer to?

(A) children

(B) eyes

(C) student

(D) teacher

Q2. According to the passage, what does Mario Pinton do?

(A) Blacksmith

(B) Goldsmith

(C) Silversmith

(D) Locksmith

Q3. Based on the contents, which of the following statements is true?

(A) Emilio Baracco was a pupil of the sculptor Amleto Sartori

(B) Emilio Baracco began his artistic activity in 1965

(C) Emilio Baracco joined the Association of Venetian Etchers in 1979

(D) All of the above

Q4. What do we learn about Emilio Baracco from this article?

(A) He is a teacher

(B) He is an Italian

(C) He is a police officer

(D) He is a goldsmith

Q5. According to the author, in 1995, whom was Emilio Baracco's work dedicated to in Piazzetta Santa Chiara, Padua?

(A) Teachers

(B) Workers

(C) Police Officers

(D) None of the above

8 藝術&文化

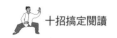
 本文中譯

雕刻大師

　　艾米力歐‧巴洛可於 1946 年生於義大利的帕度亞。他就讀於帕度亞的藝術學院並成為金飾家馬力歐‧平東與雕塑家安姆立托‧薩爾多立的學生。艾米力歐從年輕的時候就加入安姆立托‧薩爾多立的工作室並且學習雕塑的技術，以及製作即興喜劇中所使用的舞台面具。1963 年至 1967 年時他就讀於威尼斯藝術學院並接受雕塑家亞耳貝托‧維安尼的指導。1965 年他開始自己的藝術活動，艾米力歐參加了位於威尼斯的"貝維拉瓜"美術館所舉辦的集體創作展，並在這個藝術活動中獲得了雕塑類的獎項。

　　他在圖像方面的興趣驅使他，於 1974 年加入了由 Renato Bruscagliay 在烏爾比諾所創立的國際銅蝕刻技術課程，並於 1976 年時參加由卡羅‧賽西所主持的平板印刷課程。自 1975 年開始，艾米力歐就與位於威尼斯的國際版畫中心合作。他也受到位於穆拉諾的國際玻璃藝術學校的邀請，為藝術家們教授他們於此校的第一堂課，同時艾米力歐也在此校與玻璃藝術大師 Lino Tagliapietra 一起工作，並且因為他的一些玻璃雕塑作品而受到注目。他也被登錄在第 1979-9 以及 1981-11 期義大利 Bolaffi 平面設計雜誌之中。1979 年他加入威尼斯蝕刻家協會。他也被納入巴卡那卡瓦洛版畫委員會所發行全部版本的義大利雕塑家作品集 [Repertorio degli Incisori Italiani]"之中。1995 年艾米力歐因為創作位於帕度亞的聖嘉勒廣場上，為紀念這個城市殉職的警務人員紀念碑而受到眾人所矚目。他也開始與一些鑄造廠合作鑄造他的銅製雕塑作品，並自 2005 年開始從事微融合的研究，並且創作小型的銀製雕塑、紀念章與珠寶。我們可在位於義大利、歐洲及美國等地許多重要的公立與私人蒐藏中找到他的作品。

理解力測驗中譯

1. 第 2 行的單字"pupil"是何意？

(A) 孩童

(B) 眼睛

(C) **學生**

(D) 老師

2. 根據本文，Mario Pinton 的職業為何？

(A) 鐵匠

(B) **金飾家**

(C) 銀飾家

(D) 鎖匠

3. 根據內容，下列何者敘述為真？

(A) Emilio Baracco 曾經是雕刻家 Amleto Sartori 的學生

(B) Emilio Baracco 於 1965 年展開他的藝術活動

(C) Emilio Baracco 於 1979 年加入威尼斯蝕刻家協會

(D) **以上皆是**

4. 我們於本文中得知關於 Emilio Baracco？

(A) 他是一位老師

(B) **他是義大利人**

(C) 他是一位警察

(D) 他是一位金飾家

5. 根據本文作者，1995 年時 Emilio Baracco 位於 Piazzetta Santa Chiara, Padua 的作品是向誰致敬？

(A) 老師

(B) 工人

(C) **警察**

(D) 以上皆非

8

藝術 & 文化

 **本文圖解**

④ Emilio Baracco *was born* in Padua (Italy) in 1946. He *attended* the

Art Institute in Padua, ② a pupil of the goldsmith Mario Pinton ③A and of

the sculptor Amleto Sartori. From a young age he *attended* the **latter's**

latter 意思是後者，
指 Amleto Sartori

atelier and *learned* the technique of sculpting and creating theatre masks

of the commedia dell'arte. From 1963 to 1967 he *attended* the Accademia

di Belle Arti in Venice **under** the supervision of the sculptor Alberto Viani.

under 在這邊是指在…的監督之下

③B He *began* his artistic activity in 1965 with a collective exhibition at the

"Bevilacqua la Masa" art gallery in Venice **where** he won the prize for

副詞子句，說明這個地點

sculpture.

His interest in graphics *led* him to attend, in 1974, the International

Course in Technique of Chalcographic Etching in Urbino with Renato

Bruscaglia and, in 1976, the Lithography course **run** by Carlo Ceci. Since

此處 run 為過去分詞，為一分
詞片語，修飾 course

1975 he *has collaborated* with the Centro Internazionale della Grafica

[International Center for Graphics] in Venice. He *was invited* to the first

course for artists at the Scuola Internazionale del Vetro [International

Glass School] in Murano, **where** he worked with Maestro glassmaker Lino

where 指這間學校，而非 Murano

Tagliapietra and realized some glass sculptures. He *was included* in the

9-1979 and 11-1981 issues of the Grafica Italiana Bolaffi. ㉚ In 1979 he *joined*

the Associazione Incisori Veneti [Association of Venetian Etchers]. He *has*

been included in all the editions of the "Repertorio degli Incisori Italiani

[Repertory of Italian Etchers]" of the Gabinetto di Stampe di Bagnacavallo. In

1995 he *realized* a memorial in Piazzetta Santa Chiara, Padua, ⑤ **dedicated**

dedicated…為分詞構句，表
示 memorial 是用來獻給…

to the fallen police officers of the city. He *has collaborated* with a number of

foundries for the casting of his bronze sculptures and since 2005 *has begun*

a research on microfusion and *created* small sculptures in silver, medals and

jewels. His works can *be found* in important public and private collections in

Italy, Europe and the United States.

8

藝
術
&
文
化

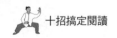

 **單字與片語**

重要單字 Key Vocabularies

① pupil （n) 學生；學徒

② sculptor （n) 雕刻家

③ collective exhibition 聯展

④ lithography （n) 平版印刷術

⑤ glassmaker （n) 玻璃工

⑥ foundries （n) 鑄造廠

⑦ microfusion （a) 微融合

重要片語 Key Phrases

❶ collaborated with 共同合作

❷ worked with 與…共事

本文解析

　　本篇文章是講述一位義大利雕刻家艾米力歐・巴洛的學習過程及後來在雕塑藝術上的成就，內容詳細部份在此不再重複。因為該篇文章背景是義大利，其中有大量的義大利文的人名及地名，念起來可能不習慣，但這可不予以理會，只要把握描述的事件及過程就可以了。

　　第一題問"pupil"的意思，該字有學生及小孩子二種意思，文中顯然是指學生之意。第 二 題 問 到 Mario Pinton 職 業， 由 文 中 ... a pupil of the goldsmith Mario Pinton... 直接可看出來是 goldsmith。第三題問敘述為真者，只要依選項中的年份及人名等關鍵字在文章中找出其出處，就可判斷出答案。第四題關於 Emilio Baracco 的背景，由第一句就可看出他是義大利人。第五題問 Piazzetta Santa Chiara, Padua 的作品是向誰致敬，由 ... dedicated to the fallen police officers of the city. 可知是向殉職的警務人員致敬。

學習重點 ➡

　　本文是關於人物傳記類 (biography) 型的文章，而讀者應該有發現，句子幾乎都是以第三人稱 he 為主詞，其實這是標準傳記類型文章的標準寫法，甚至於我們自己寫有關於自己的傳記時，除最開始說明你自己的身份外 (Dr. Wang is the professor of Taiwan University)，後面的句子也是要用 he (或 she) 來表示自己，也就是將自己當成被介紹的對象，而不是自己介紹自己，這點與我們中文的用法有很大不同。另本文有提及多個年代，不論是藝術家的出生年代、學習藝術的年代或獲得藝術界認可及成就的年代筆者建議讀者遇到出現許多年代的地方要特別注意，題目可能會從中出題來考驗讀者是否能真正瞭解文章。

學習小撇步 (Tips) ➡

　　看文章時，為加快速度，如碰到 " 補充說明 " 的地方，常常可以先忽略不看，並不會影響對文章的認知，而 " 補充說明 " 的地方都是以兩個逗點格開 (, ...,)，這時，如果將注意力專注於文句的主結構，即可充分明瞭句意，並讓閱讀流暢許多。

例如：

His interest in graphics led him to attend, in 1974, the International Course in Technique of Chalcographic Etching in Urbino with Renato Bruscaglia and, in 1976, the Lithography course run by Carlo Ceci. 讀者可試試看將 , in 1974, 及 , in 1976, 這兩個去掉不看會甚麼差別。

8
藝術 & 文化

 英文本文

Article 8.4

Paolo Tosti was born in Gubbio in 1973. He graduated from the Academy of Fine Arts of Perugia specializing in scenic design. He then attended a master class in Fashion Photography in Florence. At this point, he began a series of work collaborations with master photographers. While searching for his own personal interpretive style, he specialized in black and white photography and in the techniques of developing and printing. In 1993, he '**discovered**' infrared film and joined the Italian Association of Infrared Photography. His entrance into the world of professional photography came about in 1997 after he was realized by a number of publicity campaigns for various companies in Italy and several photographic agencies delivered his photos for magazines and newspaper. Since 1999 he have organized and directed the International Festival of Artistic Photography Paese in Photo. He is involved in several photographic project regarding traditions and folkloric events like bull-racing in Pamplona (Spain), Festa dei Ceri, and Palio di Siena in Italy. His artistic works have been displayed in numerous personal and group exhibits: Perugia, Florence, Brescia, Milan, Rome going by way of Copenhagen, Brussels, Dublin, Saint Petersburg, Prague, Villach and all the way across the ocean to New York, Los Angeles, Seattle and Tokyo as well.

理解力測驗

Q1. Regarding the information, what is Paolo Tosti's profession?

    (A) painter

    (B) teacher

    (C) photographer

    (D) director

Q2. According to the article, what did he specialize in?

    (A) fashion photography

    (B) black and white photography

    (C) publicity campaigns

    (D) filmmaking

Q3. What is the meaning of "**discovered**" in line 7?

    (A) covered

    (B) revealed

    (C) undercover

    (D) capped

8

藝術 & 文化

Q4. Based on the information, when did Paolo Tosti enter into the world of professional photography?

    (A) 1993

    (B) 1995

    (C) 1997

    (D) 1999

Q5. In this article, what is the correct description?

    (A) He had attended a master class in Fashion Photography in Florence

    (B) He specialized in black and white photography and in the techniques of developing and printing

    (C) He organized and directed the International Festival of Artistic Photography PaeseinPhoto.

    (D) All of the above

本文中譯

攝影大師

　　保羅 · 托斯第於 1973 年生於古比奧，並且畢業於義大利佩魯賈藝術學院專攻場景設計。接著，他進入位於佛羅倫斯的時尚攝影學院研讀大師講習班的課程。同時，他也開始與攝影大師們進行一系列的合作。在尋找自己的個人闡釋風格時，他沈浸並專攻於黑白攝影以及顯影與印刷的技術。保羅在 1993 年的時候"找到了"紅外線底片並且加入了義大利紅外線攝影協會。開始於一些各類型義大利公司所舉辦的公關活動中對他的認識，以及一些攝影經紀公司將他的攝影作品寄給報章雜誌，保羅 · 托斯第在 1997 年進入了專業的攝影世界。自 1999 年開始，保羅籌畫並指導主題為攝影中的禮讚的國際藝術攝影節。他也參與許多有關傳統與民俗活動的攝影企畫案，例如在西班牙潘普洛納所舉行的奔牛節，義大利的蠟燭節以及賽馬節等等。他的藝術創作也在下列許多的個人與團體展中展出：在義大利的佩魯賈、佛羅倫斯、布雷西亞、米蘭以及羅馬；並經由哥本哈根、布魯塞爾、都柏林、聖彼得堡、布拉格、菲拉赫跨海至紐約、洛杉磯、西雅圖以及東京等地。

理解力測驗中譯

1. 根據本文資訊，Paolo Tosti 的職業為何？

(A) 畫家

(B) 教師

(C) 攝影師

(D) 導演

2. 根據本文內容，他專攻於？

(A) 時尚攝影

(B) 黑白攝影

(C) 公關活動

(D) 拍電影

3. 第 7 行的"discovered"是何意？

(A) 遮蓋的

(B) **揭露的**

(C) 暗中進行的

(D) 覆蓋的

4. 根據資訊，Paolo Tosti 何時進入職業攝影界？

(A) 1993

(B) 1995

(C) **1997**

(D) 1999

5. 本文中下列何者為正確的敘述？

(A) 他曾經在位於佛羅倫斯的時尚攝影學院研讀大師講習班的課程

(B) 他專攻於黑白攝影以及顯影與印刷的技術

(C) 保羅籌畫並指導主題為攝影中的禮讚的國際藝術攝影節

(D) 以上皆是

8

藝術 & 文化

 **本文圖解**

Paolo Tosti *was born* in Gubbio in 1973. He *graduated* from the Academy of

Fine Arts of Perugia specializing in scenic design. ⑤Ⓐ He then *attended* a master

class in Fashion Photography in Florence. At this point ① he *began* a series of

work collaborations with master photographers. **While searching** for his own
                                              分詞句構句，表示當他在尋找…的同時

personal interpretive style, ② he *specialized* in black and white photography

and ⑤Ⓑ in the techniques of developing and printing. In 1993 he *'discovered'*

infrared film and joined the Italian Association of Infrared Photography.

④ His entrance into the world of professional photography *came* about in 1997 after he was realized by a number of publicity campaigns for various companies in Italy and several photographic agencies delivered his photos for magazines and newspaper. Since 1999 ⑤ⓒ he *have organized and directed the International Festival of Artistic Photography Paese in Photo.* He *is involved* in several photographic project **regarding** traditions and folkloric

分詞片語當形容詞，修飾 project，
表示關於某方面的計畫

events like bull-racing in Pamplona (Spain), Festa dei Ceri and Palio di Siena in Italy. His artistic works *have been displayed* in numerous personal and group exhibits: Perugia, Florence, Brescia, Milan, Rome going by way of Copenhagen, Brussels, Dublin, Saint Petersburg, Prague, Villach and all the way across the ocean to New York, Los Angeles, Seattle and Tokyo as well.

 **單字與片語**

重要單字 Key Vocabularies

① interpretive （a）作為說明的　　② infrared （a）紅外線的

③ publicity campaigns　公關活動　　④ folkloric （a）民俗的

本文解析

　　本文主要敘述一位義大利的攝影家保羅・托斯第學習攝影的經過及後來的一些成就及貢獻，文章中提到很多比較不常見的地名，但這點並不會影響對文章內容的理解，只要把這些東西當成一個專有名詞（地名）處理就可以了。

　　第一題問 Paolo Tosti 的職業，由文章中 he... with master photographers 可以清楚看出他是位攝影家。第二題問這位攝影家的專長，由文中 he specialized in black and white photography... 可隻專長是黑白攝影。第三題問 "discovered" 在文中是指何種意思，該文中 discovered 是指發現紅外線攝影方式在攝影藝術上的運用，並不是指他發現紅外線這項科學發現，所以用 reveal（揭露）最恰當。第四題問他進入職業攝影界的時間，關鍵字 professional photography，由文中 ... into the world of professional photography came about in 1997... 可得出答案。第五題問敘述何者為真，將這些選項中的關鍵字，找出在文中出處後即可得到答案，請參考本文圖解中的標示。

學習重點 ➡

　　本篇也是傳記文體，請讀者注意的是時態的用法，主要是過去式與現在／過去完成式的用法。過去式表示事件或狀態發生在過去，從其完成到現在之間有一段間隔（例如本文中 He then attended a master class in Fashion... ）。而現在完成式用來表示開始於過去而延續至今的動作且有可能繼續延續下去或重複性的事件（例如本文中 Since 1999 he have organized and directed the International Festival... ）。這兩種時態的動作都發生在過去，現在完成式強調動作現在的結果，過去式著眼過去的動作或狀態本身。試比較：

I have read this book.（說明我瞭解書的內容。）

I read this book yesterday.（描述昨天做的一件事，與現在無關。）

第九招 利用文義線索瞭解單字

　　做閱讀測驗時，不認識的單字是減緩閱讀速度的殺手，雖然前面提過，就算是文章中有一個或少數單字不懂，只要能掌握上下文的要旨，應該不影響閱讀。然而，如果該單字碰巧是關鍵字時，如何在沒有辦法查閱字典時，靠一些上下文的技巧來"猜"該單字的意思，就可達到充份閱讀的目的。以下提供一些利用文章本身的線索來推測單字意思的小技巧。

1. 運用同義字：文章中有時針對較難懂的字，後面會有相關補充說明，這時好好運用這些說明，就有機會推斷這單字的意思。

　　例：He is the most competent programmer in our company; he is capable of creating a lot of popular programs.

　　　　如果我們不認識 competent 這個字，我們可從其後的子句中找到一個線索 is capable of，這個片語的意思是「有能力勝任」，所以 competent 也是類似的意思。

2. 比較與對比：利用句子中相對關係或因果關係來推斷，並配合句意及一般常識來驗證不懂的單字。

　　例：With all the evidence against Tom being guilty, there would be no chance of acquittal.

　　　　這個句子一般會出現在法律的文件中．前半部是分詞片語，其中有個關鍵字 all(全部) 引導後面的 guilty 有罪的，所以後面的主要子句中 acquittal 的意思大概就是無罪才能讓句意合乎邏輯。

3. 定義或敘述：充分運用句子中本身所隱含的資訊如該單字句中的地位（主詞補語、形容詞形容以知名詞、或同位語等），來推論單字的含意。

例 3: Lin, a poor guy to take all the blame, is the scapegoat of the event.

　　要知道 scapegoat 是什麼意思，可從前面的形容詞片語找到線索，因為這二部分都是來描述 Ben 的現況。a poor guy to take all the blame(接受所有責難的可憐人) 就是 scapegoat (代罪羔羊) 的定義。

4. 語氣與場景：運用文章中，前後段文句的語氣語場景，來判斷該單字的屬性，如正／負面，樂觀／悲觀，積極／消極等作用的用語。

　　例：The streets filled with bellicose protesters. The scene was no longer peaceful and calm as the marchers had promised it would be.

　　從第一句的 protesters(抗議者) 我們可得知，這二句話是在描述抗議的場景，而第二句更明白指出，現場 (the scene) 不平靜，所以我們可想像當時的抗議者一定是火爆又不理性，所以可以推斷 bellicose 應該是與和平 (peaceful) 相反的形容詞 (形容人的好戰及好鬥)。

5. 利用已知單字的字首字尾來推敲未知單字的屬性及大意。這是大家常用來背單字使用的方法，用在閱讀測驗上一樣適用。

　　例：ab- = away, from 等意思的字首，所以 abduct(= lead) 原為引導離開，引伸為綁架之意，而 abnormal 就是脫離標準規範 (norm)、亦即不正常的意思。

　　以下是一篇運用較難單字的文章，我們將重點放在如何運用前面所述的方式來推測其中的單字意思。

⑨ 校園 & 教育

　　In 1349 it resumed in Paris, spread to Picardy, Flanders, and the Low Countries, and from England to Scotland and Ireland as well as to Norway, where a ghost ship with a cargo of wool and a dead crew drifted offshore until it ran aground near Bergen. From there the plague passed into Sweden, Denmark, Prussia, Iceland, and as far as Greenland. Leaving a strange pocket of immunity in Bohemia and Russia unattacked until 1351, it had passed from most of Europe by the mid-1350s. Although the mortality rate was erratic, ranging from one-fifth in some places to nine-tenths or almost total elimination in others, the overall estimate of modern demographers has

settled—for the area extending from India to Iceland—around the same figure expressed in Froissart's casual words: "A third of the world dies." His estimate, the common one at the time, was not an inspired guess but a borrowing of St. John's figure for mortality from the plague in.

　　首先看到 aground 這個字，由句子前面有提到這是一艘鬼船漂流在沿海 (a ghost ship with a cargo...)，而 until it 中的 it 就是指這艘鬼船，後面看到有地名，推斷該子句講的應該是該船漂到到 Bergen 那地方然後怎樣了，再看單字本身為 a-ground，由 ground 為陸地，所以推斷這應該是指船擱淺了 (船碰到陸地)。接下來看到 plague 這個字，由前面的句子無法獲的得足夠資訊，那就先判斷該字為一個東西 (名詞)，而且這是個不好的東西 (因為前面提到這是一條鬼船帶來的東西)，後面提到這東西傳遍了歐洲各地。至此，我們可以大膽提出假設：這個東西很會傳播，且會死人的應該是與疾病有關的東西，那就大概知道應該是瘟疫了。接下來看到 immunity 這個字。由該句意思可知，前面提的這個東西 (瘟疫) 橫掃了整個歐洲，只留下 Bohemia and Russia 沒被攻擊 (unattacked)，再由該字首為 im 可作為"沒有"相關含意的解釋，所以該字應該是以"沒有受到波及"之意來解釋 (而該字就是免疫)。接下來看到 mortality，該字與 rate(比例) 放在一起，所以應該是表示某種東西的比例，句子中間分號，ranging from... others, 的地方就是說明該詞，而其提到這比例從五分之一到幾乎全部滅亡 (almost total elimination)，再由前面已經得到的相關資訊，如該篇是講瘟疫的傳播，所以推斷這應該是指造成死亡的比例 (致死率)。再接下來看到 erratic，該字作為主詞的補語，且由字尾 -tic，推斷該字為形容詞，說明主詞 mortality rate，而前面已經提過分號中說該致死率由五分之一到百分之百不等，且由該詞的字首為 err 開頭，具有分散、不正確的之意，所以推斷該形容詞為"不一定的"之意。接下來看到 demographer，由字尾判斷是指某類的人，由前面 the overall estimate(全面估算)，表示是估算某類東西的人，在由後面提到 A third of the world dies(世界上三分之一的人死亡)，所以推斷該類人應該是指估算世界人口的人，或病理統計學者之類，但在此不會影響閱讀的認知，因為不管是誰，都只是指某種學者的推估之意。

　　以下是全篇翻譯，供讀者參考：

在 1349 年，它由巴黎重新開始，傳播到皮卡第，佛蘭德，以及低地國家，且從英格蘭到蘇格蘭及愛爾蘭和挪威，在那裏一條鬼船帶著一船的原木及死掉的船員們漂浮在外海直到它在靠近卑爾根擱淺。瘟疫從那裏傳進瑞典、丹麥、普魯士、冰島且最遠到格林蘭。剩下一小部份不可思議免疫的地區如波西米亞及俄羅斯沒有受到攻擊直到 1351 年，在 1350 年代中期時它經過大部份的歐洲。雖然致命率是不固定的，某些國家範圍從 1/5 到 9/10 或在其他地區幾乎完全滅絕，現代人口統計學家全面估算已經確定了─從印度延伸到冰島的這個區域─這數值大約與 Froissart's 隨意説的一樣：死了世界上三分之一的人。他的估算，在當時是個一般的估算，不是一個有根據的推測，而是借由約翰啟示錄上的瘟疫的致死率圖表，這在中世紀對人類事件最喜愛的指引。

⑨ 校園 & 教育

 英文本文

Article 9.1

A recent report published by an American education institute shows that more and more foreign students are coming to the US. Colleges and universities recorded over 700,000 students from abroad, a rise of 3% from the previous year. This is mainly because more and more students from China are coming to the US.

The number of 400,000 Chinese students that study abroad sent 120,000 to the US this year, an increase of 30%. The Communist country overtook India as number one, while South Korea comes in third. More and more Chinese middle class families can afford their sons and daughters to study abroad. International education prepares them to become leaders and top managers in their own country. When it comes to getting a good job those who can show foreign qualifications are better off.

The most popular university in America is the University of South California in Los Angeles. Almost 8,000 foreign students study there. Engineering and business management are among the most popular studies that foreign students enroll in. The report also states that more and more young people are coming to American high schools and colleges.

All in all, there are fewer students entering the US from other countries. The report says that this might be the result of the global recession and the international financial crisis of the past few years. Foreigners are becoming popular when it comes to staff jobs at colleges and universities. Over 110,000 scholars work as researchers, teachers, or professors in higher education. There are even some who have become presidents of educational institutions.

The report shows that foreign students in America are a major economic factor. Over all, they contribute about $ 20 billion to the American economy. They spend money on accommodation, books and food. Although most get the funds from their families, they get scholarships from their home countries and, thus, are able to spend more abroad.

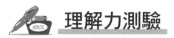 理解力測驗

Q1. What is the best title of this article?

(A) More foreign students coming to study in the U.S.

(B) Chinese middle class students coming to study in the U.S.

(C) Fewer students from other countries entering the U.S.

(D) Foreign students in America being a major economic factor.

Q2. According to the article, what is the main cause of increasing in foreign student number to the U.S?

(A) The government of U.S provides funds for foreign students.

(B) International education prepares foreign students to become leaders.

(C) More and more students from China are coming to the US.

(D) Those who can show foreign qualifications are better off.

Q3. What does the term "**all in all**" means in line 1, paragraph 4?

(A) all in one

(B) all together

(C) all the time

(D) all along

Q4. According to this article, about how many Chinese students came to the U.S last year?

(A) 400,000

(B) 120,000

(C) 90,000

(D) 8,000

Q5. According to this article, which of the following statements is NOT correct?

(A) Fewer students from other countries are entering the US except Chinese.

(B) The global recession and the international financial crisis deter many students from studying abroad.

(C) For the number of students studying in the U.S., India overtook China as the number one.

(D) The most popular universities for foreign students are engineering and business management schools.

9 校園 & 教育

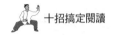

 **本文中譯**

在美的外籍學生

一項最近由美國教育機構所出版的報告指稱，愈來愈多的國外學生進到美國來，且大學及學院記錄顯示有超過每 70 萬學生是來自國外，相較於前一年增加 3%，這主要是因為有愈來愈多從中國學生來到美國。

在這 40 萬中國學生中，有 12 萬 7 千人是今年來到美國的，增加幅度為 30%。這個共產國家超越印度成為第一位，而在此同時韓國名列第三位。愈來愈多中國的中產階級家庭有能力送它們的兒女到國外留學，國際化的教育讓他們在自己的國家中成為領導及高階經理人才，當碰到要找個好的工作時，那些具有國外學歷的人就比較有機會。

在美國最受歡迎的大學是位於洛杉磯的南加州大學，大約有 8 千名國外學生在這邊念書，工程及商業管理是這些外籍學生最多選讀的科系。這篇報告也提到愈來愈多年輕學生進入到美國的高中及大學。

整個來看，從其他國家到美國的外籍學生變少了，這項研究認為這可能是因為全球經濟不景氣及在過去幾年的金融危機所造的。而在大學中的行政工作中，外籍人士變得愈來愈常見，有超過 11 萬的學者從事於研究、教學或是當高等教育的教授，有些人甚至已經成為研究教育機構的首長。

這份報告指出在美國，外籍學生是一個主要經濟因素。整體來說，外籍學生大約對美國經濟貢獻 200 億美金，他們花費在住房書籍以及飲食方面。雖然他們大多數人是從家中獲得經費，他們也從他們國家得到獎學金，因此可以在國外有更多的花費。

理解力測驗中譯

1. 本文最佳標題為何？

(A) **更多的外籍學生到美國念書**

(B) 中國中產階級的學生到美念書

(C) 其他國家愈來愈少學生來到美國

(D) 在美國的外籍學生是一個主要的經濟議題

2. 依據本文，甚麼是使得在美國的外籍學生數目增加的主要原因？

(A) 美國政府提供經費給外籍學生

(B) 國際化的教育讓外籍學生成為領導者

(C) **愈來愈多中國學生進到美國**

(D) 那些有國外文憑的人會有較好的待遇

3. 第四段第一行中的"all in all"是甚麼意思？

(A) 合而為一

(B) **從各方面來說**

(C) 總是

(D) 一直

4. 依據本文，去年約有多少中國學生來到美國？

(A) 400,000

(B) 120,000

(C) **90,000**

(D) 8,000

5. 根據本文，下列敘述何者為非？

(A) 除中國以外，有愈來愈少的外國學生來到美國。

(B) 全球不景氣及國際金融危機使許多學生無法出國念書。

(C) **就在美國念書的學生人數而言，印度超越中國成為世界第一位。**

(D) 外籍學生最喜歡的學院是有關工程及商業管理。

9
校園 & 教育

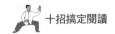

 本文圖解

A recent report **published** by an American education institute *shows*
過去分詞片語，修飾 report，表示被出版之意

that more and more foreign students are coming to the US. Colleges and

universities *recorded* over 700,000 students from abroad, a rise of 3% from

the previous year. ② This *is* mainly because more and more students from

China are coming to the US.

Of the 400,000 Chinese students that study abroad ③ it *sent* 120,000 to
of 為在…之中的意思　　　　　　　　　　　it 指 China

the US this year, an increase of 30%. ⑤ⓒ The Communist country *overtook*

India as number one, while South Korea *comes* in third. More and more

Chinese middle class families *can afford* sending their sons and daughters to

study abroad. International education *prepares* them to become leaders and
prepare 解釋為使…具備

top managers in their own country. **When it comes to** getting a good job
解釋為當談到…

those who can show foreign qualifications *are* better off.

The most popular university in America *is* the University of South California

in Los Angeles. Almost 8,000 foreign students *study* there. ⑤ⅅ Engineering and business management *are* among the most popular studies that foreign

students enroll in. The report also *states* that more and more young people

are coming to American high schools and colleges.

All in all, ⑤Ⓐ there *are* fewer students entering the US from other

countries. The report *says* that ⑤Ⓑ **this** might be the result of the global

this 指的是前面 there are... countries 這段話

recession and the international financial crisis of the past few years.

Foreigners *are becoming* popular **when it comes** to staff jobs at colleges

意思是：當一提到…

and universities. Over 110,000 scholars *work* as researchers, teachers or

professors in higher education. There *are* even some who have become

prests of educational institutions.

⑨ 校園 & 教育

The report *shows* that foreign students in America are a major economic

factor. Over all, they *contribute* about $ 20 billion to the American economy.

They *spend* money on accommodation, books and food. Although most get

the funds from their families, they *get* scholarships from their home countries

and, thus, *are able to* spend more abroad.

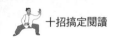

 **單字與片語**

重要單字 Key Vocabularies

① institute（n）學會，機構

② previous（adj）前面的

③ communist（n）共產主義者

④ recession（n）衰退

⑤ staff jobs 行政工作

⑥ scholar（n）學者

⑦ accommodation（n）居住

⑧ scholarship（n）獎學金

重要片語 Key Phrases

❶ better off 情況較好的

❷ all in all 從各方面來說

❸ enroll in 加入

❹ over all 總的，全部的

 **本文解析**

　　本文開始就提到愈來愈多的國外學生進到美國來，而主要是因為中國學生增加所致，中國中產階級將小孩送到美國接受教育，讓未來找工作更有機會。而其他國家的學生來到美國念書的人數變少的原因是因為全球經濟不景氣，這些學生後來也進入到相關教育機構任職。而外籍學生在美國念書，同時也對美國的經濟做出貢獻。所以本篇文章主題是講美國外籍學生增加原因及對美國的影響，所以標題以更多的外籍學生到美國念書較恰當。

　　第二題問美國外籍學生數目增加的主要原因，由文章中 ... mainly because more and more students from China are coming to the US，可知原因是因為中國學生人數增加。第三題問"all in all"的意思，該片語表示"從各方面來說"，所以以選項中的 all together 最接近。第四題問去年約有多少中國學生來到美國，這題需要稍微注意一下，因為在本文中是用 ... it sent 120,000 to the US this year, an increase of 30%. 表示今年的 12 萬人是增加 30% 後的人數，所以去年應該是要少於這個數才合理，且其幅度為 30%，但是讀者不需要真的去運算，因為這不是考數學，只要從選項中將不合理的數自去掉就行了，40 萬太大，8 千太少，12 萬是今年的數字，所以答案就是約 9 萬人。第五題是細節題，要選敘述為非者，該四個選項均有經過與原文中的句子改寫過，讀者請自行參考。

學習重點 ➡

　　文章中常可遇到動詞後面需用動名詞或不定詞當動詞受詞的情形，一般而言，以不定詞當動詞的受詞，意思為實現未來意向的動作，為較積極性的含意，而如果接動名詞的話，則為實現過去意向動作之消極性含意。

1. 後面需接不定詞作為受詞之動詞

　　afford, agree, aim, arrange, ask, claim, dare, decide, decline, desire, determine, except, expect, fail, guarantee, hesitate, hope, learn, manage, mean, offer, plan, prepare, pretend, promise, refuse, seek, take, want, wish⋯等動詞後面需接不定詞。

　　例句：He managed to complete the sales report.(他設法完成銷售報告。)

　　　　　Cindy refused to have dinner with her supervisor.

　　　　　(莘蒂拒絕與她的上級長官吃飯)

2. 後面需接動名詞作為受詞之動詞

　　admire, afford, appreciate, avoid, consider, delay, deny, discontinue, dislike, enjoy, escape, finish, forgive, mind, miss, permit, postpone, practice, prohibit, quit, recommend, regret, spend, suggest, resist,⋯等動詞後面需接動名詞。

　　例句：She finally gave up drinking.(她最後戒酒了。)

3. 後面可接動名詞或不定詞作為受詞之動詞

　　attempt, begin, cease, commence, continue, decline, dare, intend, like, love, mean, need, neglect, plan, prefer, propose, stop, remember, try⋯等動詞後面需可接動名詞或不定詞，但意思可能會有不同，一般而言，接不定詞表示「接下來要作的事」，而接動名詞表示「已經做過的事」。

4. 需注意分辨 to 在詞句中 是表示不定詞的 to ＋原形動詞，或是 to 為介係詞用。

　　例如：When it comes to getting a good job those who can show foreign
　　　　　qualifications are better off.

　　　　　when it come to 表示在說到⋯情況的時候，或當提到⋯的時候，這時 to 是個介係詞，所以後面碰到動詞需用動名詞 (V ＋ ing)，而非是 to ＋原形動詞。

⑨
校園＆教育

 英文本文

Article 9.2

For the drawing education during Japanese Colonial period, the landscape painting of colored drawing of buildings had a significant influence on the main island's folk art. In general, the main island's folk art tradition is inherited from the local characteristics in Fujian and Guangdong areas of mainland China. However, after the First Sino-Japanese War in 1895, Japan began colonizing the main island, and also gradually reformed the education system, language, habit, custom, and religion that existed in the main island from ancient times. Moreover, during this period, the most significant influence on the main island's folk art was the implementation of painting education. In 1912, elementary school students began to take painting class. It emphasized not only the inspiration of children's intelligence, but also the learning of the basic pattern and **perspective** drawing technique which means the cultivation of their observation ability. In addition, these elements can be considered as integrating the basis of western painting into the painting education, and then become one of the key factors to change the main island's folk art style during Japanese colonial period.

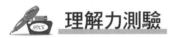 理解力測驗

Q1. According to the contents, generally where did the main island's folk art tradition come from?

(A) Japan

(B) Fujian and Guangdong

(C) Korea

(D) None of the above

Q2. Which of the following description is NOT true?

(A) The First Sino-Japanese War occurred in 1895.

(B) In Japanese Colonial period period, the implementation of painting education was the most significant influence on the main island's folk art.

(C) These elements can be considered as integrating the basis of eastern painting into the painting education.

(D) In 1912, The main island's elementary school students began to have painting class.

Q3. According to the author, what kind of capability does the cultivation for perspective imply in drawing technique?

(A) basic pattern

(B) observation ability

(C) intelligence

(D) all of the above

Q4. In this passage, what does the word "**perspective**" in line 10 mean?

(A) picture

(B) see through

(C) aspect

(D) all of the above

Q5. What do we learn from this article?

(A) In Japanese Colonial period, the landscape painting of colored drawing for buildings had a significant influence on the main island's folk art

(B) In Japanese Colonial period, Japan gradually reformed the main island's education system, language, habit, custom and religion

(C) In Japanese Colonial period, the learning of the basic pattern and perspective drawing technique was the cultivation of students' observation ability

(D) All of the above

9

校園 & 教育

 本文中譯

建築彩繪的風景畫對於台灣民間藝術影響

　　在日治時期的圖畫教育之中，建築彩繪的風景畫對於本島民間藝術有顯著的影響。一般來說，本島民間藝術的傳統是承襲中國閩粵地區的地方特色。但是在 1895 年中日甲午戰爭之後，日本開始殖民本島，並對於本島自古以來的教育制度、語言、習慣、風俗、信仰進行逐步的改革。此外，在此時期對於本島民間藝術影響最鉅的莫過於圖畫教育的施行。1912 年，本島小學生開始上圖畫課，此時期不但重視兒童智能的啟發，且學習基本圖案及透視圖的技巧，也就是觀察力的培養。而這些元素可說是將西洋繪畫的基礎放置於圖畫教育內，成為日治時期本島民間藝術風格轉變的重要因素之一。

 理解力測驗中譯

1. 根據本文內容，一般來說本島民間藝術的傳統是承襲自何地？

(A) 日本

(B) 福建與廣東

(C) 韓國

(D) 以上皆非

2. 下列敘述何者為非？

(A) 中日甲午戰爭發生於 1895

(B) 在日治時期，對於本島民間藝術影響最鉅的莫過於圖畫教育的施行

(C) 這些元素可說是將東方繪畫的基礎放置於圖畫教育內

(D) 1912 年本島小學生開始上圖畫課

3. 根據本文讀者，透視圖的技巧意味為何者能力的培養？

(A) 基本圖案

(B) 觀察力

(C) 智力

(D) 以上皆是

4. 在本文中，第 10 行的單字 "perspective" 是何意？

　(A) 圖畫

　(B) 看穿

　(C) **觀點**

　(D) 以上皆是

5. 我們可由本文得知？

　(A) 在日治時期，建築彩繪的風景畫對於本島民間藝術有顯著的影響

　(B) 在日治時期，日本逐步改革本島的教育制度、語言、習慣、風俗以及信仰

　(C) 在日治時期，基本圖案及透視圖技巧的學習，是學生觀察力的培養

　(D) **以上皆是**

 **本文圖解**

For the drawing education during Japanese Colonial period, the
for 在此為就…方面而言

landscape painting of colored drawing of buildings *had* a significant

influence on the main island's folk art. In general, ① the main island's folk art

tradition *is* inherited from the local characteristics in Fujian and Guangdong

areas of mainland China. However, after ②Ⓐ the First Sino-Japanese War in

1895, Japan *began* colonizing the main island, and also gradually *reformed*

the education system, language, habit, custom and religion **that** existed in
　　　　　　　　　　　　　　　　that 子句形容前面的 education
　　　　　　　　　　　　　　　　system... 等五個先行詞

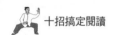
the main island from ancient times. Moreover, during this period, ⑳B the most

significant influence on the main island's folk art *was* the implementation

of painting education. ⑳D In 1912, elementary school students *began* to

take painting class. It *emphasized* not only the inspiration of children's

　　　　　　　　　　　　it 指的是 take painting class 這件事

intelligence, but also ③ the learning of the basic pattern and perspective

drawing technique **which** means the cultivation of their observation ability.

　　　　　　　　which 指的是前面提到 the learning...
　　　　　　　　drawing technique 這件事

In addition, ⑳C these elements can *be considered* as integrating the basis of

western painting into the painting education, and then *become* one of the

key factors to change the main island's folk art style during Japanese colonial

period.

 單字與片語

重要單字 Key Vocabularies

① colonial（a）殖民的　　　② characteristics（n）特色

③ intelligence（n）智力　　　④ cultivation（n）培養

 **本文解析**

　　本文一開始提到日治時期的建築彩繪風景畫對於本島民間藝術有顯著的影響，這就是本文的主旨，之後提到日本殖民統治對台灣島內的風俗生活習慣等進行改革，而小學生也在這時開始學習西洋式的相關繪畫技巧，進而成為該時期台灣繪畫藝術風格轉變的原因之一。

　　第一題問台灣民間藝術的傳統是承襲自何地，由文中第三行可看到 ... folk art tradition is inherited from the local...Fujian and Guangdong areas...，可知識傳承自福建廣東地區，要注意 come from 意思是來自於。第二題為細節題，問何者為非，可用選項內的關鍵字找到文內相關內容即可得出答案。第三題問透視圖的技巧為何者的培養，需注意的是這個題目的問法，imply 的意思是"意指"，而由 ... perspective drawing technique which means the cultivation of their observation ability. 可知學習基本圖案及透視圖的技巧可培養觀察力。第四題問單字"perspective"，該字是"透視"的意思，所以與 see through（看穿）最接近。第五題問何者是本文所提到的，各項敘述均有在文中出現，答案為以上皆是，讀者可以自行參閱。

學習重點 ➡

　　介係詞的使用是台灣學生的一大頭痛問題，特別是中文要表達在…地方、時間、地點、方位等等意思時，只需用一個"在"便解決一切，但英文中表示"在…"的意思卻需要依據不同情況考量，才能決定用 in、on 或 at。以下簡單說明這三個介係詞的基本概念：

1. 當用於指時間時

　　at 來指定特定的時間：The train is due at 12:15 p.m.

　　on 來指定日期：My brother is coming on Monday.

　　in 指定一天、一月、一季或一年中非特定的時間：

　　例如：He started the job in 1971.

　　　　　He's going to quit in August.

2. 當用於指地點時

　　at 來指定特定的地址：Grammar English lives at 55 Boretz Road in Durham.

　　on 來指定街道等名稱：Her house is on Boretz Road.

　　in 來指定陸地區域（鄉鎮、縣市、州省、國家和洲）：

9 校園 & 教育

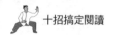
 英文本文

Article 9.3

Why then, do I teach?

I teach because I like the pace of the academic calendar. June, July, and August offer an opportunity for reflection, research, and writing.

I teach because teaching is a profession built on change. When the material is the same, I change-and, more importantly, my students change.

I teach because I like the freedom to make my own mistakes, to learn my own lessons, to stimulate myself and my students. As a teacher, I'm my own boss. If I want my freshmen to learn to write by creating their own textbook, who is to say I can't?

Such courses may be huge failures, but we can all learn from failures.

I teach because I like to ask questions. While teaching, I sometimes find good questions.

I teach because I enjoy finding ways of getting myself and my students out of the ivory tower and into the real world. I once taught a course "Self-Reliance in a Technology Society". My 15 students read Emerson, Thoreau, and Huxley. They kept diaries. They wrote term papers.

But we also set up a corporation, borrowed money, purchased a **run-down** house and practiced self-reliance by renovating it. At the end of the semester, we sold the house, repaid our loan, paid our taxes, and distributed the profits among the group.

So teaching gives me pace, and variety, and challenge, and the opportunity to keep on learning.

(abstracted from Why I Teach by Peter G. Beidler)

理解力測驗

Q1. According to the contents, the author prefers to?

    (A) To set up a company

    (B) To make profits

    (C) To be a teacher

    (D) To renovate houses

Q2. Which of the following is NOT a reason why the author teaches?

    (A) Because he likes the pace of the academic calendar.

    (B) Because he thinks that teaching is a profession built on change.

    (C) Because he likes the freedom to make his own mistakes.

    (D) None of the above

Q3. Based on the contents, who is the author?

    (A) an elementary school teacher.

    (B) a junior high school teacher.

    (C) a high school teacher.

    (D) a university teacher.

Q4. The word "**run-down**" in line 16 means?

    (A) broke down

    (B) new

    (C) energized

    (D) refresh

Q5. Who will be interested in responding to this article?

    (A) female readers

    (B) male readers

    (C) students

    (D) teacher wannabe

9 校園 & 教育

 本文中譯

為何要教書

那麼為什麼我要教書呢？

我教書是因為我喜歡學校行事曆的進度。每年6月、7月及8月提供一個讓我自己反省、研究以及寫作的機會。

我教書是因為教學是建立於改變的一種職業。當教材沒變，但我會改變，更重要的是我的學生也會改變。

我教書是因為我喜歡自由的，犯我自己的錯誤，學習我自己的課業，激發我自己與我的學生。身為一個老師，我是我自己的主人。如果我要求我的新生們，由他們自己所創造出的教科書來學習寫作，誰說我不能這樣做呢？

這樣的課程也許會是非常的失敗，但是我們都能從失敗中來學習。

我教書是因為我喜歡發問。當我在教學中，有時候會發現一些非常好的問題。

我教書是因為我享受於發現方法，以將我自己和我的學生們帶出象牙塔而進入這個真實的世界中。有一次，我教授一堂名為"在一個科技社會中自力更生"的課程，我的15位學生們閱讀了愛默生，梭羅以及赫胥黎等大師的作品。他們寫下日記及學期研究報告。然而我們也設立了一間公司，借了些錢買了一間破舊的房子，並重新整修來體驗自力更生。在學期末時我們賣掉了這間房子，支付完我們的借款，並且把獲得的盈餘分給組員。

所以，教書給予我道路，多樣化和挑戰，以及持續學習的機會。

（摘錄自 Peter G. Beidler 的 Why I Teach）

理解力測驗中譯

1. 根據本文內容，作者喜歡？

    (A) 設置公司

    (B) 賺取利潤

    (C) **當老師**

    (D) 整修房子

2. 下列何者不是作者為何教書的原因？

    (A) 因為他喜歡學校行事曆的進度

    (B) 因為他認為教書是建立於改變的一種職業

    (C) 因為他喜歡可以犯錯誤的自由

    (D) **以上皆非**

3. 根據本文內容，作者為什麼人？

    (A) 小學老師

    (B) 國中老師

    (C) 高中老師

    (D) **大學老師**

4. 第 16 行的"run-down"是何意？

    (A) **破損**

    (B) 新穎

    (C) 有活力

    (D) 更新

5. 下列何者會對本文有興趣？

    (A) 女性讀者

    (B) 男性讀者

    (C) 學生

    (D) **想當老師的人**

9
校園 & 教育

 本文圖解

Why **then**, do I *teach*?
　　 then 在此意思為那麼

I *teach* ㉒Ⓐ because I like the pace of the academic calendar. June, July, and

August *offer* an opportunity for reflection, research, and writing.

I *teach* because ㉒Ⓑ teaching is a profession **built** on change. When the
　　　　　　　　　　　　　　　　 過去分詞片語修飾 profession，
　　　　　　　　　　　　　　　　 意思為根植於…
material is the same, I *change*-and, more important, my students *change*.

I *teach* because ㉒Ⓒ I like the freedom **to make** my own mistakes, **to learn**
　　　　　　　　　　　　　 三個不定詞片語修飾 freedom...

my own lessons, **to stimulate** myself and my students. As a teacher, I'*m*

my own boss. If I want my freshmen to learn to write by creating their own

textbook, who *is* to say I can't?

Such courses *may be* huge failures, but we *can all learn* from failures.

I *teach* because I like to ask questions. While teaching, I sometimes *find*

good questions.

I *teach* <u>because I enjoy finding ways of getting myself and my students</u>

<u>out of the ivory tower **and into** the real world.</u> I once *taught* a course "Self-

連接詞 and 連接 get... out of 及 get... into，
但第二個 get 省略

Reliance in a Technology Society". My 15 students *read* Emerson, Thoreau,

and Huxley. They *kept* diaries. They *wrote* term papers.

But we also *set* up a corporation, *borrowed* money, *purchased* a run-

down house and *practiced* self-reliance by renovating it. At the end of the

semester, we *sold* the house, *repaid* our loan, *paid* our taxes, and *distributed*

the profits among the group.

So teaching *gives* me pace, and variety, and challenge, and the

opportunity to keep on learning.

(abstracted from Why I Teach by Peter G. Beidler)

 單字與片語

重要單字 Key Vocabularies

① pace (n) 步伐；進度

② reflection (n) 反省

③ profession (n) 專業；職業

④ stimulate (v) 激勵；刺激

⑤ ivory tower 象牙塔

⑥ Self-Reliance (n) 自立更生

⑦ run-down (n) 破敗的；失修的

⑧ renovating (v) 更新；改善

⑨ variety (n) 多樣性

⑩ challenge (n) 挑戰

重要片語 Key Phrases

❶ get... out of 從…離開

❷ set up 設置

❸ keep on 持續做…

本文解析

　　本篇是一位作家的文章節錄。主題從第一句話就可以看出來這是一篇有關於為何喜歡教書的文章，文中詳列了一些作者喜歡從事教學工作的原因及理由，因為其為散文文學作品，故沒有嚴謹的結構，但最後作者還是給了結論，那就是書給予我道路，多樣化和挑戰，以及持續學習的機會。

　　第一題問作者喜歡甚麼，答案很清楚是當老師教書。第二題問何者不是作者喜歡教書的原因，選項中各項均能在文中找到相關敘述，所以都是喜歡的理由。第三題問作者是哪類老師，從文中 ... getting myself and my students out of the ivory tower and into...，一般用象牙塔表示大學的學術環境，所以可以推論作者是大學老師。第四題問片語 "run-down" 在文中的意思，run-down 為用完、耗盡的意思，在文中用來描述 house，故應該是指破敗的 (房子) 之意。第五題問何者會對本文有興趣，因為全篇講的是喜歡從事教職的原因，所以對想當老師的會有興趣。

學習重點 ➡

　　本篇文章使用大量的 I teach because ＋子句的句型，這是一種非常簡單並常用的句型，表示對於一件事情的因果關係的描述，讀者可充分運用於寫作中。另外，本文句型構造雖然簡單，然而在有些單一句子中使用多個動詞或受詞等用法，使句子看起來有些異於一般性文章要求簡潔有力用語，但這是一般文學作品常見的用法，只要瞭解句子結構就好。

例如：

I teach because I like the freedom **to make** my own mistakes, **to learn** my own lessons, **to stimulate** myself and my students.

→ to make，to learn，to stimulate 三個不定詞片語共同修飾名詞 freedom

But we also **set up** a corporation, **borrowed** money, **purchased** a run-down house and **practiced** self-reliance by renovating it.

→ set up，borrowed，purchased 及 practiced 四個動詞用於單一句子中。

So teaching gives me **pace**, and **variety**, and **challenge**, and the **opportunity** to keep on learning.

→ pace，variety，challenge，opportunity 四個名詞同時當雙賓動詞 give 的直接受詞。

⑨
校
園
&
教
育

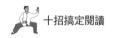
 英文本文

Article 9.4

A research report says that virtual worlds can be important places where children practice what they will do in real life. They are also a powerful and attractive alternative to more passive adventures like watching TV. The research was done with children using the BBC's Adventure Rock virtual world, aimed at those aged 6-12. It surveyed and interviewed children who were the first to test the game.

The online world is a theme island built for the BBC's children channel by Belgian game maker Larian. Children explore the world alone, but they use message boards to share what they find and what they do in the different creative studios, and what they find around the virtual space.

At times children were explorers and at others they were social climbers eager to connect with other players. Some were power users looking for more information about how the virtual space really worked. The children could try all kinds of things without having to be afraid of the consequences that would follow if they tried them in the real world. They learned many useful social skills and played around with their identity in ways that would be much more difficult in real life.

According to the study what children liked about virtual worlds was the chance to create content such as music, cartoons, and videos.

The publishers of the report say that virtual worlds can be a powerful, engaging and real interactive alternative to more passive media. They **urged** creators of virtual spaces for children to get young people involved very early on because they really do have good ideas to add and they are very good critical friends.

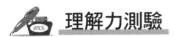 **理解力測驗**

Q1. Virtual worlds can be important places for children because

(A) they can watch TV.

(B) they can use the BBC's Adventure Rock virtual world.

(C) they can practice what they will do in real life.

(D) they can be the first to test the game.

Q2. Who is Larian?

(A) a game player

(B) a BBC's programmer

(C) a game maker

(D) a online Belgian write

Q3. What is true about "the online world"?

(A) Children always explore the world with others.

(B) It is a theme island built for the BBC's adventure channel.

(C) Children could try all kinds of things without worrying about the results in the real world life.

(D) Children can't tell others what they find and what they do in the virtual space.

Q4. The term "**urged**" in line 3, paragraph5 probably means

(A) pleaded

(B) argued

(C) deny

(D) acknowledge.

Q5. According to the article, we can know that

(A) Children liked real worlds for the chance to create content.

(B) Passive media is more powerful, engaging and real interactive alternative to more virtual worlds.

(C) Creators of virtual spaces must find younger involved very early because they are crucial.

(D) Children learned many useful social skills through virtual worlds.

9

校園 & 教育

本文中譯

虛擬世界

　　有一項研究顯示讓在小孩子在虛擬世界中練習真實生活是重要的，相較於一些被動方式如看電視而言，它是一項有用且具有吸引力的替代品。這項研究是讓小孩子經由使用 BBC 的探索搖滾虛擬世界來進行的，主要針對那些 6-12 歲的孩童來作的，並訪談這些第一次測試這項遊戲的孩童。

　　這線上世界是一個主題島，它是由比利時的遊戲製作人 Larian 為 BBC 的兒童頻道所創設的。兒童們單獨探索這世界，但他們可以在虛擬空間中所發現具有不同的想像力的工作室內，用訊息板來分享他們發現及所做的事。

　　孩子們有時候會是探索者，而其他時候他們會是渴望去與其他玩者連結的社交攀附者，有些則是權力的使用者，他們找尋更多如何在虛擬空間運作真正有用的資訊。這些孩子可以做各式各樣的嘗試，而不需擔心如果他們在真實社會做這些事的後果。他們學習到許多技能，並且用一些在現實社會中會比較難做到的方式表現出他們的獨特性。

　　依據這項研究，小孩子對虛擬世界最感到喜愛的，就是有機會可以創造出一些東西，例如像音樂、卡通及影像。

　　這項報告的發表者說，虛擬世界是一種有用的、吸引人的、且對多數被動媒體來說是真正互動的替代品。他們強力主張給小孩子的虛擬空間創造者在初期就要讓年輕人來參與，因為他們確實有許多好主意可以加入其中，且是非常好的良師益友。

理解力測驗中譯

1. 虛擬世界對小孩很重要是因為

(A) 他們可以看電視

(B) 他們可以使用 BBC 的搖滾探索虛擬世界

(C) 他們可以練習那些在真實世界要做的事

(D) 他們可以當第一個試玩遊戲的人

2. 誰是 Larian ?

(A) 一個遊戲玩家

(B) BBC 的節目製作人

(C) 一個遊戲創作人

(D) 比利時的線上作家

3. 有關"線上世界"何者為真?

(A) 孩子們都可以總是與其他人探索世界。

(B) 它是一個為 BBC 的探索頻道創設的主題島。

(C) 孩子們可以嘗試各種事情而不用擔心在真實社會中會有何後果。

(D) 在虛擬世界中孩子們不可告訴其他人它們發現甚麼或他們要作甚麼。

4. 再第六段第二行中"urged"這個字可能意味著?

(A) 請求

(B) 爭論

(C) 否認

(D) 認同

5. 依據本文,我們可以知道

(A) 孩子們喜歡真實世界因為有創造東西的機會

(B) 被動的媒體比起虛擬世界是更有力量、活力及互動的替代品。

(C) 虛擬空間的創造者必須要去找很早就涉入的年輕人因為他們是關鍵。

(D) 孩子們經由虛擬世界學習到許多有用的社交技巧。

9

校園 & 教育

 **本文圖解**

A research report *says* ① that virtual worlds can be important places

where children practice what they will do in real life. They *are* also a powerful
what 引導名詞子句當 practice 受詞

and attractive alternative **to** more passive adventures like watching TV. The
介係詞 to 在此表示相較某方面而言

research *was done* with children using the BBC's Adventure Rock virtual

world, **aimed** at those aged 6-12. It *surveyed* and *interviewed* children who
分詞構句，修飾前面所提的 virtual world

were the first to test the game.

③B The online world *is* a theme island **built** for the BBC's children channel

by ② Belgian game maker Larian. ③A Children *explore* the world alone but ③D

they *use* message boards to share what they find and what they do in the
二個 what 引導的名詞子句都當 share 的受詞

different creative studios **they find** around the virtual space.
形容詞子句省略關係代名詞 which

At times children *were* explorers and at others they *were* social climbers

eager to connect with other players. Some *were* power users looking for
省略關係代名詞及 be 動詞 who are

more information about how the virtual space really worked. ③C The children

could try all kinds of things without having to be afraid of the consequences

that would follow if they tried **them** in the real world. ⑤D They *learned* many

them 指的是 things

useful social skills and *played* around with their identity in ways that would

be much more difficult in real life.

According to the study ⑤A what children liked about virtual worlds *was*

the chance to create content such as music, cartoons and videos.

The publishers of the report *say* that ⑤B virtual worlds can be a powerful,

engaging and real interactive alternative **to** more passive media. They *urged*

介係詞 to 在此表示對某方面而言

creators of virtual spaces for children to get young people involved very early

on ⑤C because they really **do** have good ideas to add and they are very good

助動詞 do 在此為強調語氣

critical friends.

⑨

校園 & 教育

單字與片語

重要單字 Key Vocabularies

① virtual （a）虛擬的　　　　② alternative （n）替代品

③ adventure （n）冒險　　　　④ survey （v）調查

⑤ interview （v）訪問　　　　⑥ theme （n）主題

⑦ message （n）訊息

⑧ social climbers　想加入上流社會者；攀高枝者

⑨ consequences （n）結果　　　⑩ identity （n）一致性

⑪ content （n）內容　　　　⑫ urge （v）催促，極力要求

重要片語 Key Phrases

❶ do with　處理

❷ at times　有時候

❸ connect with　與…聯繫

❹ play around　玩耍，玩弄

❺ get involved　參與

❻ early on　初期

本文解析

　　本文是一篇有關於虛擬環境運用，讓兒童在一個由 BBC 電視台所創造的虛擬主題島中練習並探索未來真實世界，該虛擬世界讓兒童可以盡情嘗試探索，而不需擔心在真實世界中會發生的後果，他們可以單獨探索，也可以結伴來訓練社交能力，而作者結論中認為虛擬世界的設計者應該要參考那些很早就涉入虛擬世界的年輕人的意見。

　　第一題問虛擬世界對小孩很重要的原因，該題直接從一開始：virtual worlds can be important places... do in real life 可得知答案。第二題問誰是 Larian，由 ...

Belgian game maker Larian. 可知他是一位 game maker。第三題問有關"線上世界"何者為真,這是一題細節題,由各選項中的關鍵字在文章中找相對應處即可找出答案,請自行參考本文圖解所示。第四題問"urged"的意思,該字是"強力要求"的意思,選項中以 pleaded(懇請)最接近。第五題問本文中可知道的事,這也是細節題,一樣由各選項中的關鍵字在文章中找相對應處即可找出答案,但要注意改寫的意思,如選項 (C)Creators of virtual spaces must find younger involved very early because...,該句的意思是廠商要去找尋那些很早涉入其中的年輕人…,與文中表達的意思是不同的,讀者需留意。

學習重點 ➡

關係代名詞在句中是當受格用時可省略,但當關係詞是主格,且後面是 be 動詞＋Vp.p. 或 be ＋ adj 時,常常將主詞語 be 動詞一並省略掉(但不能只省略關係詞),形成 Vp.p. 當形容詞的結構。

【錯誤】She sat down in a corner was formed by two houses.

說明:句中應該有形容詞子句 which was formed by two houses,which 為主格,不可單獨省略,但本句中可與 be 動詞同時省略。

【正解】She sat down in a corner (which was) formed by two houses.
（她在二間房子形成的角落裏坐了下來。）

例句:

The computer game(which) I just played is much fun.
（我剛剛玩的電腦遊戲很好玩。）

The man (whom) you just met is a teacher.(你剛剛碰到的那個人是個老師。)

本文中例句:

At times children were explorers and at others they were social climbers eager to connect with other players. eager 前面原應該是有關係代名詞及 be 動詞 (who are),但依上述規則省略了。

9 校園＆教育

第十招 廣泛閱讀，注意重點文字

最後還是要回歸到測驗的最終本質——整體閱讀能力的提升。

文章的領域或相關內容是你所熟悉的將有利於應考，而各類文章中，多少會有一些關鍵字是常會出現的，而有些關鍵字雖然常見到，但畢竟比不上真正知道它的意思來得迅速。所以只要在準備的時候，注意這些相關用字，在考場上再見到它的時候，會感覺一見如故。筆者依據本身參加各類考試中，常見的閱讀測驗內容，舉例各類型主題常見探討內容及相關字詞如下：

在自然及科學中，如氣候變遷的問題，可能會提到如地球暖化 (global warming)、溫室效應 (greenhouse gas effect)、臭氧 (ozone) 層破壞、溫室氣體如二氧化碳 (carbon dioxides) 及甲烷 (methane)、環境保護 (environmental protection)、太陽能 (solar energy) 發電，水力 (hydraulic power) 發電等等。再如地球演進 (evolution)，可能提到古生物學 (paleontology)、達爾文的演化論 (theory of evolution)、恐龍滅絕 (distinguish of dinosaurs)、彗星 (commit) 或小行星 (asteroid) 撞地球，哺乳類動物 (mammals) 及兩棲類動物 (amphibian)，一些常見動物如蜥蜴 (lizard)、章魚 (octopus)、烏賊 (squid; ink fish)。在現代科技中，可能提到宇宙 (cosmos) 及銀河 (galaxy) 等天文學 (astronomy) 的發現、基因改造食品 (genetically-modified food, GM food)、奈米科技 (nano-technology)、雲端運算 (Cloud Computing)、無人飛機 (Unmanned Aerial Vehicle,UAV)、無人水下遙控載具 (Remotely Operated Vehicle，簡稱 ROV) 等等。

在人文及社會科中，如全球化 (globalized) 問題，可能提到在地化 (localization)、

貿易保護主義 (protectionism)、關稅壁壘 (tariff wall)、金融 (finance) 與資本 (capital)、市場壟斷 (monopoly) 等。在宗教問題上，可能會提到各種宗教，如基督教 (Christianity)、佛教 (Buddhism)、道教 (Taoism)，恐怖主義 (terrorism)。社會議題上，可能會提到貧富差距 (poverty gap)、工會 (labor unit) 發動的罷工 (strike; walkout)、示威 (demonstration) 活動、勞資雙方 (labor and management) 的問題、二黨政治 (two-party system; bi-party political)、獨裁或民主 (democracy or dictatorship) 的政權 (regime)、官僚體制 (bureaucrat)、公投 (referendum)、反核運動 (anti-nuclear campaign) 關注的核子災害 (nuclear hazard)。

在歷史與文化方面，可能提到各地的遺跡 (historical remains)、文化傳承 (cultural inheritance)、世界文化遺產 (world cultural heritage)、各朝代 (dynasty) 或帝國 (empire) 中的戰役及版圖 (campaign and territory) 等。另外像是原住民文化 (aboriginal culture)、風俗習慣 (customs; manners)、慶典儀式 (ritual; ceremony)。在教育及藝術方面，可能提到各種工藝 (technics; craft)，如雕刻 (sculpture; engrave)、書法 (calligraphy)、油畫 (oil painting; canvas)、各地美術館及博物館的展覽 (exhibition)，讀寫能力或識字能力 (literacy)。

在生活及休閒方面，如提到住房問題中的各種集合住宅 (collective housing)、公寓 (condo)、國民住宅 (public housing) 等，交通工具中的渡輪 (ferry)、客機 (airliner; passenger plane)、休旅車 (Sport Utility Vehicle, SUV)，旅行中產生的時差 (time difference; time lag)，各類加盟或經銷權 (franchise)、仲介或代理人 (agency broker) 及其佣金 (commission) 等字眼。在各種休閒活動中，可能會看到體適能 (Physical fitness)、職業運動 (professional sport) 的觀眾 (spectator) 或粉絲 (fancy)、青少年 (adolescent; juvenile) 的肥胖及糖尿病 (diabetes) 問題等字眼。在各種旅遊 (tour) 中的活動中，如各地的漁人碼頭 (fisherman's wharf)、搭遊輪 (cruse) 中的賭場 (casino)，免稅 (duty-free) 商店，以及最近火紅的廉價航空 (budget airline 或 Low-cost Airline) 等。

因限於篇幅，無法將所有常見的字詞都列出 (事實上也不可能)，但讀者可以從上列舉的內容中，理出一個頭緒，知道在看到各類文章中，應該注意的字詞方向。

⑩ 職場生涯

 英文本文

Article 10.1

By the time of December 31st, 2005, 453 non-US enterprises had been listed in the largest stock market in the world, New York Stock Exchange (NYSE), which accounted for 33.81% of the total market value (market capitalization). As the globalized phenomenon of capital market has become more and more intensive, the regulations of financial statement that promulgated by Securities and Exchange Commission, US (US SEC) made many non-US enterprises **halt** their process of listing in US. Based on the ground of protecting investors, US SEC will demand that non-US enterprises should provide a Form 20-F with reconciling the earnings and shareholders' equity governed by their national accounting standards to the earnings and shareholders' equity regulated in Generally Accepted Accounting Principles in the United States (US GAAP). Undoubtedly, the regulations of US SEC caused the increase of operation costs for enterprises, but has the quality of financial statement been upgraded? To view from the previous researches, some empirical results support the viewpoint that the quality of earnings will be more optimal under the relatively strict accounting standards and legal system in US. However, some scholars thought that each country's accounting system has been developed for a long time by cooperating with its national condition and culture, and among different countries, all situations, including tax law, company governance, ownership structure or other systematic factors, are different to each other. Therefore, the profit that compiled in accordance with the regulations of its national accounting system is probably more useful than the financial information that yielded from US GAAP.

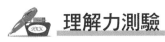 **理解力測驗**

Q1. According to the article, by the time of December 31st, 2005, how many US enterprises had listed in NYSE?

  (A) 450
  (B) 451
  (C) 452
  (D) No mention

Q2. Why many non-US enterprises halt their process of listing in US?

  (A) Globalized phenomenon of capital market has become more intensive.
  (B) Regulations of financial statement issued by US SEC.
  (C) Different national conditions and cultures.
  (D) All of the above.

Q3. What does the term "**halt**" in line 7 refer to?

  (A) proceed
  (B) continue
  (C) cease
  (D) move

Q4. Based on this article, what is the percentage accounted for total NYSE market value by U.S. enterprises listed in NYSE?

  (A) 12.31%
  (B) 20.81%
  (C) 33.81%
  (D) 66.19%

Q5. According to the writer, based on the ground of protecting investors, what information will US SEC demand non-US enterprises to provide?

  (A) Form 20-I
  (B) Form 20-S
  (C) Form 20-B
  (D) Form 20-F

 **本文中譯**

盈餘與股東權益

　　截至 2005 年 12 月 31 日，全球最大股票市場－紐約證券交易所計有 453 家非美國企業於當地掛牌，佔了總市值的 33.81%。雖然此資本市場全球化的現象有日益激烈的趨勢，但美國證管會對財務報表的規定卻使得許多非美國企業望而卻步。美國證管會基於保護投資人的立場，要求非美國企業必須提供一份 Form 20-F 的資料，將其母國會計準則下的盈餘與股東權益調節至美國會計準則下之盈餘與股東權益。美國證管會的規定無疑的使企業增加了許多作業成本，但財務報表的品質是否真的提升了？ 由以往的研究來看，有的實證結果支持在美國較嚴格的會計準則與法規制度下，盈餘數字品質較佳的論點；但也有學者認為，各國的會計制度是在配合其國情文化下長期發展出來的。而不同國家間，稅法、公司治理、所有權結構或其他制度性因素不同，根據其本國會計制度之規定所編製出的盈餘數字可能比根據美國會計準則下所產生的財務資訊更有用。

理解力測驗中譯

1. 根據本文資訊，截至 2005 年 12 月 31 日，紐約證券交易所計有幾家非美國企業於當地掛牌？

(A) 450

(B) 451

(C) 452

(D) 沒有提到

2. 為何許多非美國企業對於在美國掛牌望而卻步？

(A) 資本市場全球化的現象愈演愈烈

(B) **美國證管會對財務報表的規定**

(C) 不同的國情文化

(D) 以上皆是

3. 第 7 行的單字"halt"是下列何意？

(A) 前進

(B) 繼續

(C) **停止**

(D) 移動

4. 本文中在當地掛牌上市的美國企業佔美國股市總市值的多少？

(A) 12.31%

(B) 20.81%

(C) 33.81%

(D) **66.19%**

5. 根據作者，美國證管會基於保護投資人的立場，要求非美國企業必須提供何種資料？

(A) Form 20-I

(B) Form 20-S

(C) Form 20-B

(D) **Form 20-F**

⑩ 職場生涯

 本文圖解

① By the time of December 31st, 2005, 453 non-US enterprises *had been listed* in the largest stock market in the world, New York Stock Exchange (NYSE), ④ which accounted for 33.81% of the total market value (market capitalization). As the globalized phenomenon of capital market has become more and more intensive, ② the regulations of financial statement that promulgated by Securities and Exchange Commission, US (US SEC) *made* many non-US enterprises halt their process of listing in US. **Based**

分詞構句，當副詞用，表示基於…原因

on the ground of protecting investors, ⑤ US SEC *will demand* that non-US enterprises should provide a Form 20-F with reconciling the earnings and shareholders' equity **governed by** their national accounting standards

分詞片語，修飾 equity，表示被…管理

to the earnings and shareholders' equity **regulated in** Generally Accepted

分詞片語，修飾 equity，表示被…規範

Accounting Principles in the United States (US GAAP). Undoubtedly, the regulations of US SEC *caused* the increase of operation costs for enterprises,

but *has* the quality of financial statement been upgraded? To view from the

previous researches, some empirical results *support* the viewpoint **that** the

> that 引導的名詞子句為
> viewpoint 的同位語

quality of earnings will be more optimal under the relatively strict accounting

standards and legal system in US. However, some scholars *thought* that

each country's accounting system has been developed for a long time by

cooperating with its national condition and culture, **and among** different

> and 連接第二個子句，後面 among 為
> 一介係詞片當副詞用，表示在…之中

countries, all situations, including tax law, company governance, ownership

structure or other systematic factors, are different to each other. Therefore,

the profit that compiled in accordance with the regulations of its national

accounting system *is* probably more useful than the financial information

that yielded from US GAAP.

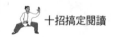

 單字與片語

重要單字 Key Vocabularies

① market value 市值

② phenomenon（n）現象

③ capital market 資本市場

④ intensive（a）密集的

⑤ financial statement 財務報表

⑥ halt（v）停止

⑦ reconciling（v）調和

⑧ shareholders（n）股東；持股人

⑨ empirical（a）實務上的

⑩ relatively（adv）相對地

重要片語 Key Phrases

❶ By the time 到…時候

❷ stock market 股票市場

 本文解析

　　本文首先提到紐約證券交易所是全球最大的交易所，但許多非美國企業想去掛牌時，美國證管會要求這些公司需提供一份 Form 20-F 的財務報表的規定，讓許多企業因而止步，作者認為該規定加重了企業成本，有學者認為這些會計準則會使企業有較佳盈餘表現，但一派學者認為各國國情及制度不同，依本國會既準則下編製出來的報表應該會更真實。所以該篇主要討論美國證管會的一項規定造成的不同反應。

　　第一題問紐約證券交易所計有幾家美國企業於當地掛牌，這題需看清楚題目問的是美國企業，而文中提到的是非美國企業的數量（... 453 non-US enterprise...），所以答案在文章中並沒提及。第二題問為何許多非美國企業對於在美國掛牌望而卻步，由 the regulations... by (US SEC) made many non-US enterprises halt their process，知是因為證管會頒布一項規定所造成，注意選項中用 issue，有頒布發行意思。第三題問單字 "halt"，該字是動詞 "停止"，所以與 cease（停止）最相近。第四題問當地掛牌上市的美國企業佔美國股市總市值的比例，這題也要看清題意，題目是問 US enterprises listed in NYSE，而文章中是說：non-US enterprises... which accounted for

33.81%...，所以非美國企業的比例為 33.81%，而相對的，美國本土企業的比例就是 66.19%。第五題問證期會要求非美國企業必須提供何種資料，由 Based on the ground of protecting investors, US SEC will demand that non-US enterprises should provide a Form 20-F 可看出答案。

學習重點 ➡

　　介係詞片語是由介係詞起頭，名詞或代名詞結尾的兩個或兩個以上的字群所組成。可當名詞或形容詞的地位，或當副詞使用，修飾動詞、形容詞、其他副詞或修飾整句，例如 at first(一開始)，except for(除…以外)，at a cost of (以…價格)…等。片語動詞則是動詞與介係詞的習慣性用法組合，例如 account for(導致於)，make up for(賠償)，take part in (參加)…不勝枚舉，平時就應留意記憶。

例句：

I'm in charge of this store.(我管理這家店。)

In case of an earthquake, turn off the gas and stove.
(當地震時，關閉瓦斯及爐子。)

Turn in your assignment by the end of this weekend.
(在週末前交出你的作業。)

Our president contribute money to charities.(我們董事長捐款給慈善機關。)

本文中例句：

Each country's accounting system has been developed for a long time by cooperating with its national condition and culture, and among different countries, all situations, including tax law, company governance, ownership structure or other systematic factors, are different to each other.

　　其中 cooperating with(與 … 配合) 為一片語動詞，而 among different countries 為一介係詞片語當副詞用，修飾全句。

10
職場生涯

327

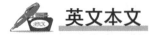 英文本文

Article 10.2

In an announcement Monday, Mr. Willian Math, senior marketing director of Mobile Ltd, stated that the company had developed a new type of mobile phone with additional **sophisticated** communication devices.

Math said that the new mobile phone had taken almost five years to produce, and he also announced that the company would be launching it onto the global market. Its marketing strategy involves building up a collaborative network of several major electronic device companies.

Some industry exports have expressed doubts about the large-scale marketing of the new product. One analyst said we are unlikely to see a large market for this type of product.", adding that the majority of the customers would not need the additional features. Other analysts thought the customer today prefers a cheaper and reliable mobile phone to expensive and complex one when considering the sky-high prices of this product in the sluggish economical situation.

There are other market researchers who hold a different view, however. One of the researcher commented: "by using a network shared by large electronic companies, Mobile Ltd may provide customers' satisfaction to many high-end users in the international market in the long term."

According the company's scheme, the product may go to market in the next second quarter, and there will be a large-scale promotion. Mr. Math is quite confident that this product will be a hot sale in the market because buyers will be fascinated by its incomparable wireless connection features.

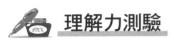 **理解力測驗**

Q1. What is Mobile Ltd going to do?

(A) Product a new sophisticated communication model.

(B) Build a major mobile phone manufactory.

(C) Sell new mobile phones for domestic customers.

(D) Market new cell phones in different countries.

Q2. What is implied about the new mobile phone?

(A) The company did not spend more than five years developing it.

(B) The company will be introducing it through web marketing.

(C) The company might not want to form a collaborative network initially.

(D) The company has engaged in advertising collaboratively.

Q3. what does the analyst probably think about the new product?

(A) It might have defects.

(B) It might not match client's needs.

(C) It needs additional promotion.

(D) It will not be small enough.

Q4. What do market researchers NOT claim about the new product?

(A) The company will not benefit from the new product.

(B) The company may use a network by large electronic companies.

(C) The company will build a network center.

(D) The product might attract some customers.

Q5. Which of the followings has the closest meaning with the word "**sophisticated**" in the line 3 of first section?

(A) complicated

(B) ignited

(C) amazed

(D) irritated.

 本文中譯

新聞報導

　　威廉瑪斯先生，行動裝置公司資深市場主管，在星期一的一則消息宣布中說該公司已經發展一款具有精密通訊裝置的新型行動電話。

　　瑪斯說該新型電話大約花費五年時間來生產，而且他也宣布該公司將把該產品推向全球市場。它的市場戰略牽涉到與一些主要電子設備公司合作網絡的建立。有一些業界專家已經對這項新產品的大規模市場表示存疑，有一位分析師說到：我們看不到這個產品有多大的市場，他並補充大部分的顧客並不需要這些而外的功能。其他分析家認為在這經濟停滯狀況下且產定價是如此高之高，消費者應該寧可要一隻便宜且實用的手機，而不會想要昂貴且複雜的手機。

　　然而，有一些市場研究員抱持著不同的觀點，其中一位評論說到："經由與大的設備公司網絡分享，行動裝置公司在長遠的未來也許可以讓高端消費者感到滿意。"

　　依據該公司規畫，這項產品將於明年第二季問市，且將會有大規模促銷。瑪斯先生非常有信心認為這項產品將會在市場上熱賣，因為買家將會被它無與倫比的無線網路連接功能所吸引。

理解力測驗中譯

1. Mobile 公司要做甚麼？

    (A) 生產一種新的複雜通訊模型

    (B) 建立一個主要的行動電話生產工廠

    (C) 銷售新的手機到國內市場上

    (D) 在不同國家銷售新的手機

2. 關於新手機有提到甚麼？

    (A) 這間公司研發它的時間不超過五年

    (B) 這間公司將把它經由網路來推銷

    (C) 這間公司一開始並沒有要形成一個合作網絡

    (D) 這間公司已經合作進行廣告了

3. 有些分析師認為這個新產品如何？

    (A) 它可能有瑕疵

    (B) 它可能無法滿足顧客需求

    (C) 它需要額外的促銷

    (D) 它不夠短小

4. 市場研究員對這產品沒有宣稱的是？

    (A) 這家公司將不會從這項產品獲利

    (B) 這家公司可能會使用大的電子公司的網絡

    (C) 這家公司將會建立一個網路中心

    (D) 這產品將吸引一些消費者

5. 下列何者與第一段第三行的"sophisticated"這個字的意思最相近？

    (A) 複雜的

    (B) 點燃的

    (C) 吃驚的

    (D) 激怒的

 **本文圖解**

In an announcement Monday, Mr. Willian Math, senior marketing director

of Mobile Ltd, *stated* that the company had developed a new type of mobile

phone with additional sophisticated communication devices.

Math *said* that ② the new mobile phone had taken almost five years to

produce, and ① he also *announced* that the company would be launching

it onto the global market. Its marketing strategy *involves* building up a

collaborative network of several major electronic device companies.

Some industry exports *have expressed* doubts about the large-scale

marketing of the new product. ③ One analyst *said* "we **are unlikely to** see
　　　　　　　　　　　　　　　　　　　　指不大可能發生的事

a large market for this type of product", **adding** that the majority of the
　　　　　　　　　　　　　　　　分詞構句，表
　　　　　　　　　　　　　　　　示附加說明
customers would not need the additional features. Other analysts *though*

customers today prefer a cheaper and reliable mobile phone to expensive

and complex one **when considering** the sky-high prices of this product in
分詞構句，表示當考慮…情形

the sluggish economical situation.

There *are* other market researchers who hold a different view, however.

One of the researcher *commented*: "④ By using a network **shared** by large
分詞片語，修飾 network，
表示與…所共享

electronic companies, Mobile Ltd *may provide* customers' satisfaction to

many high-end users in the international market in the long term."

According the company's scheme, the product may *go* to market in the

next second **quarter,** and there *will be* a large-scale promotion. Mr. Math
一年分為四季，每季稱一個 quarter

is quite confident that this product will be hot sale in the market because

buyers will be fascinated by its incomparable wireless connection features.

單字與片語

重要單字 Key Vocabularies

① announcement（n）宣布

② senior（adj）資深的

③ sophisticated（adj）精密的

④ communication（n）通訊

⑤ device（n）設備，裝置

⑥ launch（v）著手進行，送出

⑦ strategy（n）策略

⑧ collaborative（adj）合作的

⑨ features（n）功能，特點

⑩ sky-high　極高的

⑪ comment（v）評論

⑫ satisfaction（n）滿意

⑬ scheme（n）計畫

⑭ promotion（n）促銷

⑮ hot sale　熱賣

⑯ incomparable（adj）無比的

重要片語 Key Phrases

❶ in the long term　長遠來說

❷ go to market　上市

 本文解析

　　本文先提到行動裝置公司將發表型新的行動電話，且將與主要的設備商合作來推銷到全球市場上。有分析師質疑其市場規模，認為產品功能太多，而一般人不需要這麼多功

能，況且景氣不好消費者也不需這麼高端的手機。但有市場研究員抱持不同看法，認為經由與設備廠商合作，可以滿足高端消費者，而該公司對產品仍抱持信心，認為其功能強大將會吸引買家。所以本文最主要是述說市場對該項產品的未來看法不一。

第一題問該公司要做甚麼，這由第二段第一句可知該公司要將產品賣到全球，需注意 launch（送出，出發）這個字的意思。第二題是關於新手機有提到者，選項中除了 (A) 以外，其他都沒提到，注意文中用 ... had taken almost five years...，表示幾乎 (almost) 花了五年時間，故推論應該不到五年。第三題問分析師認為這個新產品如何，由第三段 One analyst said...，得知分析師認為產品不是顧客需要的，其它選項都沒提到。第四題問市場研究員對這產品的意見，由 ... market researchers who hold a different view... 這段可看出該題選項中除 (C) 以外，其他都有提到。應注意該公司是要與大設備商建立合作網絡（building up a collaborative network），而非自己建立網路中心（build a network center），需區分清楚。第五題問 "sophisticated" 這個字的意思，它是 "精密、複雜的" 之意，所以與 complicated（複雜的）最相近。

學習重點 ➡

這篇是講報商業報導的文章，其句型結構單純，要注意到的是動詞時態的運用。報導的文章中如果引述他人的說法，因為都是已經說過的話，所以動詞一般都是用過去式。而如果講到過去的二件事，其先發生（距離現在較遠）者用過去完成式，後發生（距離現在較近）者的用過去式，例如：... senior marketing director of Mobile Ltd, stated that the company had developed a new type of mobile phone...，說這段話的時間是在後，所以用過去式 stated，而發展完成是在前，所以用過去完成式 had developed。另外，於過去時間表示未來將要發生的事，過去時間動詞用過去式，而未來時間要發生的事，動詞用 would ＋原形動詞（或進行式）來表示過去的未來式，例如本文中：he also announced that the company would be launching it onto the global market。

10
職場生涯

 英文本文

Article 10.3

After a **sluggish** performance over the last years, recent sales in the IT and computer sector have shown some recover. In fact, the level of sales in the high tech sector from October to December has risen slightly more than those during the same period last year. Economists say that this is due to the introduction of new lap-top computer models and software, especially products marked intensively through November and December. As a result, some economists have argued that business figures have been improving.

However, other IT and computer industry analysts are skeptical about future trends. At present, they claim that recent, newly-launched computer models are merely modified versions of previous computers and that they offer limited improvement in capacity. Moreover, a large-scale business research project conducted through a nationwide survey of managers in the computer industry supports this view. It indicates that senior managers of major IT and computer companies are not so optimistic about the apparent recent trend.

Thus, although improved income on the part of computer companies has been reported, this is by no means certain to lead to a major growth in sales for the industry in the future. According to one survey, it may also say that caution needs to be exercised when interpreting recent news regarding IT and computer company sales figures.

理解力測驗

Q1. What is the article mainly about?

(A) Positive sales figures for computer and IT companies.

(B) The uncertain situation in the IT and computer firm sector.

(C) Caution needed when think about the recent general economical trend.

(D) Positive results of company's business plans.

Q2. What can be inferred about the business performance from October to December?

(A) It didn't show very high growth.

(B) It did show some recovery but was no better than the same business period last year.

(C) It showed slight improvement based on the recent economic boom.

(D) It did not indicate any growth at all.

Q3. What can be said about the view held by IT and computer industry?

(A) They think that IT and computer firms showed positive recovery to a certain extent.

(B) They think that IT and computer forms can deal with the economic problems in the industry.

(C) They think that some minor growth will continue in the future.

(D) They think that major recovery seems to be unlikely.

Q4. Which is NOT mentioned about the large-scale business research project?

(A) It was disseminated to both academics and business managers.

(B) It was study based on questionnaires sent to major companies through the nation.

(C) It results were based on returned surveys sent to major IT and computer firms.

(D) Questionnaires were completed by senior managers in major companies

Q5. Which of the followings has the closest meaning with "**sluggish**"?

(A) slippy

(B) inactive

(C) oppressive

(D) burdensome

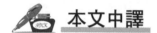 **本文中譯**

資訊產業報導

在經歷過去幾年的銷售蕭條後,近年來 IT 及電腦部門在銷售已經呈現一些復甦,事實上,相較於去年同期十月到十二月,高科技部門在銷售量上已經有微幅上升,經濟學家說這是因為新推出的筆記型電腦以及軟體,特別是在十一月及十二月密集推出的產品。因此,有些經濟學者認為經濟前景已經較為改善。

然而,其他電腦產業分析師對於未來趨勢感到疑慮,目前,他們聲稱最近新上市的電腦只是以前電腦的修改版本,且在容量上增加有限。況且,一項經由訪查全球的電腦產業經理人的大規模的產業研究計畫也證實這項看法,這顯示主要 IT 及電腦產業的資深經理人也同樣對目前表面上的趨勢不表示樂觀。

因此,雖然電腦公司的營收增加的報告已經出爐,這不必然意味著這個產業在未來在銷售量會有較大成長,根據一項研究指出,在解讀最近的有關 IT 及電腦公司的銷售數字時需要特別注意。

理解力測驗中譯

1. 本文主要談到甚麼？

(A) 電腦及 IT 公司的正面銷售數據

(B) IT 及電腦公司方面的不確定情形

(C) 考量最近一般經濟趨勢必須注意的情形

(D) 公司經營計畫的正面結果

2. 從十月到十二月的營運表現中可推斷的是為何？

(A) 營運表現沒有很高成長

(B) 營運表現有些回溫但沒有比去年同期更好

(C) 營運表現姬於最近經濟繁榮而有一些進步。

(D) 營運表現一點都沒成長

3. IT 及電腦產業所持的觀點是甚麼？

(A) 他們認為 IT 及電腦公司有一定程度的正面復甦。

(B) 他們認為 IT 及電腦公司可處理產業中的經濟問題。

(C) 他們認為未來仍繼續會有小幅成長。

(D) 他們認為大幅成長幾乎不可能。

4. 何者非為有關於這項大規模產業研究計畫所提到的？

(A) 這項研究普及到產業界及學術界。

(B) 這項研究是以問卷送給全國的主要公司來做的。

(C) 研究結論是以給全國主要 IT 及電腦公司回收問卷而得的。

(D) 問卷是由主要公司的資深經理人填寫完成。

5. 第一段第一行中"sluggish"這個字與何字意思最接近？

(A) 靈活的

(B) 遲鈍的

(C) 壓迫的

(D) 令人煩惱的

 本文圖解

After a sluggish performance over the last years, recent sales in the IT and computer sector *have shown* some recover. In fact, ② the level of sales in the high tech sector from October to December *has risen* slightly more than those during the same period last year. Economists *say* that this is due to the introduction of new lap-top computer models and software, especially products **marked** intensively through November and December. As a result,

分詞片語修飾 products，表示那些上市的產品

some economists *have argued* that business figures have been improving.

However, other IT and computer industry analysts *are* skeptical about future trends. At present, they *claim* that recent, newly-launched computer models are merely modified versions of previous computers and **that** they

名詞子句 that... 為動詞
claim 的第二個受詞

offer limited improvement in capacity. Moreover, ④A a large-scale business research project **conducted** through a nationwide survey of managers in

分詞片語修飾 project，表示被執行之意

the computer industry *supports* this view. It *indicates* that senior managers

of major ③ IT and computer companies are not so optimistic about the

apparent recent trend.

Thus, ① although **improved** income on the part of computer companies
過去分詞當形容詞修飾 income，表示已經增加的

has been reported, this *is* by no means certain to lead to a major growth in

sales for the industry in the future. According to one survey, it may also *say*

that caution needs to be exercised when interpreting recent news **regarding**
分詞片語修飾，
表示關於某方面
的消息

IT and computer company sales figures.

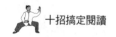

單字與片語

重要單字 Key Vocabularies

① sluggish (a) 停滯的

② performance (n) 表現

③ sector (n) 部門

④ economist (n) 經濟學家

⑤ lap-top (n) 筆記型電腦

⑥ analyst (n) 分析師

⑦ skeptical (a) 懷疑的

⑧ version (n) 版本

⑨ capacity (n) 容量

⑩ survey (n) 調查

⑪ optimistic (adj) 樂觀的

⑫ interpret (v) 解釋為…，解讀為…

重要片語 Key Phrases

❶ be due to 由於

❷ at present 目前

❸ by no means 絕不，一點也不

本文解析

本文先提到電腦的銷售在近期似乎有好轉的跡象，因此有人認為經濟前景已經改善，然而，有其他人對產業前景不表樂觀，而且對於一項針對資深經理人的調查也顯示出同樣的答案，作者在最後結論提到雖然營收有增加，但這不必然意味著這個產業在未來在銷售量會有較大成長，也就是前景仍然不是很確定，這是本文的重點，也是第一題的答案。

第二題問十月到十二月的營運表現，該題直接從文中 … October to December has risen slightly more than during… 可得知答案。第三題問 IT 及電腦產業所持的觀點，由第二段先談到 IT and computer industry 分析師都對於未來趨勢感到疑慮，且該段後面也提到對目前表面上的趨勢不表示樂觀，綜和研判未來大幅成長幾乎不可能。第四題問何者為非的細節題，由第三段 a large-scale business research project… recent trend. 都是該題答案範圍，要注意該文中提到研究是 nationwide survey of managers，並沒提到 academics and business managers，所以該選項為錯的。第

五題問單字"sluggish"的意思，該字是"遲緩的"之意，所以選項中以 inactive（遲鈍的）最接近。

學習重點 ➡

比較用法是商業文章喜歡用的語法之一，要作比較需為同樣的事物才能進行，否則就不合邏輯，所以在比較級句子中一定要注意比較的對象是否對等，也就是橘子比橘子，頻果比蘋果，不可以拿橘子比頻果。

例如：The rooms at the Regency Hotel are larger than the Rex Hotel.

本句的中文翻譯為：Regency 飯店的房間都比整個 Rex 飯店來的大。常識判斷這應該不合邏輯，本句錯誤的原因是比較的對象不對，不可拿飯店的房間跟整個飯店來比，應該要房間比房間，所以該句需修正為：

The rooms at the Regency Hotel are larger than those at the Rex Hotel.
(Regency 飯店的房間都比 Rex 飯店房間來的大。)

以本文中的 ... the level of sales in the high tech sector from October to December has risen slightly more than those during the same period last year.。該句比較對象是 level of sales（銷售狀況），用 has risen slightly more（已經稍微增加），表示銷售狀況的增加，而這是跟去年同時期相比的，所以用 than those during the same period last year，注意：those=level of sales.

學習小撇步 (Tips) ➡

前面雖然提過，大部分文章都是從第一段前一二句便可看出文章大意，但還是有些文章會將不同的觀點先寫出來，然後再舉更多的證據或數據來推翻前述的論點，這時就要注意一些用法，例如它可能用有些 someone thought that... ; However, other said...，這時就要注意語氣的轉折處，且要注意比例原則，也就是以提到的多，且真正強調的東西為主，而非一直拘泥於前面先提到的論點。

職場生涯

 英文本文

Article 10.4

The newspaper industry is entering a new era. The Seattle Post-Intelligencer has become America's first newspaper to stop printing and become the first newspaper to appear online only. The newspaper was 146 years old, the oldest in Washington State.

Only about 20 people work for seattlepi.com, the Internet version of the newspaper. Once over 150 people worked in the newsrooms of Seattle's most famous paper. There is only one daily newspaper left in Seattle, The Times. Many people think that it could follow the Post-Intelligencer by going online only too.

Among other big cities in the US, Denver only has one daily newspaper because the Rocky Mountain News closed a few weeks ago. Some newspapers around the US are afraid of going bankrupt. Among these are the Chicago Tribune and the Los Angeles Times.

One of the main problems that printed newspapers face today is advertising. Big local newspapers earn a lot of their money with ads. But that market has moved to Internet advertising which is either free or costs very little. Another reason is that many newspapers have become bigger and bigger. They have spent too much money expanding and buying up other papers.

Newspapers are reducing costs wherever they can. In Detroit daily newspapers are delivering their papers on only three days a week. In Ohio the state's largest **newspapers are sharing stories.** Almost 8,000 jobs have been lost in the newspaper industry.

Newspapers have lost millions of readers in the past years because a new generation of readers has emerged. Much of the news that people get online still comes from newspapers and most of them publish it for free. While newspapers have fewer reporters in big cities and abroad, observers say that they have lost much of their quality. The question is: Will they find a new home on the Internet?

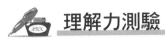 理解力測驗

Q1. What is the best title of this article?

(A) The Seattle Post-Intelligencer on line

(B) The reducing costs of newspapers

(C) The declining of printed newspaper

(D) The Internet version of the newspaper

Q2. How many employees worked for The Seattle Post-Intelligencer in the past?

(A) 20

(B) 146

(C) 150

(D) 8000.

Q3. According to this article, how many daily papers were there in Denver one month ago?

(A) 1

(B) 2

(C) 3

(D) No mention.

Q4. What does the term "**newspapers are sharing stories**" refer in this article?

(A) Other newspapers are delivering news.

(B) Other newspapers are sharing costs.

(C) Other newspapers are making stories.

(D) Other newspapers are doing the same.

Q5. Why does the author say "will they find a new home on the Internet?"

(A) Because many reporters have lost their job.

(B) Because people get online still comes from newspapers.

(C) Because newspapers have lost millions of readers.

(D) Because reporters have lost much of their quality.

本文中譯

實體報紙的衰落

　　報紙產業現正進入一個新世紀，西雅圖的智者郵報已經成為美國第一份沒有印刷而只出現在網路的報紙。這份報紙有 146 年歷史，是華盛頓州最古老的報紙。

　　只有約 20 名員工在 seattlepi.com，也就是這家網路版的報紙上班，以前曾經有多達 150 人在這家西雅圖最有名的報紙的新聞室工作。西雅圖只有一家日報，也就是時代，許多人認為它也會步上智者郵報只有線上版的腳步。

　　在美國的大城市中，丹佛目前只有一家日報，因為洛磯山時報在幾週前關門。一些美國境內的報紙擔心會破產，這些包括芝加哥論壇報及洛杉磯時報。

　　這些實體報紙目前面臨的其中一個主要問題就是廣告。大型區域性報紙可以靠廣告賺錢，但是這個市場已經轉移到免費或是只要很少費用的網路廣告上面去了。另一個原因是許多報紙變得愈來愈大，他們花費了許多錢在擴充以及併購其他報紙上。

　　報社也竭盡所能的在縮減開支。在底特律，報社的日報每週只有三天遞送，在俄亥俄州的最大報社正在做同樣的事，大約有 8000 個工作報紙業的工作職缺已經消失了。

　　由於新一代的讀者出現後，報紙業在過去幾年已經流失了數以百萬計的讀者，許多人們從網路上得知的新聞還是來自於報紙，且報業把這些新聞免費發佈。而當在大城市以及國外報業的記者變少了的同時，觀察家說他們失去了原有的品質，問題是：記者們可以在網路上找到一個新家嗎？

理解力測驗中譯

1. 本文最佳標題為何？

(A) 線上的西雅圖智者郵報

(B) 正在減損價值的報紙

(C) **實體報紙的沒落**

(D) 報紙的網路版

2. 西雅圖智者郵報以前有多少位員工？

(A) 20

(B) 146

(C) **150**

(D) 8000

3. 依據本文，丹佛一個月以前有多少家日報？

(A) 1

(B) **2**

(C) 3

(D) 沒提到

4. "newspapers are sharing stories"這段用語在文中指的是甚麼意思？

(A) 其他報紙正在放出消息

(B) 其他報紙正在分攤費用

(C) 其他報紙正在製造消息

(D) **其他報紙正在做同樣的事**

5. 為何作者問說"他們可以在網路上找到一個新家嗎"？

(A) **因為許多記者失業了**

(B) 因為人們從線上得到的消息還是來自報社

(C) 報紙業已經流失上百萬的讀者

(D) 因為記者的品質下降很多

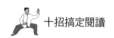

 本文圖解

The newspaper industry *is entering* a new era. The Seattle Post-Intelligencer *has become* America's first newspaper to stop printing and *become* the first newspaper to appear online only. The newspaper *was* 146 years old, the oldest in Washington State.

Only about 20 people *work* for seattlepi.com, the Internet version of the newspaper. ② Once over 150 people *worked* in the newsrooms of Seattle's most famous paper. There *is* only one daily newspaper **left** in Seattle, *The*

分詞片語，修飾 newspaper

Times. Many people *think* that it could follow the Post-Intelligencer **by** going

by 表示用…方式

online only too.

Among other big cities in the US, ③ Denver only *has* one daily newspaper because the Rocky Mountain News closed a few weeks ago. Some newspapers around the US *are* afraid of going bankrupt. Among these *are* the Chicago Tribune and the Los Angeles Times.

One of the main problems that **printed** newspapers face today *is*

printed 為過去分詞當形容詞，修
飾 newspaper，意思是實體報紙

advertising. Big local newspapers *earn* a lot of their money with ads. But that market *has moved* to advertising on the Internet which is either free or costs very little. Another reason *is* that many newspapers have become bigger and bigger. They *have spent* too much money expanding and buying up other papers.

Newspapers *are reducing* costs wherever they can. In Detroit daily newspapers *are delivering* their papers on only three days a week. In Ohio the state's largest newspapers *are sharing* stories. Almost 8,000 jobs *have been lost* in the newspaper industry.

Newspapers *have lost* millions of readers in the past years because a new generation of readers has emerged. Much of the news that people get online still *comes* from newspapers and most of them *publish* **it** for free.

them 指的是 newspapers，而 it 是指 news

⑤ While newspapers have fewer reporters in big cities and abroad, observers *say* that **they** have lost much of their quality. The question *is*: Will they find a

they 指的是 reporters

new home on the Internet?

⑩ 職場生涯

 **單字與片語**

重要單字 Key Vocabularies

① era （n）年代
② newsroom （n）編輯部
③ bankrupt （n）破產
④ printed newspaper （n）實體報紙
⑤ advertising （n）廣告
⑥ share （v）分攤，共享
⑦ observer （n）觀察家
⑧ emerge （v）出現

重要片語 Key Phrases

❶ buy up 買進
❷ for free 免費地

 **本文解析**

　　本文先提到，西雅圖的一家報紙已經變成完全的網路報，且該市的另一家報社也可能會跟著轉型成網路報。而其他地方的實體報紙也面臨經營問題，因為報紙的主要收入來源廣告都轉移到網路上去了，所以各家報社只能儘量減少開支，網路免費新聞的結果造成記者的工作機會也沒了，所以本文最主要是描述實體報紙因網路的興起而沒落了，也是第一題的答案。

　　第二題問西雅圖智者郵報以前有多少位員工，該題需注意 in the past 就是指過去的意思，由 Once over 150 people worked in... 可得知答案。第三題問丹佛一個月以前有多少家日報，由 Denver... Rocky Mountain News closed a few weeks before. 知一個星期前另一家報紙才關門，所以一個月前應有二家報紙。第四題問"newspapers are sharing stories"這段用語在文中的意思，shear 是分享的意思，分享故事指的就是前面題的每週送三天報紙，也就是做同樣的是的意思。第五題問作者為何問說"他們可以在網路上找到一個新家嗎？"，當報業已經因為網路興起而無法生存時，所以記者也會沒有工作而失業，所以除非他們能在網路上找到一個新家，他們才能生存。

學習重點 ➡

　　這篇是講報紙相關的文章，其中要注意到用語之間的關係，例如 news 是指新聞、或消息等，雖然字尾有加 s，但其實是不可數名詞，要用單數，而 newspaper 當名詞用時是報紙，但也能當成報社來解釋；而其也能當動詞用，當成辦報紙或採訪新聞之意，所以需要將一字多意的字的用法在文章中需清楚，才能順利讀懂文章。例如本文中的這段話：Much of the news that people get online still comes from newspapers and most of them publish it for free. 文中第一句的 it 指的是 news(新聞)，而 newspapers 是多家報社的意思，所以該句中的 them 指的就是這些報社 (newspapers)，而非報紙本身，因為報紙不會自己印自己。

　　另外，提到一段時間以前的用法時，需注意 ago 與 before 的差別：

1. ago：以現在為基點往前推算，與過去式連用，不與完成式連用，
　　例如：It happened a few minutes ago.(那是幾分鐘以前發生的事情)
　　　　　It was seven years ago that Steve Jobs introduced the iPod to the world.(史帝夫賈斯伯七年前發表 iPod)

2. before：從過去某一個時間點往前推算，或者單指以前 (沒有搭配明確時間)
Eventually, Mrs. Ibanez's thirty-five-year-old daughter Cecilia arrived and explained that her mother had been in a state of emotional upset since her father had left home two weeks before. (Ibanez 太太 35 歲的女兒 Cecilia 最後終於來了，說她母親自從父親兩個禮拜前離家出走後心理就一直很不穩定。)

The year before last he won a gold medal, and the year before that he won the silver.(他前年贏得一枚金牌，大前年贏得一枚銀牌)

10
職場生涯

Leader 012

十招搞定閱讀

作　　者　方定國、張慧文
封面構成　高鍾琪
內頁構成　華漢電腦排版有限公司

發 行 人　周瑞德
企劃編輯　劉俞青
執行編輯　陳韋佑
校　　對　陳欣慧、饒美君
印　　製　大亞彩色印刷製版股份有限公司
初　　版　2015 年 02 月
定　　價　新台幣 349 元
出　　版　倍斯特出版事業有限公司
電　　話　(02) 2351-2007
傳　　真　(02) 2351-0887
地　　址　100 台北市中正區福州街 1 號 10 樓之 2
E - m a i l　best.books.service@gmail.com

港澳地區總經銷　泛華發行代理有限公司
地址　香港新界將軍澳工業邨駿昌街 7 號 2 樓
電話　(852) 2798-2323
傳真　(852) 2796-5471

國家圖書館出版品預行編目(CIP)資料

十招搞定閱讀 / 張慧文, 方定國著. --
初版. -- 臺北市 : 力得文化, 2015.02 面 ;
公分. -- (Leader ; 12)
ISBN 978-986-91458-2-4(平裝)
1. 英語 2. 讀本
805.18　　　　　　　　　　104001321